SPELLBOUND IN SPUD CITY

TWISTED TALENT SERIES

E. R. JENSEN

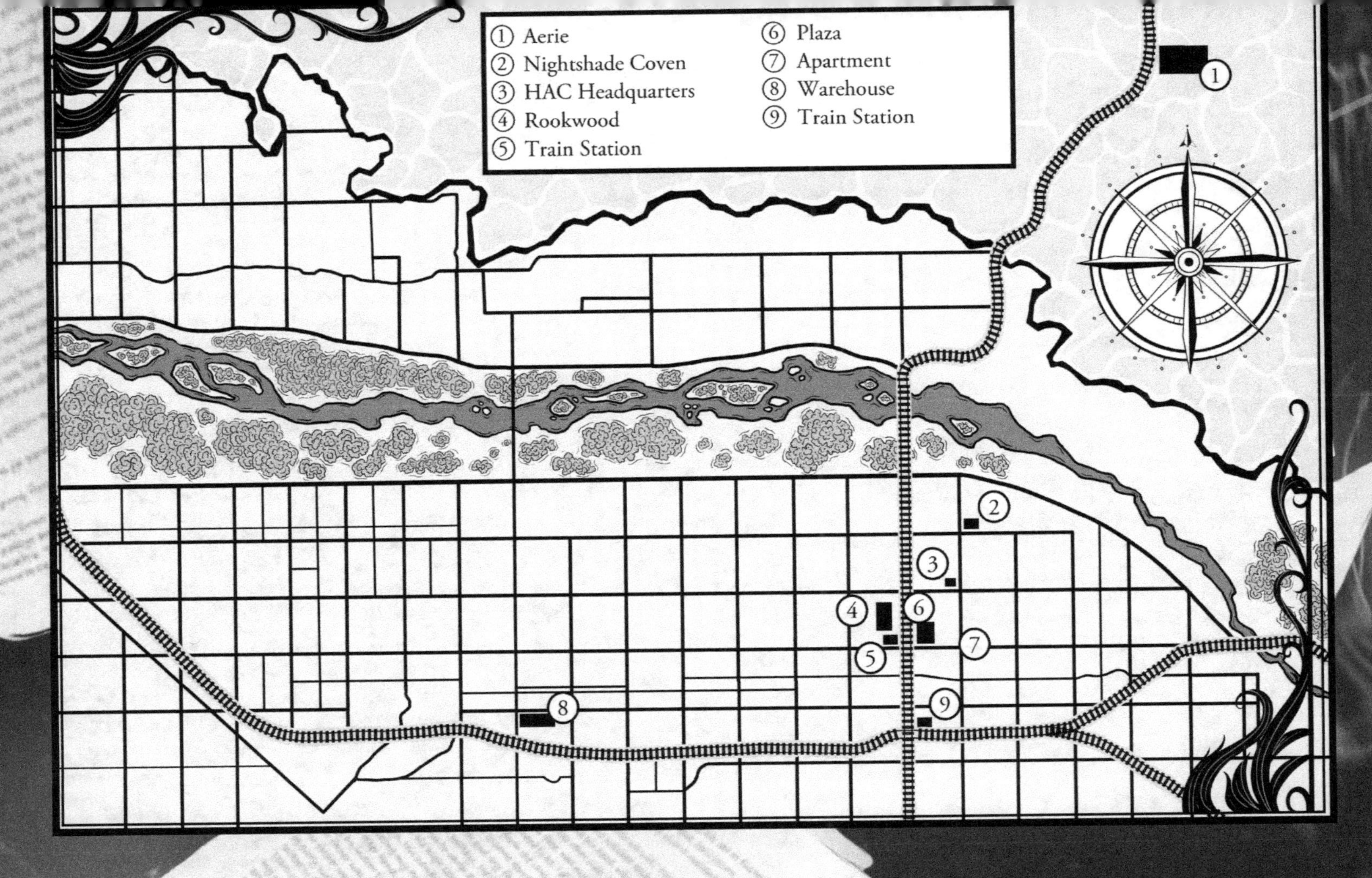

1 Aerie
2 Nightshade Coven
3 HAC Headquarters
4 Rookwood
5 Train Station
6 Plaza
7 Apartment
8 Warehouse
9 Train Station

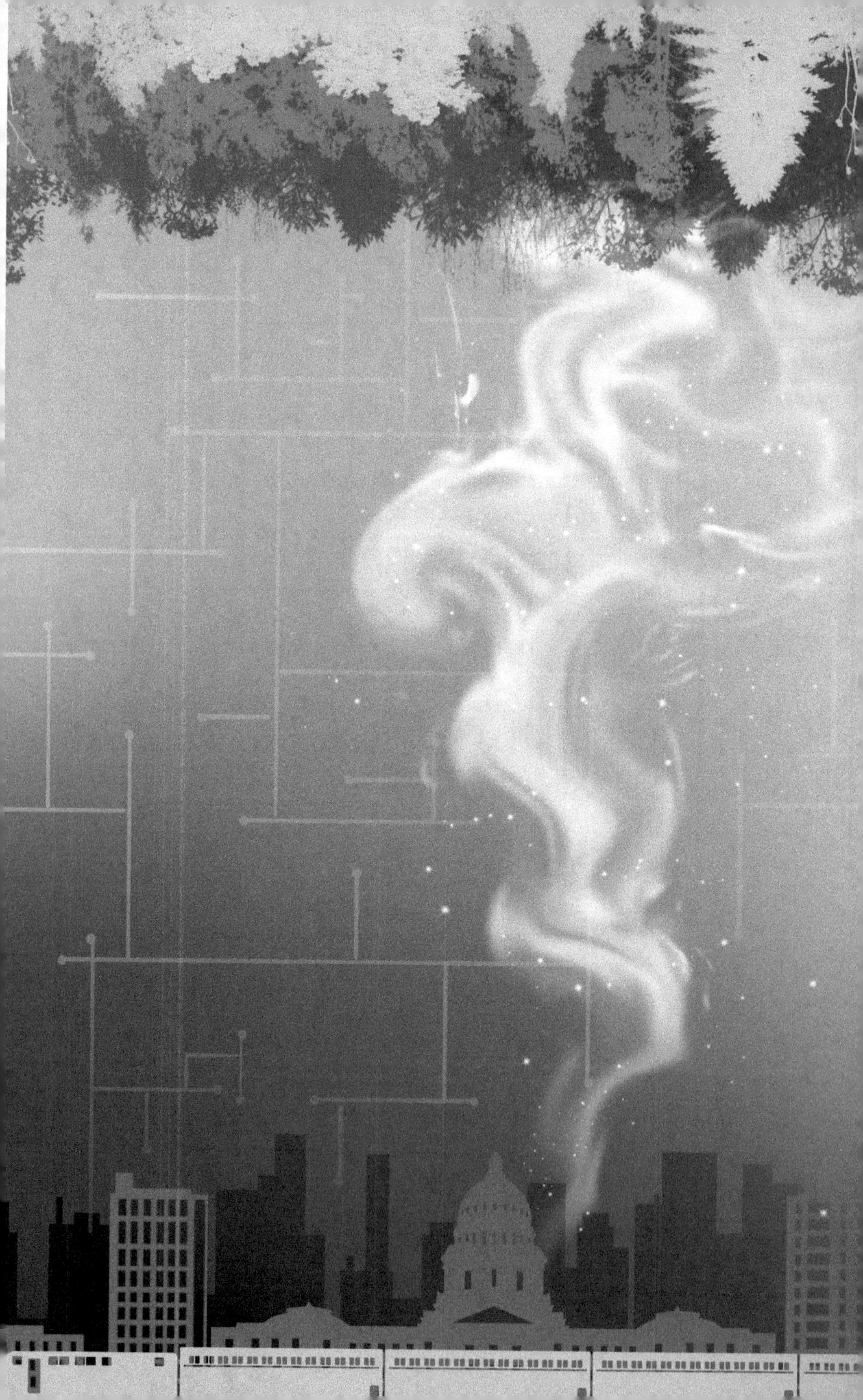

ONE

ELYSE
July 20, 2125

On a sweltering summer afternoon in Jackson County, Georgia—sixty miles northeast of downtown Atlanta—Elyse Hutchinson, twenty-one, walked to the horse paddock where her golden mare, Honey, and Josh Everly's black gelding, Fork, were waiting. The past four weeks had been stressful, requiring Elyse to step outside of her comfort zone and embrace the fact that not only did magical talents exist in the United States, but that she possessed one that allowed her to see the past and the future.

It had seemed simple. Go on a blind date with a guy her best friend Quinn described as "delicious," and try to learn more about her family. Upon reflection, the problems had begun to crop up as Elyse dove deeper into discovering who she was. She was not *just* Elyse Hutchinson, horse rancher of Jackson County; she was also Elyse Hutchinson, great-granddaughter of Archibald Cornelius, the man many believed was the primary scientist behind the COVID-50 pandemic, which devastated more than eighty percent of the country's population—and, as she had recently learned, introduced magical talents to the world.

Elyse still had many unanswered questions about her great-grandfather and his research. She was unwilling to believe that one person could be held accountable for something as significant as COVID-50, and she was determined to find out everything she could to prove that her great-grandfather was not the only person involved. Dariusz Sierżęga stating during the masquerade ball that he had done something to the virus to make it spread magical talents supported her theory. Her body tightened as she thought about Dariusz, the vampire who was the leader of Hellfire and Chaos. He wanted her because of her magical talent and had admitted that he wanted to turn her into his slave.

Yet Elyse found she could not completely escape the influence of HAC because the woman who had agreed to help them get to safety was none other than Catrina Fox, one of the HAC lieutenants. No matter how many times Josh tried to reassure her that Catrina was truly on their side, Elyse still had her doubts. Especially when Catrina had demonstrated that she was willing to use any means necessary to carry out her orders—orders Elyse suspected Dariusz gave her.

As she walked toward the horses, her thoughts churned. *Catrina hasn't told us where we're going or if we'll ever be back. Can I really trust her to not just sell Aunt Grace out the moment we're gone? Can I trust her enough to let her teleport me somewhere that she claims is safe?*

Her feet stopped moving, and Josh Everly, former FBI agent—and possibly her new boyfriend—gave her hand a gentle tug, reminding her they had to get the horses and go before Dariusz showed up and stopped them.

Elyse took a deep breath. *I already decided I would trust Catrina. It is not going to help matters if I start questioning that decision.*

Josh gave her hand another squeeze before letting go. Elyse smiled at the two horses in the paddock. Honey and Fork were a good match for each other, and since Catrina recommended bringing horses for transportation instead of relying on acquiring some once they arrived at their destination, Elyse thought it would be best if they both had horses they got along with. While it would be devastating if something happened to Honey or Fork, she knew how critical it could be to have a reliable mount—although who knew what passed for "reliable" to Catrina. Since the vampire could teleport wherever she pleased, Elyse doubted that Catrina had much use for horses, or cars for that matter. Elyse hadn't argued since she had no idea where they were going. Still, she was comforted to know that they would be bringing two of her best horses along.

Elyse picked up Honey's saddle, and Josh did the same with Fork's. They entered the paddock and quickly tacked up the horses.

"What are you thinking about?" Josh asked, leaning toward her for a light kiss. Her lips tingled where they touched. He kept it light and brief. Elyse realized he must have noticed her long silences. Every time they touched, no matter how briefly, she couldn't help but want more—a longer kiss, a longer hug, even the lightest of touches in passing. Part of her thought it was crazy. No one, man or woman, had ever made her feel like that. Not even her best friend Jessica, whom she loved with all her heart. Until she had given Josh a second chance, she hadn't realized how different her feelings were for him than for Jessica.

Elyse found herself blushing. "Just wondering what the horses would think of being teleported. Since I didn't know magic existed until a month ago, it's not something I have been able to desensitize them to, like I do with everything else."

Josh chuckled. "Fork and Honey seem to take everything pretty well that we've done so far."

Elyse rolled her eyes. "Firing a gun is not the same thing as using a magical talent with a horse."

"I know. I was just saying they seem to handle themselves pretty well. Why are you worried?" Josh said with a shrug.

"If you had seen the desensitizing process, then you would understand. But I am confident in your riding skills. I'm sure if he takes off bucking that you will stay on just fine," she said and gave his arm a pat before tying her saddlebags on and double-checking everything.

A cough came from behind them. Elyse glanced behind her and saw Catrina watching them with an impatient frown.

"Are you done yet?" the vampire asked.

Elyse reluctantly nodded. She was ready, but that didn't mean she had truly come to terms with what their leaving meant. When Josh had explained Catrina's proposal to get them somewhere safe, he had also stressed that he had no way of knowing when they could come back. The last thing Elyse wanted was to bring danger to her ranch, but she'd never had the opportunity to travel. Horse ranching was a full-time job. Horses didn't stop needing to be fed or watered just because a human wanted to disappear for a few days. It was one of the reasons why Elyse had never acquired an apartment in downtown Atlanta and had kept her visits to a few hours at a time. The ranch was an all-consuming lifestyle.

Not that there is anywhere to travel to, she reminded herself. If she was being honest, she wasn't sure how someone would get from Atlanta north to New York or Washington, DC, or west to Texas. She had clients who had come from farther than that to buy the horses she bred, but she had not had the opportunity to study a map to know what routes someone would take.

"Then come out of the paddock so we have enough space," Catrina ordered.

Elyse pinched her lips together at Catrina's tone. Now wasn't the time to get the vampire riled up, not when they were depending on her to take them somewhere safe, away from Atlanta and Jackson County, so that Dariusz Sierżęga would be led away from her ranch and family.

Elyse took a deep breath and followed Josh out of the paddock. When they had enough space to turn both horses around and stand comfortably, she looked to Catrina for the next instruction.

Catrina gave them a grim smile. "Take your reins in one hand and then grab my hand with your free one."

Elyse moved to Catrina's right side, and Josh stood on her left. She gripped Honey's reins tightly, having no idea how teleporting really worked and not wanting to lose the mare in transit. She held her hand out for the vampire to take and was surprised by how cold Catrina's hand was. The vampire gripped Elyse firmly.

"You didn't tell us where we're going," Elyse said softly, and then the air started to shimmer.

"To Terrance in Boise," Catrina replied. The shimmering increased, surrounding all three of them and the horses. The air twisted and the darkness sucked them in.

A roaring sound filled Elyse's ears, and she staggered forward, falling to her knees. The motion jerked hard on Honey's reins, and the mare nickered in protest. The black gleaming air disappeared, and in its place was a huge waterfall. Gravel dug into her knees. With a groan, Elyse leveraged herself up. Keeping her eyes on the waterfall, Elyse found that for some reason it looked vaguely familiar, but she had no idea why. Then it dawned on her. When she was about ten, she had become fascinated by natural waterfalls and had begged her mom to help her find all the information she could on them. Some boxes had been in the shed that surprisingly had information on waterfalls across the country from various trips that her ancestors had taken.

"Shoshone Falls," she whispered in awe. "The Niagara of the West."

Elyse heard something to her left and knew she should look to see if Josh and Fork were okay, but she was having trouble tearing her eyes away from the impressive waterfall. Even though it was summer and historically water levels were reduced because of agriculture, it still had to be close to full capacity, over 212 feet tall and almost 900 feet wide.

"Are you just going to stand there with your mouth hanging open, or are you going to help me?" growled Josh.

Elyse whirled at the tone but then started laughing. Josh had somehow gotten tangled up in the reins. They were wrapped around his left arm and right leg. Fork was standing with his ears flat out to the sides, clearly unhappy. Elyse's chest filled with pride that Fork was able to recognize Josh needed help from a human and that it would be safer if Fork didn't lend a hoof. Though Elyse could see as the gelding's nose twitched that he really did want to help Josh.

"I guess you do need help." Elyse walked over to them and gave Fork a pat before turning her attention to Josh. She gave him a kiss. "I'll have you sorted in no time. Promise." Then, she unbuckled one of the reins and proceeded to unwrap Josh. When he was finally free from the rein, she reattached it to the bridle. Then she stepped into his arms, and he encircled them around her. She might have an idea of where they were, but that knowledge did not give her comfort like she had hoped. Josh's arms around her helped Elyse settle her thoughts and try to relax again.

She wished they could stand there forever gazing upon Shoshone Falls, but she knew that they were out in the open, easy to spot by any passerby and far from "safe."

"Do you know where Catrina went?"

Josh shook his head. "No, and she never really said anything about the plan before teleporting, only that we would be going to Terrance in Boise. Which to be honest is pretty typical for Catrina, at least in my experience. I heard you say Shoshone Falls. Does that mean you know where we are?"

Elyse snuggled deeper into his arms and leaned her head back onto his shoulder. "Yes, or at least I know roughly where we are."

"Which is?" Josh said, loosening his arms.

Elyse sighed as he relaxed his hold, but she knew he was right and they needed to be on their way. She turned around so that she could face him and his arms settled lightly on her waist. It seemed he too craved the touch.

"Twin Falls, Idaho," Elyse replied somewhat hesitantly.

"Twin Falls?" Josh said, eyes widening. "Why the hell would Catrina take us to Twin Falls?" He stopped his rant as suddenly as he started it, then gazed around, and Elyse followed his gaze with her own. A few trees and a gravel road or whatever they were standing on were next to the huge waterfall and its canyon. "You said you know this is Shoshone Falls. Do you know how to get to Boise from here?"

Elyse gave Josh an amused look. "Well, the good news is that we are in the correct state, but I thought as an FBI agent, you knew how to get everywhere."

Josh rolled his eyes. "*Former* FBI agent. I know how to get places within Atlanta and Manhattan since I have lived in both cities the longest, but everywhere else I require some sort of instructions. Yes, I have been to Boise, so I can probably manage somewhat once we're there, but I've never been to Shoshone Falls, nor do I know how to get from Shoshone Falls to Boise, given that I have no idea where we are in the state of Idaho."

Elyse blew out her breath, wondering why he was getting frustrated with her. *Josh just admitted to having been to Boise before. I've never been out of Georgia. Shouldn't I be the one fussing?* "Boise is west of here. In fact, if we follow the Snake River, it should lead us right there."

"Really?" Josh said incredulously.

"Yes, really." Elyse reached out and gave his arm a squeeze. His arm was hard like concrete. *He's nervous,* she realized, studying his face and seeing the tension in his expression. Focused on Josh, she let go of the reins without a thought and threw her arms around his neck, pressing her body tight to his and kissing him. At first, it felt like kissing a rock, but slowly she felt the tension draining from him. She could tell he was recovered when she felt his cock hardening against her. She pulled back, glancing knowingly at the bulge in his pants.

"Maybe we can find somewhere to take care of that," she offered with a smirk.

Josh grimaced. "I really don't want our first time to be out in a field on hard ground, Elyse. I'm not saying no. I'm just saying I want a proper bed."

Elyse stuck out her lower lip in a pout, but she knew he was right. As much as she was turned on right now, she really didn't want to have sex in a random field either. He leaned forward again and kissed her before he snagged Honey's reins off the ground and offered them to her.

"Thanks," Elyse said, stepping closer to Honey and swinging her leg up into the saddle. She waited for Josh to mount before clucking to Honey and setting off in the direction she was confident would take them west to Boise.

Elyse led them on a narrow trail that hugged the rim of the canyon holding the Snake River. She let Honey do most of the work, allowing herself to look around. *Idaho, not a place I ever wanted to visit ... but here we are.* She bit her lip, thinking about the events of the past month and how many things had happened that should have been impossible. Even now she still battled with her emotions.

A month ago, Elyse had been focused on breeding, raising, and training horses for her clients, continuing the horse ranch in Jackson County that had been in her family for over one hundred years. She had been clueless to magical talents existing at all, much less that she had one. Precise control of it still eluded her though.

She had discovered through a box of journals and the help of her best friend Jessica that her great-grandfather had worked for one of the labs in Atlanta, Georgia, largely responsible for the mutation of COVID-50—a lab her uncle Albert had been employed by until his death at the hands of Dariusz.

And then there's Josh, she thought. They had had some intense romantic moments over the past month, and she knew she was falling for him hard, but the simple relationship she had thought they would have had been nowhere near simple, except for maybe the first two dates. Elyse glanced over her shoulder at Josh. He was wearing a light tan cowboy hat that obscured his blond hair, a blue-and-white plaid button-up long-sleeve shirt, and jeans. His sidearm was in a holster on his belt, clearly visible. She could still see the slight stiffness in his posture and the way he held the reins, but it was only noticeable if someone was looking for it. To most, he appeared like he rode a horse all the time and was perfectly comfortable, which had been the plan.

Catrina wouldn't have insisted on them bringing horses if having them would make Josh and Elyse stick out once they arrived at their destination. Elyse knew Idaho was conservative, although not necessarily in the exact same way that Georgia was. But she felt certain there would still be distinct differences between the city-dwellers and the farmers. The biggest question was going to be whether Boise was run by the government or if another organization had a bigger—more visible—foothold.

I really have no idea how much of a foothold HAC has in Atlanta, just that they operate in the shadows, not in the open.

Elyse closed her eyes for a moment, trusting Honey to take care of her. Inhaling deeply, she could smell the fields of alfalfa they were passing by. Taking a second breath, she opened her eyes and realized that her magical talent had taken over and she was in a vision.

A woman of medium height with dark chin-length hair, golden eyes, and warm brown skin paced in a small room. She wore tight-fitting black pants and a black tank top that seemed to be made of Kevlar or something similar, with an assortment of weapons strapped to her legs and waist, including what Elyse thought could be grenades.

Terrance, *Elyse realized with a jolt.* The woman is Terrance.

Suddenly, Terrance turned sharply. The vision refocused so that Elyse could see the person who walked through the door.

The man who entered was huge. He had to be at least seven feet tall. The long-sleeved shirt he wore did nothing to hide how muscular he was. Like Terrance, he had weapons strapped to him, though he mostly had guns of various sizes.

"What the hell, Cory? I am supposed to meet Elyse and Josh, and you're keeping me from leaving. Why?" Terrance snarled.

Growling low in his throat, Cory shoved Terrance backward into the wall. "You have no idea what kind of mess you've made, do you?"

Elyse was surprised that Terrance let him push her without retaliating.

"I guess that depends on what you're calling a mess ... I know Mariah and Vic are not happy that Catrina Fox decided to bring them here."

"It's more than that," Cory said in a low undertone.

Terrance's lips twitched. "Are you going to make me guess, or are you going to get to the point?"

Another low snarl and then Cory opened his mouth and spoke, but Elyse couldn't hear anything.

She pinched her arm, hoping that would help her hear; instead she found herself in the saddle on Honey's back. Blinking rapidly, she tried to make sense of where they were. *Still following the Snake River. I guess Josh didn't notice anything I was doing changed. I will have to tell him what I saw when we stop.*

Elyse could see a creek that fed into the Snake River just ahead and thought that would be the perfect place to stop and water the horses. She knew that she could ride for hours, day after day, because she'd been doing just that her whole life, but she wasn't sure if Josh's body could handle that kind of abuse. A short break with a chance to stretch out his legs would likely be welcome. She guided Honey to a large tree that created a small patch of shade by the edge of the creek.

"You must have read my mind," Josh said from behind her. She heard the creak of the saddle as he dismounted. Elyse hopped off Honey and loosened the girth on the saddle. They weren't going to be stopped for long enough to justify completely untacking the horses, but at least they could give them a moment to relax.

Elyse led Honey to the creek and sat down at the edge of the water, allowing the mare to wade farther into the water to cool off. Fork practically dragged Josh into the water in his eagerness to follow Honey's lead. Elyse chuckled.

"How far away do you think we are from Boise?" Josh asked.

Elyse shrugged. "Honestly, I'm not sure. I think Shoshone Falls is about one hundred miles or so from Boise, but we've been mostly just walking, so at our pace, it'll probably take a couple of days."

"We could go faster if you want. We might be safer if we get there sooner. Out here it feels rather exposed," Josh admitted.

Elyse nodded. She had been hesitant to suggest that they go faster, but she was pleased that Josh felt it would be a good idea. Out in the fields she felt exposed, and if someone wanted to eliminate them, it would easy. Theoretically, they should be able to see someone coming, but she knew better. With the frequent crops, including corn, it would not be difficult for someone familiar with the land to remain undetected.

She dug in her pocket and pulled out a small bag of salted nuts. She took one before offering the bag to Josh.

He shook his head. "I already snacked some. I'm fine."

"Okay," Elyse said and ate another nut. "I had a vision."

Josh's gaze intensified as he looked at her. "What did you see?"

"Terrance. I actually think it was the present or recent past because based on the conversation I overheard, she was trying to leave to reach us, but things are happening there that are preventing her from doing so," Elyse explained.

"Did you see or get a name of the person she was talking to?" Josh asked, scratching his chin in thought.

"Cory. He was huge, muscled, and likely over seven feet tall," Elyse said.

Josh chuckled. "Yes, Cory is huge. Was anyone else there?"

Elyse shook her head. "No, but they did mention Mariah and Vic." She twisted a finger through a strand of hair. "I got the feeling that they have stuff going on, and we have just been dropped in the middle of it."

"Hopefully that won't cause too much of a problem," Josh said with a grimace.

"But maybe Terrance will meet up with us before we get to Boise," Elyse said hopefully.

"Eh … she probably has no idea where we are. When we get close enough to Boise, I know Terrance has scouts. So someone should tell her where we are, and then she'll find us. As long as she's not tied up." He smirked.

"What?" Elyse replied, eyebrows arched.

"Oh, just that Cory likes to tie Terrance up, Catrina told me," Josh said, wagging his eyebrows suggestively.

Elyse shook her head. "I don't think I want to know." Even as she said it, an image of Josh tied to her bed naked came to her. She wiped her hands on her pants, trying to distract herself, and glanced at the horses. They looked mostly asleep standing in the creek.

"We can try trotting for a while if you want. With the heat, I don't think cantering would be ideal, but a trot should be okay. As long as we are careful and don't wear them out too much, which would require us to go even slower."

Josh shrugged. "Whatever pace you think is best. I'll let you set it. We'll get there when we get there."

Elyse gave a gentle tug on the rein and Honey's head popped up, then the mare made her way out of the creek. Fork followed right behind her. Once they were clear of the creek, Elyse and Josh both mounted, and Elyse clucked, urging Honey into a brisk trot and continuing their trek west on the Snake River.

TWO

JOSH

Elyse was in the lead, her long red hair hanging down her back. Josh admired how effortlessly she rode Honey. They were still following a narrow trail on the edge of the canyon that held the Snake River. Most of this part of Idaho was farmland and fairly flat. In the distance, Josh could see the mountains: the Sawtooth Range to the northeast and Owyhee Mountains to the southwest.

From the position of the sun, Josh was fairly certain they'd been riding for about eight hours, give or take, since they left Shoshone Falls. He just didn't know how fast they were traveling or how far they had to go. Since they had stopped at the creek, Elyse had increased their pace with stretches of trotting mixed with walking. Everything ached from the amount of time they had spent in the saddle. Before they had left Elyse's ranch, he had been slowly building up his stamina and could ride for two to three hours without any discomfort, but eight hours was more than he was ready for.

He was a little surprised they hadn't come across anyone yet. He knew based on the farms they had passed that there had to be people not too far away. All the fields appeared well tended, and the crops they had passed—wheat, corn, and alfalfa—seemed healthy.

Although what do I know about crop health? Elyse probably would be a better judge of it than I am.

Sweat trickled down his back, and his damp shirt clung to him. It was hot. Way hotter than he had expected. The one time Josh had been in Idaho, it had been October and the weather had been low sixties with sun. His thoughts drifted back to that trip.

Josh kept his face blank and his back straight. He could feel the comforting weight of his gun on his right hip and the knife hidden under his left sock. He knew if Assistant Director Gerald Fernway found out about the knife, he would likely be reprimanded, but Josh didn't care. He was more concerned about his ability to perform his duty as one of four FBI agents assigned as Fernway's escort for his trip to Boise to meet with the governor of Idaho, Paul Beechwood.

The escort, Fernway had said, was more of a formality than anything, but it was Josh's first big assignment. The FBI office in Los Angeles had gotten a request to send Josh to Atlanta to be a part of the escort detail. Josh thought that the cost of transporting him from Los Angeles to Atlanta was a little over the top, but what did he know.

The meeting had lasted only a few hours, and Josh had stood outside of the room with the other three agents. When it concluded, Assistant Director Fernway and his escort got back on the helicopter and returned to Atlanta.

Josh shook his head. He never had figured out how exactly they had managed the trip with a helicopter and not a normal airplane—if those even existed anymore. Helicopters couldn't fly almost three thousand miles without refueling, and they were slow compared to the speeds a plane could achieve. He had always assumed some sort of magic was involved, but none of his questions were ever answered. Unlike that perfect October day seven years ago, the weather was not nice today in any shape or form. Even though it was not humid like Atlanta, he was pretty sure he'd never been anywhere this hot before. Elyse hadn't commented, so he wasn't sure if she just didn't care about the temperature or didn't feel like complaining.

He let go of the reins with one hand and wiped his sweaty palm on his jeans before picking the reins back up. Fork, with his black fur, was completely drenched in sweat, poor horse. Josh gave the gelding a pat. As he leaned down, something flickered at the edge of his vision. Keeping his body tipped, Josh slightly adjusted his head, hoping to give whoever it was the illusion that he didn't know he or she was there while he was actually trying to see them better.

At the far side of the cornfield they were passing, another rider was on horseback. Josh couldn't tell from this distance if the rider was male or female, but he could definitely make out the rifle strapped to the back, the handgun at the waist, and the third gun, possibly a shotgun, in the person's hand. Josh flicked his eyes forward to see if Elyse had noticed they were being watched, but her eyes were focused on the trail ahead, and her posture hadn't changed.

Josh sighed. *It could be nothing. Just a farmer protecting his land. The last time I saw Terrance, I didn't bother asking her how things were around Boise, so I have no clue what the state of things is here, whether the United States government has control over the city or if it is Hellfire and Chaos or someone else entirely.* He knew that every big city that still existed was not operating the same way it had been. Each one had some amount of government presence, but not all were as rigidly controlled as Atlanta was.

He nudged Fork lightly with his legs, urging him to speed up into a trot so they could pull up next to Elyse. When they were side by side, Josh reached over and gave Elyse's hand a light tap.

"We have company. Don't look," he said softly. He didn't want to make any quick moves in case the farmer decided that shooting them was in his best interest. In Josh's experience, people didn't pack three guns if they weren't willing to use them. Whether or not they had good aim was another story, but he did not want to gamble with getting shot.

"Are we going to do anything about it?" Elyse asked, her voice equally soft, though he thought he heard a slight edge to it.

"Not unless the farmer makes a move first. I was hoping by now either Catrina would have reappeared or that Terrance would have found us. I don't like that we're going into Boise blind," Josh explained. *Not like I can do anything about it. Neither one of us can teleport, so we are stuck unless Catrina decides to show up and take us somewhere else, or if we find someone else who can teleport.* He shuddered at the thought of letting anyone else teleport him. There were few people he trusted. Hell, he wasn't even sure he completely trusted Catrina, and look where that fragile trust had gotten him.

His handgun was a reassuring weight in its holster, but Josh was not naïve; a handgun and two exhausted horses were no match for a rifle. Even if he wanted to urge Elyse to run, it would be useless. They wouldn't make it, and it could encourage the farmer to take action against them. However, if they kept their cool, then maybe the farmer would just ignore them, and they could continue on their ride west without any conflict.

As they rode side by side, Josh felt certain more people were gathering, he just couldn't see them. The skin on the back of his neck prickled. The path they were on dipped, and he couldn't see the far edge, only what was below them and the upward slope. Suddenly, not one but three riders appeared on the rim, all equipped with numerous guns, and each had one weapon leveled at either him or Elyse.

Honey and Fork both stopped in their tracks. Josh itched to grab his gun but knew it wouldn't help matters and could result in one of them getting shot.

"Are you Josh Everly and Elyse Hutchinson?" the rider in the middle called. He wore a black cowboy hat and a faded green T-shirt and was holding a large shotgun.

Josh plastered a fake smile on his face. "Yes. Who's asking?"

The riders exchanged a look. "I'm Devin Shaw. Terrance told me to help you if you came my way."

"Terrance Basak?" Josh asked uncertainly. He was having trouble believing they'd found someone who wanted to help them.

Devin nodded. "Yes. She runs the Hellfire and Chaos branch in Idaho."

Interesting that HAC is more open about their presence … unless he was just ordered to introduce himself that way. Josh ran a hand over his leg, thinking. "I want proof the Terrance you're talking about is the Terrance I know. Tell me something that isn't common knowledge."

Devin shrugged. "She can turn into a Siberian tiger."

Josh shook his head. He was not surprised that was the first thing Devin offered. "You could just know of her and be aware she can shift. I need something else, something more personal."

Devin's eyes narrowed. "She is mated to Cory."

"Thank you," said Josh and nudged Fork forward with his legs, closing the distance between them. "Now, how are you planning on helping us? You don't happen to have someone who can tele-port us, do you?"

Devin smirked. "No, but … well, you'll see. I won't spoil the sur-prise for you." Devin spun his horse around and spurred it hard. The three riders shot forward at a gallop.

Josh rolled his eyes in annoyance and made a kissing sound to Fork. The gelding eagerly sprang forward, clearly forgetting how hot and miserable he had been just moments before. *I really hope we're not running very far.* Instead of following the trail that Josh and Elyse had been on, Devin led them in a sharp turn to the left, away from the river and toward the fields. Closest to them was alfalfa hay, but they were making a beeline for a cornfield, which was tall enough to make it difficult to see what was on the other side.

To Josh's surprise, Devin and his companions flowed into a sin-gle-file line and galloped *into* the cornfield. He could feel Fork stiffening underneath him as the horse reacted to Josh's apprehension at running blindly through corn. Elyse seemed to have no reservations. She snuck ahead of Josh and followed Devin and his cohorts dutifully.

Josh sent up a prayer and loosened his grip on the reins. As the corn closed in, he realized with a gasp that they were on a hard-packed path, about the width of two of the rows of corn, that seemed as though it was used often. *So it's not just random.* He still wasn't sure what to make of the group or the path they were taking when the corn abruptly disappeared and the group ahead of him halted. Josh rocked back, dropping his weight into his saddle as Fork dropped his hind end and literally slid to a stop, sending up a cascade of dirt in his wake.

Josh blinked a few times, trying to clear the dirt from his eyes, certain he was mistaken about what he was seeing. Devin turned toward him, a smirk on his face.

"Is that what I think it is?" asked Josh.

"Depends on what you think it is," Devin retorted.

"A train?" Josh replied.

Devin clapped. "Good job! You know what a train looks like, but do you know how it runs?"

Josh shook his head. *How did I not notice they had a train when I was here last time?* He rolled his eyes at himself. *Duh, because the helicopter landed on top of the building the meeting was in, and we went inside, and then went back into the helicopter.*

"It runs on a mix of magical talent and solar power," Devin replied.

"Who has control over it?" Josh asked, curiosity piqued.

"Over this particular train, HAC, but there are a couple of other trains, and for the most part, they are operated by the local government for the use of its residents," Devin replied. "Now, if you don't mind, we should get on board."

Josh glanced at Elyse, assuming she was wondering the same thing. How were the horses getting on the train?

One of the other riders dismounted and walked over the train. He tapped on the side twice, and the panel opened and a ramp unfolded. "The horses will go up the ramp."

Josh dismounted and followed Devin up the ramp with Fork. Elyse slipped behind him. When everyone was on board, the panel shut.

THREE
TERRANCE

It took all of Terrance Basak's willpower to keep her hands from curling into fists on top of the table. As lieutenant of the Northwest division of Hellfire and Chaos, she was not obligated to share her plans with any of her members. *Yet I do*, she reminded herself. Which was how she had ended up in the conference room at HAC headquarters in Boise with her mate, Cory, a tiger shifter, and her third-in-command Pierre, a wolf shifter, both looking like they wanted to take a bite out of her.

"HAC doesn't need the money," Pierre said.

"This isn't an HAC plan," Terrance replied.

"Fine, *you* don't need the money," Pierre replied, his fists clenched.

"This is not the first time I've agreed to a private contract. I don't see why you have a problem with it. Or honestly why it matters to you at all, Pierre," Terrance said, keeping her eyes on Pierre and not on her mate. Cory had originally told her that he didn't care if she took the contract to find the Snowflake, yet now that Pierre had an opinion about it, Cory seemed inclined to have one too. *Men.* She bit her lip, knowing if she rolled her eyes and Pierre thought it was directed at him that she'd be in more trouble.

"My issue isn't that you took out a contract. It's that you did so to retrieve the Snowflake. I am not sure if you just have no idea what the Snowflake is and that's why you accepted the contract, or if you do and don't understand all of the risks associated with it," Pierre explained.

Terrance blew out her breath. She had done her own research before accepting Trey's contract to acquire the Snowflake. The device had been created to essentially hack into the government's computer system that exclusively controlled all the electricity-generating farms throughout the country, such as the solar farm west of downtown Atlanta and the wind farms in Boise. Theoretically, if an individual had the Snowflake, then they had the ability to control access to the electricity for the entire country. But Terrance knew enough about the government and computer hacking to not believe that a single device could be that powerful. Or that the government would be stupid enough to allow something like the Snowflake to exist.

"I accepted the contract knowing what the Snowflake is rumored to be capable of doing. However, I don't feel as though a single device would be capable of such a task. Not after HAC, with our own Yolanda at the helm, has failed to successfully gain control of a single wind or solar farm with an on-site attack," Terrance said.

Her thoughts drifted back to the operation three years ago to take control over the wind farm in the foothills of the Owyhee Mountains south of Boise. Yolanda had been convinced she could break through the encryption locking down the control panel for the wind farm. But even using her magic, nothing Yolanda had done had worked. Terrance remembered Yolanda describing it as "impenetrable." The operation was intended as a show of power to the Idaho governor, but it had failed miserably. Instead, Terrance had been forced to approve the backup plan, which was to destroy half of the wind farm.

The rolling blackouts throughout the state had lasted for more than two months. While Terrance had still been able to show the governor that she was not someone they wanted to mess with, she had caused problems for her own organization as well. The backup generator system at her HAC headquarters was sophisticated and allowed for talents to recharge it, but that only worked for so long. The talented had to rest and replenish their stores.

"Ter." Cory snapped his fingers in her face.

Terrance blinked. "What?"

"I asked you a question. But clearly you were focused on something else. Care to share?" Cory said.

"No, it's not important. I don't know why you have your panties in a twist over this contract, Pierre, but the deal has been made. In fact, I am going to retrieve the Snowflake in a few hours," Terrance said firmly, then stood up, bracing her hands on the conference table. She met Pierre's blue eyes with her golden ones and held his gaze until he looked away. As Alpha of the Treasure Valley wolf pack, Pierre seldom had to back down to anyone. Anyone except for Terrance or Cory. Terrance knew it was the only way he would let go of whatever his issue was with this contract, by forcing him into submission. Thankfully, long gone were the days that she had to fight him into submission.

There was a knock on the door. Terrance turned her head toward it but made no move to open it.

The door opened and Pierre's sister, Sienna, peered around it. "Devin has found Josh and Elyse."

Terrance raised her eyebrows. "They weren't supposed to arrive until tomorrow."

Sienna shrugged. "Well, they're heading to the train now."

Terrance sighed. "I will have to meet them later then." She checked her watch. "I need to go." She glanced over at Pierre, wondering if he would say anything else.

"Let me know if you need me," her third-in-command said, not meeting her eyes. He slipped past Sienna and out the door.

Terrance waved Sienna off, and the wolf shifter shut the door behind her. Arms wrapped around her waist, Terrance turned, tilting her head back to gaze at her mate. She knew they looked comical together in their human forms, Cory seven feet tall and her barely five foot two. When they shifted, though, they were almost the same size, four hundred pounds of Siberian tiger each.

Cory dipped his head down and brushed his lips lightly on Terrance's. "Be safe."

Terrance deepened the kiss before reluctantly pulling back. "I will do my best to stay safe." Cory's hands loosened around her waist, and Terrance stepped back, bumping the table. "Love you." She slid past him and out the door.

Terrance had caught the train from outside HAC headquarters and ridden it into downtown Boise, disembarking at the station by the state university. She watched the train depart before checking her phone.

> *W0lfL0v3r99: Sit on the bench for 5 minutes before moving the stone at the base of the statute.*

The instructions had been sent in pieces across several types of media to avoid being discovered by anyone they didn't want to interfere with the transaction. Unlike her deal with Trey, the deal with W0lfL0v3r99 was trading the Snowflake for weapons that Terrance and Cory had acquired in a heist two months ago. Cory had wanted to destroy the weapons immediately, but Terrance had decided to wait just in case they needed them for something. Now she was glad she had postponed their destruction.

Terrance strolled down the sidewalk. She was approaching the park that bordered the Boise River. The path she traveled was shaded, offering some respite from the heat. This morning, the weather report had indicated that they were going to possibly hit new record highs for July in the next two days. It was currently almost 110 degrees. Being under the trees cut at least five degrees. It was just a touch more bearable.

Not that if I shifted I'd be faring any better, not in the summer, she reminded herself. Siberian tigers were definitely not made for hot climates, whether it was dry or humid heat. During the winter snowstorms, if they didn't have any HAC business to attend to, Terrance and Cory would often go "camping" in the mountains for a week. Those who knew them well knew that they spent most of the time either playing in the snow as tigers or in each other's arms.

Terrance blinked, forcing herself to focus on the task at hand. The Snowflake. Just up ahead she could see her destination—a bench with a statue of a dolphin behind it. She had always thought it odd that the bench wasn't facing the statue so that people could sit and admire it. When she reached the bench, she sat down and checked her watch.

After waiting five minutes, she stood up and walked over to the dolphin statue. Pressing her foot down on the concrete at the base of the statue, she was rewarded with a click as the piece of concrete lifted up. Kneeling down as though to tie her boot, Terrance lifted the concrete gently. Underneath was a small, thin box. She pulled it out and shoved it into her pocket, then replaced the piece of concrete and pressed it down to close it. Satisfied that it was not obvious the concrete could move, Terrance walked east along the river.

She followed the path along the river until she reached the wooden bridge. She crossed it and walked up the hill, to the other side of the university. When she was far enough from the park, she pulled out the box and opened it. Sure enough, the Snowflake was inside: a thumbnail-sized chip in the shape of a snowflake.

I will have to confirm this is the real Snowflake when I get back, she thought. Then, she shut the box and returned it to her pocket. Terrance made her way to the train station.

Terrance sat near the door of the train. The train car was empty, and there were two stops from downtown Boise to the station closest to HAC headquarters. She stared at the floor, letting her thoughts drift, when someone sat down next to her. She stiffened, and her knife was in her hand before she had even figured out who it was.

"I thought you were napping," Agent Florence said.

Terrance met the FBI agent's eyes and caught the smirk. "You're lucky I didn't strike first." She loosened her grip on the knife and studied the woman next to her. Black hair in a severe bun at the nape of her neck, fitted black suit with a white silk blouse, dark olive skin, and her voice carried a faint Italian accent. "Since you're sitting next to me on an empty train, I assume there's a reason?"

Agent Florence nodded. "Yes. I have a proposition for you. Or I should say Governor Beechwood does."

Terrance's lips twitched. She did not like it when the governor took notice of what she was doing and she made an effort to ensure she seldom had direct encounters with the man. His agenda was maintaining the state of Idaho, while hers was running a division of HAC that operated in four different states and frequently engaged in illegal activities.

"I'm not interested."

Agent Florence rolled her eyes. "You have no idea what I'm going to say. How can you already say no?"

"Easy. My answer is no," Terrance said and stood up, turning her back to the FBI agent, fiddling with her knife.

Agent Florence didn't follow her. Instead, she stayed in her seat. "He knows about Trey and is willing to give you ten times as much."

Terrance swiveled back toward Agent Florence but kept her hand from falling down to her pocket. If the governor knew about her deal with Trey, it was possible Agent Florence knew she had the Snowflake on her. "Is this a joke?"

Agent Florence shook her head. "No."

The train was slowing. They had to be approaching Terrance's stop. The doors slid open, revealing the train station. Terrance hesitated, not sure what to say.

"Just think about it. You know how to reach me if you want to move forward," Agent Florence said.

The train doors started to shut, Terrance gave the FBI agent a nod and slid through the doors before she got stuck on the train. On the platform, she glanced around, trying to regain her bearings. Seeing Agent Florence on the train had been unexpected, but over the years she would occasionally meet with Terrance to offer opportunities that were not always on the books. What had caught Terrance off guard was that the governor was offering her ten times the amount that Trey had for her to acquire the Snowflake. *This is going to require a discussion with Cory.*

Terrance headed for the apartment she shared with Cory inside HAC headquarters. She was hoping he would sense her intentions through the mating bond and meet her there. Terrance unlocked the apartment door and stepped inside, locking it firmly behind her.

Cory was sitting on one of the stools at the bar-height counter in their kitchen.

"Hey," she greeted. He nodded in acknowledgement but stayed silent. "I'm going to put this in the safe."

Without waiting for his response, Terrance went into their bedroom closet and opened the safe. She pulled the box the Snowflake was in out of her pocket, placed it on a shelf, and shut and locked the safe.

"I could tell you were stressed out on the train. What happened?" Cory asked, diving right in.

Terrance filled up a cup of water in the sink opposite Cory's stool and took a sip before replying. "I was able to get the Snowflake no problem, but Agent Florence was on the train."

"Did she ask if we wanted to do a new joint operation?" Cory asked.

Terrance pursed her lips. "Not exactly. Governor Beechwood knows we have the Snowflake, and he has offered us ten times what Trey did—one hundred million dollars—to give him the Snowflake instead of giving it to Trey."

Cory's eyes widened, and his jaw dropped open. Terrance's breathing hitched slightly as the realization of how much money that was came crashing down on her too. Saying the number aloud let it really sink in.

"That's a lot of money," Cory said cautiously.

Terrance blew out her breath. "I know. But it also makes me wonder why the governor wants the Snowflake. What is he intending to do with it, or what does he think Trey is going to do with it?"

Cory drummed his fingers on the counter. "You originally said that you didn't care about the why and were doing it just to get some extra money. Which, if that is the case, then there would be no reason to not go with Governor Beechwood's offer."

"Aside from the fact that I already made a deal with Trey. I am sure he is not going to let me renege without consequences," Terrance pointed out. One hundred million was a *lot* of money. *Enough to consider getting out entirely once we have it*, she thought but wasn't sure if Cory would agree. They rarely discussed plans for the future unless it was an upcoming HAC operation or one of their winter camping trips. In fact, they had never really discussed if they wanted children.

"We have enough firepower here that we can withstand any retaliation Trey might try. Since you made the initial deal, I'll let you make the decision," Cory said diplomatically.

Terrance met his gaze. For once she couldn't get a read on what Cory was thinking through their bond. "Have you ever thought about leaving this all behind?"

Cory searched her face with a frown. "Getting a new apartment outside of headquarters?"

Terrance lightly swatted his hand. "No. I mean retiring from HAC."

"Can you do that? Would Dariusz let you quit?" Cory asked.

Terrance sighed; he had a valid point. "I don't know."

"How about this," he said, resting his hand on top of hers and giving it a gentle squeeze. "See if Trey will give you more money, and if he won't, then take the governor's deal. When the dust settles, we can have a serious discussion about our future."

Terrance nodded. "Okay. I will arrange the meeting with Trey and see whether or not he will go for the new amount."

Cory leaned over and gave her a light kiss. "Good. I need to get back to the training session I was in the middle of. Keep me posted."

Terrance watched Cory leave and then sent Trey a message requesting another meeting. When she was done, she realized that Elyse and Josh would be arriving soon and she had to finish her preparations for their arrival.

FOUR
ELYSE

Elyse gazed at the train. It was sleek black with rounded sides; the front and back ends looked identical, and she assumed it could go in either direction on the track without having to turn around somewhere. As she studied it more, she realized that the roof wasn't actually metal at all. It was tiny solar panels, presumably allowing the train to charge continuously, just as her car did. *When it's not in the shed,* she thought, then remembered that her shed and car had exploded a week ago at her ranch. With a big sigh, she let go of her thoughts about the ranch and focused once again on the train. It had what appeared to be four separate cars, although she was not sure if they were truly separate or not. The metal panels changed where they merged, almost like the hide of an armadillo. *Probably so it can go around turns and flex.*

It was far from what she had expected to see on the other side of the cornfield; she had anticipated a road, perhaps with a large truck and horse trailer or something along those lines. *I suppose a train track is very similar to a road.* Though a train was probably more realistic as a form of transportation if they weren't going to use a car or teleportation, she mused.

She watched the door open and create a ramp. Inside, she could see what looked like some sort of material for stall bedding, which led her to believe that this was a common way of transporting the horses longer distances. *I wonder if any states other than Idaho have trains or if this track is just local. Josh seemed very surprised by the train, so it's likely he wouldn't know.*

Devin led his horse in and motioned for Elyse to follow. Honey stepped right onto the ramp as though she had seen a train before and it didn't bother her one bit. *Hopefully, Fork cooperates too.* She was about to glance back at Josh when the interior of the train caught her eye. It was set up with an aisleway on one side and six stalls on the other. They weren't huge by any means but large enough for transporting. *Much like a horse trailer,* she thought, for those of her clients who could afford to ship their new horse and not have to ride or walk it home themselves.

She had to admit she had just assumed that other large cities in the United States operated much like Atlanta did: the wealthy living in the downtown area with the luxury of electricity and cars and everyone else living in rural areas without electricity, riding horses for transportation, and farming. Perhaps that was also because she was new to the world of magic and magical talents. She didn't have any idea about the full range of tasks that magical talents could be used for. So far, she had personally come across a tiger shifter, vampires, a healer, and Josh—whose talent made him stronger and faster. *Maybe I should ask Josh when we get a moment alone.*

Elyse got Honey settled in one of the stalls, and Josh did the same for Fork, who seemed completely unfazed by the train. The train began to move. At first, it was so silent that Elyse wasn't sure that it was moving.

Devin cleared his throat. "If you want, we can leave the horses here and go to the next car. It has seats and windows."

"That sounds great. Thanks," Elyse replied without checking with Josh first. She knew that arriving at Shoshone Falls had really thrown him off, and he seemed out of his element. But they were on a moving train; she didn't have a ton of options. Being able to see where they were sounded appealing. At least if they had to bail suddenly, they would know they weren't jumping into the river canyon.

Devin pushed a button on the wall and the door slid to the side. Devin had said the next car had seats, but he omitted any details. Elyse was surprised to see that the "seats" were luxurious-looking couches arranged so that she could see out of the large panoramic windows and still be comfortable.

"The train didn't seem to have windows when we were outside," Elyse said quietly.

Devin nodded. "Yes, a metal protective cover slides over them. It comes in handy when you're under attack."

"What do you mean 'under attack'?" Josh said, voice tense.

Devin pursed his lips. "Well, I don't know what Atlanta is like, but around here, things are not always peaceful. This train belongs to HAC, so the organization has taken some measures to ensure that the people inside the train are not easy targets."

"Who around here would have the balls to attack HAC?" asked Josh.

Devin chuckled darkly. "Idaho's governor holds Boise in … I guess you could say a partnership with HAC. There are other people in the area, including a clan of bear shifters, who disagree with it. Also at times, there are conflicts, as I'm sure you're well aware, that are internal to the organization." He paused. "Besides, I would think that someone with experience like you have, Josh, would know it's better to be prepared for any scenario than not."

During their exchange, Elyse found her attention drawn to the window. They were going at a moderate speed, faster than they could ride for any prolonged period of time but slower than a car would go. Which meant she could see where they were. The train tracks seemed to drift closer to the Owyhee Mountains than the Snake River did, which she supposed made sense if the intention was to keep the train hidden. Up ahead, she could see what looked like buildings, but she was surprised to see them so soon. She hadn't thought they had ridden more than thirty miles since they left the falls.

One of the other riders who had been with Devin sat down next to her on the couch. He extended a hand for her to shake. "I'm Nathan."

Elyse gave him a smile and took his hand. "Elyse."

Nathan's hand squeezed hers, and then everything faded.

Elyse was in a small café she didn't recognize. The walls were made of old red bricks, and the mortar was falling out in some places. A woman with medium-brown skin and short, cropped black hair sat at a table with a steaming cup of coffee in front of her. Terrance, Elyse realized. Terrance was sitting across from someone Elyse didn't know—a thin man with dark beady eyes, greasy blond hair slicked against his head, and a wisp of a goatee on his chin.

The thin man spoke first. "We had a deal, Terrance."

Terrance snarled low in her throat, and her skin rippled slightly. "The deal has changed, Trey."

Trey gave her a sharp smile. "Unfortunately, it doesn't work like that. You can't just back out or change the terms because you no longer like them."

"Too bad. Here's the new deal. We want double. Or I will destroy it," Terrance said firmly.

As Terrance flexed her fingers against the cup, Elyse saw claws growing out of them.

Trey must have noticed them too because his reply was hasty. "I will have to see if my boss will agree to double."

Elyse thought Trey would call or contact his boss, but instead the man stood up and stepped away from the table.

Terrance growled. "When will you know?"

Trey looked at Terrance, his face unreadable. "Either you'll be dead in the next twenty-four hours, or you'll be paid. It should be pretty obvious."

Elyse expected Terrance to demand to know now, but the shifter let Trey walk away. Elyse kept her eyes focused on Terrance, watching as she flexed her fingers and the claws extended and retracted. If Elyse had to guess, Terrance was not pleased with the outcome of the meeting, which led Elyse to wonder what the deal was and who it was with. Is it Terrance herself or Terrance representing HAC? *Elyse huffed out a breath.* I don't even know if this is past or future.

The café faded, and Elyse assumed she'd end up back in the train. Instead, she was with Terrance again. Gone were Terrance's business clothes; she wore a sports bra and athletic shorts. Her skin was slick with sweat. This time, though, Terrance was doing some sort of mixed martial arts fight with a man who was almost seven feet tall. Realization dawned on Elyse. This was Cory.

Terrance feinted with her left hand and pivoted, delivering a roundhouse kick with her right leg. Cory was ready. He grabbed Terrance's ankle and twisted, flipping her onto the mat. Terrance didn't hesitate. She bounced back to her feet and sped up her attacks, doing a quick series of jabs to his abs and then following that up with another kick.

The fighting was so quick that Elyse had trouble following all the moves. One moment it seemed like Cory still had the upper hand, and the next, he was flat on his back with Terrance straddling him, her hands around his throat, fingers turning into claws as she dug them into Cory's neck. His hands moved from being pinned under her legs to caressing her hips. As Elyse watched, Terrance's hands loosened around his throat, and the claws retracted. In one deft movement, Cory flipped over and Terrance was the one pinned, but

Elyse was pretty sure Terrance didn't mind, given her lips were locked with Cory's in a very intense kiss. Cory's hands trailed over Terrance's body before settling on her breasts.

Elyse felt a shiver run through her. She bit her lip. I need to get laid, and soon, *she thought, annoyed at her body's response. She closed her eyes, not sure she really wanted to watch any more of the vision as Cory was quickly removing his pants.*

Elyse opened her eyes and thrust herself backward in surprise when Josh's deep blue eyes were only a few inches away from her green ones.

"What the hell?" she gasped.

"You were shaking hands with Nathan when your eyes went vacant. He was worried and called me over," Josh explained. "Did you have a vision?"

Elyse nodded in confirmation, but she wasn't sure if she trusted Devin and Nathan to tell them what she saw.

"And?" Josh prompted.

Elyse scratched her chin, debating how to respond. "I saw Terrance and Cory. Terrance was complaining about not being able to meet us as she had planned," Elyse replied, settling for using the old vision Josh already knew about. She hoped he would understand that she didn't feel like she could share what she saw in present company. Besides, she really had seen Terrance.

Josh nodded. "Well, it is clear that Terrance is not here to meet us." Thankfully, he did not ask any further questions.

Devin walked over. "Terrance didn't say that you could see the past."

Elyse shrugged. "Do you walk around telling everyone about your magical talent?"

Devin frowned. "No, of course not."

"Then why would you think that Terrance would go around telling everyone about mine?" Elyse replied, annoyance causing her voice to raise.

"She usually tells me things like that if they're important to my assigned task," Devin said, keeping his voice light.

Elyse was still annoyed. "Escorting me shouldn't require you to know what my magical talent is, unless you are not just escorting us, and something else is going on instead." She kept her eyes on Devin.

Devin took a step back, letting his hands drop to his sides in a more relaxed position. "I am just escorting you. If this is supposed to be anything other than that, then I have not been informed. I have heard that Catrina likes keeping her people in the dark, but Terrance is not like that."

Elyse took a deep breath. She didn't want to create a problem with Devin and Nathan if there wasn't a reason to. But she wasn't sure she could trust them, either. If she was being completely honest, the only person on the train she trusted was Josh. They had had a rocky start, but she had forgiven him for things, such as her uncle Albert's death, that had been out of his control.

Catrina had promised she'd take them somewhere safe, somewhere Dariusz couldn't find them. It was now dawning on Elyse that what Catrina considered safe might not be the same as what she considered safe. At first, when Catrina had made the offer, Elyse had had this vision of being taken to a cabin somewhere off the grid and just living with Josh there. Everything they needed to survive would be at the cabin, and they could manage indefinitely. Such a scenario would certainly have allowed them to explore their relationship more.

Elyse shook her head ruefully. *I shouldn't have been naïve enough to assume she had a hidden cabin somewhere to stash us.* The train slowed. Elyse glanced around, wondering if they were already close enough to Boise to disembark from the train. She could see what appeared to be an old residential area that looked largely abandoned. But she could also see that the sky was rapidly darkening, with huge, almost black thunderclouds coming their way. The wind picked up outside. She could see pieces of debris starting to drift between the houses. Tiny dust devils were also stirring up.

"We're going to have to wait out the storm," Devin announced.

"Why?" Elyse asked. She was well versed in southern thunderstorms; a little rain and wind wouldn't hurt the train.

Devin shook his head. "You'll see soon."

As soon as the words were out of his mouth, a huge boom sounded, and thunder rolled across the valley. Large streaks of lightning forked down from the sky, and the wind intensified. The train came to a complete stop. Elyse could feel it vibrating from the wind. Small trees were ripped up by the roots and tossed in the air. Anything that was loose became airborne. The sky was almost pitch-black, so it was difficult to see the chaos outside except for in the flashes of lightning that were at increasingly shorter intervals.

Boom! Boom! There was a flash followed by a huge crack and a pop as a tree at the end of the residential street they were next to got hit by a bolt of lightning and split in half with smoke curling out of it. The skies opened, releasing a torrent of rain. Even with the flashes of lightning, no one could see anything outside the train. It shuddered under the onslaught of wind and rain. Pieces of something slammed into the side of the train a few times, but it remained secure on its track.

Elyse was shocked by the intensity of this storm. They had impressive ones in Atlanta, but this was quickly outranking those as the worst she'd experienced in her life. Just as fast as the storm began, the rain stopped, the wind died down, and the dark clouds continued rolling eastward. The train stayed stationary for another five minutes, as though its driver was making sure the storm was truly gone. When it began moving again, the train was going at about half the speed as before.

"We are almost there," Devin announced.

"Do you get storms like that often?" Elyse asked.

"That is pretty much what our storms are like, crazy and short," Nathan replied.

"Are they natural?" Josh asked.

Nathan seemed surprised by the question. "Of course they're natural."

"You say that as though you are sure it can't be unnatural. I take it that you've never come across anyone with a magical talent that permits them to manipulate the weather?" Josh said in an amused tone.

"No one has a magical talent like that," Nathan replied, though Elyse could hear the doubt in his voice.

"I have come across one person. Though I believe she died. I've always assumed that if there was one person with the magical talent to influence the weather, that there is likely at least one more person with that ability too," Josh said.

"Let's go back to where the horses are. Terrance should be waiting for us at the station," Devin suggested.

Elyse and Josh followed him back to the train car with the horses. Both Fork and Honey seemed relaxed, nibbling on the hay in their stalls as though they had been entirely unaware of the crazy storm. *Maybe they didn't know it was outside. Since the train is controlled by magic, it would make sense if they could also shield the horses from the noise outside that could stress them out more.*

The horses unloaded just as smoothly as they had loaded. The train station was tiny with stairs at one end. Because they had the horses, they did not unload onto the platform but in the space behind it. Just as Devin had said, Terrance was waiting for them.

Elyse wasn't sure how to greet the tiger shifter. She settled for a slight wave, which to her relief Terrance did in return. Josh opted to shake hands, but he at least had met Terrance more than once.

"Devin told me you've had a well-rounded introduction to our summer weather," Terrance said with a smile.

Josh rolled his eyes. "I guess you can call it that. The storms I don't mind. It's the heat. How do you live here every summer, year after year?"

Terrance shrugged. "You get used to it. I'd much rather have it be one hundred and fifteen degrees and dry heat than ninety degrees with ninety percent humidity like you get in Atlanta."

"I guess you adapt to the climate wherever you end up living," Elyse chimed in.

"Yes, most people do, or they're just miserable," Terrance replied. "Now, let's head to the stables, and then I can get you to your residence while you're here."

"The stables are near where we're staying?" Elyse asked.

Terrance nodded and started walking. Elyse fell in step beside her. "Yes. They are nearby, and they do have an exercise pen, so the horses can get out to stretch their legs daily and aren't stuck in a stall if you're not going for a ride."

"Do you find that people use horses or cars more here in Boise?" Elyse asked.

Terrance shook her head. "Neither really. Most people either walk or use the train. A minority have horses and cars, but with the train, most areas are readily accessible. I guess it just comes down to personal preference and finances. From what I have seen, a lot of people around here would prefer to spend their money on having a fancier house than having a car."

"If we want to ride, are there places to tie the horses if we want to go into a store or anything like that?" Elyse asked.

From what it sounded like, Boise could not even really be compared to Atlanta. It was so different, from the climate to the way the city was organized. In Atlanta, everyone had cars. Even if they could walk, they preferred to use cars. Elyse had had a car because riding a horse sixty miles from Jackson County into downtown Atlanta was too far and risky. The downtown area had not been designed to accommodate horses and made them ideal targets for theft.

"Yes, there are hitching posts and whatnot. There are certainly people in this city who rely on horses and cars. All I was saying is walking is more common, and as you'll soon find out, many of the streets are still rather narrow and do not accommodate cars very well," Terrance explained. "The train tracks run north-south and east-west. The main east-west track is where the old Interstate 84 was. When the decision was made to install a train track, it seemed simplest for the local government to use the already-established freeway and just convert it to accommodate the train instead of building something entirely new. In my opinion, it's one of the best decisions they've made. There are times where it would be nice to have a track that would serve as a ring road, too, but our population here is much smaller than what you have in Atlanta, so we make do with what we have."

Elyse was intrigued by the idea that people walked or rode the train everywhere. Since Terrance led them on foot, Elyse decided it would be rude to ride, but by the time they got to the stable, her legs were protesting, though Josh seemed to enjoy the walking far more than the long ride.

The stable was a short, squat metal building with a large rolling door. Elyse got a view of a long row of stalls flanking a wide aisle that had been freshly swept. Terrance led them inside. The sound of the hooves echoed on the concrete. She stopped in the middle where two side-by-side stalls had open doors. Inside, Elyse could see clean shavings and a pile of fresh hay.

"These two are for you. There is a locker where you can store your tack. It has saddle racks, and there's a key so you can lock it and keep your items safe. There is a camera in each stall as well as at all entrances and exits, so when anyone arrives or departs, we have a record of that. No one will take your horses or gear. As I said before, you are free to come and go as you please," Terrance explained.

"Are there any restrictions on what hours we can take the horses out?" Elyse asked.

Terrance gave her a curious look. "No. But I'm not sure why you would want to go for a ride in the middle of the night."

Elyse shrugged. "I've done things like that before. It's probably not the best idea in an unfamiliar city, but sometimes it helps when I'm really stressed out to just spend time with Honey. Can you show me the paddock you mentioned for turnout?"

Terrance nodded. "Of course."

They continued out the other side of the barn, and sure enough there was large pen with sand footing.

I could probably ride in there if I did want to go on a moonlight ride, Elyse told herself.

"This place looks great. Thank you for finding a place to house Honey and Fork. We really appreciate it," Josh said. "Now, what about us poor humans?"

Elyse rolled her eyes and gave him a light shove. "I'm sure that's where we're going next, Mr. Impatient." Josh caught her by the waist and started to kiss her, but just before his lips touched hers, he yawned. Unable to help herself, Elyse yawned too.

"If the two of you are done here, we can go to the apartment and you can go to sleep," Terrance said.

Elyse turned toward her and realized that the shifter was waiting for them by the door they had entered through.

Elyse took Josh's hand in hers, and they resumed following Terrance.

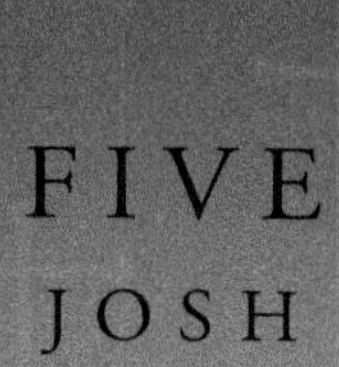

FIVE

JOSH

Terrance opened the door to the small apartment that Josh was supposed to share with Elyse. Josh walked inside with Elyse close on his heels. With what he had seen so far of Boise, Josh was anticipating that they would not need the horses, which made him wonder why Catrina had insisted they bring them. *Unless her intention all along was to drop us off at Shoshone Falls instead of in Boise itself.*

He ran a hand over his face. He was exhausted. He knew teleporting was tiring, but he had expected to be taken directly to their destination, not to teleport, spend eight or more hours riding, then get on a train—and also have to be sociable—for several more hours.

Terrance was still standing by the door, and Josh turned to face her. "What is the plan?"

"Right now? For you and Elyse to rest. Remember, you are here because you are supposed to stay safe and out of trouble. There is nothing that you are needed for," Terrance said coolly.

Josh eyed her. The way she phrased her sentences made him suspect there was a lot she wasn't telling him. At that moment, though, he was too exhausted to care about asking for details.

50

Instead, he gave her a tired smile. "Thank you for the help. I'll see you tomorrow."

Terrance returned the smile, although he could tell it was somewhat forced. "I'll see you tomorrow. There's food in the fridge and the pantry, so you should have everything you need." With that, she turned on her heel and walked out.

Josh shut the door and locked the deadbolt. He peered around. It seemed safe. If the locks were any indication, it had been set up to be a safe house of some sort. He had no doubts that if an attack was imminent, it would protect them long enough for them to have a chance to defend themselves or run.

Josh took a tour of the apartment. There was a bedroom with two beds—a twin and a king—and an open-concept living area with a couch, an L-shaped kitchen, and a dining table for four. He would have peeked in the bathroom, but Elyse seemed to have snuck in there already, and he could hear the shower being turned on.

He was grateful there were two beds but was not totally sure what to think about them being in the same bedroom. On one hand, it made it easier to ensure she was safe, since anyone trying to attack in the middle of the night would wake him up; on the other, it meant they had minimal privacy from one another if that was something they required. After Elyse's uncle's death at Dariusz's hands, they had essentially agreed to restart their relationship. When Elyse had forgiven him for rescuing her at the cost of her uncle Albert, he had vowed to himself to let Elyse set the pace for whatever they had between them. Lately, that seemed to involve him taking cold showers.

Josh took a deep breath, trying to let his mind go to anything other than Elyse in the shower and how badly he wanted to join her. He was pretty sure Elyse knew how he felt and felt the same way, but … lasting relationships weren't built on sex alone. He had committed to waiting until Elyse was ready, however long it took.

At Shoshone Falls, she was ready, he reminded himself. *Was she, though? Or was it just fear talking, fear that they might only have one chance to be intimate?* He shook his head. It didn't matter. They were safe now in an apartment with two beds. If Elyse wanted to take the next step while they were here, he was not going to say no, but until then, he would let her take the lead in how slowly or quickly they got there.

Josh sat on the couch and squeezed his eyes shut, running over everything that happened since they arrived in Idaho. He realized that Elyse had had not one, but two visions, one of which happened while they were on the train, and she hadn't wanted to tell him about it in front of Devin and Nathan. *We're alone, so it would be a good time to discuss it.* Just then a yawn ripped through him, then another. *Or I am just going to pass out before I can say anything to Elyse at all?*

His eyes popped open when he heard a giggle. Elyse was wrapped in a white towel, her long red hair cascading around her shoulders.

"Why don't you pick a bed and go to sleep?" she asked softly. Then, she walked over to him and leaned down, kissing him.

Josh wrapped his hands around her waist and pulled her onto his lap, deepening the kiss. Elyse adjusted on his lap so she was straddling him and wiggled. His cock hardened till it was almost painful. A moan escaped his lips.

Elyse nipped his lower lip playfully. "I thought you were falling asleep."

"Does it feel like I'm falling asleep?" he asked, voice rough as he tried to get control over his cock.

Elyse giggled. "No. But maybe I should let you go to sleep."

"If you think I can sleep like this, then you're sorely mistaken," Josh muttered and bit his lip. He did not want to come in his pants, but if Elyse kept wiggling on top of him, he was going to lose what little control he still had. He set his hands on her hips and began lifting her off of his lap.

"What are you doing?" she asked, surprised.

"I can't stand up with you on my lap. Before today, you have been dead set on waiting. Tonight, I think we're both too tired, and honestly, I don't want you to do something you're going to regret later. Which means I need you to move before I lose control," Josh said and shifted her onto the couch, then stood up. He took a few steps away from Elyse and the couch before turning around to face her.

"I'm going to go take a shower," he said abruptly and then took off for the bathroom before she had a chance to reply. He knew he wasn't being completely fair, that maybe she was more awake than he was and had been completely aware of what his reaction would be when she sat on his lap in only a towel. Either way, this wasn't how he wanted their first time to be. He wanted it to be special because Elyse was special. He knew that she had had her fair share of men in her bed. Not that he felt like he had to compete with them. He just wanted to be sure that she knew she was his and only his. It would not be quick and dirty.

He shed his clothes and then turned the shower on, on cold, and hopped in. It felt like someone was dumping bucket after bucket of ice water on him, but it had the desired effect. All thoughts of Elyse and yanking the towel off of her slid from his mind, as did the other plans that had been surfacing for how he would take her. When he was sure that he was not going to relapse, Josh shut off the water and grabbed a towel. He quickly dried off and slid his dirty clothes back on. Not really what he wanted to do, but the cold shower would have been pointless if he walked out there in nothing but a towel and Elyse came after him again.

Josh opened the door and was surprised to see there was only a small light over the sink still on, just enough light to make sure he didn't run into the furniture on his way to the bedroom. The bedroom also had a small lamp turned on next to the king-size bed. It appeared Elyse had decided to sleep in the twin-sized bed. He wasn't sure if that was because she felt like she'd be less tempting in the small bed or that she was being nice. He knew that the small bed would suck for either one of them. She was six feet tall, and he was six foot two.

Tomorrow I will have to discuss that with her. He decided he was not going to let a woman—his girlfriend or otherwise—take the small bed so he could be comfortable. He just didn't operate like that.

Josh slept better than he expected. He woke up and peered at the clock. It was eight a.m. He glanced over at the other bed and saw that Elyse was not in it. For a moment, concern flooded him that something had happened and he had been too tired to notice. Upon further inspection of the bed, he noted that the covers had been pulled up and tucked in, almost as though no one had slept there at all. Which definitely meant Elyse had made the bed and gotten out of it of her own accord. Relaxing at that realization, he stood up and ran through some quick stretches, trying to loosen his muscles that were stiff from all the riding the day before. In a chair at the foot of the bed, he spied his saddlebags.

He rummaged through them and pulled out a clean pair of jeans, boxers, and a red T-shirt. Taking a quick sniff, he decided the cold shower definitely had not been sufficient. Josh rolled his clean clothes around his toiletries and headed to the bathroom for a hot shower.

The hot shower had been refreshing. Taking a moment to get himself back together after yesterday was worth it. Josh quickly put his dirty clothes and toiletries back in the bedroom and then went over to the small dining room table where Elyse was sitting.

He had not expected her to make them breakfast, but she had and was clearly waiting for him to eat. Both plates had scrambled eggs with cheese, spinach, and bell peppers in them. There were also a couple of sausage links and steaming cups of coffee.

"This smells amazing," Josh said, smiling at Elyse and then sliding into his seat.

Elyse just shrugged and fiddled with her blue cloth napkin. "When I saw you head for the shower, I figured I could make us some food. It's not like I have anything better to do."

"After we eat, I'd like to hear about the vision you had on the train. I know it must have been something you didn't feel comfortable discussing in front of the people we were with, which is fine. Considering everything you've been through the past month, I think your assessment of proceeding with caution is a great one. I think we can trust Terrance, but I don't know any of the people who work for her. Catrina we can trust only as long as our interests align," Josh said.

Elyse nodded and took a bite of her food. Josh decided to follow suit. Eggs were always better when they were hot. Besides they didn't have anywhere they had to be, so there was no reason to discuss the vision first. He knew if it had contained urgent information Elyse would have found a way to tell him when they were on the train. The fact that she waited indicated to him that while it might be useful information, it would not have changed anything they did last night.

Josh worked his way through everything on his plate. Terrance had been serious when she said the kitchen in the apartment was well stocked. Elyse seemed to have found a selection of spices, for the eggs were very flavorful, and a perfect balance to the hint of maple in the sausage. When his plate was empty Josh set his fork on it and picked up his cup of coffee.

Elyse, who finished her food a moment or two after Josh, gave him an amused smile. "I guess we were both hungry. Maybe I should make more?"

Josh shook his head. "No, I'm full now. You made the perfect amount."

"Okay," Elyse replied and took a sip of her coffee, then set it down. "The vision. I was shaking Nathan's hand, and that's when my talent took over. What I saw was in some sort of café. Terrance and a man named Trey. Trey was talking about a deal that he had made with Terrance, and Terrance supposedly changed the deal and now wants double. Trey wasn't happy about that. Terrance put pressure on him and said that she would 'destroy it' if he didn't agree to pay double."

"'Destroy it'?" Josh repeated. "Did they ever say what the object was?"

Elyse shook her head. "No, they didn't. Trey just said he would have to get a response from his boss, and either the money would be in Terrance's account or she would be dead in twenty-four hours."

Josh took a sip of his coffee, digesting what Elyse described. He wasn't sure if he should be concerned that Terrance had a deal with this Trey fellow or if he should just ignore it. *Besides, we have no idea if that was in the past or future.* He set down his coffee. "Did you see anything else?"

Elyse blushed, causing Josh to raise his eyebrow. "Terrance and Cory were working out or something and then got romantic."

Josh chuckled. "They are mated, you know. Usually, sex is part of that."

Elyse blushed deeper, her cheeks turning bright red. Instead of replying, she picked up her coffee cup and took a long drink.

Josh took a small sip of his coffee, giving Elyse a chance to regroup. "Let's say worst case scenario that what you saw was today—Terrance is meeting with Trey today. Then, she has some object." He paused. "Or it's not an object. It's a person." He blew out his breath, mind whirling at the possibility that Terrance could possibly be trading one of them to Trey.

He shook his head; the idea was crazy. What reason would Terrance have to turn either one of them over for a payday? It seemed ridiculous that she would go to all the trouble of helping them, preventing Dariusz from taking Elyse as his slave, to just turn her over for cash on the side.

Running a hand over his face, he peered over at Elyse, who was watching him. Her face had returned to its normal color. "I think we have to assume that whatever deal Terrance has with Trey has nothing to do with us. We don't have enough information. Unless you want to practice your magical talent and see if you can get another vision that relates to the deal."

He watched as Elyse bit her lip, and her eyes lowered to the table. He had to admit it would be nice to know more about the deal, but he also didn't want to push Elyse to use her talent if she didn't want to. They had practiced a few times at the ranch with mixed success. It seemed for the most part that if she was trying to find out information directly related to her past or future, it worked well. If they wanted to know about someone else, she was just as likely to have her talent not work or get a vision about something totally unrelated to what they wanted to know. Elyse had started writing down her visions in a journal so that even if they seemed unimportant at the time, if anything came back up later, she would have a record.

"It might be worth trying. At least we know if it relates to me directly, I should be able to get more information," Elyse finally replied.

Josh nodded and stood up. He gathered both plates and the empty coffee cups and took them to the sink. He stuck the plates in the sink before realizing that the apartment had a dishwasher. He set them in the dishwasher and then refilled the coffee cups and carried them over to the coffee table in front of the sofa. Then, he took a seat on one side of the sofa.

Elyse sat down and snuggled against his side. Not her usual position when she was trying to use her talent.

"Is there something else you wanted to discuss first?"

"Yes," she replied.

"I will answer any question you have about any topic if I have relevant information," he offered.

"On the train ride you mentioned different types of talents and that weather is one of them. I was wondering what else there is," Elyse said eagerly.

Josh blew out his breath. While not an easy question, he had been expecting her to ask him something personal. "I believe you recall I'd previously told you that talents seemed to have manifested differently in various regions throughout the United States. The East Coast seems to have favored talents that involve the mind. So you can see the past and future. Others can move objects with their minds. I can prevent vampires from reading my mind. Mind reading, some forms of healing talents, stuff like that. The Midwest has many different types of elemental magic—earth, fire, water, and air. The Pacific Northwest—including Idaho—seems to be home to different types of shapeshifters, and California has the largest population of vampires."

"Do other kinds of talents exist aside from that list?" Elyse asked.

Josh nodded. "Yes, that is not an exhaustive list. When I was at the school with other magically talented teenagers, I came across individuals who could become invisible, walk through walls, create electricity. I even met one who could fly."

"Wow, that's quite a variety of talents," Elyse said.

"It is," he murmured. Elyse was almost in his lap. He kept his hands still, not entirely sure what she was doing. He had thought the plan was for her to try using her magical talent to discover more information about Terrance, but now he wondered if she just wanted to make out.

"Cat got your tongue?" Elyse asked with a smirk.

He shook his head. "No. I'm just trying to figure out what you're doing."

"Snuggling," she replied simply.

"What does this version of snuggling entail?" he asked, eyebrow arched and a smile tugging at his lips.

Instead of answering, she kissed him.

SIX
ELYSE

Josh was running his hand down Elyse's back, and she was having trouble thinking of anything other than the feel of his hands on her and where else she wanted them.

Suddenly, she could no longer feel his lips on her mouth. She opened her eyes and found herself riding Honey bareback. Josh was next to her on Fork. They were galloping through the largest pasture at her ranch in Jackson County. She could feel the wind tugging at the sweat-dampened strands of her hair. It was just enough to make the humidity bearable.

"Elyse," Josh's voice called. He snapped his fingers in front of her face, close enough for her to feel the air moving. Her eyes popped open.

"Are you okay?" Josh asked with concern in his voice.

"Yes. Though I wish my talent didn't seem to be inclined to work at such inconvenient moments. I was quite enjoying what your tongue was doing," she said, blushing slightly.

"We can continue that later, promise. I thought we were sitting on the couch to try to figure out more about what was going on with Terrance and that Trey fellow in your vision. Now don't get me wrong, I would happily spend all day with you in my arms if that's what you really want to do," Josh said.

Elyse bit her lip. His invitation was tempting, but she was also concerned about what she had seen and the implications it might have for the time they were in Boise. If they were not as safe as they assumed, then they would need to take more precautions.

She reached for her coffee mug and took a long sip. It was still hot and blazed a scorching trail down her throat. She then set it down. She couldn't get a vision while holding a cup of coffee—or any beverage for that matter—without dumping it all over herself.

Elyse sat on the couch, close to Josh but not touching him. In their experiments, they found if she touched him, her magical talent would direct the vision toward her and Josh, not whatever she was trying to focus on, as she had just demonstrated. She wiggled, trying to get in a comfortable position. The couch was firmer than she would have liked. When she was as comfortable as she could get, Elyse set her hands on the tops of her thighs and let her eyes flutter shut.

Terrance and Trey. Terrance and Trey, she repeated over and over in her mind. Elyse could tell when her talent was starting to work because it felt like little sparks across her skin. One moment with her eyes shut, all she could see was black.

> *The next, Elyse found herself standing in the same café with brick walls from her first vision. Trey was sitting at the same table he had been at with Terrance, but no one was sitting across from him. He had an untouched blueberry muffin on his plate and a mostly empty glass of water. Trey's phone was on the table, and he seemed to be staring at it as though waiting for a phone call. Sure enough, it rang. He waited until the third ring to pick it up.*
>
> *Unfortunately, Elyse could not hear what was being said on the other end of the phone.*

Trey stayed silent for over a minute, then spoke. "Consider it done." He set the phone back down on the table and stood up. He pulled a couple of bills out of his wallet and left them on the table, then grabbed the phone.

Elyse found she was able to follow him as Trey walked out the door and made his way down the street. He paused at a black metal trash can and dropped the phone into it. The vision faded.

Elyse opened her eyes and ran a hand over her face.

Josh was giving her an expectant look. "Given the amount of time you weren't moving, I am assuming your talent worked and you saw something."

Elyse nodded. "I did, but I'm not sure how helpful it was. I saw Trey at the same café. He got a phone call, said 'Consider it done,' and then walked out of the café and threw the phone in the trash." She paused. "Why would someone throw away a phone? They're really expensive."

Josh waved a hand in dismissal. "Burner phone. Fairly common practice for people working in organizations like the FBI or HAC."

Elyse raised her eyebrows. "Really? Wouldn't you be worried someone would just grab the phone out of the trash?"

Josh chuckled. "I mean, I suppose someone could, but who likes digging through trash?" He took a breath. "Did you see anything that gave any clues for what day it was, or what year?"

"No, sorry. I know it wasn't useful, but I did see one of the two people I was trying for, and in the same location as before, so I feel like it wasn't a complete failure," Elyse said uncertainly. She'd spent her whole life assuming these feelings she got were just that, weird feelings. Less than a month ago, when her magical talent unlocked, she discovered she could see the past and future and that her feelings were a part of her talent trying to manifest.

Too bad no one gave me an instruction manual. Elyse was quickly learning that it was a lot of work to figure out how to control her visions and get useful information, not just random bits and pieces that made no sense.

Josh took a sip of his coffee. Elyse could see the faraway look in his eyes and assumed he was running through whatever process he had used as an FBI agent with a new case, trying to glean as much information as possible even when there wasn't much there.

"Okay, so we know that Trey has a boss. Terrance didn't seem overly concerned with the consequences by deciding to require double the payment. Which to me means she does not view Trey's boss as a threat, or she has something on Trey's boss that she feels gives her enough leverage to keep him from following through with his threat to kill her." Josh paused. "What we don't know is whether Trey is also HAC or a different organization. The fact that he has a boss makes me feel as though it is an organization, not just a one- or two-person crew."

Elyse nodded. It made sense, but what she didn't know was what he wanted to do about it. "Are we just letting it go, or did you want me to try again and see if I get any additional information in another vision?"

Josh scratched his chin. "I will admit part of me really wants to know who this Trey fellow is and what he wants, but the other part is concerned that if we find out more it will put us in the middle of something else that we should not be in the middle of. We were brought here to stay safe. Jumping into a conflict doesn't exactly sound like staying safe."

Elyse considered his words. Josh was right. They were supposed to be steering clear of any possible conflict. If they ended up neck deep in whatever was going on with Terrance, it would likely draw Dariusz's attention to Boise, the last thing either of them wanted.

"Maybe we should just wait and see what happens. If the visions were from the past, then they shouldn't be relevant to us being here in Boise anyhow. If it is in the future, I suppose we will have to trust that Terrance will inform us if it is no longer safe for us or if she needs our help," Josh said.

Elyse took a deep breath. "I know you want to keep me safe, Josh, but if Terrance asks for help, I owe her. She was instrumental in us escaping at the masquerade."

"And what if this whole thing is a trap?" Josh prompted.

"Then it probably won't matter what we decide," Elyse responded. As the words came out of her mouth, she realized how true they were. If this was a trap, then they were already here without an easy way to leave.

"Then it's settled. We will see how things play out here," Josh said and drained his coffee, setting the cup down with a loud thump. Elyse smiled and drank her cup of coffee at a much slower pace, savoring the rich flavor.

An hour later, Elyse was over waiting for Terrance to show up. An idea occurred to her. "Terrance said that we could go see the horses or take them out for a ride whenever we wanted. Why not do that now? I'm sure if the stable has as sophisticated a security system as she described, she would easily be able to track us there if she came calling while we were out."

Josh looked like he was considering objecting, but she knew he was bored too. "Fine. We can groom them and put them out for a bit in the pen."

"No ride?" Elyse asked, disappointment clear in her voice and expression.

"Maybe later, after we see Terrance, or tomorrow. I just don't want to go too far when she said she would come by. I know she will know if we are at the stables, but I doubt HAC has cameras all over the city that would allow her to track our every movement," Josh replied.

The way Josh mentioned the cameras made Elyse wonder if he thought the opposite of what he said, that there was such a system in place. She shuddered at the thought of people she didn't know being able to observe every place they went and every task they did. One of the things she loved about her horse ranch was the privacy. No houses were nearby. No one to yell at her if her music was too loud or to chastise her if she decided to run across the field naked. In the city, whether here or downtown Atlanta, the buildings were so close together, she felt like all she had was an illusion of privacy. Walls protected her, but if a window was left uncovered, someone could easily catch a glimpse of whatever was happening.

Elyse slipped her boots on and gazed around the room, trying to figure out if she was forgetting anything, but nothing came to mind.

"Ready?" asked Josh.

Elyse agreed. "Yep!"

They headed out of the apartment and down the path out the back, retracing their steps from last night. A few minutes later, the stables were in sight. The rolling door was shut at this end. Elyse walked up to it and gave a light tug. The door moved, and she stood back as it rolled up. Nickers of greeting came down the aisle toward them. It seemed that Fork and Honey were still the only horses in residence for the time being, which suited Elyse just fine.

She let herself into Honey's stall. The mare stepped forward, and Elyse threw her arms around her, inhaling the sweet scent of hay and clean shavings. She felt her talent beginning to work. She could feel the tingle of sparks going up and down her arms. She braced herself, unsure of what vision she would get.

Elyse could feel Honey's soft fur, but instead of it being under her cheek, it was under her legs. She was riding bareback in shorts. Her hair cascaded around her in red waves. Peering around, she recognized her best friend Jessica's farmhouse. Moments later, Jessica appeared from the back side of her barn riding her brown horse, Moon. Her dark skin was a stark contrast to Elyse's lightly tanned pale skin. Jessica's curly black hair fanned out around her face, just brushing the top of her shoulders, and she was wearing jean shorts and a button-up denim shirt tied so that her bellybutton was visible. Both were barefoot. Elyse sighed as she remembered the phase they had gone through when they were obsessed with baring as much skin as possible. Jessica's parents had quickly put their foot down when they'd tried to go for a ride in bikinis, deciding that since Elyse's parents were dead, they could at least ensure that she went around properly dressed.

"Ready?" Jessica said, riding up alongside Elyse.

"Yep!" Elyse smiled.

Without being prompted, the two mares leaped forward into a lope. Laughing, Elyse urged Honey to speed up even more. As they raced around the bend in the driveway, the sun started dropping behind the tree line, shedding blinding light on the road ahead. Elyse glanced over at Jessica; neither one of them was wearing a hat or sunglasses, and she was having difficulty judging where the path was. They'd have to slow down when they approached Cubed, which was where Elyse assumed they were going, but Jessica's family owned most of the land between where they were and the bar, and the two horses had been this way many times before.

"Race to the bridge?" Elyse challenged, before wondering why the hell she would have been that dumb, asking Jessica to race if they couldn't even see where they were going. But with her magical talent bent on showing her this vision of the past, there was nothing she could do except be a bystander.

Jessica answered by speeding up and pulling ahead of Elyse. Honey let out a big snort and gave a small buck before digging in with her hindquarters and shooting forward.

Elyse felt Honey's neck once again beneath her cheek. *I wonder who won that race,* she pondered. They had raced almost every day together for a few summers, though not always the same route. There had been more than a few times where they weren't able to see, and things had gone sideways. The horses were far smarter than the teenage girls who had been riding them.

"Is everything okay in there?" Josh called. From how his voice sounded, Elyse assumed he was inside of Fork's stall grooming the gelding.

"Yes, I'm fine. Just had a memory of one of the races Jessica and I used to have," she replied.

"Anything exciting happen during the race?" Josh asked with amusement in his voice.

"I'm not sure. It ended before I found out. But the setting sun was blinding us, so it's likely," she replied.

"Are you ready to put them out in the pen?" Josh asked.

Elyse nodded, then realized he couldn't see her. "Yes," she called and slid the halter on Honey's head, then led the mare into the aisleway.

Josh was in the aisle already waiting with Fork. The aisle was wide enough for them to walk side by side with the two horses and still have room to spare.

When they reached the pen, Elyse swung the gate open and walked inside. Josh followed her.

"Take off the halter," she instructed. As soon as she stepped out of the pen and secured the gate, both horses took off at a gallop, racing around the pen, sending up huge clouds of dust and sand.

Elyse started coughing and backed up toward the barn. Josh followed her with an arm over his nose. They stopped when they had escaped far enough away from the cloud that the air cleared a little.

"I guess they wanted to get some wiggles out," Elyse murmured.

SEVEN
TERRANCE

It took Terrance a while to figure out where Cory was. When he had woken up, he mentioned something vague about practicing and then had disappeared. Through the mating bond, she could tell he was still in headquarters, but she had been unable to pinpoint a precise location. She had been about to shift to see if she could track him better as a tiger when she stumbled across him in the security office. Cory was sitting in front of the wall of monitors reviewing the cameras. To the left, she could see one that showed Elyse and Josh at the stables. The other screens showed various parts of Boise, including all of the train stations, the Plaza, and downtown around the capitol building.

"What are you doing in here?" she said, slightly exasperated.

Cory turned in his chair, his surprise clear on his face. "My job."

Terrance stuck out her tongue at him. "You have many 'jobs,' and most of them don't require you to monitor these screens."

Cory shrugged. "Have you heard anything back from Trey?"

Terrance shook her head. "No, I haven't. When I met with him yesterday, I couldn't get a clear read on whether or not he was confident the new amount would be approved or not. He did say I'd have an answer in twenty-four hours, and we're quickly approaching that time."

"Are you worried that he is not going to agree?" Cory asked.

"No, I just don't like having loose ends," Terrance replied.

Cory stood up and pulled her into his arms. "I love you," he murmured.

"I love you too," she replied.

He tipped his head down and kissed her deeply. Terrance leaned into him. He picked her up, and she wrapped her legs around his waist. She found it much more comfortable to kiss that way. Cory took a few steps, and her back pressed into the wall, he ran his hands down her sides and then began unzipping her pants.

There was a cough behind them. Cory stopped messing with her zipper and cast a scathing look over his shoulder at whomever was at the door. Terrance couldn't see much around Cory.

"I'll come back later," Sienna said, amusement clear in her voice.

Terrance unwrapped her legs from around Cory, and he loosened his grip on her so she could stand on her feet. "You can say whatever it is you need to say now."

Sienna pushed the door open farther and stood in the doorway. "I was just wondering how you wanted to handle security for Josh and Elyse when you take them to the Plaza. Which we are doing soon, right?"

Terrance blew out her breath. She had gotten distracted this morning and forgot that she had intended to go over there first thing. *I fail as a host.* She could feel Cory's eyes on her, and when she looked at him, she could see his desire. "Yes. We are doing that soon."

"And your plan for security is?" Sienna prompted again.

Terrance blinked, trying to make herself focus on Sienna's question. The wolf shifter needed an answer that wasn't "let me fuck my mate and then get back to you." "I was thinking that we should have Mariah, shifted, on overwatch, and you and Pierre can wander around the Plaza and keep an eye on things. I am not expecting anything to happen, so three should be enough."

Sienna nodded. "Okay, I will get everyone prepped. How long till you want to head over there?"

Terrance bit her lip, debating. *They have already been waiting for so long, what's a little longer?* "How about twenty minutes? Then, when I leave to go get them, the three of you can head to the Plaza. I'd rather make it feel like they're not being watched, not just for their sakes, but also in case anyone else is paying attention to Josh and Elyse, we won't give them cause to take action."

"Sounds good. I'll see you in twenty," Sienna said and then turned on her heel and departed quickly.

Cory shut the door and locked it, then turned back to Terrance. She shivered as his gaze slowly went from the top of her head to her toes, possessive and full of heat. A low growl escaped from her as she waited for him to make the first move, but he stood there a few feet from her, motionless. Terrance decided if she was going to be ready to go in twenty minutes, then she was going to have to speed things along herself.

She reached for the edge of her shirt and slowly pulled it over her head. Her black lace bra revealed far more than it hid of her ample breasts. Next, she undid the button at the top of her pants. As her fingers gripped the zipper, Cory stepped forward and covered her hands in his. In one smooth motion he unzipped her pants and slid them off. Terrance started to reach for his pants, but Cory beat her to it. She smirked as she realized that neither one of them had chosen to wear underwear this morning. *Is that because we knew this was going to happen or because we just don't like underwear?*

Cory stepped forward and picked her up. Once again Terrance wrapped her legs around his waist, though this time she could feel his cock brushing against her inner thigh. Cory kissed her and swiftly undid her bra clasp, tossed the bra over his shoulder, then pressed her back into the wall again. With one quick thrust he was inside of her. A moan escaped her lips. With each thrust, he drove them both closer to the edge. She had thought he might rush since she had told Sienna that she would be ready to go in twenty minutes. But Cory did not like to rush, and today was not any different. As the pressure built, his strokes became quicker and even deeper. Suddenly, Terrance gasped as pleasure exploded within her. A moment later, Cory followed; she could feel him sag slightly at the release. But then, to her surprise, he began the rhythm again.

"Again?" Terrance teased.

Instead of answering, Cory kissed her roughly and gave one more thrust. Terrance screamed as a second, much larger wave of pleasure rocked through her body. Cory chuckled against her lips. "I do know what I'm doing, love."

Terrance kissed him instead of replying, wishing they could just stay like this forever, with their bodies entwined. She wasn't sure how long Cory had held her against the wall when he reluctantly backed up a step and slid her off of his cock and onto her own two feet.

"Can't we just take a day off?" Terrance whispered.

Cory gave her an unreadable look. "I am not the one who invited Catrina to bring Josh and Elyse here, nor am I the one who decided to become a lieutenant of HAC. But … you are the boss, so … *boss*, can you take the day off?"

Terrance made a face before kneeling to grab her pants and bra off the floor. "I will have to add that to our schedule for tomorrow. How's this sound … Terrance and Cory Fuck Day?"

Cory was in the middle of buckling his belt and burst out laughing. "It's very to the point."

Terrance couldn't help herself; she giggled, then pulled her pants on, trying to school herself into being serious. "I truly wish we could do that, a day off, but you know how it goes. Especially with everything going on right now."

There was a light tap on the door.

"Shit," Terrance growled and glanced at the clock; it had been twenty-five minutes. "Coming!" she yelled and yanked on her shirt before slamming her feet into her boots and pulling the door open.

"Bye!" Cory called from behind her as she took off at a run down the hallway, laces slapping the linoleum floor noisily.

When Terrance reached the foyer, Sienna gave her a knowing look and Pierre wouldn't meet her eyes. Terrance debated asking Pierre about taking a day off for a fuck day but decided he might bite her if she did. He tended to prefer if everyone kept their personal lives to themselves and focused exclusively on their work when they were together. Except the fact that not only were Terrance and Cory married, they were mates, which made it difficult at times for Terrance to keep personal things to herself. Pierre was at an advantage because his wife did not work for HAC, allowing him to keep any romantic parts of his personal life completely private. Instead, he just had to deal with his sister Sienna around the clock.

Terrance looked at the two wolf shifters and then turned her gaze to Mariah, a peregrine falcon shifter.

Mariah shrugged dismissively. "We're ready when you are, boss."

Terrance hastily tied her boots and then said, "Let's head out. I don't want to keep them waiting any longer."

EIGHT

ELYSE

Elyse and Josh let the horses run around the pen at the stables for about an hour before deciding to head back to the apartment. Elyse had hoped that Terrance would find them at the stables. She wasn't sure how long she would be able to hold off from going for a ride if all they were going to do was sit and wait forever.

Josh made a fresh pot of coffee, and Elyse felt like she had inspected every inch of the apartment and was very ready to go out and do something, anything other than being cooped up. Just as she was about to start pacing again, Josh caught her hand in his and offered her a cup of coffee.

"I know you're bored. I am too, but maybe we should use this as a chance to get to know each other better," Josh suggested.

Elyse looked at him, surprised, but acknowledged he did have a good idea. Most of the time they had been dating they had either been in the middle of dangerous situations or surrounded by other people. They had not had a lot of opportunities just the two of them.

"Okay. Let's alternate so we each get to ask a question, and it isn't lopsided. Deal?"

Josh nodded. "Deal. You can go first."

Elyse pursed her lips in thought. "On one of our first dates, you said that you liked to drive vintage cars and go to the gym. Have you ever had any other hobbies? I mean, hobbies that you chose, not that you had to participate in because of an assignment."

Josh shook his head. "Not really. Growing up in Manhattan, I'd tinker with whatever old car or motorcycle parts I could find. I learned a lot but was never able to build an entire car. Kickboxing is something I was introduced to also in Manhattan, and I found that I really enjoy it, not only because of the physical exercise, but because it also gives me the opportunity to discipline my mind."

"Okay. I guess I understand that, and I know how busy you were with the FBI, so I imagine that a lack of time has also played a role over the years preventing you from picking up another hobby. Your turn. What do you want to know?" Elyse asked.

"I already know you like to paint and dance. Why don't you tell me how you and Jessica met?" Josh asked.

Elyse laughed. "That's your first question?" Josh nodded. "Okay. Well, our moms were best friends. When they got pregnant within a few weeks of each other, both with their second child, it forged an even closer bond between them. You know we're only a week apart in age? I think they got lucky, though, that Jessica and I became as close as they were. Though we did go through a phase where all we did was bite each other."

Josh sputtered and almost spit out his coffee. "You bit each other? Do you actually remember doing that?"

Elyse laughed. "No, I don't remember doing it. But Mom told me all about it. I think that phase lasted several months where every time they got us together, we would fight and bite. I actually have a scar," she said and lifted up her shirt slightly to reveal two small marks just over her left hip.

"If I didn't know better, I'd say it almost looks like a vampire bite," Josh teased.

Elyse rolled her eyes. "Jessica is not a vampire. She just bit me extra hard." She took a sip of her coffee, hoping Josh would drop the subject. She realized that Josh knew a lot about her family since he had been helping her learn things, but she knew very little about his. "I'd like to know about your parents."

Josh's smile faded, and Elyse wondered if he would tell her anything. He had been the one to suggest they ask questions. He must have expected she'd ask about his family at some point if they were serious about their relationship.

He licked his lips, then spoke softly. "My mom left when I was twelve. She just went to work one day and never came back. My dad never gave me an explanation. I don't know if that is because he didn't have one or didn't feel like sharing. He was not the type you would question if he wasn't going to provide information."

Elyse opened her mouth to speak, but Josh kept talking. "My dad was retired military. He served for thirty years before he met my mom on one of his ops. They fell in love. When they found out she was pregnant, he retired, although I have since found evidence showing he was forced out."

"Because he got your mom pregnant?" Elyse asked, surprised.

Josh shook his head. "No. Because she was known to have a magical talent, and it was considered taboo in the military to mix with the talented population. From what I have been able to discover, the military gave him only one option. Which was retire, move to Manhattan, and find a low-key job there. As long as he didn't make any noise, they would leave him alone."

"What do you mean by 'make noise'?" Elyse said.

"He worked on many top-secret operations within the United States and in other countries. They wanted him to stay silent and accept his retirement. Essentially, they would stay out of his business if he didn't reveal anything about theirs," Josh explained.

"Your mom was okay with that?" Elyse said.

"She loved Dad too much and was willing to go anywhere with him. Because Manhattan was set up as a place for the talented to live, they assumed it would be safer than living in a city like Atlanta where it wasn't okay if you walked around showing off your magical talent. By the time they discovered that Manhattan wasn't any safer than the other large cities, it was too late to get out of the arrangement," Josh said.

"What kind of talent did your mom have?" Elyse asked.

Josh shook his head. "I don't know. She never showed me what she could do, and I was too afraid to ask my dad about it."

Elyse reached out and squeezed Josh's hand. "I'm sorry that you had to go through that."

Josh raised her hand to his lips and kissed it gently. "Most people face challenges in their lives. My mom left. Your sister and then both of your parents died in accidents. Those events have shaped us into who we are. I have realized over the years that as much as I miss my mom and hope to one day find her, there are so many things that might have happened differently if she hadn't left. I am not sure I would want to erase those from my life."

Elyse bit her lip. He had a good point. "Like what?"

"You," he said. "I wouldn't want to erase you from my life. I know our relationship has had some bumps, but believe me when I say I am all in, and I will wait for you however long you need to feel the same way."

But I do, she wanted to say, but something held her back from voicing the words. She wasn't sure what. Maybe it was fear that he would find someone who was less complicated than she was. Having a girlfriend who sporadically got visions of the past and future had proven rather disruptive at times.

Instead, she just said, "I know, and I appreciate it."

She stood up, needing to walk and settle her mind more. Walking soon turned into pacing.

Her pacing took her from the door into the apartment to the window above the couch and back to the door. It was the only path that didn't have furniture to weave around. Josh shot her looks of annoyance.

Maybe because I started pacing before he did.

On her third lap, there was a knock at the door. Elyse rushed forward, hand gripping the doorknob eagerly, when Josh coughed behind her. She let go of the doorknob and glared back at him. "What?"

"Did you forget that it might not be Terrance?" Josh chided.

Elyse rolled her eyes but stepped back away from the door. He was right *and* happened to have a gun in his hand. She continued to retreat, giving him room to maneuver.

Elyse watched, breath caught in her throat, as Josh slowly opened the door about an inch. He braced his foot against it to keep it from being shoved open the rest of the way.

"Who's there?" Josh demanded through the crack.

Elyse strained her ears but couldn't make out the muffled reply. Josh evidently was comfortable with whoever was on the other side of the door because he shoved the gun back in its holster and yanked the door open the rest of the way.

"Jumpy much?" came Terrance's voice from the hallway.

Elyse stepped out of the shadows. "Good afternoon," she greeted. Terrance had said she'd come by in the morning, but it was almost two p.m.

Terrance walked the rest of the way into the apartment, and Josh shut and locked the door behind her.

"I'm sorry it took so long. I had some other things come up I had to deal with," Terrance said. Elyse kept silent. It was rude to pry, and most likely Terrance would tell them if it was relevant to them being in Boise.

Terrance pulled one of the chairs out at the table and plopped into it. Elyse could see the other woman visibly relaxing, which intrigued her. *Why would Terrance be more relaxed around us than her own people? Or maybe she had another meeting with Trey and came here immediately afterward.* Elyse bit her lip. *Not my business,* she reminded herself again.

"I would like to take you over to the Plaza. We can walk if you want. It's about half a mile," Terrance announced.

Josh sat down at the table and motioned for Elyse to do the same. Elyse sat down and waited for someone else to speak, knowing she was out of her element.

"What is the state of things around here?" Josh asked. "Is it like Atlanta where there is a clear difference between the individuals who live in the downtown area and those who are more rural, or is Boise fairly well mixed?"

Terrance's lips twitched. "Valid question. I guess you could say it's more mixed here. The agricultural land that is way out by Shoshone Falls to the east and Ontario in the west are more similar to Jackson County, where Elyse is from. But unlike in Georgia, most people here know magical talents exist, and magic is used more openly. The train, for example, is widely used by the whole valley, and everyone is aware it requires magic in addition to solar power to run. Of course, you have some people who are unwilling to believe in magical talents. Those individuals refuse to use the train at all."

"What about the government?" Josh inquired.

Terrance shrugged. "The officials have their headquarters in Aerie. It's a self-sustaining community that the government took over when COVID-50 hit and evicted any nongovernment officials from their homes. Initially, there were a lot of issues, but as head of HAC here in Boise, I have been able to negotiate with the Idaho government, and we typically stay out of each other's way."

Josh raised his eyebrow. "You're telling me there is no conflict and that HAC just follows all of the laws of the state without causing problems?"

Terrance chuckled. "If the FBI never finds evidence to pin anything on HAC, then there would be no obvious conflict."

Elyse narrowed her eyes. "So you just pin all of your illegal activities on some poor, unsuspecting people?"

Terrance rolled her eyes. "No. The individuals the FBI locks up for HAC's illegal activities are most definitely guilty. Maybe not of what the FBI accuses them of, but they are far from good citizens.

Most of them belong to one of the local gangs. Sometimes I think that Agent Florence knows what I'm doing and just looks the other way."

"Who is Agent Florence?" Josh asked.

"The FBI agent in charge here in Boise. Unlike Atlanta, we don't have someone with a big fancy title like *assistant director*," Terrance said with a slight growl in her voice.

Josh ran a hand over his face. "I don't think you would want someone like Fernway here. You know very well how involved he was with what was happening in Atlanta. If Agent Florence is locking up real criminals, then at least she is doing her job, no matter how she gets them. Assistant Director Fernway's betrayal has had me questioning whether there is any good blood in the FBI at all or if the whole organization is corrupt."

Terrance snorted. "Most of it is corrupt, just like the government. You're really stupid if you believe otherwise."

Josh sighed. "I'm not stupid. I just think that it has taken me this long to realize things that felt not quite right over the years really *haven't* been. It wasn't until I met Elyse that everything began to make sense." He reached over and grabbed Elyse's hand, giving it a squeeze. "I don't know how much you know about me, but I was found by Mr. Pascal when I was seventeen in Manhattan, New York, and sent to the school in upstate New York for four years. The school is run by the government, and then from there, I went straight to working for the FBI. Which is where the majority of the graduates end up, either in the FBI or some other government job, depending on what their skills are."

"Ah," Terrance said. "I'm surprised you figured it out after all this time. In my experience, graduates from that school either die in the first two years or are completely loyal, no matter what happens to the government."

Josh shot out of his seat, sending the chair toppling to the ground. Elyse yanked her hand back to balance herself so she wouldn't fall out of her chair. Josh walked away, leaving the chair on the floor. Elyse wasn't sure what to do. She looked at Terrance, who shrugged, and then back at Josh, who was pacing and not looking their way.

Elyse had a feeling Josh was not going to settle quickly. She decided that maybe asking Terrance more about Boise would help distract Josh from whatever dark thoughts he was having. "Terrance, you said earlier that here in Boise people tend to inter-mix more. What do you mean by that?"

Terrance shot Elyse a grateful smile. "With trains as transportation, people do not have to be able to afford a car to be able to access places that use electricity. Most of the trains are able to transport horses, and they can make going out to dinner or to the mall more accessible to even the farmers. Magical talents are accepted, so you will see people walking down the street juggling balls of water or objects floating through the air. Shapeshifters tend to be more private about shifting in public, but you will occasionally see someone shift as well."

Elyse tried to imagine what it would be like seeing people casually using their magical talents while at a mall and wasn't sure what to think. It just sounded so strange to her. Even all the time she'd spent in downtown Atlanta over the years, she had never seen anyone openly using magic.

"Okay, this plaza place you're going to take us to, it's safe? Are we going to need an escort?" Elyse asked tentatively. She knew they were supposed to be hiding from Dariusz, but part of her really wanted to move freely around the city.

"No, you won't need an escort. I'll take you there and point out where everything is that might be of interest, and then you can spend as much or as little time there as you want. I would not recommend straying too far from the Plaza, but the walk from this apartment to there is fine. Which reminds me." Terrance dropped two phones on the table. "These are for you. My number is pro-grammed into both, as are your own phone numbers, and just in case, I put Cory's number in as well. Your other phones, computers, et cetera should remain here in the safe box."

"Safe box?" Josh asked. Elyse knew they hadn't found anything like a safe while inspecting of the apartment.

"Yes. Here, let me show you." Terrance stood up and led them into the bathroom, of all places. She opened the medicine cabinet, then pushed what Elyse had thought was just part of the latch mechanism for the mirror. The back of the cabinet opened, and beyond that was a black metal door with a pad that took what looked like a fingerprint. Terrance put her finger on the pad and there was a beep, then the black metal door swung open. Inside were three shelves. It had more space than Elyse had expected given it was no larger than the medicine cabinet.

"It's keyed to my fingerprint and your fingerprints. The thumb and forefinger. You can use either one," Terrance explained.

Elyse decided not to ask how Terrance had their fingerprints without their knowledge. She glanced at Josh and he didn't seem to care, or at least wasn't outwardly showing it.

"Okay, I will go grab our other phones," Josh said and walked to the bedroom.

"Don't forget your computer!" called Terrance.

Elyse shook her head. "We didn't bring one. It's just the two phones."

Terrance quirked her eyebrow as though surprised. *I wonder why?* thought Elyse. *Or maybe everyone here has computers.* Elyse walked back to the kitchen and waited for Josh to place the phones and lock the safe. The bathroom was barely large enough for one person, so having three in there felt very cramped.

When Terrance and Josh emerged from the bathroom, Terrance walked straight to the door. "You two ready?"

Elyse nodded eagerly. "Yes."

"Then follow me," Terrance said and headed out the door. Elyse quickly followed, leaving Josh to shut and lock the door.

NINE

JOSH

The walk to the Plaza was quick, as Terrance had said, but it gave Josh time to let go of the anger that had welled up when Terrance had mentioned graduates from the government school for the magically talented were either dead in two years or loyal to the extreme. He was angry with himself for having been so naïve when he was seventeen and had been recruited. *At least now I am free from the government.* He took a deep breath. *But I don't know if I still owe HAC anything after what happened in Atlanta. If I ask, then there's a good chance I won't like the answer.*

Josh focused on their surroundings as they walked toward the Plaza. The street they went down was lined with large trees with small, bright green leaves that looked as though they were trimmed up a couple of times a year to make sure people could walk under them. The hard dirt street had likely been paved at some point, but with the lack of materials, it seemed Boise, like other cities, had opted to switch to dirt instead of the continuous maintenance of paved or concrete streets.

A rider on a horse was headed down the road in the opposite direction, and other than that single rider, they did not see any other people until they reached the Plaza.

The trees on the street they were on just disappeared, giving way to an empty manicured grass lawn up to the edge of the buildings that Josh presumed were the beginning of the Plaza. He could see the copper spires from some buildings beyond the first one. The first one had an old cinema sign on it, although it seemed as though it was not used for that purpose any longer. But he supposed the auditoriums that movies were held in seventy-five years ago would be ideal for presentations, meetings, or even a live show. If Terrance was right that the Plaza was as safe as she made it out to be, it would be a logical place for meetings to happen in neutral territory.

They worked their way around the cinema and into what he surmised was the heart of the Plaza. In a large centralized courtyard was a large pond with several bronze statues and feeder creeks. Outdoor seating and several restaurants surrounded the pond. From his position closer to the cinema, it appeared as though the buildings, which were three stories on the perimeter, kept going, and then the center on the opposite side of the pond had a shorter two-story building. It seemed as though a lot of thought had been put into the original design of this place, whenever that was, and that someone local had felt it was worth maintaining even through the disaster of COVID-50.

Terrance appeared at ease here in the Plaza. Josh wasn't sure if that was because she was faking it or truly was relaxed because she felt confident that the Plaza was indeed a safe space. *But then again, maybe she feels confident in her own city, especially when she can turn into a deadly four-hundred-pound cat.*

"I am going to leave the two of you here and attend to some business on the other side of Boise. If you need me, I am just a phone call away," Terrance said.

Josh brushed his fingers over the new phone that Terrance had given him. It was smaller than the one he was used to, but she was right, it would work to call her if something happened. "I'm sure we will be fine. We don't need a babysitter."

"I wasn't saying you can't handle yourself. Only that you're in an unfamiliar city and should something arise that you want help with, you have a way of reaching me. Or Cory. You can try him if for some reason I don't answer," Terrance replied.

Josh took a deep breath. A night of sleep and then waiting hours for Terrance to give them something to do had not settled him as much has he had hoped. Now, Terrance was dropping them off somewhere "safe," but he still hadn't had a chance to really get his bearings in this new city. It dawned on him that he had been in far worse situations. They had friends here and were in a safe space. Which if he was being honest was far better than some of the situations he'd been dropped into. "Okay. What is the plan for later this evening?"

"Just be back at the apartment by eight p.m. and you should be fine," Terrance said.

"Okay," Josh replied. "That should be easy enough." Instead of asking her more questions, Josh decided to just let her go. *Whatever happens after eight p.m. is not my concern. I am a guest in Terrance's city, and if she needs us to be back in the apartment by a certain time to keep us safe, then we will accommodate her request.*

Elyse slipped her hand into his and gave it a gentle squeeze. For most of the walk, Elyse had been slightly behind Josh, he had assumed to give him a chance to talk to Terrance about any matters that could be important during their stay in Boise. Josh had to admit he still wasn't sure what to make of the place or the concept of where they were. The Plaza. As they stood by the fountain, people filtered in and out of the restaurants and other shops. He hadn't seen any obvious magical talents being used, but that didn't mean they weren't. Hell, most people who looked at him would never know he had talents, and the same went for Elyse.

They stood there watching Terrance head toward the train station that she had mentioned.

When she finally disappeared around the building, Josh turned to face Elyse. "What do you want to do?"

Elyse shrugged. "We could check out the stores and at least see what they have. I'm not really in the mood to shop, but a chance to walk more would be welcome."

Josh gave Elyse a light kiss on the lips before walking toward the first store they saw, Cat's Meow. From the display case, Josh was not sure what the store sold. There were some paintings and photos of cats in gaudy gold frames, and the inside of the shop was hidden with red brocade curtains.

He opened the door and walked in with Elyse just behind him. It quickly became obvious why the inside of the shop was hidden from the exterior. A female mannequin was wearing a red sheer robe over a red leather corset. Josh bit the inside of his lip, stopping his thoughts of what Elyse would look like in that corset before they could lodge themselves in his mind. This was not the best store for him, especially since they were taking their relationship slow.

Elyse took the lead since he must have paused too long in front of the red corset. They did a quick circuit around the shop, and then went back outside. Josh found himself taking several deep breaths of fresh air.

"Not your cup of tea?" Elyse teased.

Josh chuckled. "Not unless you're going to model for me."

"Maybe someday," Elyse flirted.

Josh let the subject drop. The last thing he wanted to do was push her away. Some days he felt starting over was working and that things were great between them—a budding romance. Others, he wasn't sure. Over the years, Josh had been with many women. He had even had a girlfriend for about six months. But he had never met anyone who made him feel like Elyse did. He wanted to be a better person for her.

They walked past a gym. Through the window, Josh could see what looked like a mat for some sort of match. *I wonder if anyone in there kickboxes.* His fingers twitched. They passed a small jewelry store and were about to cross the street when Elyse pulled him to the side.

"We could go in the gym and ask if anyone kickboxes. Terrance said the Plaza is safe," Elyse offered gently.

Josh sighed. "No. I'm fine. I can find other things to keep me occupied."

"Are you sure? I really don't mind," Elyse replied.

"Yes, I am sure," he said, more firmly this time. He really did appreciate that Elyse wanted to give him a chance to practice, but he could run through some basic stuff in the apartment. There was no need to drag her to the gym. He wasn't comfortable enough in Boise to feel as though he could leave her alone.

Josh raised Elyse's hand to his lips and kissed it before urging her to continue onward. The Plaza was set up as an oval with businesses on the perimeter and in the middle. They completed the circuit finishing where they had started, in front of the large fountain. The other stores they had passed had included a children's clothing store, a women's clothing store, a kitchen store, and a bookstore, as well as several more restaurants. About one-third of the main-level business spaces were empty and had For Lease signs posted on them.

It was impossible to tell if the apartments and offices above had people in them, unless he caught a telltale glimpse of a curtain moving or someone walking in front of a window. Josh had made note of the locations of all of the security cameras. Every business had a camera at its entry door as well as across the street angled also toward the door. It was a logical setup, he surmised, especially if they were trying to deter or capture any possible thieves. But there should have been more cameras. *Unless I can't spot some of them,* he reminded himself. For Terrance to consider the Plaza a very safe place, he was surprised by the lack of visible security. *What prevents someone from being violent here? What am I missing?*

Josh absentmindedly ran his thumb over Elyse's hand while he pondered the security at the Plaza. *There could be magical protections in place that I have not been able to detect.*

They walked around slowly, following the street around the entire oval. "I am sorry if it felt like I was pressuring you earlier. That was not my intention," Josh said.

Elyse shook her head. "It wasn't you. It was me. I just got caught up in my own thoughts."

Josh wasn't sure he believed her. "I know when we were in Atlanta I made some bad choices, and maybe those are making it difficult for you to trust me when I say that I will do anything, including wait for you. You have to understand that for years I have been loyal to the FBI. It wasn't until Catrina blackmailed me into becoming a double agent and I was given you as a recruitment assignment that I began to see how messed up the orders I had been receiving over the years were. My dad, as I told you earlier, was retired military. As soon as I could understand, I was taught not to question orders I was given. He discouraged me from thinking for myself. As an FBI agent, I had to take orders without question but also rediscover how to think independently to successfully unravel the cases I was assigned.

"The more undercover ops I did, the more independent thinking I had. I know this is probably a bad analogy, but think of being undercover as when you had to take over running the ranch after your parents died. You no longer had anyone telling you what to do. You became the boss of yourself. Undercover ops are much that way because Assistant Director Fernway wasn't there on the op with me. He had to allow me to make my own decisions. Then, on the date when I tried to recruit you and you reacted so badly, I realized how wrong what I was doing was, and I didn't really know what the FBI wanted with you. Some of the talented people I recruited over the years did become my informants, but others just vanished."

Elyse frowned. "So you're saying the reason you like me is because I allowed you to realize that the FBI was giving you orders that were really terrible?"

Josh sighed. She was making this harder than he had hoped. "No. I'm saying you made it possible for me to finally break through the veil that Fernway was hiding behind. I like you, Elyse, because you are a beautiful, intelligent woman who pushes me to be a better person and has taught me that there is more to life than just a job. That there are times when friendships must come first, no matter the circumstances. Since we met, I have changed, and I like the new me. So thank you for being part of that." He gave her a light kiss, but her lips remained rigid. "What can I say or do to make this better?"

Elyse gave him an irritated look. "Just give me time to think. You just dumped a lot of words on me and then expect me to smile and say everything is fine."

He nodded and silence fell between them as they continued their route around the Plaza. They had made almost another entire lap before Elyse had them stop and turned to face him. Their eyes were almost level.

"I am glad that I have helped you change. I just want to make sure you are in this relationship because you want me for who I am, not because I am the person responsible for your awakening."

"Of course. That's what I was trying to say," Josh said.

Elyse quirked an eyebrow up at him. "Well, you threw in a lot of extra words that I had to muddle through before you got to the point."

"Sorry," he said softly before pulling her close and kissing her. This time, her lips welcomed his.

TEN
TERRANCE

Terrance took a deep breath and kept walking. She had sensed they were being followed the moment she stepped out of the apartment with Josh and Elyse, but she hadn't wanted to give anything away, either to Josh or the person following her. Because of Josh's years in the FBI, she knew he was quicker to pick up on behaviors or mannerisms. She was confident the Plaza was safe; it had been for the past fifty years. Though she had not been part of the negotiations that had established it as neutral ground, all the organizations within Boise who wanted to carve out a larger piece of the valley to grow their territory knew to leave the Plaza alone.

Just ahead was the last building in the Plaza, and then she would be able to see the train station. Her destination was Rookwood, a neighborhood on the other side of the tracks where there were fewer prying eyes. One of the ways the Plaza stayed safe was that the Boise government had cameras everywhere within its boundaries. The cameras were monitored by the local FBI division, and Cory, with the aid of their tech guru, had hacked into the FBI's computers and was able to watch the cameras as well. Which meant a lot of people knew what was going on in the Plaza. She was also aware that HAC and the FBI had significantly different protocols for how to handle a situation should their members choose to violate the Plaza's rules.

As one of the primary modes of transportation around Boise, the train stations also had an extensive security system, including a myriad of cameras and around-the-clock security teams. The west side of the train station, however, was a different matter entirely. That was where she was heading.

Doing her best to look as though she was just casually going to the train station, Terrance kept walking at a brisk pace. She entered the train station and took the stairs to the upper level two at a time, then crossed the bridge over the tracks and went back down. There were enough people in the train station that it was possible for her to shake her tail. *I guess we shall see.* She wove her way through the crowd and then slid out a side door marked Employees Only in bold . The door opened to the outside. She jumped down the four steps and took off at a run. Ahead was the long-crumbling wall, her entry point into Rookwood, and on the other side, old houses—some missing their roofs, others with trees or vines growing in the middle of them.

Terrance debated if she should shift or not. As a Siberian tiger, she could shred most enemies, but running long distances was not easy, though she could sprint very short distances and jump. In her human form, she was much nimbler and able to cover lots of ground quickly. *If I need to shift, I will shift,* she told herself. Speeding up her pace, she jumped over the wall, clearing it with room to spare, and glanced over her shoulder to see if they were following.

A snarl escaped her lips as she saw not one but three people following her, and they were also running. Terrance took off at a sprint, pushing herself as fast as she could while still keeping her ability to weave through the houses and trees and over uneven ground. Trying to make herself harder to find, she rounded a corner and skidded to a halt when she spotted a young boy who looked no more than ten years old in the middle of the street.

She approached him slowly. "What's your name?" she said softly.

He gave her a blank look, then replied, "Ben."

She took a few steps closer to him, reaching out to him with her right hand, but he did not take her hand. Her left was loosely over her gun in its holster. She wasn't afraid of the boy, but she wanted to be able to defend them both if the people in pursuit caught up to them.

"C'mon, let's go hide," she said.

The boy shook his head. "I am hiding."

If this takes much longer, they will find us for sure, she chided herself. Terrance bit her lip. She didn't understand. She grabbed for his hand, but hers just passed straight through.

"Hologram," she muttered. A clatter of rock behind her. Terrance spun, gun raised.

She had never seen the men who faced her before. Neither in person nor on camera, which was strange. She made a point of being able to recognize everyone who belonged in her city. The man on her right was tall and skinny with pale skin, dark-red eyes, and short, spiked black hair. He wore a long black trench coat, which was absurd in the sweltering heat of the Boise summer. The man to her left was the complete opposite. He was short and rather round with dark-brown skin, a full black beard, and a shaved head. He was wearing a short-sleeve, navy-blue button-up shirt and Bermuda shorts. Though as she looked them over, she was not sure how the short fat one had been able to keep up with her. *Unless his power is like Josh's, and he is fast.*

Terrance kept her gun drawn, ready to fire if either of them made a move toward her.

The tall skinny one narrowed his dark-red eyes at her and tsked. "Where's the Snowflake, Terrance?"

Deciding it would be better to play dumb, she replied smoothly, "I don't know what you're talking about."

The tall skinny one gave her a toothy grin, revealing to her chagrin a set of very pointy teeth. *Shit, shit, shit.* A small growl escaped from her lips, and she felt fur starting to sprout along her arms as she started to lose control over the tiger. If the vampire noticed, she was in trouble. Terrance adjusted her hold on the gun and took a deep breath, willing herself to get a grip.

"I know you're lying. Because," the vampire paused heavily, "Trey told me you have it."

"There's no fucking way Trey told you I have the Snowflake, because I don't have it," Terrance replied before she could stop herself.

The vampire chuckled. "You're right. He didn't, but I am confident that you do know where it is, so thank you." Then, the vampire disappeared.

Terrance felt something sting her shoulder, like a bullet had been fired from behind her. She completely lost control of the tiger. Terrance turned and sprinted for the nearest house. Mid-stride, she went from human to great cat. Bullets whizzed through the air. She could feel something else as well but could not quite pinpoint what it was. When she was in her tiger form, she was more in tune with when people used their magical talents. Sometimes, it was just a vibration through the ground; other times she felt it in her body. The air crackled with energy. Terrance spun around, claws ready, and leaped onto the man—no, woman—who had fired the bullets. Her razor-sharp claws sliced through the woman's flesh like it was nothing. Terrance leaped off the body of the woman, barely sparing a glance for her and the growing pool of blood.

Terrance followed the feeling of the magic being sucked somewhere. Just when she thought she had figured out where it was coming from, a bolt of electricity went straight through her. She snarled as her whole body twitched and closed her eyes. *I am not this easy to kill.* When she opened them again, she was surprised to see the short fat man standing only a few feet away. She lunged, jaws open. Just before she connected, he unleashed all the magic she presumed he had been pulling in. Terrance snapped her jaws shut on his throat and ripped as her body convulsed. She fell to the ground with a thud and lay there twitching, unable to move of her own accord. Blood dribbled out of her mouth from ripping out the mage's throat. Then, everything went black.

Terrance woke up with a start. She was still in tiger form with a bandage wrapped around her right front paw. As she peered around, willing to her eyes to focus, she determined she was definitely not in the dilapidated Rookwood neighborhood the fight had happened in, but she was struggling to figure out where she was since her eyes refused to cooperate. After a while, she squeezed them shut. A headache was forming, and she was really hoping it would go away if she quit trying to see.

It took Terrance a moment to realize that just because she couldn't use her eyes didn't mean her other senses had stopped working. She inhaled deeply, sorting through the scents. She could smell whatever they had cleaned her wound with, although Terrance didn't recall injuring her arm before she shifted or after. The sheet underneath her smelled fresh, as though it had been recently changed. *Which means either I haven't been here for long, or they were able to lift four hundred pounds of sleeping tiger.* Her thoughts paused. *Either they aren't afraid of me or were more concerned about getting whatever mess my body was in cleaned up.*

As she continued to sort through other smells, she picked up the sound of shoes on linoleum. The way the person walked was familiar. The footsteps entered the room.

"You're awake," came a deep voice, a voice she would know anywhere. Her mate, Cory.

Terrance opened her eyes and let out a frustrated growl when they still wouldn't focus. She flexed her claws and heard the cloth underneath them ripping. Suddenly, Cory's hands were in her fur.

"Easy, Ter," he murmured before he started to purr. She closed her eyes and rubbed her head on his hand, wondering why she hadn't been able to tell he was nearby. They could always feel each other through the mating bond. One of the benefits and down-sides of it, to be so in tune with one another.

"You can try shifting. I don't know if it'll help. Doc said that sometimes any lasting effects of magic will go away once you shift to human," Cory said softly.

Terrance licked his hand and let her body go limp as she focused on shifting back. A minute later, she had goosebumps on her bare skin. Tentatively, she opened her eyes and found to her relief she could see Cory and the rest of the room. They were still a little blurry but it wasn't as bad as it had been.

"Where are we?" she asked, still feeling out of sorts. A shiver ran through her, and she realized that she hadn't kept her clothes in the shift. Whatever that mage had hit her with had really done a number on her shifting talent for her to not be able to shift with her clothes still on.

"In the healing suite at headquarters," he replied, his voice rumbling through his purring, which had gotten even louder.

Terrance heard Cory say they were in the healing suite, but nothing in the room looked familiar. Part of her wanted to tell him that she didn't remember—the other part knew he had been worried and needed reassurance that she was fine. "You okay?"

Instead of answering, Cory and wrapped his arms around her, touching their foreheads together. "You scared me," he said softly.

Cory gently ran his hands across her shoulders and back, massaging her tight muscles. Terrance closed her eyes, enjoying his touch.

"Mmm," she murmured against his chest. She started to roll over to give him better access to her back and a wave of dizziness went through her. She grabbed his hand. "How long was I unconscious for?"

"Twenty-four hours," he said, kissing her hand and then climbing into bed next to her.

Terrance closed her eyes as a headache pressed behind her forehead.

"Do you think you can lie on your stomach?" Cory asked.

Terrance rolled over instead of responding. He waited a few moments to see if she would object to the position before he straddled her legs and began massaging in earnest. Slowly, Terrance's tight muscles loosened.

Cory gave her a kiss on the cheek, and she sucked in a breath. The headache was turning into a migraine.

Cory paused and sat upright. "What's wrong?"

"Nothing," Terrance mumbled, burying her face in the pillow.

Cory bit her lightly on the neck. "It's not nothing if you can't even answer me."

Terrance sighed and rolled over so she could see Cory instead of the pillow. "My vision is still fuzzy, and although the massage is helping, I also have a massive migraine."

Cory lay down on the bed beside Terrance and pulled her into his arms. "Then you can rest here with me until you feel better." He gave her a light kiss on the lips and pulled the sheet over both of them.

Terrance woke up curled up against Cory with his arm draped over her. She was surprised he had fallen asleep and stayed with her. It gave her some insight to how worried he had been. She started to scoot out from under his arm when his hand clamped down on her.

"Where are you going?" he said roughly.

"To the bathroom. You better let me up unless you want me to pee on you," Terrance warned him tartly. The arm instantly retracted, allowing her to bounce out of bed and out the door. She tried to remember what the layout of the healing suite was. Her mind still felt fuzzy, which was concerning. She opened the door to the room and sheepishly said, "Where is the bathroom?"

Cory shot off the bed, swept her into his arms, and carried her to the bathroom. She shut the door firmly behind him and saw to her needs. *He knows more rest did not help as much as he'd hoped and is going to fuss,* she thought as she washed her hands.

When she opened the door, Cory was there waiting patiently, a pair of baggy black sweats hugging his hips and a stack of clean clothes in his hands. "Do you remember where we are?"

Terrance peered around the hallway and shook her head. "No." She pointed to the door to the room. "I know that's the large healing room, but I don't remember where this hallway goes."

"Do you remember what happened?" Cory asked, eyes narrowed in concern.

Terrance sighed and ran a hand over her face. "Mostly. But can we sit down? I still have a bit of a headache." She took the offered clothes. Using his arm to brace for balance, she got dressed.

"Sure." He took her hand in his and led her into the waiting room. He sat on the couch and then pulled her into his lap, running his fingers through her hair. She leaned into his bare chest, relishing their closeness.

"I took Josh and Elyse to the Plaza as we had discussed. When we were there, I felt like I was being followed. I left Josh and Elyse and crossed through the train station heading into Rookwood, and then I saw this illusion of a boy, his name started with a B. It distracted me and allowed a vampire, a short fat guy, and a woman to surround me. The short fat guy is the one who hit me with the electricity. I had shifted, so I could feel him using his talent to draw on the residue of magic that was still present in some of the houses. As I killed him, he released what he had collected. The closest thing I can compare it to would be a stun gun, but it was so much more powerful than that," she said, shivering at the memory.

"I thought it might have been electricity that hit you based on how you were still twitching when we found you, but I wasn't completely sure. Doc couldn't tell. He just repaired whatever damage he could find and said rest would help you recover," Cory said before nipping at her neck.

Terrance poked him in the ribs, and he stopped messing with her neck. "Did he put a restriction on any physical activities?"

Desire clear in his eyes, Cory captured his lips with hers, avoiding the question completely. Though by the way he was behaving, she assumed that Doc had said something along the lines of as long as she was up to it, they could do whatever they wanted. She let her mate kiss her and enjoyed it, but when he began reaching for her waist, she put her hand on top of his to stop him.

"I love you. But as Doc said, I need to rest. Maybe if I can sleep more, I will feel normal again."

Cory sighed and reluctantly backed off. "I know I can be pushy, but you scared me."

"I scared me," she whispered, knowing he would hear her. She knew that if her memory of the events that resulted in her getting zapped was intact that she would likely soon recover the memory of their apartment and shake off the feeling of fuzziness. What she really wanted almost as much as sleep was to know who it was who had attacked her and why. Something at the back of her mind was tickling her. She thought she might be forgetting an important detail, but cozy in Cory's arms, she could not get her mind to work. She took a deep breath, and before she could count to ten was fast asleep.

ELEVEN
ELYSE

Elyse leaned back in her chair. They had walked around the Plaza for a few hours, checking out several stores and stretching their legs before finally they both got hungry enough to get some food. They decided on a quick service restaurant with Asian food. Since Terrance hadn't given them any recommendations before she departed, the two of them had been on their own for deciding which restaurant appealed the most.

Elyse selected the teriyaki chicken over fried rice, deciding to go with a safe option. Josh chose to be a little more adventurous and selected Kung Pao chicken, which had two little peppers by the name indicating it was moderately spicy. Within five minutes of ordering, their number was called. Even with the sun going down, it was still hot outside, so they had agreed to sit inside since there were large fans running and it seemed cooler. Elyse found herself wondering if most of the restaurants in Boise had quick service like this or if they had full-service ones too. While she appreciated the speed with which they got their food, she also felt that the whole experience was lacking.

Maybe this is another difference between Boise and Atlanta, she pondered.

The two of them settled into their chairs and dug into the food while it was still hot. While she ate, Elyse watched the people around them. There was a family with two young girls and a teenage boy. The girls were throwing a ball of water between them with occasional droplets of water splashing their shirts sending them into a fit of giggles. The teenage boy appeared to be doing his best to ignore the girls and avoid getting wet. Elyse found it intriguing that the parents did not feel the need to correct the girls for their open use of their magical talent in a restaurant.

Ever since they sat down with their food, Elyse had noticed a change in Josh's behavior. He was on edge, more alert than he had been earlier, but for the life of her Elyse could not figure out why. *He must have noticed something that I am oblivious to,* she surmised. *If I need to know, I'm sure he will tell me.*

Decision made, she polished off the rest of her food. Glancing at her watch, Elyse saw they had about forty-five minutes before they had to be back in the apartment. But she wasn't sure what else they would want to do. Just walk slowly back? They had gone in every store as well as walked the oval many times, and part of her was almost craving the apartment over the possibility of walking one more lap.

Elyse jumped when Josh tapped her foot with his. "Sorry," he said softly.

Elyse shrugged. She was the one who wasn't paying enough attention to what he was doing. She stood and picked up her plate, then walked around to his side to grab his.

As she leaned over, Josh spoke in a whisper, "We are being watched. The two women in the back corner by the fireplace. Don't look. Just put our plates in the trash, and then we will leave. Follow my lead."

Elyse kissed him on the cheek, then took both plates to the trash. When she returned, Josh stood up and took her hand in his, then kissed her lightly on the lips. She returned the kiss, barely brushing his lips with hers, trying to keep focused on the fact that Josh had said they were being watched. He led them out of the building and across the bridge so they could stand close to the pond. This position had multiple escape routes, unlike the restaurant, where they were essentially in a glass box.

Josh pulled her around to face him and wrapped his arms around her in a hug. He brought his lips close to her ear. "They followed us out of the restaurant. Terrance said to be back by eight p.m., but I don't want to lead our tail right to our apartment."

Elyse wrapped her arms around him, burying her head in his shoulder. "We could go shopping. Make it look like we're boring, and maybe they'll go away," she said, keeping her voice low. As much as she was over this place, he had a valid point about not wanting to lead their tail right back to the apartment. It was not a good way to ensure they would stay safe. She felt him nod, his chin grazing her shoulder. Slowly, she unwrapped her arms from around Josh, and he slid his hand back into hers.

She pursed her lips. "I think I want to check out that clothing store we went by earlier. Birds and Bees?" she said in her normal voice so that whoever was following them would hear.

"If that is where you want to go, then sure," Josh replied with a slight smile.

Elyse knew very well that he did not enjoy shopping in women's stores, but she wasn't sure which other store to go to. She didn't want to scare him away by suggesting they go into the jewelry store and look at rings. *Maybe someday.*

When they finally made it back to the apartment, it was closer to nine p.m. But once the people following them at the Plaza disappeared—about thirty minutes into their adventure in Birds and Bees—they did not have any others pop up to replace them.

Josh entered the apartment first, hand on the holster of his gun. After Terrance's warning about returning after eight p.m. and being followed while they were in the Plaza, she knew that his caution was warranted. When Josh gave the all clear, Elyse stepped inside and shut the door. Her eyes immediately went to the dining room table where there was an oddly familiar box labeled "Cornelius."

Elyse raised an eyebrow as she realized that it wasn't just familiar. It was in fact the box of her great-grandfather Archibald Cornelius's journals. "What are these doing here?"

Josh reached into the box and grabbed a piece of paper off the top. "Here."

Elyse took the note.

> Dearest Elyse,
>
> I thought you might like to continue reading your great-grandfather's journals. I know it is not possible for us to communicate directly while you are staying safe, but there are still more answers here.
>
> I also have faith that as you develop control over your magical talent that you will be able to find the answers you're looking for beyond the journals.
>
> Love always,
> Aunt Grace

Elyse set the note down on the table. To be honest, the past couple of days she hadn't thought much about what she had learned about her great-grandfather. She ran a hand over her face and sat down in one of the dining chairs.

When she had read the journals previously, they had led to her having visions, which she now knew was part of her magical talent. Most of the visions had been related to the events described in the journals, though some had not. Taking a deep breath, Elyse sorted through the information she did have on her family, specifically her great-grandfather Archibald Cornelius.

Archibald's team at the lab had been directly involved in the research of COVID-50 when it first appeared in July 2050. His team had been tasked with finding a cure. At some pivotal point, things in their research had changed, as had the virus. Dariusz had done something magical to the virus, which had resulted in surviving babies born from mothers who contracted the virus and then died in childbirth being blessed—*Or cursed,* she thought—with magical talents.

A thought dawned on her as one of her dreams tied to the journals flashed back.

> *The lights flickered in the lab.*
> *"Not again," muttered the woman.*
> *The power went out. A whirring sound could be heard, then the backup generators kicked on, with the lights following moments later.*
> *"See? It came back on, like it always does," Archibald said. He opened the door of the fridge closest to him and gave a satisfied nod that it was still running. Just then, a huge flash of light illuminated the room before everything went black. Archibald let out an unearthly scream as the fridge he had been peering into collapsed on top of him.*

Elyse shook her head. Was it really that simple that a big storm had caused a power outage and zapped the fridge all the samples were in? *I suppose it doesn't have to be complicated, if simple works. People who were more familiar than I am with COVID-50 associate the name Cornelius with it, yet Archibald was just someone who worked in the lab. Wasn't he?* she wondered. *Or is there more to it?*

Elyse's great-grandfather and recently deceased uncle Albert had both worked for Evermore Genetics, a laboratory that had been dedicated over one hundred years to the advancement of biological engineering and was known for being at the forefront of virus genetic research. Prior to a month ago, Elyse had never thought that her uncle or great-grandfather working in a laboratory had been very remarkable.

With the appearance of the journals here on their dining table in Boise, Elyse regretted not doing more research before they had left Atlanta. Not only had she missed out on asking her Aunt Grace what she knew about the family, she also missed out on using Josh's computer, which he'd left at the ranch.

Elyse jumped when there was a light touch on her shoulder, almost knocking the chair out from under her. "Are you okay?" Josh asked with concern in his voice.

"Yeah, why?" Elyse asked uncertainly.

"You've been quiet for a while. I wasn't sure if the journals were stirring up some bad memories or what," Josh said with a shrug.

Elyse shook her head and gave Josh's hand a squeeze. "No. I'm fine, I promise. I just haven't really thought much about my great-grandfather or the journals the past week, and it made me realize how little I still know. You had promised to help me, but with everything that happened leading up to us leaving, we didn't have time."

Josh nodded. "You're right, and I'm sorry I couldn't help more. I'm sure Terrance has a computer we can borrow."

Elyse smiled. "That was my first thought too. But I would like to see where we get if I use my magical talent."

"That's a great idea. Good practice too," Josh agreed. "What would you like me to do?"

Elyse pursed her lips in thought. "Just be ready with a pen and paper to write down anything I see."

Elyse set her hands flat and relaxed on the top of the table. She didn't want to touch Josh because she was worried that would influence her talent to show her the wrong thing. She closed her eyes and took a deep breath, letting it out on a count of ten. Then, she focused on her talent and what she wanted to see. *Show me*

Evermore Genetics, she commanded herself. There was a tingling sensation.

> *When Elyse opened her eyes, she was standing on a sidewalk that looked vaguely familiar. Peering around, she tried to get her bearings. On the opposite side of the street was a large high-rise building. The front entrance had large, bright blue words that said Evermore Genetics. Elyse crossed the street to get closer to the building. The glass next to the sliding doors read 1222 NW Peachtree Blvd.*
>
> I know where I am, *she thought.* Downtown Atlanta.
>
> *Elyse glanced at her surroundings, but no one else seemed to be around. She went up to the doors expecting them to open, but they didn't. She tried to go through them, since sometimes she could just walk through walls if she was in a vision. This time, however, nothing happened.* Odd.

Elyse opened her eyes and blinked rapidly. She was in the apartment in Boise. Josh was sitting opposite her.

"Did it work?" Josh asked.

Elyse smiled ruefully. "I suppose it did. I guess next time I need to be more specific. I just wanted to see Evermore Genetics. I literally got to see the building in downtown Atlanta."

Josh's eyes widened. "So you saw the lab?"

Elyse shook her head. "No, I couldn't get into the building. I just saw the outside."

"Hmm … maybe focus on something a little more specific. Evermore Genetics and the lab or your great-grandfather or uncle … maybe it was too broad and your talent had too many options," Josh suggested.

Elyse nodded. They were treating her talent as though it had a mind of its own, but sometimes that was exactly how it felt. Maybe one day when she obtained complete control over her talent, it would no longer feel that way. Josh had more experience with magical talents since as an FBI agent, one of his primary tasks had been recruiting magically talented people. She rolled her head and shoulders to loosen back up, then set her hands on the table.

Closing her eyes, Elyse took a deep breath and found her magical talent was there, almost eager for her next request. *Strange.* She shrugged and made herself focus on the task. *Evermore Genetics and Archibald Cornelius.*

Elyse opened her eyes and found herself once again directly across the street from the Evermore Genetics building in downtown Atlanta. She crossed the street and was about to try the front doors again when a young white man in his early thirties, wearing a suit and square glasses with thick black rims, walked out of the building talking to a light-brown-skinned man with short, cropped black hair in a navy blue suit with a deep bass voice. Their conversation looked rather animated, and the white man—who Elyse realized must be Archibald—seemed very excited.

Elyse quickly moved closer, wanting to hear what they were saying.

The man in the navy suit was speaking. "I will send over a formal offer with all of the details, but it sounds like we have come to an agreement, Dr. Cornelius?"

Archibald nodded. "Definitely. After seeing the lab and what resources you have in person, I am convinced this is the right fit."

"Good. Then all that's left are the minor details and paperwork." The man in the navy suit offered his hand for Archibald to shake.

"Thank you, Dr. Tierney," Archibald said, shaking hands. Then, with a big smile, he headed south down the sidewalk.

Elyse started to follow, wanting to know where he was going, when everything began to fade.

Elyse opened her eyes and gave Josh a small smile. "That worked, mostly." Josh opened the book they were taking notes in, pen ready. "I was back in downtown Atlanta in front of the building, but this time a young Archibald and Dr. Tierney were having a discussion. From the bits I heard, I believe that was when he accepted the offer to work for Evermore Genetics."

"Well, that's good. I take it you focused on Archibald and Evermore Genetics?" Josh asked.

Elyse yawned and nodded. "Yes."

"Did you want to try again?" Josh asked.

Elyse shook her head. "No, I'm exhausted. We can pick this up tomorrow."

Elyse slipped into the bed and pulled the covers around her chin. She had been quick with her evening routine and offered to go first to keep Josh from requesting that she take the large bed again. The smaller bed didn't bother her. It was comfortable, and she was tired. Wrapped snugly in her cocoon of blankets, she fell asleep.

Elyse was on the opposite side of a lab bench where a lean, wiry man with thinning gray hair and a small gray mustache, wearing a lab coat over a light blue button-up shirt and gray slacks, was looking over the shoulder of a young man with long blond hair pulled back in a ponytail. Elyse couldn't tell much about his face since he was peering into a microscope.

The older man Elyse recognized almost immediately as a younger version of Uncle Albert. This has to be fifteen years ago or so, she thought, *based on how his hair was gray rather than white and his skin was not as papery-thin as it had been the past few years.*

"What do you think, Thomas?" Uncle Albert asked.

Blond ponytail answered, "The blood from sample A seems to be eating—for lack of a better word—the blood from sample B. Once it consumes a cell of sample B, then its structure also seems to change. I've never seen anything like this before."

Uncle Albert chewed on his lip in thought. Elyse watched him intently. "I thought perhaps what I saw was a fluke, but you're the third person who has witnessed these two samples reacting the same with each other. Four times is too many to be a coincidence."

Thomas pulled back from the microscope. "What does it mean?"

Uncle Albert shook his head. "That is the million-dollar question. I'm not sure."

"Where did you get the samples from?" Thomas asked.

"Dr. Tierney informed me when they arrived. I was asked to run them through the usual tests and then to report my findings. Until I started putting the different samples together, though, none of the results were remarkable," Uncle Albert explained.

"Are they all blood samples?" Thomas asked.

"Yes. Why?" Uncle Albert asked.

"Was it indicated what species they're from?"

Elyse smiled at his questions. It appeared these two had been through this situation before and had an established rapport.

Uncle Albert shook his head. "Unfortunately, no. When I asked, I was told it was not important." He tapped his fingers on the table. "Though at this point, I think that because we do not know what species the blood is from, it is difficult to produce any additional information that will be useful. As I'm sure you know, some species—or even blood types within a species—are not compatible."

Thomas peered around the room as though worried some-one would overhear him, before he proceeded to speak in a whisper. "I have heard rumors that magic exists."

Elyse was surprised when Uncle Albert didn't even twitch at the mention of magic. He knew all those years ago?

"I see. So you are aware of this," Thomas said, continuing to speak in a whisper. "How do we rule out that it's not magic at work until we know what species the blood is from?"

Uncle Albert pressed his lips together in a thin line, as though debating whether or not he should reply. Finally, he drew a breath and spoke in a soft voice. "You are right. Knowing what species it is would help, especially where magic is concerned, but I do not have any way of testing for magic or determining what species it is. When the computer that did the genome sequencing stopped working last month, we lost that ability."

"Can't they repair it?" Thomas asked, seemingly grasping for straws.

Uncle Albert shrugged. "Maybe, maybe not. But until they do, I don't have any way to identify the species unless we are given the information. Which means all I can do is write up this final report and see what Dr. Tierney does with it."

Elyse rolled over and opened her eyes. She was on the very edge of the twin-sized bed in the apartment. A few feet away, she could hear Josh lightly snoring. The room was almost pitch-black thanks to the room-darkening curtain over the sole window. She wasn't sure how long she'd been asleep for but was sure there was still plenty of night left for her to return to sleeping. *Maybe without the weird dream.*

Elyse took a deep breath and slowly exhaled, counting backward from ten. She wasn't sure if she made it to one before she fell deeply asleep.

TWELVE
TERRANCE

Terrance was sitting at her desk in their headquarters with her feet propped up, reviewing the report again from Pierre on how things went with Elyse and Josh once she left them in the Plaza. They had not yet been able to identify the people who had been following them or the organization they belonged to, but her best tech-talented member, Yolanda, was on the job.

Yolanda was a shadow mage whose talent somehow also gave her an edge with technological stuff. It was something Terrance didn't quite understand, but over the years it had proven quite useful.

Weeks ago, when Catrina Fox, another lieutenant of Hellfire and Chaos, asked for help with acquiring Elyse Hutchinson because of her desirable magical talent of seeing the future and the past, Terrance had known that getting involved would not be a simple matter. Individuals with talents to see the future were one in a million, and once discovered, anyone in a position of power wanted to gain control over them. Which meant agreeing to help Catrina was highly likely to result in a mess Terrance probably wouldn't come out of unscathed.

Terrance's decision to travel to Atlanta had been for personal reasons. She had a history with Catrina, and although she hesitated to call Catrina a close friend, they had gotten into and out of a number of tight situations. Terrance had known if she had made the request for help, Catrina would have dropped everything and come. Terrance felt obligated to do the same.

Catrina ran her part of HAC with a tight fist. She gave orders and everyone who worked for her obeyed unconditionally. When they didn't, there were consequences. Terrance suspected much of that came from the number of years Catrina had spent working directly with Dariusz, the leader of Hellfire and Chaos and the oldest living vampire.

Terrance, on the other hand, had been raised by her father and a group of parents who also had children who had become shifters in the Pacific Northwest.

As a natural leader, Terrance found people wanted to follow her, even when she really would prefer to not have them do so. Her father told her that it was one of the things she had learned from her aunt Cecelia, her mother's sister who had helped take care of her when she was young. Then her aunt had done something—Terrance could not remember what—that her father had considered unforgivable and had forbidden them from seeing each other again. Years later, Terrance had reached out to her aunt hoping to reconnect, but her aunt had not been interested. She had been too wrapped up in her research to spare time for her niece.

Regardless of what her father said, Terrance believed her natural leadership tendencies had come from him. She saw how he was with the parents of her friends, how he encouraged them to stick together and survive the challenges one was presented with when the infant they thought was going to be a cute and adorable human suddenly was able to turn into an animal too. Frequently at inconvenient times. Even when she knew he was frustrated with her and the others, he never lost his temper or raised his voice. She had vowed if she ever had the opportunity to lead anyone that she would do so as he had taught her, by cultivating unyielding loyalty and friendship.

Sometimes Terrance wondered if her methods worked better because of where she lived. The residents of Boise knew about magical talents, and the differences between the farmers and city-goers was blurrier. Terrance knew the trains influenced this, since the city and its resources were not as difficult to access for the farmers as they were in Atlanta. The trains provided her with unique opportunities to be able to have a much larger network of people working for her. Which allowed her to keep closer watch on the other organizations in Boise. She knew that was a two-way street; the other organizations likely also kept close tabs on her.

In addition to the government-operated FBI, which served as local and federal law enforcement, there were two other organizations: Ursus Aureus—the Golden Bears—and Nightshade Coven, a clan of vampires. UA was a family of bear shifters who offered protection to the farmers in the western side of the valley. Terrance had always suspected that UA had some illicit operations as well, but if they did not interfere with HAC business, it was not her concern.

Nightshade Coven was another matter altogether. They were constantly stirring up trouble. Terrance suspected it was someone from Nightshade Coven who was following Josh and Elyse at the Plaza. The fact that she had encountered a vampire immediately after leaving the Plaza added further fuel to that assumption.

Which was where Yolanda came in. She created and managed the whole HAC database of people. Similar to the way an FBI agent could look up information on individuals, the HAC database did the same thing. The biggest difference being that HAC knew way more about the magically talented.

A light knock on the office door snapped Terrance out of her thoughts.

"Sorry," said Yolanda.

Terrance shrugged. "I wasn't doing anything important. Did you figure out who was following Elyse and Josh?"

Yolanda nodded and handed Terrance a computer, a thin piece of glass about the size of a sheet of paper. The technology had been developed just before the COVID-50 outbreak. With the scarcity of materials, no one had deemed it important enough to develop more advanced computers in the past seventy-five years.

On the screen were two photos one of Tabbitha Griffin, a woman of large stature, six feet tall, three hundred pounds, and formidable. She had long purple hair, tan skin, and bright green eyes. Terrance didn't recognize her but had a nagging feeling she'd heard of the woman before.

The second woman, Emma Dalton, was average height and build with medium-brown skin, dark-brown eyes, and short black hair.

Terrance could see right away why Emma would have been selected to follow Elyse and Josh. She blended in. She wasn't sure why Tabbitha would have been selected because with the purple hair and her height, she would be way more obvious.

Terrance looked up at Yolanda. "Okay, so we know their names. Do we know who they work for?"

Yolanda shook her head. "No. That's where it gets weird. From what I can find, they are just mercenaries for hire."

"Part of a larger group?" Terrance inquired.

Yolanda shook her head again. "No. Or at least not that I can tell. I've done a deep dive on both and haven't found anything particularly useful."

"Maybe Tabbitha Griffin and Emma Dalton are just aliases," Terrance suggested.

Yolanda nodded in agreement. "That is where my thoughts are headed as well. I just haven't had any luck so far. Now, the individuals who attacked you after you left the Plaza are another matter entirely." Yolanda tapped the computer screen a couple of times and brought up three different photos. The first was Artur Hagi, the tall and skinny male with pale skin, dark-red eyes, and short, spiked black hair. In the photo, he wore a black T-shirt and jeans. The second, Gustabo Borra, was short and rather round with dark brown skin, a full black beard, and a shaved head. In the photo, he was wearing a black suit, a far cry from the casual clothes he had been in the other day.

"Artur is a vampire, and Gustabo has a magical talent for lightning and electricity, maybe something else too. Artur said they had been sent by Trey to retrieve the Snowflake, but I am not sure if he has a connection to Trey or if he just knows that Trey has a contract with us for the Snowflake. Either way, it is concerning that the number of people who know we have it is increasing."

Terrance leaned back in her chair, tapping her fingers on the desk.

"I was able to dig up more information on Artur. He is a member of Nightshade Coven. The FBI has some open cases where he is listed as a possible suspect, but they don't have enough proof to bring him in. Though I am not sure they would if they did. Unless they can build a case involving more than one member of the coven." Yolanda paused. "Gustabo is not a vampire, though it seems as though he did receive some money from one of the coven's accounts, so I feel confident stating that he was definitely hired by them."

Terrance sensed Cory's approach as he walked down the hallway, likely coming to join the meeting. Thanks to the mating bond, she'd known he was coming as soon as he made the decision. Their connection came in handy in situations like the one yesterday, when Cory had sensed her distress over the bond and used it to track her location after she'd been attacked. On the downside, it made it difficult to be sneaky.

Terrance smiled as Cory walked in as though he owned the place, which he did—at least according to him. Since Terrance had been part of HAC before she and Cory had become mated, most of their group considered her the sole leader, which is how they were viewed in the HAC hierarchy. Terrance was one of Dariusz's lieutenants, and Cory was her second-in-command. Cory walked behind the desk and a gave her a light kiss on the cheek before leaning against the wall behind her chair.

"I find it troubling that Nightshade Coven has the Snowflake in their sights. When you first told me about the contract with Trey, it had seemed straightforward, especially since we already had a lead indicating the Snowflake was here in Boise. But at this point, I think you chose to omit some things." Cory gave Terrance's shoulders a warning squeeze.

Terrance sighed. "I didn't think the other information would matter."

Cory snarled softly. "I strongly disagree. Knowing that Josh Everly was working on a case in Atlanta that involved Octavien Boutin and the Snowflake was a huge giveaway that it would not be simple."

Terrance stood up to face Cory. She had to tip her head up to meet his eyes. "Josh has worked on big cases before. I don't see why that is important."

Cory bared his teeth at her, which were starting to elongate. "I'm not talking about Josh's involvement. I'm talking about Octavien Boutin. If I know who he is, you *must* know."

Terrance wrinkled her forehead, not understanding his anger. "He's one of Dariusz's underlings, not tied to HAC. What about it?"

Cory closed his eyes in frustration. Terrance could see his skin rippling as he fought to not shift. "Octavien is deeply involved in Dariusz's affairs in Europe. I thought you knew that."

Terrance shrugged. "No, I didn't."

"Josh found the connection—" Cory started.

Terrance growled. "Josh and I are acquaintances. I am not sure why you think he would have openly shared information with me on a case he was working for the FBI, or why you would think I would automatically ask him for additional information before accepting a contract. If you thought I made a wrong call when I told you about the contract with Trey for the Snowflake, then you should have said so at the time. That was over a month ago. We cannot change the past."

Cory moved away from Terrance and the wall and paced on the other side of the room, staying far enough away from Yolanda that she had room to do what she needed with the computer.

"We can't change the past," Terrance repeated. "So, what is it that you came in here to say? It can't be just to criticize choices I made that we can't change."

"Josh knows about Octavien and the Snowflake. I think he would be a good asset, and he's here in Boise. If Nightshade Coven is involved, then we're going to need all the help we can get. Especially since it is clear that Trey's boss has not accepted your deal and they are out for your head," Cory explained.

Terrance frowned. "Josh and Elyse are here to stay away from Dariusz. How is Josh helping us going to keep them safe?"

"They weren't safe the moment Catrina left them at Shoshone Falls, not with the Snowflake here," Cory replied matter-of-factly.

"That's not true," Terrance protested weakly, but she knew Cory was right. The question was whether Catrina had known that Boise was not going to be the safe place for Josh and Elyse she had promised. Terrance blew out a frustrated breath. She hadn't anticipated what she considered a simple contract—retrieve and turn over the Snowflake—to become such a big deal.

Yolanda coughed, and both tiger shifters focused their attention on her. "Do you want me to keep digging and just notify you when I find more useful information?"

Terrance nodded. "Yes, that seems like the best course of action for now. Thanks."

Thankfully, Yolanda took that as a dismissal and shut the door on her way out, allowing them to keep the meeting fairly private. Terrance braced her hands on her desk and gazed at Cory, knowing he was still angry with her. She just had no idea what he was going to *do* with his anger.

"I want Josh to come with me to go talk to Willow Kelly. Normally I would take you with me, but with a contract out on your head, I think that would be the wrong move," Cory said in a tight voice.

Terrance nodded. Talking to the leader of Nightshade Coven was a good place to start.

"Are you only taking Josh?" Terrance asked mildly.

"If I take more than Josh, then they might view us as a threat. I just want to talk, see if she will tell us what they want, and also confirm that Artur was operating under her orders," Cory explained.

Terrance eyed her mate. He was still really tense and looked like he was about to punch something. "Maybe you should hit the ring first. You know Josh kickboxes. Maybe you can strategize and let off some steam. I am sure that Willow is not going to take kindly to your intrusion if you go in like you are now."

Cory took a step forward, then another. "Maybe I want to accomplish that in a different way." His eyes raked over her from the top of her head to her waist; the rest was hidden by the desk. Desire flooded his gaze, and Terrance had to struggle to keep her own in check, especially as images of what he wanted to do to her invaded her mind through the mating bond.

"How about this? You go get some exercise with Josh, talk to Willow, and then when you return, we can see about those other thoughts of yours," Terrance said with a wicked grin.

Cory grumbled under his breath. "Fine. Besides, you're probably right. The vampires are more active at night, so I'll be more likely to get an audience if I show up tonight instead of waiting until tomorrow."

Cory closed the distance between them and gave her a demanding kiss with a promise for what was to come later. Terrance shivered in anticipation, then bit her lip. They had a plan and needed to stick to it. Thankfully, her mate left before they could make good on the promise.

Her lips still tingled from the kiss. Terrance glanced at her desk without really seeing the papers on it. Yolanda had given her the names of the two women, Tabbitha Griffin and Emma Dalton, who had followed Josh and Elyse at the Plaza. She rolled the two names around and around her mind. *Why do they sound familiar?*

Terrance opened a desk drawer and pulled out a computer. She turned it on and did a quick search for the two women, pulling up the information Yolanda had already found. With their information up, she opened another screen and typed in "Ursus Aureus members." A lengthy list began to load, and she started to scroll through the names. The group of bear shifters was one of the oldest organizations of magically talented people within the Boise area. She heard rumors of them when she was a child, and her dad always reassured her that they were safe as long as they stayed away from the western farms.

On the list were Griffin Taylor and Deborah Emanuel. *I wonder.* She clicked on Griffin Taylor. Sure enough, a photo of a woman who looked similar to Tabbitha Griffin appeared on the screen. She then checked the file for Deborah Emanuel, and the same thing happened for Emma Dalton. She quickly sent both of those files to Yolanda.

"They're bear shifters," she mused aloud. "Why are they making a move now?"

There was a light knock on the door, and Yolanda entered. "I think Trey hired them," Yolanda announced.

Terrance gave her a sharp look. "He hired bear shifters to go after Josh and Elyse?"

Yolanda shook her head. "No, I think he hired them to follow Josh and Elyse to send you a message. That he knows they are here and how to find them."

"He had Josh and Elyse followed *and* paid to have me attacked? That doesn't track," Terrance replied.

"If you were supposed to die in the attack at Rookwood, then the message was likely meant for Cory. That he took you and was gunning for Josh and Elyse too. But what if they are not related? Maybe Trey has nothing to do with Rookwood and it is merely a warning to you that he agrees to pay double but isn't willing to entertain to any more changes to the deal," Yolanda said.

Terrance tapped her fingers on the desk. Yolanda did have some strong theories. The Ursus Aureus members did hire themselves out to stir things up occasionally. From what Terrance could tell, the clan enjoyed being in the spotlight, even if it resulted in some of their members dying. It could even be worth going out and confronting them. Usually flashing money around loosened the tongues of someone in UA. She always thought it was weird that they were only loyal as long as the money was flowing the right way but would eagerly sell any information to the highest bidder.

It also makes them dangerous, she reminded herself. Because any information the clan gathered was for sale. The tricky part was knowing what information UA had access to and justifying investing resources to finding out.

Maybe I should suggest that Cory and Josh go out to meet UA. Josh's presence might intrigue them enough to gain us an audience. Mind made up, Terrance shut down her computer, returning it to its place in her desk.

As she walked down the hallway toward her apartment, Terrance found her thoughts going back to Trey and his guns for hire. *Trey must have found out about the offer Governor Beechwood made and assumed I would go for the highest bid instead of upholding the original contract.* But she realized that she still did not know who was pulling Trey's strings. She was confident he had a boss, but the question was who. *Could it be the vampires?* she wondered, knowing it would explain why Artur Hagi had attacked her. But Terrance wasn't entirely convinced that the situation fit what they knew of Nightshade Coven.

Terrance sighed and forced herself to focus. She realized she was now in front of her apartment door and that her plan had been to get a snack and go to sleep.

THIRTEEN

JOSH

Josh's eyes snapped open, and he found himself reaching for his gun on the nightstand. He took a deep breath, trying to settle himself. *I am in the apartment that Terrance offered us as a safe house. Nothing is wrong.* Then he heard the noise again. A light tapping on the door.

Josh glanced at the clock. It was midnight. He swung himself out of bed and checked his gun, making sure it was fully loaded, and flipped the safety off before padding quietly to the front door. After being followed at the Plaza, he was still on edge, and given the hour, he didn't think anything good was going to happen if someone was at his door. One of the things he missed about his apartment in Atlanta was that it was difficult to access unless you knew exactly where you were going. The levels that had residential apartments were not labeled with the names of the residents, only by number. Without an invitation or hacking into the building's computer to acquire the list of residents, no one knew who lived where, which meant there were no unwanted visitors. He suppressed a chuckle. *That's not entirely true.* Some of his visitors—like Catrina Fox—were unwanted, but at least he knew who knew where he lived.

118

Here, just like at Elyse's ranch, anyone could show up. No security was in place to prevent solicitations. The light tapping came again, jarring him out of his thoughts.

Josh braced his foot against the door and opened it slightly.

"Who's there?" he demanded quietly. He didn't want to alarm Elyse.

"It's Cory," came the reply. Josh opened the door wider, and sure enough, the large tiger shifter was standing there.

Josh ran a hand over his face and let his hand with the gun relax a bit. "What can I do for you, Cory?"

Josh could've sworn Cory looked embarrassed as he replied, "I was wondering if you wanted to go practice kickboxing or something and then come with me to talk to the leader of Nightshade Coven."

Josh scratched his chin and then glanced back over his shoulder; even though he hadn't heard anything, old habits died hard. "It's late. This can't wait until tomorrow?"

Cory shrugged. "The vampires around here prefer to not be awake during the day. Elyse will be safe if that's what you're worried about. Pierre and Sienna, two wolf shifters, came with me and will guard the building."

Josh took a deep breath and let it out. Cory had answered all his unspoken questions, and the offer to spar was very appealing, even if agreeing to go with Cory meant he'd likely get no sleep tonight. Perhaps Cory would shed more light on what was going on in Boise, since he was pretty sure it was not *nothing*, as Terrance kept saying.

"Okay, I'll do it. Let me get dressed and throw some things in a bag so I can change later. Just give me a few minutes," Josh said. When Cory nodded, Josh shut the door and set his gun on the table, safety on.

He quickly stuffed a pair of clean jeans, boxers, and a T-shirt into a bag as well as several extra clips of ammo, followed by a water bottle and tape to wrap his hands. Bag packed, he slid on a pair of green athletic shorts and a light-gray shirt.

He wrote a quick note and left it on the dining room table. They'd likely be back before Elyse even woke up. But he knew that if there wasn't a note and she woke up, she would panic, thinking the worst had happened. Not something he wanted to put her through for no reason.

Josh slid his gun into the back of his waistband and opened the door. Cory was leaning against the opposite wall and stood up straight when Josh came through the door. "I've got everything."

"Good," Cory said and led them down the stairs and through the back door into an alley.

"Where are we going? There was a gym in the Plaza," Josh asked.

Cory shook his head. "We have a gym at headquarters. It's safer to go there than to the Plaza."

Josh raised his eyebrow. "Terrance said the Plaza is safe."

Cory chuckled. "It is, usually. But when you're co-leader of the Boise division of HAC, people notice when you're out and about."

"Ah," Josh said in understanding. He'd never been in a position where anyone paid much attention to him. Or not that he was aware of, anyhow. He had been one of many FBI agents based out of the downtown Atlanta office under the hand of Assistant Director Fernway. Because of his continuous success in recruiting magically talented people to the FBI, every time he had put a request for a promotion, it had been denied. His boss had been content with Josh right where he was. Josh had never cared enough about moving up the ladder to put pressure on his boss, not that he was sure that would have helped his odds of being promoted.

He did find it interesting that Cory operated with enough of a high profile in Boise that people were aware of his movements when he was in public places. Like many things here, it was much different than in Atlanta. The FBI had had trackers in all of its agents' cars, but beyond that they did not routinely monitor everyone's movements within downtown Atlanta. There were just too many people, even with the insanely high decrease in the population across the country due to COVID-50. Atlanta and the three rural counties around it were home to over one million people. Whereas Boise and its surrounding valley had less than two hundred thousand.

Cory hadn't been kidding when he said that they had a gym at headquarters. Josh swept his eyes over the large gym, which had a surprising amount of equipment in addition to a well-marked fight ring in the middle. The sheer size of the space made Josh wonder how many members answered to Terrance and Cory. He knew she was one of the HAC lieutenants, but he had always been under the impression that there were more than just her and Catrina Fox. Maybe he had been wrong, or perhaps Cory just liked having a large space to work out in with a variety of equipment to suit many tastes and training levels. It was getting close to one a.m. and the gym was empty. Josh didn't mind. He usually just tuned the background noise and activities out anyhow.

Josh dropped his bag on a bench at the side of the ring, and they both went through their warmup routines in silence.

"You warmed up enough?" Cory asked, then took a swig of water.

"Yep, ready when you are," Josh said and walked over to the center of the ring.

"I want a real match," Cory said firmly.

Josh grinned. "Given that you came knocking at midnight, I assumed it wasn't just for a light match."

"Good. Just making sure we're on the same page," Cory said. "Now. The main reason I wanted to use our gym is this." Cory raised a little black thing that Josh hadn't noticed he'd been holding. Cory pushed a button and a dome of magic fell into place over the ring. When it settled it was almost invisible, just a slight blur. Josh gazed at it, not sure what to think, when words appeared to his right: "Josh" in blue and "Cory" in green.

"It keeps score," Cory said offhandedly.

"Is that necessary?" Josh asked. He'd never had anyone want to keep score when they were sparring for fun. Only in the real fights where he got paid.

Cory shrugged. "I like keeping score. It also will give a warning if one of us is having severe health problems. There are sensors embedded in the mat that allow it to track our heart rate, temperature, and so on. It's a mix of magic and technology. I find that it helps me not go overboard in a fight."

"That sounds like something Terrance would say," Josh replied.

Cory smirked. "You're right. That is what she said when she installed it and told me if I wanted to keep practicing, I would have to use it."

"I'm sure you could find other places to practice that she wouldn't know about," Josh replied.

Cory rolled his eyes. "I guess you're not familiar with the saying 'happy wife, happy life'?"

Josh laughed. "No."

"Well, you might want to get familiar with it if you're serious about Elyse," Cory informed him.

"I will keep that in mind. Now, are we going to spar or just stand around chatting all night?" Josh inquired.

"Right. Phyllis, start the count down," Cory ordered.

Josh was confused for a moment until he realized the technology or whatever must answer to Phyllis. *Odd.*

The dome flashed as it counted down: three, two, one.

Cory didn't waste any time. He leaped forward with a left jab followed by a straight right hand. Josh blocked easily and followed with a right jab, left hook, and straight right. As the fight progressed it was clear to Josh that he was evenly matched against Cory.

Deciding to end the match, Josh quickly shifted into a left jab, then lifted up his left knee as though he was going to kick. Unfortunately, Cory must have been familiar with this combination. Before Josh could use his superman jab, Cory had a hold of his knee with both of his hands. He twisted, slamming Josh into the mat hard.

The air blasted out of Josh's lungs, leaving him coughing, unable to breathe. As Josh was sitting on the mat, he peered up at the dome and saw that it had been flashing "not breathing" before moving to the word "recovering." *Interesting.*

"You ready to keep going?" Cory asked in a slightly amused tone.

Josh could feel the sweat trickling down his back as he regrouped and tried to figure out what his next move should be. He still hadn't decided what he was going to do when Cory attacked from the left, crouching low and aiming for Josh's stomach and thighs. Josh made a decision and turned his right hip toward Cory, then went into a crescent kick, which grazed his abdomen, and followed it with a spinning right crescent kick that sent Cory backward onto the mat.

Josh glanced at the dome, looking for Cory's vital information, but when he looked back at the mat, Cory was gone. Thickly muscled arms wrapped around Josh's torso as Cory grabbed him from behind. Josh thrust his left elbow back hard. It connected with Cory's abs and felt like hitting a rock wall. The arms around him stayed where they were.

Mumbling some nonsense words, Josh stomped down with his heel on Cory's instep. Cory snarled in pain and let go. Josh danced out of the way and threw a left low hook, aiming at Cory's kneecap. His fist slid over the knee, but he recovered and followed up with a right roundhouse kick. If he had been a moment later their legs would have collided, as Josh could see Cory's weight starting to shift for a kick of his own.

Josh took a couple of steps to the right. Cory took that as an invitation to strike and leaped toward Josh, fists and feet flying. Josh was able to block, but he could not find an opening to get a strike of his own in. He also knew the relentless onslaught couldn't last forever. Finally, an opening presented itself. Josh watched as

Cory rocked back on his left heel and started to lift his right leg. Josh stepped forward, closing the gap between them. Right jab, left jab, right jab, then a left superman straight into Cory's unprotected jaw.

As Cory fell, Josh saw the dome flash a warning that Cory was unconscious.

I don't think I hit him that *hard.* Regardless, Josh stepped away from Cory to give him a chance to wake up. Cory's eyes didn't stay shut for long.

"I see what you mean by Phyllis being helpful," Josh said conversationally.

Cory stood up, lightly touching his jaw. Josh thought he could see the hint of a bruise forming. "It's been a while since someone's gotten me that good. We should do a rematch sometime. But we need to go before we run out of darkness if we want Willow to agree to talk to us."

As though Cory had spoken to Phyllis, the magic dome disappeared completely. Josh walked over to his bag and water. He took a long swig.

"The locker room is over here," Cory said and motioned for Josh to follow him.

Josh and Cory walked at a brisk pace down the street. It was tempting to walk in silence, but after being in the gym, Josh had questions.

"Why is your gym so big?"

Cory chuckled. "We do have a lot of people who report to us, but it is rare that more than a handful of us are in there at one time. Primarily, it is because I wanted to have enough equipment that four or five people could be doing the same type of workout but never interfere with one another. But if you thought that was big, then perhaps I owe you a tour of headquarters. Maybe tomorrow you and Elyse can swing by, and I'll show you both around.

We actually have an Olympic-sized pool as well as a full-sized basketball court."

"Really?" Josh said, surprised.

Cory nodded. "Yes. When Terrance and I built this place, we really wanted to make sure it felt like somewhere we could come together as a community. I'm sure you're aware many of our members are shifters. We do a lot of outdoor activities too, but it's nice to have some indoor options and the ability to include non-shifter members."

"What else do you have at headquarters?" Josh asked.

"I'll save the rest for the tour," Cory said.

Josh wasn't sure what else to say, so they slid into a comfortable silence. When they had walked for about ten minutes, Josh debated asking how much farther it would be. *Not like I have anywhere else to be ... other than sleeping,* Josh reminded himself. Instead, he tried to focus on his surroundings, or as much of them as he could see in the moonlight. The street they were on was narrow and lined with large pine trees. Behind the trees were tall wooden walls which, with more trees on the other side, made it difficult for Josh to tell what was beyond the street. *This would be a great place to ambush someone.* Josh bit the inside of his lip. Cory was not going to lead him into an ambush, or at least not intentionally. He also knew the tiger shifter had far superior hearing than he did and likely would know much earlier if they were in imminent danger. His gun was tucked in the back of his waistband. Since he wasn't familiar with the area and Cory wasn't holding a gun, Josh didn't want to cause any trouble by holding his.

"We're almost there," Cory announced, slowing his pace.

At the end of the street, the wooden fence and pine trees abruptly stopped, making way for a large wrought-iron gate attached to a stone wall. The wall itself had lights on top of it. Josh assumed they were for both decorative and security purposes. Beyond was a massive Mediterranean-style house that felt out of place in Boise. It most certainly would have been out of place in Atlanta, where anything that wasn't a high-rise tended to be colonial style. The stone wall was red brick, which was common in Boise, but didn't match the style of the house.

The closer they got to the house, the heavier the air felt. *Magic,* Josh thought. Cory walked right up to the gates, either not able to sense the magic in the air or not concerned enough to change their plan, with Josh about a stride behind. The gates swung open as though the inhabitants were waiting for them.

Cory strode forward, pretending to be completely comfortable here. *Maybe he is,* Josh mused. *It's not like I asked him how well he knows the vampires of Nightshade Coven.* One thing he did find intriguing was that Catrina, a vampire, was an HAC lieutenant based out of a city that as far as he knew had a minimal number of vampires or shifters. Yet Terrance was an HAC lieutenant and a shifter based in a city that seemed to have a significant population of shifters and vampires. He knew in some cities the vampires and shifters did not get along, though that did not appear to be the case here in Boise or between Catrina and Terrance. Unless they got along on the surface and things were not as they seemed underneath.

Josh peered around as he followed Cory up the long cobblestone driveway that meandered around until ending in a large circle in front of the house. Josh knew the estate must look much different in daylight, but it felt rather stark bathed in moonlight.

Cory walked right up the three steps and lifted the large brass knocker. He knocked three times before stepping back, hands behind his back, to wait. Josh, his back to Cory, kept an eye out for anyone who might try to approach from behind. It would be a good trap: guests go to the front door, and while they're occupied, take them out from behind. Given it was a tactic that he had used several times in the FBI, he knew how useful it could be.

Josh heard the door open, and Cory exchanged a few words with someone, likely a vampire.

"Come on. Willow will see us," Cory said from the doorway. Josh reluctantly turned and followed Cory inside. He couldn't help flinching when the door shut firmly behind him. The entryway was reminiscent of an Italian villa, with reddish-brown floor tiles, a double staircase with decorative wrought-iron rails, and a large blown-glass chandelier. Some art was on the walls, but their escort did not give Josh enough time to examine it.

They were led deeper into the house, past the kitchen, though Josh couldn't figure out why vampires would need a chef's kitchen when they didn't eat normal food. The house kept going; Josh expected to turn one direction or another, but they proceeded straight back. Finally, they halted at what seemed to be a room set up for entertaining. There was a grand piano with sofas scattered around. If Josh's estimate was correct, thirty or so people could fit in the room without any trouble.

"You can sit if you like," their escort said in a heavy Italian accent.

Josh stepped to the side and finally got a good look at the man. He was average height and build. His skin had a pallid tone but looked like it might be medium-brown. He had wavy dark-brown hair and dark-red eyes.

Vampire. That would explain why he seems pale.

"What is your name?" Josh asked.

Cory threw him a sharp look, as though he wasn't supposed to talk. They hadn't discussed what Josh was supposed to do, so he didn't feel bad about annoying Cory.

The vampire's posture stiffened, but he replied, "Tiberio Sellitti."

"Are you from Italy?" Josh asked.

"My parents were born in Italy. I have never been though," Tiberio replied.

Josh opened his mouth to ask another question, but Cory caught his eye and silenced him. *I wonder why he doesn't want me asking questions.*

"Willow will be here shortly. Make yourselves comfortable," Tiberio announced, and then he walked away.

"Now what?" Josh asked.

"You can sit if you want," Cory said.

"Are you going to sit?" Josh asked.

Cory curled his lip, showing a canine tooth that was longer than it should have been— the only indication Josh had that Cory was not as calm and collected as he had thought. *Standing it is.*

Cory's demeanor led Josh to believe that he might be right in assuming that beneath the surface of the genial relationship Cory's HAC group had with Nightshade Coven, there was tension and distrust. Not that Josh was surprised. Vampires were terrifying, even when they were playing nice.

Bullets made out of holy water, Josh thought—the only thing aside from beheading he had found over the years that was guaranteed to kill a vampire. Everything else tended to have mixed results. A wooden stake through the heart was effective about fifty percent of the time. If it was tipped in holy water, then it was one hundred percent effective. Josh attributed that to the holy water, not to the stake, though. Cutting the head off was an ideal way of killing most humans and animals. Without a head, it was game over. However, beheading was not as simple as some thought, which was why it was not Josh's first line of defense. Typically, he would use his gun, hoping to injure an opponent, and then if beheading was required, use that as a last resort.

Josh took a deep breath and let it out slowly. By the time he had taken a second one, the air in front of them had darkened with swirls of blackish-gray smoke. A form materialized and then solidified.

This must be Willow Kelly, Josh thought as he looked at the vampire who led Nightshade Coven. Willow wore a white blouse with billowing sleeves, a wide black belt, and a tight black skirt. Her long blond hair fell in sheets down to her waist. Her eyes were crystal blue rimmed in dark red. Wisps of the black smoke curled around her, though the majority of it had disappeared.

"Willow," Cory said with a formal bow. Josh hastily bowed too.

"Cory," Willow said with an incline of her head, then turned her attention to Josh. "Josh Everly."

Josh kept his face blank. He was not surprised she knew who he was.

"Now, let's sit and discuss what it is that you came here to ask me," Willow said, sweeping her arms wide to indicate the couch.

A large wingback chair in black fabric appeared, and she sat in it. When Willow sat, Cory moved around to the front of the couch and took a seat perching on the edge. Josh sat a little bit farther back on his couch cushion, trying to seem more relaxed.

"I want to know why your man Artur Hagi was involved in an attack on Terrance," Cory said firmly.

Willow tapped her lip with long, manicured nails. "It was not sanctioned by me."

"But you did know about it," Cory pressed.

Willow's eyes narrowed. "I found out after the attack that it had happened, yes."

"So, you are officially denying your involvement?" Cory replied.

"Yes. He was not under orders to attack Terrance. Do you think I would do something that stupid and provoke your wrath? Our alliance has been critical for both of us," Willow said.

Josh noticed that Cory flinched when she said alliance, as though that was her interpretation of the coven's relationship with this division of HAC but not his. Anticipating the next question, Josh focused on Willow.

"What about the Snowflake?" Cory asked. Josh caught the very subtle twitch of Willow's eye followed by her hand dropping into her lap.

"The Snowflake?" Willow asked, laughing, "You mean the ridiculous computer chip thing that is supposed to allow whoever has it to operate any of the power generation facilities held by the government?"

Cory nodded. "Yes, that Snowflake."

"I've heard of it, of course, but I always thought it was nonsense. Who would have been foolish enough to create something like that?" Willow replied.

As Josh observed Willow, he noticed how every response was quick, like she had already planned what she was going to say ahead of time.

"Clearly Artur believes the Snowflake is legitimate because he attacked Terrance to get his hands on it. Artur was accompanied by Gustabo Borra, who has done work for Nightshade Coven. It seems like quite a coincidence for them to be working together without your knowledge," Cory explained patiently.

Willow's eyes flashed completely red. "Are you accusing me of hiring a hit on Terrance?"

"Did you?" Cory asked, flexing his fingers.

Willow hissed and bared her teeth at him. "I already told you I did not order Artur to attack Terrance."

Josh made sure to keep his expression serious. He had expected Willow to deny any involvement. Since he didn't know Cory well, he had not been able to guess how the shifter would handle the encounter, Josh only hoped he would tread carefully and that they wouldn't have to fight their way out of a building full of vampires.

"You said earlier we have an alliance. I did not think that allies were supposed to allow the leaders of their ally's organization to be attacked by one of their members. In fact, you should have felt obligated to stop it before it happened. I don't believe the bullshit you're spewing about not knowing. You know every move of every vampire in your coven. I will ask one more time, what is your interest in the Snowflake?" Cory demanded.

Willow stood up, the black swirling around her more as her temper rose. "How dare you come into my house and accuse me of lying. I am sorry that Terrance was attacked, but I do not like what you are implying. We are done. Leave immediately. I will not guarantee your safety if you choose to linger." The black swirls flared up, encasing her completely, and then she disappeared.

Josh stood up and pulled his gun out of his waistband. Cory glanced at his hand before settling his gaze on his face. "You shouldn't need that. But we need to go."

Cory led the way out of the house. Josh followed right on his heels. They did not encounter anyone else. Cory kept walking, almost breaking into a jog once they were past the front gates. It wasn't until they were off the tight pine-lined street and in more open space that Cory checked his speed.

"Is your alliance or whatever you had over?" Josh asked.

Cory nodded. "Probably. I don't think she was being completely honest with us about the Snowflake. But vampires can be very touchy to deal with. I guess today Willow was angry that I was implying she had organized the attack on Terrance."

"Was your alliance that important?" Josh inquired.

Cory shrugged. "It wasn't really an alliance. Mostly it was an agreement that we'd stay out of their business, and they would stay out of ours. Given she knew but didn't directly order Artur's attack, I would say it's safe to assume the agreement has come to an end anyhow."

"I was surprised she thought we would believe her spiel about the Snowflake being nonsense," Josh admitted.

Cory shrugged. "I'm not. There have been times where I felt like Willow really feels as though vampires are far superior and that anyone else is just not capable of her level of intelligence. What concerns me, though, is her plan for the Snowflake. Historically, Nightshade Coven has stayed mostly low profile."

"Maybe her motives are the same as whoever is buying it from you," Josh said. "I still can't believe that you found it and are selling it."

Cory ducked into the shadows of a tree. They were close to the headquarters. "What would you do with it?"

"Destroy it," Josh said resolutely.

"Don't you think that someone other than the United States government should have control over the source of electricity for the whole country?" Cory demanded.

"I may not agree with the government policies all the time, but I am worried about the people and businesses who still rely on the electricity these wind and solar farms generate," Josh replied.

"Maybe it's time everyone took a page out of the farmers' books and live without it entirely," Cory suggested.

Josh gave Cory an incredulous stare. "Yet you rely quite heavily on that electricity for your organization. Do you think you could handle your operations without it?"

"We run drills to prepare for losing our connection to power. We have a couple of magically talented individuals who have been able to essentially mimic electricity with their talent and can either run devices directly or channel into a battery or generator that will then power things," Cory explained, surprising Josh. Though he supposed if they knew of the Snowflake's existence, it would make sense to prepare for the possibility that it would get into the hands of someone who wanted to control the electricity in the country and potentially prevent people from accessing it.

"What is the plan now, since Willow wasn't much help?" Josh asked.

"Go forward with the contract to turn over the Snowflake and just be prepared for another attack. Backing out would probably be just as detrimental as following through," Cory said.

The sky was starting to lighten. Josh wasn't sure what time it was, but maybe he could get an hour or two of sleep before Elyse woke up and wanted to do something. "Do you need me for anything else?"

Cory shook his head. "No, that should be it for now. I'll keep you posted if there are additional developments."

Josh was surprised when Cory stopped walking again. He stifled a yawn and looked around. They were in front of the apartment building where he and Elyse were staying. *I must be tired if I didn't recognize where we were.*

"Thanks for including me," Josh said softly. He gave Cory's arm a squeeze and hurried inside.

FOURTEEN
TERRANCE

Terrance was sitting at the desk in the living room of her apartment, riffling through a stack of papers. She had slept for a few hours after Cory had left but had been restless, getting just enough of his emotions through the mating bond to let her know he was physically okay.

The alliance she had made with Willow was a fragile thing, and she would be surprised if Cory came back and told her it was still intact. Most of the time the alliance meant that if they had a similar target, whoever got there first would get to keep the target, with the other organization backing off. Nightshade Coven had been linked primarily to human trafficking and drug manufacturing and distribution, whereas Terrance's division of HAC focused on weapons, magical objects, and information. Of course, Agent Florence and the local FBI wanted to stop the activities of HAC and Nightshade Coven. With Terrance's working relationship with Agent Florence, she had found herself enlisted to help solve some of the larger human trafficking cases.

Her thoughts went to one operation two years ago.

The weight of the gun comforted Terrance as she hid behind the corner of the building. Agent Florence was going to flush out Willow, and Terrance was going to incapacitate her if she came this way. Because of Terrance's "alliance" with the vampires, she was dressed in FBI gear with a mask and hood on obscuring her features. Several of the other FBI agents were wearing masks and hoods to make it look as though that was their tactic for the operation, not just a way of hiding one identity.

Terrance could hear the sound of running feet long before anyone reached her. Willow, long blond hair flowing behind her, ran around the corner. Terrance leapt, tackling Willow and shoving her hard into the sidewalk. Terrance had ahold of one of Willow's arms, but the vampire rolled onto her back, forcing Terrance to loosen her grip. Long nails dug into Terrance's neck as Willow wrapped her hands around her throat. A growl escaped Terrance's lips before she could stop it. The vampire's eyes widened as though she might have recognized Terrance. Out of the corner of her eye, Terrance saw a flash of purple magic. It hit Willow in the head, and her hands went limp. Terrance flopped onto her back on the sidewalk, breathing heavily.

Agent Florence was towering over Terrance and reached a hand down. Terrance gripped it and pulled herself up. "Thanks."

Agent Florence shrugged. "If you hadn't been there, we wouldn't have caught her. The other vampires just gave themselves up, and we have a team going to retrieve the ten people that Willow was preparing to ship to California."

Terrance blinked. Their timing had been quite close. If they had apprehended the vampires even a few hours later, they would not have been able to prevent the captives from being sent to California. She shuddered. She hadn't been there herself, but she knew that a good portion of the state was controlled by one or two very large vampire covens. With the huge Sierra Nevada mountain range as a physical barrier and no easy way to travel there from Idaho, Terrance had never had a reason to find out more about California, especially given the animosity that most vampires and shifters had for each other.

Terrance looked up. The doorknob was turning. She ran a hand over her face and shuffled the papers on her desk. The door opened, and Cory stepped through, shutting it firmly behind him. Terrance stood up. Her nightshirt slid to the side, revealing her shoulder. The bottom edge skimmed the tops of her bare thighs. She walked toward him. His whole body was tense. "How did it go?"

Cory growled. Terrance wrapped her arms around his waist and laid her head on his chest. The growl was still rumbling through his body. He set his hands around her waist and picked her up. She wrapped her legs around his hips and kissed him, and he bit her lip hard, drawing blood. She pulled back and licked her bleeding lip, meeting his golden eyes with her own.

"I made you a promise earlier," he said and captured her lips with his. With her legs wrapped around his hips, she could feel his cock hardening against her. She ran her hands down his back in encouragement. Without breaking their kiss, he reached between them and unbuckled his pants, letting them slide down. He took one step and was free of them. Two more steps and her bare bottom slid against the dining room table. She smiled against his lips and laid back onto the table. With one quick thrust, he was inside her.

Terrance moaned in pleasure as Cory sped up, quickly driving her toward the edge. Since her attack, he had been reluctant to have sex for fear of hurting her. So, she was pleased that he felt comfortable enough with her recovery to be aggressive in their coupling. One more thrust and pleasure exploded throughout her entire body. She felt Cory shudder as he got his release a moment after hers.

Terrance kissed him lightly, relishing the feel of their joined bodies. She wasn't sure how long they were there, draped across the table, before Cory took a step back and gave her room to reluctantly sit up.

"Let's get in bed," she suggested and took his hand.

Cory gave her hand a gentle squeeze and followed her into the bedroom. They both climbed into bed and lay facing each other. As Terrance gazed into his eyes, she wondered how she'd ever gotten this lucky, to not only find a man to love but to have the mating bond as well. She couldn't imagine life without Cory at her side and wasn't sure how she had managed for so many years without him.

Cory closed his eyes for a moment and then opened them. "Willow denied any involvement, even when I pushed."

"Isn't that what you expected?" Terrance replied.

"Yes. I was just hoping that she would admit to something, so we would have concrete answers. The only thing I accomplished was making her angry. We need to make sure we don't drop our guard," Cory said.

"I will make sure everyone is aware that we have a higher-than-normal threat level with both Nightshade Coven and Trey wanting a piece of us," Terrance replied.

She leaned over and kissed him, letting her hand blaze a path from his shoulder down his muscled chest and abdomen.

FIFTEEN
ELYSE

Elyse woke up and glanced over at the large bed where Josh was sprawled, looking like he was in a very deep sleep. Usually, they had the same sleep schedule, so she was surprised to see him that out. Shaking her head, she thought, *It's not like we have anywhere to be.* Elyse slid her feet into a pair of pink fuzzy slippers and a matching pink robe and padded into the kitchen. As she walked past the dining table, she saw the note and picked it up.

> ELYSE,
>
> CORY ASKED ME TO GO WITH HIM TO THE GYM AND TO A MEETING. I SHOULD BE BACK BEFORE YOU'RE AWAKE.
>
> YOURS,
> JOSH

Elyse set the note down, wondering when he had left. She turned her attention to making a fresh pot of coffee. Humming to herself as the coffee brewed, she inhaled, relishing the scent.

Steaming mug in hand, Elyse snagged a journal out of the box and headed for the couch. She thought maybe the journals would give her a better idea of how to direct her talent when searching for answers about Archibald Cornelius.

Taking a long sip of coffee, then setting the cup down and snuggling into her robe, Elyse found a comfortable position and opened the journal. It was dated 2055.

September 1, 2055

We are still trying to develop new vaccines for COVID-50. The virus continues to mutate at alarming rates, and every time we think we have something that works, it changes. Almost as though the virus is learning. I sound completely insane even writing that as a possibility. A virus is not intelligent, or at least it doesn't have human intelligence.

We are short-staffed, and there is still a severe shortage of supplies. The continued rate at which people are contracting COVID-50 and dying is far worse than anyone had expected. COVID-19 might have set a precedent, but no one was prepared for what we are facing now. I have heard rumors that the virus is unnatural, but I am not sure what the implications of that are. Whether the virus was created in a lab or found in the environment, it is a product of nature. There is no other explanation for what it could be. The science explaining the existence and biology of viruses is straightforward.

Mom, thank God, is still taking care of Albert and Brianna. I am not sure what I would do

if she decided she no longer wanted to raise
her grandkids. I miss them, I do, but sometimes I just can't bear to look at Brianna.
Renee would never have gotten sick if I hadn't
been working in the lab and coming home. If
I had just stayed away, they would have both
been safe.

September 15, 2055

I had lunch with Dr. Carver, and he brought
up the rumors about COVID-50 being unnatural.
He said that not only had he heard it referred
to as unnatural, but he had also even heard
some whispers of magic. How crazy is that?
Magic doesn't exist.

Elyse blinked rapidly. She had not been expecting the mention
of magical talents in a journal dated from 2055. She reached for
her coffee cup and took a sip, savoring the slightly bitter flavor
before returning to the journal.

February 1, 2056

Today at the lab, we received an updated
report on the number of deaths proven to have
been caused by COVID-50. The count is up to a
hundred million people across the country. Almost
one-third of the population is gone. The disease
is fast and brutal, which is why we have been
pushing so hard to develop a vaccine.
Dr. Tierney wants me to go to Boise, Idaho,
to a meeting at one of their smaller offices.
The lab there is closer than we are to making

> a vaccine and seems to have discovered a way
> of slowing the virus long enough for the vac-
> cine to work. Or at least that is what I have
> been told. We will see.
> There has been rioting in downtown Atlanta,
> and some are starting to suspect that
> Evermore Genetics is tied to the development
> of COVID-50. Perhaps the trip to Boise will get
> me out of the line of fire.

Elyse almost dropped the journal. *Archibald came here to a lab owned by Evermore Genetics?* She went to turn the page when everything around her got blurry and then faded out.

Elyse found herself inside of a small private jet that was taxiing at an airport. Archibald Cornelius was sitting in the chair facing her, looking worn out. His brown hair was shot with strands of gray, and his square-rimmed glasses were slightly crooked on his face. His left hand curled around the handle of a dark brown briefcase. Elyse peered around the airplane and was surprised to see that no one else was there. The plane had four plush seats with a table in between each pair. There was a door to the rear marked Bathroom and then the door at the front, which she assumed went to the cockpit and the exit.

They sent him by himself. Was that because they couldn't spare anyone else or because the boss wasn't overly invested in the outcome of this trip? *Elyse wondered.*

The plane finally stopped moving and the front door opened.

A pilot became visible. "Dr. Cornelius, you're here. We'll see you in two days."

Elyse's great-grandfather nodded and mumbled something she didn't quite catch before making his way out of the plane. A dark sedan waited for him on the tarmac, hovering silently. It looked very similar to the car Elyse had had back in Jackson County, with a dome-shaped piece of metal on the bottom half, windows all the way around the top, and a black roof that was also a solar panel. The escort stepped out of the car and took Archibald's suitcase, depositing it in the trunk before going around to the front door and opening it for him. She was surprised the woman wanted him in the front seat. Elyse went through the back car door as though it weren't there and sat down.

The screen in the car flashed "return to lab." The woman tapped the screen and the car began to move. She turned to face Archibald.

"Dr. Cornelius, it is good to finally meet you," she said and offered her hand for him to shake, which he did. "I am Dr. Cecilia Basak. As I mentioned on the phone, I have found a way to slow COVID-50's mutation down, and it has enabled me to develop a vaccine that works even on the newest version of the virus that's running rampant in Boise. I have successfully cured over one thousand mice. The trial on the monkeys has just been given the green light. If it is successful, I should be able to start human trials within two months."

Archibald did nothing to hide his surprise. "What exactly did you do to slow the rate of mutation?"

"I used blood," Dr. Basak said softly.

Archibald's jaw opened in shock. "What do you mean you 'used blood'?"

Dr. Basak continued as though she was used to reactions like his. "You had made a note in one of your reports that you felt that the virus seemed like it could be intelligent. Which got me thinking, that perhaps we needed to take a different approach. Maybe the nutrients that we typically put in the medium we grow viruses in are not sufficient, and it keeps mutating because it must continuously adapt to not having adequate food. Through trial and error, I explored a variety of potential food sources ranging from other viruses, bacteria, plants, and meat. When I got a positive response from raw beef, I decided to try cow blood, and that seemed to do the trick."

Archibald openly stared at Dr. Basak. "You're telling me that you feed the COVID-50 virus cow blood and that it then stops mutating and is responsive to a vaccine? That sounds …" He paused as though searching for the right word. "Far-fetched."

Dr. Basak shrugged. "Perhaps. But results are results. You of all people should know that sometimes organisms do very unexpected things. I am sure over your career you have seen all sorts of things and are more open than some to the possibility that what I have discovered is legitimate."

Archibald snapped his mouth shut, grinding his teeth. Elyse wasn't sure what to think or what he was going to say. The car was taking them, presumably, to Dr. Basak's lab.

Several minutes went by, and the tension in the car grew. Finally, Dr. Basak broke the silence. "C'mon. You have an undergraduate degree in bioengineering and an MD-PhD in biomedical engineering."

Archibald gave her a strange look. "What does my college education have to do with me believing you have been successful where I have failed?"

Dr. Basak looked taken aback. "Sometimes you just need to take a step back to be able to get a fresh look at things."

"Fine, I will try to stay open-minded. But I want to see all your results. If I am going to report to Dr. Tierney that this is the real deal, then I need to be able to get a thousand percent behind it," Archibald said.

Dr. Basak nodded. "Understood. Now, here we are."

Elyse had been watching their faces and hadn't realized they pulled up to a building. They appeared to be in downtown Boise. There were a few high-rise buildings, and she could see what was obviously the capitol building at the end of the street they were on. It always seemed like the capitol buildings of various states had similar architecture. The building Dr. Basak led them to didn't have any large fancy logos on it. In fact, it was one of the shortest buildings on the street, although from the exterior it appeared to boast at least six stories.

The small print on the door read Evermore Genetics, along with a handful of other businesses that had offices in this building. Dr. Basak and Archibald went for the elevator. Inside, a sign listed each level and what businesses would be found there. Evermore Genetics was the sole occupant of level five.

The doors opened, and they walked into a large reception area with a receptionist at the desk.

"Dr. Basak," the receptionist greeted.

Dr. Basak gave her a slight nod and kept walking down the corridor to the right. There were several offices and then a door at the end. She swiped her keycard and led them into a massive laboratory. A few machines were running and filled the room with a low hum. Elyse had been expecting a tech or someone to greet them, since there had been a receptionist, but no one appeared.

Archibald must have had similar expectations. "Where is your assistant?"

Dr. Basak frowned. "He died two weeks ago."

"I'm sorry," Archibald said.

"He was lucky, I suppose. It wasn't COVID-50 that got him, but a car accident," Dr. Basak explained.

Archibald shuddered. "Either way. It's unfortunate he is dead. Do you have any other help?"

Dr. Basak shook her head. "No, it is just me and Gladys—the receptionist. If I need a second set of hands, she will fill in. But for the most part I'm just a one-woman show."

"How do you manage that with your ... daughter?" Archibald asked uncertainly.

Dr. Basak smiled slightly. "Terrance, she's my niece. My sister-in-law's family helps a lot. They know how important the research I'm doing is and fill in as needed."

Archibald walked around the lab. Inspecting, Elyse supposed. She wasn't sure if he had been there before, although it seemed as though he knew enough about Dr. Basak to know there was a young child in her life.

Elyse started shaking. She looked around, wondering if there was an earthquake or something in the lab.

Josh was shaking her arm. Elyse opened her eyes and found herself wedged between the couch and the coffee table, journal gripped in her hand so hard that her knuckles were white.

"Are you okay?" Josh asked, worried.

Elyse offered him what she hoped was a reassuring smile, then stood up and stretched, trying to get the kink out of her back. "I was reading the journals, and I guess my magical talent took over." She gave him a light kiss on the cheek. "How did last night go?"

Josh ran a hand over his jaw, making a face. "It went okay. Before you lose the details, let me write down what you saw in the vision."

Elyse watched as he retrieved the notebook from the dining table and opened to a blank page, pen ready.

"Archibald went in a private plane to the Evermore Genetics lab in Boise. He was met by Dr. Basak." Elyse paused when Josh looked surprised, but he didn't say anything, so she kept going. "Dr. Basak claimed to have found a solution to their issue creating a vaccine. Her solution was feeding the COVID-50 virus cow

144

blood, which slowed the rate of mutation. You shook me out of the vision before I got to the part where she shared the detailed results of her studies on mice."

Josh stopped writing and shut the notebook. "Do you know what year it was?"

Elyse offered him the journal, which had a large 2055/2056 on it.

"I didn't realize that Terrance was that old. I always thought she was a second-generation shifter," Josh blurted out.

Elyse gasped. She hadn't quite made the connection between Dr. Basak and Terrance the tiger shifter. "You know Dr. Basak?"

Josh shrugged. "I know of her. Her research, along with Archibald's aid, led to the development of the first viable COVID-50 vaccine. But by the time it went into mass production, it was too late. At least for most of the population in the United States. It might have helped citizens in other countries. I am not sure."

"What do you mean too late?" Elyse asked.

"It took them over six years to develop a viable vaccine. I don't know how much you know about COVID-19, but with that pandemic, it took under a year for the first vaccines to be available. COVID-50 was way deadlier. After a six-year wait, the population suffered immensely," Josh explained.

Elyse sat down on the couch. She knew of course that millions had died from COVID-50. She just hadn't realized it was not only due to how severe of an illness it was but also how long it took for anyone to be able to effectively combat it. She ran the vision and notes from the journal back through her mind over and over, looking for anything she might have missed.

"Dariusz admitted to creating COVID-50 ..." Elyse started.

Josh gave her a surprised look. "I'm not sure when he mentioned that if he truly meant he created it or if he just changed it so that it had the ability to give people magical talents. Either way ... what are you thinking?"

"I just wonder if his plan was to demolish the country's population, shake things up by adding magic into the world, or if he had some other motive," Elyse said.

"Asking him might get us an answer, but I am not sure I am ready to face him again. Not when we barely escaped last time," Josh said, reaching his arms over his head in a stretch. "What would you like for breakfast?"

"Pancakes?" Elyse asked hopefully.

Josh gave her a wry smile. "If the ingredients are here, I would love to make you pancakes." He sauntered into the kitchen and made a big show of searching the cupboards.

Elyse gave him a smug smile when he had collected all the necessary ingredients and put them on the kitchen counter. "While you do that, I'm going to read more journal entries."

"Sounds good," Josh replied over his shoulder.

Elyse settled herself back on the couch and flipped through the journal pages until she reached the entry after the last one she had read.

February 10, 2056

I get the feeling that there is something Dr. Basak is not telling me about her research, but I am not sure what. The reports I have seen all confirm what she told me. The vaccine she has developed works. I was even able to watch her inject mice with the disease yesterday. This morning they were showing symptoms, and then she administered the vaccine, and by the time we were ready to leave for the day—eight hours later—the mice were already showing signs of recovering.

I am less worried about convincing Dr. Tierney we need to move forward with the vaccine

than the implications of distributing it when
we get to that point. The country is an utter
mess. With such a high mortality rate and
everyone terrified of getting sick and dying,
there has been a lot of chaos in the past few
years. Some of the larger cities like Atlanta
and Boise are faring better since the government already had a strong presence, but other
more rural areas are not as fortunate. Don't
even get me started about the state of supply
chains.

February 11, 2056

Of the hundred mice we vaccinated yesterday,
eighty percent seem to be fully recovered, fifteen percent are still improving, but not cured,
four have relapsed, and one has died. Those
statistics match the previous tests that Dr.
Basak has conducted.
Finally!
When I get back to Atlanta, I have a meeting
tonight with Dr. Tierney, and then I get to
go to Mom's for a long weekend. It will be
nice to have a chance to just relax and forget about the lab for a while. If the weather
cooperates, maybe we can all go trail riding.
Mom warned me when she agreed to take
Albert and Brianna that she was going to
do everything in her power to make sure her
grandchildren were hooked on horses. She seems
to be successful so far.
The plane is about to land. More later.

March 1, 2056

I should have petitioned to have a few more days at the ranch when I returned to Atlanta. Things have been insane at the lab since we now have a viable vaccine in our crosshairs. Dr. Basak is not able to conduct large-scale trials on monkeys in Boise due to space limitations.

Lucky for us, Evermore Genetics bought the entire Atlanta Zoo when COVID-50 hit and the zoo lost its funding to take care of the animals, so we have animals and a holding facility that is not too far away to conduct the trials on. I am sure if the public knew what stuff happened behind the walls of the zoo there would be outrage, but they would have to know first.

Honestly, I try to stay as far away from there as possible. For the most part, trials done on the larger animals are out of my jurisdiction. Occasionally, they will send samples over for me to run tests on, which suits me just fine.

I might be making another trip to Boise, though I am unsure why.

Elyse snapped the journal shut, fuming. "Did you know Evermore Genetics bought the Atlanta Zoo so they could conduct testing on the animals?"

Josh turned around, spatula in hand. "No, but they have done some shady things. It's a lab. They have to get animals to conduct trials on from somewhere."

"Doesn't that make you angry?" Elyse said, an edge in her voice.

"Of course, but I wasn't around when it happened, and I am just a single former FBI agent. What is one person against a corporation as large as Evermore Genetics?" Josh replied, turning back to the griddle with the pancakes.

Elyse dropped the journal on the couch and walked over to him, wrapping her hands around his waist from behind. "Why did people let it happen back then?"

Josh patted her arm and went back to flipping the last two pancakes. "I imagine they were too worried about dying from COVID-50 or their belongings getting stolen to care a whole lot about a corporation that didn't directly affect them."

Elyse unwrapped her arms from around Josh and grabbed plates from the cupboard and silverware from the drawer. She set the table and then poured two mugs of coffee while Josh finished with the pancakes. Coffee at the table, Elyse settled into her chair to wait. A minute later, Josh walked over with a plateful of pancakes.

"What did you put in them?" Elyse asked, noting the pink tinge and odd lumps.

"Raspberries. I know they're one of your favorites, and I figured it would add some good flavor to the pancakes," Josh said, setting the plate in the middle of the table and then sitting down in his chair.

Elyse made a pile of three pancakes on her plate and liberally doused them in syrup before digging in. They were delicious. Josh's decision to add the raspberries had been a good one, adding just a hint of tartness, which she balanced out with the syrup.

The two of them sat in silence, eating and drinking their coffee. Elyse hadn't realized how hungry she was. She glanced at the clock and was surprised to see it was eleven a.m. *No wonder I'm hungry! It's almost lunchtime.* Since she hadn't been keeping track of the time after she woke up, Elyse wasn't sure if she had spent that much time reading or what.

Hunger satisfied, Elyse took a sip of her coffee just as Josh set his fork down. They had polished off the whole stack of pancakes.

"Good thing I estimated high. I made a little more than usual, and they're all gone. But … it is eleven. I suppose this is more brunch than breakfast," Josh said.

"Are you going to tell me what happened last night?" Elyse asked.

"Nothing terribly important. Cory just wanted company," Josh replied offhandedly.

Elyse peered at Josh, not sure she believed him. "Then you should have no problem telling me what you did."

Josh sighed. "If you really want to know, we went to the gym at the HAC headquarters and did some kickboxing. After that, we paid a visit to Willow Kelly, the leader of Nightshade Coven, and she denied being involved in an attack on Terrance, then told us to leave."

"Terrance was attacked?" Elyse replied with a gasp. "By whom?"

"A vampire and a magically talented man, both of whom have ties to Nightshade Coven. But as I said, Willow denied that they had received orders from her to attack." He snapped his mouth shut as though he was originally going to say something else but had decided against it.

Elyse waited, but Josh didn't add anything. "Why was Terrance attacked?"

"Are you sure you want to know?" Josh asked.

"Of course. Why else would I have asked you for more information? I thought we had agreed to be open with each other. If Terrance is in trouble, then that could cause problems for us since we are here in Boise under her protection," Elyse pointed out.

Josh closed his eyes for a moment before opening them and meeting her gaze directly. "They were after her because she has the Snowflake. The object that her meeting with Trey was about in your vision."

Elyse's mouth popped open and formed an O. "Did Cory give you any more information on what the deal was with Trey or why they made it?"

150

"No, only that it was a personal deal," Josh replied. "On a different note, Cory offered to give us a tour of their headquarters today if you're interested."

"Sure, it's something to do," Elyse replied.

Josh blew out his breath in relief. "I believe we can just head over there whenever we want."

Elyse nodded. "Okay, then let's clean up and we can head that way."

SIXTEEN
ELYSE

The tour of Terrance and Cory's HAC headquarters sounded interesting, but Elyse also wanted to see if she could discover any new information using her talent. *I guess I will have to wait to do that.* Elyse and Josh walked down the street, in the opposite direction of the Plaza, toward HAC headquarters—a large three-story building whose entryway had a big atrium with sunlight streaming through it.

Josh walked up to the intercom and pressed a button. Elyse expected someone to speak, but no one did. The door just buzzed open. As they passed through it, she noticed there was a camera at the intercom allowing whoever was manning the door to get a visual of the person asking for entry.

They walked inside. Elyse's attention was drawn toward the windows overhead. She was surprised that the building was not warmer with as much sunlight as was coming into the room. There were potted plants around the perimeter of the entryway, which upon inspection she determined were fake.

As they were still peering around, Cory came down the stairs that were almost hidden against the wall on the left side. "Welcome," he said, smiling.

As he approached, Elyse realized how huge he really was. He made her feel small. Her thoughts drifted, wondering how Cory and Terrance's mating bond worked. Josh had never really discussed that with her.

Josh shook Cory's hand, and Elyse did the same.

"I thought we would start at the top and work to the bottom. Though a warning, the upper two levels aren't very interesting," Cory offered.

"It's your house. I'll let you decide," Josh said.

Cory nodded and then gestured for them to follow him back up the two flights of stairs. "The top level is primarily residences. We have a couple of vacant ones, so I can show you. I guess you could best describe them as studio apartments."

He led them down the hallway. The doors had numbers on them and locks that required a thumbprint to gain access. When they were about halfway down, Cory placed his thumb on the lock. It scanned his print and then blinked green, and the door popped open.

"Go ahead and check it out," Cory said, waving them inside.

Elyse took the offer and entered the apartment. It was a large, almost-square room with a bed on one wall, a kitchenette on another, a dresser, and a curtain blocking off what she assumed was the bathroom. *A lot like Jessica's cabin at the Johnsons',* she mused.

When she was done examining the apartment, they continued down the hallway to another staircase. They went down one level and proceeded down another hallway. The only difference between this one and the upstairs one was that the flooring was gray instead of blue.

"This level is a mix of offices, storage, and more residences. Should we ever need to expand the number of apartments, we can use the space on this level to do so. Though I hope we never need to. We have thirty apartments already and have never been at full capacity," Cory said. They quickly proceeded down the hallway.

"How many people live here right now?" Josh asked, voicing the question Elyse had hoped to have answered.

"In the building? I think twenty. A few of those are couples though," Cory said as he made a beeline for the staircase into the atrium.

"How many people does Terrance oversee?" Josh asked.

"I think around one hundred now. Though several of those are not actively involved in HAC. They just are available if we need a larger group for something. A few tend to travel throughout the entire Pacific Northwest and report here every six months," Cory explained.

They reached the bottom of the stairs and Cory paused as though debating which hallway to take them down. On the main level there were two options: one directly under the upper floors where they had just been, and one that went to the left. Cory moved over to the start of the hallway under the upper floors, but he did not walk down it.

"Down there is a large office with individual computer stations. The server room is at the end. The healer suite at this level is for basics. There is a surgical suite downstairs just in case of emergencies. I have found over the years that regular hospitals, even here in Boise where talents are out in the open, often do not have the skills to help someone recover from a magic attack. They're still too reliant on traditional Western medicine techniques." Cory led them toward the hallway on the left.

As they crossed the threshold from the atrium into the hallway, Elyse could feel the difference. It also seemed to wake up her talent because it made her skin prickle. She stopped following Josh and Cory and closed her eyes. She took a deep breath, hoping that if she relaxed and let whatever was going on in this hallway settle, her talent would stop doing whatever it was doing.

Elyse opened her eyes. Cory and Josh were nowhere in sight. The hallway was lined with long windows. Beyond them on the right side was a room with mirrors and a barre like one might find in a dance studio. To one side, there was what looked like gymnastics equipment: a set of tall and short balance beams, a pommel horse, uneven bars, and a neat stack of mats.

She could hear claws skidding across the slick floor. A wolf and a tiger were chasing each other down the hallway. Elyse jumped out of the way but wasn't quick enough. The tiger ran right through her. That was when she realized she was in a vision. She turned to follow the tiger and wolf, but they had simply vanished.

"Elyse, are you coming?" called Josh.

Elyse jumped, startled. Shooting a quick glance around her, she saw that she was next to a room with mirrors and gymnastics equipment, but unlike in her vision, the equipment was set up and someone was practicing on the balance beam. Josh and Cory were waiting for her at the end of the hallway.

"Haven't you seen someone on a balance beam before?" Cory asked.

Elyse offered him a strained smile. "Yes. Why does this hallway feel different than the other ones?"

Cory gave her a sharp look. "You can feel it?"

"What is *it*?" Josh asked uncertainly.

"Because it takes us to the lower levels, this hallway has several layers of protection on it. But we've never had anyone be able to detect it. It shouldn't be possible," Cory said.

Elyse didn't know what to say. "I know you're aware that I can see the past and future with my talent." Cory nodded, and she continued, "I have been working on being able to control it so that I can get the visions when I want. But it doesn't always work that way. When I set foot in the hallway, I could feel my talent waking up. As though I was trying to have a vision, but I hadn't done anything. I'm assuming it was triggered by whatever protections you have in place."

"Does that mean you saw something?" Cory asked.

"Yes, I saw the room with the gymnastics equipment, but the equipment was stashed to the side, and no one was in there. Then, a tiger and a wolf were running down the hallway," Elyse explained.

"Terrance and Pierre," Cory muttered to himself, shaking his head. Elyse wondered how often they played chase in this hallway, disrupting others. "She considers it a training exercise, but … if you ask me, they're just screwing around. They play hide-and-seek too."

"Nothing says training can't be fun too," Josh replied.

Cory shot him a look but didn't say anything.

"I'm sorry I disrupted the tour. Did I miss anything?" Elyse asked.

"No. Come on." Cory led the way. The next set of windows showed what was at the level below: an Olympic-sized swimming pool with a tiger in it.

"Is that Terrance?" Elyse asked.

Cory shook his head. "No, that is Vic."

Elyse dragged her eyes from the swimming tiger and turned to see what was on the other side of the hallway. Another set of windows showed a full-sized basketball court below, which meant the building was way larger than she had initially thought.

A door opened somewhere ahead of them, and they heard footsteps approaching before they could see their owner. Cory smiled, which led Elyse to assume that Terrance was on her way.

"I thought you would have made it farther," Terrance said.

Elyse couldn't help but smile. She thought the tour was moving along at a nice speed, but then again, she was genuinely curious about their headquarters.

"I was saving the good part for when you joined us," Cory replied.

"I never said I was coming," Terrance said tartly.

156

"Did you forget, love, that I can feel you through the bond? I knew you were coming as soon as you decided," Cory said, stealing a kiss before Terrance could protest.

Elyse bit her lip to keep from giggling. "What is the 'good part'? I think everything you've shown us so far is fabulous."

"We have a space where we can practice tactical scenarios both with and without magic. You can see it from the hallway since there isn't a session running. When we do run them, the windows up here are blacked out." Terrance led the way.

Once they cleared the end of the pool and basketball court, the walls were empty for a while. Then they passed a door labeled Stairway. The hall in front of them ended in a large room with a continuous window across the whole thing. It offered a large panoramic view of the space below them. Elyse could see the tops of walls that seemed maze-like. The room itself seemed to have multiple levels. There were staircases and walkways that spanned the upper two levels as well. She gave Josh a sidelong glance and could see how bright his eyes had gotten. Then, his fingers twitched toward his gun.

"I think Josh wants to know when your next session is," Elyse said to Terrance.

Terrance peered over at Josh and smirked. "I would say you're right. Perhaps if nothing comes up in the next day or two, we can put something together."

"How often do you train in there?" Elyse asked.

"Usually once a month unless there is a particular event that comes up that we need to train for. For example, breaking into a safe and escaping in a set amount of time," Terrance said.

"Hmmm," Elyse murmured. "Do you break into safes often?"

"No, it was just one of the last ops we did," Terrance said.

"To retrieve the Snowflake?" Elyse pressed.

Terrance hesitated before answering. "No."

Instead of giving Elyse the opportunity to ask more questions, Terrance backtracked till they got to the door to the stairwell, then led their group inside and down two flights of stairs to the bottom of the building.

Terrance led them past the pool and basketball court into a large, square room. It had a wall full of hundreds of screens showing footage from cameras. Elyse recognized some of the places being watched as part of the Plaza and the train station they had arrived at. But there were many other locations that she had no idea about. It seemed HAC was very thorough in their surveillance of Boise.

Terrance walked through the center of the square room, giving a brief wave to a few people and continuing into the next room. *The armory.* No other word fit to describe the walls and shelves full of weapons and tactical gear. Elyse was mind-blown by how much they had. Like they expected a war to break out in Boise.

"This is quite an impressive place you have," Josh said from behind her with awe in his voice.

"The FBI didn't compare?" Cory asked.

"Not even close. Perhaps somewhere they have a place outfitted like this, but not anywhere in Atlanta that I am aware of. From what I've seen, it seems like you're prepared for all possible outcomes," Josh said.

"Which is precisely the point," said Terrance. "Prepare for any situation to arise. I cannot rely on assistance from Catrina or another lieutenant. We are not in constant contact, and while I am not saying I would not request help, I cannot assume it would show up in time or at all."

"Are the two of you hungry at all?" Cory asked.

Elyse and Josh both shook their heads. The pancake breakfast had been very filling.

"Good. If you don't mind, Elyse, I was hoping I could borrow Josh to go check out a lead we got regarding who was following you two at the Plaza," Cory said, glancing between the two of them.

Elyse shrugged. "If that's what you want to do, I'm sure I can find something to entertain myself with while you're gone."

Terrance chimed in, "I have a few ideas."

"I'd love to hear them," Elyse said, stepping toward Terrance.

Josh snagged her hand and dragged her back to him. "Not so fast, missy." He kissed her. "I'll see you soon."

Elyse returned the kiss and then extracted herself from Josh, wondering why he suddenly needed to give her a goodbye kiss. *Is he worried he won't come back?* It wasn't something they usually did. *Have we even really left each other since I agreed to accept his help at the ranch and we decided to try to make things work between us?* That was when she realized that they hadn't had any time apart from each other—or not where they were far enough away that yelling loudly wouldn't be sufficient to get the other's attention.

Terrance led her down the hallway and back through the room with all of the screens, past the pool and basketball court. The door she stopped in front of was, Elyse assumed, a door into the area where they practiced ops. She wasn't sure why Terrance would take her in there though. Elyse knew how to fire a gun, but she wasn't particularly interested in learning how to run or participate in a coordinated team op. She pulled up short when the door shut behind them, and she found that they weren't in the training area, but a room outfitted much like a living room in a house would be, with several sofas and comfortable-looking chairs.

Terrance turned to face Elyse. "I thought you would like to just hang out and chat. If you'd like, maybe I can help you practice with your talent while the boys are out meeting with UA."

Since Terrance mentioned hanging out, Elyse took that to be an open invitation to choose a place to sit. The hot pink couch, though too flashy for her taste, looked quite comfortable, and she sank into it.

"Who is UA?" she asked, figuring she'd start with something simple.

"Ursus Aureus. It's a clan of bear shifters who live on the western side of Boise. They operate a large logging operation up in the mountains, as well as about half of the farms to the west," Terrance explained.

"Sounds like they have a significant foothold here," Elyse said.

Terrance raised her hand, rocking it from side to side. "Sort of. They also have one of the largest drug operations in the Pacific Northwest, and the majority of the members enjoy meddling in other people's business when it suits them."

"Should I be concerned about Josh and Cory going out there just the two of them?" Elyse asked, unable to hide the worry in her voice.

Terrance shrugged. "I don't think so. They're also taking a lot of money with them. The only thing UA consistently does is sell things for large sums of money, whether it's drugs, trees, or the agricultural goods produced on their farms. They also will be unarmed."

"Going in unarmed sounds stupid," Elyse snapped.

Terrance clicked her tongue in disapproval. "It's quite smart. If they were to go in there packing weapons, they'd be dead as soon as they set foot in UA territory. However, both of them are highly skilled in hand-to-hand combat. Whether or not you know it, Josh has won almost a million dollars over the years from underground fights. Cory has had to keep a lower profile since he is my mate, and it would be considered bad press if he was discovered do be doing paid fights. Plus, the opportunities around here are slim."

Elyse was struggling to believe what Terrance was telling her.

"Cory was planning on going by himself, till I suggested Josh go with him," Terrance offered.

"Is it supposed to comfort me that you would be okay with Cory going there by himself?" Elyse replied, frustration still riding her.

Terrance sighed. "Think of it this way. It's like one of Josh's undercover operations. You know he typically operates alone, without a partner. He can handle this, I promise. You need to trust me." She paused and then continued to speak. "I think part of the problem is that you and Josh really have not had that long to get to know one another, and the circumstances haven't been normal."

Elyse realized that Terrance was right. Even though at times it felt like she and Josh had known each other forever, there were others, like now, when it was the exact opposite. Obviously he was skilled at getting out of tight situations or he would not have survived being an FBI agent for ten years.

"Let me send out a few messages. I really think it would help you to watch us run one of these practice operations. If you could see Josh in his element, then maybe it would help you understand how well trained he is," Terrance said.

Elyse gave a slight nod of agreement, her thoughts pulling in, while Terrance focused on sending out messages to arrange the practice op. Elyse knew her concern was probably overkill, but she was not used to having someone she cared deeply about choosing to go into dangerous situations. It was going to take some getting used to.

Elyse felt as though she was relaxing some. "How long have you and Cory been together?"

Terrance slid her phone back into her pocket before smiling. "Thirty years."

"Really? You both look like you can't be much more than thirty," Elyse said.

"I have discovered that shapeshifters seem to have a longer lifespan than the average human. However, since I am one of the oldest shifters that is alive, we don't have any data on how long our lifespans are," Terrance replied.

Elyse noticed that she refrained from stating how old she actually was.

"When did you know you were mated?" Elyse asked, hoping that this would not be considered too personal.

"In shifters, it seems about one-fourth of us experience the phenomenon of a mating or soulmate bond. At first, I thought it was just related to shapeshifting talents, but over time I have heard a few stories of non-shifters also bonding. I also know that the bond differs between pairs, so I can only speak on my personal experiences," Terrance said. "I hated Cory for a long time. He was arrogant, popular, and used to getting what he wanted. Dariusz paired us together for an op, and Cory saved my life twice during it. After that, things changed, at least between the two of us. I am not sure if the bond clicked into place because he saved my life, but we got married a few months later."

"When did you know the bond existed?" Elyse asked.

Terrance tugged on her lip in thought. "I knew the first time we had sex because there were a few moments where instead of seeing him through my eyes, I was seeing me through his. That's when I knew something had changed, because shifter talents do not allow you to swap bodies."

"I saved Josh's life when his car exploded," Elyse murmured, more to herself than Terrance.

Terrance asked, "Have you slept together yet?"

Elyse turned deep red in embarrassment. She wasn't even sure why the question was affecting her. She was used to being pretty open about the status of her relationships. "No."

"Sorry, I didn't mean to pry."

Elyse shook her head. "It's fine. But your assumption is partly why we haven't." Terrance gave her a quizzical look. "What I mean is that both Josh and I, in prior relationships, have been quick to jump into bed, instead of trying to create a lasting relationship. I wanted to do things differently and Josh agreed. Then, everything went sideways in Atlanta, and I almost walked away for good. I really like Josh, and I think that it's possible we can have a lasting relationship like what you have developed with Cory, but we have had few opportunities to really work on us as a couple. Or at least not in situations that resemble a traditional date."

Terrance smiled. "Then maybe we should add that to our list of things for you to do while in Boise—go on a date."

Elyse's eyes widened in surprise. "Is that safe? It seems like there is way more going on here than we originally thought."

Terrance shrugged. "If you are only willing to wait until it is perfectly safe, then you might have to wait too long and risk losing Josh. He loves you, you know. But most men won't wait forever."

"Loves me?" Elyse whispered.

"Can't you see it?" Terrance replied.

Elyse bit her lip. She wasn't sure what she saw when she looked at Josh. *Are these feelings I have for him love?* "I don't know. I have never been in love. How do you know?"

"Trust me, you will know," Terrance said, and left it at that.

SEVENTEEN
JOSH

Josh and Cory walked side by side down the street, heading for the train station closest to HAC headquarters. It was about a ten-minute walk to the station. The trees cast shade, a welcome relief from the heat. They passed by several neighborhoods, some abandoned and some inhabited. Cory stayed silent, which surprised Josh, since last night he had been willing to chat.

Before they had left headquarters, Cory had thrown about one hundred thousand dollars into two backpacks. Cory wore one, and Josh wore the other. Cory had explained why they couldn't wear weapons, but Josh was not concerned. After their sparring match, he was confident that together they could fend off most attacks, and in the worst-case scenario, Cory could shift.

They reached the station as a westbound train was pulling up. After boarding, they only had to wait about thirty seconds before the doors shut and it accelerated. Josh peered around the train, which was significantly different from the HAC train. It had rows of seats with two seats on each side, facing opposite directions.

Cory sat down, and Josh sat in the row on the other side of the aisle. Since the train was almost empty, Josh didn't think it was worth squeezing together on the same side. "How long does the train take?"

"Probably thirty minutes or so. We get off at the last stop," Cory replied.

Josh settled in to wait. He closed his eyes and drifted off into a power nap.

Josh's eyes snapped open as the train slowed down. Cory was already standing up. "This is us."

Catching on to Cory's urgency, Josh sprang to his feet, ready to get off as soon as the doors opened. He was a little surprised that the tiger shifter wanted to get off the train quickly, but given that they were in UA territory, he decided against questioning the plan. His opinion was irrelevant.

They stepped into the station. Much like the station where they had initially arrived in Boise, this one was not much more than a platform. There wasn't even a roof to protect a person from the weather while waiting for a train. The tracks continued for another fifty feet or so with several track splits allowing the train space to change tracks. At the very end, though, was a large brick wall.

I guess that answers whether or not the train can travel beyond the borders of Boise. It can't to the west. Twenty to thirty feet on either side of the trainyard was cleared land, and then the agricultural fields started. To the south of the track were cornfields, and to the north, what looked like potatoes, but he wasn't entirely sure. He was confident one of the train cars at the far side of the yard did hold potatoes because it was uncovered, and he could see the familiar brown shapes over the rim.

A few other people disembarked from the train, but Josh lost track of them when he was examining their surroundings. He adjusted the backpack on his shoulders, then focused his attention on Cory, who was already off the platform and waiting for him on the sidewalk.

Josh was intrigued that there were paved sidewalks surrounded by agricultural fields. *Perhaps the fields weren't originally this close to the freeway.*

Cory made a motion to follow, and Josh sped up his steps so he fell in just behind. When they reached the end of the potato field, the sidewalk kept going west and turned north. Cory chose to take the turn to the north. Josh caught a glimpse of what looked like a farmhouse ahead.

As they got closer to the farmhouse, Josh became aware of movement in the alfalfa field surrounding the house. It took him a few moments to realize that what he was seeing were bear shifters in their bear forms. They were keeping their distance … but watching. Josh had no misconceptions that if he or Cory made a wrong move, they would get attacked.

The large farmhouse was two stories with white siding and hunter-green trim. It had three steps and a large porch. Cory went up the steps and waited. Josh stayed at the bottom of the stairs, keeping his eyes peeled.

Heavy footsteps came from within the house, followed by a gruff, "What do you want?"

"Tiny, I wanted to see if we could meet with Griffin Taylor and Deborah Emanuel," Cory said.

Josh could hear whispering voices but was unable to make out any of the words between Tiny and whoever else was with him at the door. Finally, after what seemed like ages, Tiny, the owner of the gruff voice, replied, "You can't talk to them, but you can talk to me. Perhaps I can provide you with whatever it is that you seek?"

"Perhaps," replied Cory.

"Then come on in, and we shall talk," Tiny said.

Josh heard the door open and took it as his cue to head up the stairs. He followed Cory inside. The screen door slapped shut behind them. Josh immediately recognized the woman following them, Deborah Emanuel, from a photo Cory had shown him. She had been at the Plaza following him and Elyse. She was memorable given her formidable stature and long purple hair. He could only see the back of the man leading them into the house, but he made Cory's seven feet look average.

They stopped at a room with a long dining table. Tiny took a seat at the head of the table and gestured for Josh and Cory to sit. Deborah remained standing. Josh wasn't sure he liked the idea of having a bear shifter at his back.

"What was it that you wanted to ask Deborah and Griffin?" Tiny said

"I was hoping to find out why they were following my friend Josh and his girlfriend Elyse when they were at the Plaza two nights ago," Cory said.

Josh kept his gaze on Tiny, who did not so much as blink when Cory mentioned the Plaza. *Either he already knows and potentially gave the orders for them to be there himself, or he doesn't care.*

"The Plaza is a safe place. It is not a crime for Deborah and Griffin to be enjoying an evening there," said Tiny.

"I did not say I was investigating a crime," Cory replied smoothly. "Merely inquiring why my friends were being followed."

"They were not being followed," Tiny said firmly.

Cory pulled the backpack from his shoulders and set it on the table, then slid it down to Tiny. Tiny tilted his head from side to side, as though weighing his options, and opened the backpack.

"Does that change your mind?" Cory asked.

Tiny shrugged. "I told you. Deborah and Griffin were not following anyone."

"Does that mean you didn't order them to be there?" Cory pressed.

Tiny narrowed his eyes. "Why does this matter to you?"

Josh watched as Cory swallowed hard, likely to rein in his temper, before answering. "Terrance was attacked and could have died. Any information we can get that might be pertinent could lead to us apprehending her attackers."

Tiny stood up, bracing his tree-trunk-sized arms on the table. Josh knew he did not want to be on the receiving end of a punch from this man. "No one in my clan attacked Terrance."

Cory stayed in his seat. "Then tell me what you do know, and I will get out of your hair. Here," he said and gave Josh the sign. Josh pulled his backpack off and slid it down the table.

Tiny opened that back and counted its contents. A pleased smile was on his face when he finished. "Deborah, tell these men what you know."

Tiny stood up and departed with both backpacks in his hand. Josh exchanged a glance with Cory. Deborah walked over to the seat that Tiny had vacated and sat down. "Griffin and I were paid twenty thousand dollars to go to the Plaza and follow Josh and Elyse. We were supposed to report who they interacted with and if anyone else seemed to be following them."

"Who hired you?" Cory demanded.

"He called himself Trey, but I didn't get a last name," replied Deborah.

Josh slumped into his chair. Trey, the person who had made the deal with Terrance for the Snowflake, wanted to keep tabs on him and Elyse, but why? *Leverage,* he surmised. *Or to ensure we would not interfere with the attack on Terrance.*

"Were you supposed to do anything else?" Cory asked.

Deborah shook her head. "Nope. It was one of the most boring jobs I've taken, but the pay was great. Now. I don't have anything else to tell you, so it is time for both of you to leave." She got up and waited for them to also stand.

"Are you sure that's it?" Cory asked.

Deborah ignored the question and herded them out the door.

When they were safely away from the farmhouse, Josh turned to Cory. "What do you think?"

Cory shook his head. "I don't know. Maybe Trey was just trying to scope you out in case things went wrong with his attack on Terrance. The more he knows about people she cares about, the more options he has. She is to do the exchange tomorrow morning."

"This felt like a waste of time," Josh replied.

Cory responded, "We did get information, and now we know that they were just there to observe. Oh, Terrance sent me a message and says that she was able to get enough people together to run through a practice op this afternoon if you'd like."

"Sure, that would be great. I saw the room you had set up, but how do you normally run them?" Josh replied.

"We can use paintball guns, but we also have equipment that uses lasers and sensors, so no ammo, though we do have the option of grenades if we want. Mostly it just depends on how messy you want to be," Cory explained.

They were approaching the train station. This time there wasn't a train pulling in or waiting for passengers, which meant they'd be waiting for the next train to show up, however long that would take. Both men settled on a bench to wait.

"What was it like growing up in Manhattan?" Cory asked, causing Josh to jump slightly.

Josh tapped his fingers on his knee, considering the question. "There were times it was fun, and other times it was lonely."

"Isn't that how most childhoods are?" Cory replied.

Josh chuckled. "I suppose. Though how many people do you know who live in a city that has a wall around it making it difficult to leave?"

Cory shrugged. "Just you and Celine."

Josh's eyes widened. "How do you know Celine?"

"There have been a few operations that we have had over the years where we needed the services of a talented healer, and she offered to assist," Cory explained.

"I know you have a healer at headquarters," Josh said.

Cory picked at a hole in his jeans before meeting Josh's eyes and replying, "We do, but not all talented have the same skill set or experience for every situation."

Josh nodded in agreement. He knew all too well how true that statement was. "For a while there were three of us growing up, Celine, Ben, and myself. We all shared the same dream, to get out of Manhattan."

"Understandable. Usually, people want to leave the place they are forced to be in," Cory replied.

"Did you have many friends growing up?" Josh asked.

Cory pinched his lips together in thought. "By nature, tigers tend to be solitary animals. As a tiger shifter, there are many times when the animal side dominates. As a youngster, I struggled to overcome the tiger's desire to be on its own. There was an entire year I lived in the mountains as a tiger."

Josh opened his mouth to reply, but the train was approaching the station. Cory stood up and Josh followed him out.

A couple of hours after they had left to talk to UA, Josh and Cory finally made it back to headquarters. Elyse and Terrance met them at the entrance and led them to the conference room where a lunch buffet was laid out.

"You did all this?" Cory asked Terrance.

Elyse smiled. "It was my idea. I wanted to cook for you, since the two of you have been so generous with your time and facilities."

Josh examined the food. Elyse had prepared a mix of options. There was a platter of fried chicken, seasoned fries, and creamed spinach, as well as grilled chicken breasts, a tossed salad, and fresh rolls. It smelled delicious.

"Everything from scratch," Elyse said. "Let's eat before it gets cold."

Josh led the way and filled his plate, then found a seat at the conference table. When the four of them started eating, more people began filtering in. Pierre, Sienna, Devin, Georgina, and some others Josh didn't recognize.

"I thought we could have lunch and then split into teams for the training op," Terrance explained. "It'll be five on five. Elyse helped me determine some of the parameters. Hopefully you're feeling up to the challenge."

Josh focused his gaze on Elyse, intrigued that she had taken part. She shrugged. "I didn't want to make it too easy."

Terrance laughed. "It won't be easy."

"Is it fair that you're participating if you set the parameters?" Cory teased.

"Yes, because I told Elyse how to start it once both teams are in position," Terrance said.

Josh was confused. "How to start it?"

Cory set down his piece of chicken. "Yes. We have the option of letting the computer randomize an op. In this case, I'm assuming that what is getting randomized are our starting points."

Terrance nodded. "Yes."

Josh still didn't really understand. *Didn't they just enter in one spot?*

Elyse smiled. "Each team gets into a box, which doubles as an elevator. The system will move the box into a randomly selected starting position once I hit the start button. The parameters I chose were multiple levels, so the ramps and stairs are a critical part, and paintball—I wanted to be able to get a better idea of how things were progressing, and the lasers sounded interesting, but are harder for a bystander to track. The objective is to retrieve the flag and get it back to your base. Whoever gets the flag to their base first wins."

"Sounds straightforward," replied Josh.

Everyone around the table smiled at Josh's comment. *What am I missing?* he wondered.

Josh peered at the four other people with him in the black box that was lit by a small red light. They were wearing standard-issue Kevlar body vests, helmets, and protective goggles. Josh's team had blue Velcro squares on the front and back of their vets; the other team had green. Each was armed with an assault rifle and a handgun. One person in each group had been randomly selected to carry two smoke grenades and one "real" grenade. Josh had been relieved when he was not chosen to carry the grenades, mostly because he had not really understood what the one they called "real" was supposed to do since this was a simulation.

The box began to move. His group included Terrance, Pierre, Sienna, and Devin—the HAC member who had found them on their way from Shoshone Falls and led them to the meet with Terrance.

"What's the plan?" Josh asked.

"The objective is to get the flag and return it to our home base. The problem is we won't know where our home base is until the box opens," explained Terrance.

"Or where the flag is," replied Pierre with a wicked grin.

"Each starting point is equidistant from where the flag is, and the most direct route would take the exact same amount of time from either base. The problem is since we know that multiple levels are involved, we could end up almost anywhere," Terrance explained, then gave Josh a wink. "We will split up. Three going for the flag and two hanging back for support."

The box stopped abruptly, and Josh could feel it swaying slightly, as though a breeze had caught it. He could not tell in the red light whether the others reacted to the swaying and if it meant something or not. The box slid to a final halt, and the door popped open. Terrance led the way out of the box.

They were on a metal mesh platform, about ten feet by ten feet, at the top of the building. There were three walls mostly obscuring them from view and then the fourth side was open onto a ramp with a slight downward angle. The ramp started out wide and gradually narrowed until it reached the next platform that was in the dead center of the building. From there, one had a variety of choices. Josh marveled at how much the space had changed since the tour. When Terrance had said that they could manipulate the different pieces to create a vast number of training scenarios, she had been serious.

The bottom level had walls, and from this height, he could easily see the other team in their base, which had a mesh roof on top, making it possible to tell there were people inside but impossible to get a clean shot. However, the path out of the base had a solid roof overhead until it reached a branching point, much like the platforms up here did. The more he studied the layout, he realized that it was set up as a reverse mirror image. Which meant the flag was likely in the dead center, which was the second-lowest platform.

"Pierre, Josh, and Devin, make a run for the flag. Sienna and I will find positions on the perimeter to help," Terrance said. Josh started toward the exit of the base. "Remember: the first five minutes, no kill shots. After that, it's a free-for-all. First to get the flag to their base or first to take out the entire opposing team wins."

Josh nodded in understanding and took off at a jog. The ramp he was on was remarkably silent under his boots. He had expected the metal to squeak or clank as they ran down it, but it did not make a sound. However, they were visible from below because the rails were basic and didn't hide them from view.

When they reached the first platform, Josh hesitated. There was a staircase that went straight down to the next level and ramps that would take them to the perimeter.

Pierre ran past him down the steps. "C'mon."

EIGHTEEN
TERRANCE

Terrance watched as Josh, Pierre, and Devin worked their way down to the flag. She was also tracking Cory's progress as his team wound its way through the maze of walls headed for the stairs that would take them up to the second platform. Except, she realized, the stairs were blocked from the lower and upper sides. *Interesting.*

"Let's go," she said to Sienna. They walked instead of running down the first ramp. Instead of heading down the stairs, they split up. Sienna took the ramp to the right and Terrance took the one to the left.

Terrance hesitated for a moment and shots rang out. She ran as the ramp behind her was peppered with paint as the shots missed her. She was almost off to the safety of the plywood wall up ahead when a well-aimed shot hit her in the calf. She grimaced at the green splatter, knowing that she was going to bruise, but kept her footing and made it to safety.

She cautiously peered out and could hear the pop-pop of shots Sienna was firing and hear stifled moans from the other team. *This is why we split up.* With Cory's military background, he preferred to keep his team as a single unit. Terrance had tried to copy his strategy for several years before realizing that the only way she could beat him was to use a strategy that suited her abilities best. From her viewpoint, she watched as Cory slung his gun over his shoulder and started scaling the outside of the platform. His legs were dangling, and he had to rely solely on his upper body strength. She couldn't help but admire her mate and relish the thought that he was *hers* and no one else's.

Josh was running around the third platform, peering over the edge and trying to shoot at Cory but missing because of the bad angle. Then, Terrance realized she had the perfect shot. *If I can stop being distracted.* She raised her assault rifle and with Cory in her sights, fired twice. He didn't even glance her way.

"Cocky bastard," she muttered under her breath. She could feel his chuckle through their mating bond. Rolling her eyes, she aimed for his helmet. They hadn't reached the five-minute timer allowing for kill shots, but she wanted him to know she could.

She fired once, and it hit the back of his helmet. She watched as his head snapped forward from the impact, and he hit his face on the support column.

"Terrance!" Cory roared.

Giggling, she slipped back to safety behind the wall. Several more shots were fired, though she could not hear anyone else yelling, so she assumed they had missed their marks.

"Got it!" came Josh's triumphant shout.

Terrance walked to the edge of her hiding place, preparing to run to the next protected area. She heard shots, then the computer loudly announced, "Kill shots are now permitted."

Shots rang out. Some bounced off the various metal parts; others made their marks. *One, two, three!* Terrance sprinted for the other end, slowing only long enough to lay some cover fire for Pierre as he leaped onto Georgina, who currently had possession of the flag.

As he leaped, Terrance belatedly wondered why he had opted to leap instead of just shooting the mage instead. Not wanting to waste precious time contemplating Pierre's decisions, she focused instead on Vic, who was trying to sneak up behind Pierre. Terrance didn't hesitate. She fired and hit Vic squarely the back of the neck. He turned, sending a scathing look up at her, and sat down with his gun in his lap. Once a participant was "dead," they had to stay where they were killed until the op was over.

There was a flash of movement to her left and Terrance realized that someone was up here, slinking around. *Probably Cory.* She slowly backed up.

Pop! Pop! She stumbled forward with the impact, face slamming into the mesh floor. The first shot had hit her in the hip and the second in the head. Whoever had taken her out decided to retreat before she could discover who it was. She sucked a breath in through her teeth. Her body hurt, which was usually the downside of practicing with the paintball guns.

Face still in the mesh, she could see shapes below her and the pop of guns being fired. Suddenly, there was a loud *boom!* The metal she was on vibrated. *I guess someone used a grenade.*

Lights in the room flashed. "Game over!" the computer announced.

Who won? That seemed awfully fast, Terrance thought as she pulled herself up to standing, massaging the back of her neck. Everyone made their way down to the bottom where the exit was.

When Terrance reached Cory, he flashed her a wicked grin, which she ignored. "Who won?"

Cory laughed. "You'll love it. Josh got his hands on a grenade, and everyone died before the flag could make it to a base. I guess you failed at explaining what the grenade would do, Ter."

A smile tugged at her lips. This was an outcome they'd never had before, *everyone dying.* Or at least not when it was two teams in open combat. When they were doing run-throughs of a very specific op, they usually had several failures before they successfully made it through all of the parameters and were allowed to do it for real.

When they reached the exit room, Elyse was laughing so hard tears were streaming down her face and she was clutching her side. Terrance's gaze went right to Josh. He was covered from head to toe in blue paint.

"Next time I will explain the grenades better," Terrance promised.

Josh shook his head. "That would be nice."

"Let's go get cleaned up," Terrance suggested. The men followed Cory and the women Terrance as they headed for their respective locker rooms.

NINETEEN
ELYSE

Elyse and Josh were sitting on the couch in the apartment. After the practice op and showering at HAC headquarters, they retreated home for some quiet time. Elyse had been reading a book when she'd gotten lost in her thoughts.

Ever since being followed at the Plaza, she had been on edge and so had Josh. Regardless of how often Terrance reassured them that they were safe, Elyse felt anything but safe here. The more they learned about the deal Terrance had set up with Trey to exchange the Snowflake for a large payday, the greater her concern had become. Yet, part of her wasn't sure if she wanted to dig deep enough to find out what exactly it was. She was one of those people who, if she knew there was a problem and she could help resolve it, then she would, no matter the cost to her.

"Penny for your thoughts," murmured Josh, before giving her a light kiss.

"Do you really think we should stay out of Terrance and Cory's business?" Elyse asked.

Josh sighed. "I think at the rate we're going we are already involved in it, whether they want to fully admit it or not. The visit to UA did not give us as much information as we hoped, other

178

than confirming that the two women following us are members and had hired themselves out for the evening. I am more concerned about why we were being watched and that we still don't have the answer. Terrance and Cory have been oddly quiet about the whole matter."

"Would she have said something, though?" Elyse pressed.

"Yes, she is not sloppy. The people following us were being sloppy. If Terrance wanted to have us followed, she'd either have told us directly or we would have never known her people were there. The Pacific Northwest is home to many kinds of shifters, not just tigers. I am confident that she has someone who can spy on us from a significant distance if she chose to do so," Josh replied.

Elyse flipped back a few pages in her book, realizing that she had not been paying attention to what she was reading and had no idea what had happened in the story. Josh ran his thumb lightly over her ear before starting to massage her shoulders. A groan escaped her lips as his fingers worked their way through the tension she hadn't realized was there. As her muscles loosened up, the massage changed to more of a caress than anything. Desire crept through her. She wasn't sure whether or not Josh knew what effect he was having on her. Elyse closed her eyes and took in a slow breath. As she counted backward from ten, Josh's lips lightly trailed kisses on her neck.

Unable to resist anymore, Elyse set the book down and twisted, capturing Josh's lips with hers. Encouraged by her reaction, Josh let his hands slide down her sides and then back up, lingering on her breasts. Under his featherlight touch, her nipples hardened. She deepened the kiss, their tongues dancing while he played with her breasts.

Elyse gasped as he lightly pinched her nipple through her shirt. Heat flooded her body, and all she could think about was getting Josh inside of her as soon as possible. She reached down and fumbled with his belt buckle, causing Josh to chuckle. He pulled back far enough to study her eyes.

"Are you sure?" he asked.

Elyse ran the tip of her tongue over his lip and nodded. "Yes. I want you, Josh, here and now."

He flashed her a wicked grin and gently removed her hands from his belt. Elyse watched as he quickly unbuckled it and stood up, stepping out of his pants. His shirt came next, then his boxers. Elyse slid out of her pants as she watched Josh undress. She could see how hard his cock already was, ready for her just as she was for him. She reached under the edge of her shirt and pulled it off. Then she reached for her bra, but Josh beat her to it, undoing the clasp and letting it slide to the floor with the rest of their clothes.

Josh took a step forward, over their clothes, and pulled her into his arms. His kiss was demanding. Without their clothes between them, the press of his cock against her abdomen was almost enough to send her over the edge. She didn't want to beg, but it had been far too long since she'd had sex.

Apparently, she made a noise of some sort. Josh smiled against her lips and picked her up, wrapping her legs around his waist. In this position, his cock was brushing the edge of her folds.

"Josh," she moaned softly as he carried her over to the bed, letting her back fall onto the mattress. With her legs still around his waist, he braced himself on the edge of the bed, and with one thrust he was inside of her. The orgasm hit her like a tidal wave. A gasp escaped her lips, but Josh kept going. He thrust in quick and slowly pulled out. Elyse was confused at first. Why wasn't he wasn't trying to just finish? It was what Derek had done. Then, she felt it, her pleasure building again. Each time he pulled out, what she was feeling intensified. He leaned down, adjusting her legs again, and took her right breast into his mouth, sucking and teasing. He then switched to the left before turning his attention to her mouth. As he kissed her, his thrusts quickened. It felt like they were merged as one as deep as he was going. With one last thrust, he sent them both cascading over the edge. Josh lowered himself carefully on top of her. Elyse smiled. His weight felt reassuring.

Elyse opened her eyes, realizing that she must have fallen asleep. She glanced to her side, and Josh was in the bed, napping. *I guess we both were tired.* She stifled a yawn with her hand, then slid out of the bed. She didn't want to wake Josh up. They both had been under a lot of stress recently, and she knew he needed as much sleep as he could get.

The curtains were still drawn behind the couch, so she was safely out of view as she padded naked over to the pile of clothing in front of the couch. She sorted hers out and got dressed, then folded Josh's clothing neatly.

Elyse smiled to herself. She wasn't sure what she had expected it to be like to sleep with Josh, but she was certain she'd never had sex that good before. *The guys I've been with weren't terrible. I bet if I ask Josh if that was the best sex he'd ever had, he would likely lie to make sure I'm happy. It's not like people usually go around telling their current partner that they've had better sex with someone else. That's a good way of ensuring that they don't ever have sex again.*

Elyse was lost in her thoughts about old boyfriends and one-night stands. She jumped when she felt a gun in her back.

"Don't move," came a voice from behind her. The gun pressed harder into her. Elyse sucked in a breath, her mind whirling. Josh was in the bedroom napping, but how the hell had someone gotten inside the apartment? It was secure.

"We're going to walk out of here, and you are not going to say or do anything. If you do, I'll shoot you and it won't be fatal, but you will be paralyzed from the waist down," the voice said.

Elyse gave a slight nod and walked quietly toward the door. She glanced wistfully at her shoes as they passed them but made no move to retrieve them. She did not want to gamble with being paralyzed for a pair of shoes.

They reached the door, which was slightly ajar. Elyse pulled it open, wincing when it squeaked ever so slightly. The gun bumped into her, and she walked through the door and into the hallway. The person with the gun must have tugged the door shut because she heard a click as the lock slid into place.

The pressure from the gun lessened, and a hand roughly grabbed her. She gazed down at the hand and realized it belonged to small boy. *A small boy captured me?* When they got out of the apartment building, Elyse stopped and refused to move forward. The boy stepped in front of her, giving her an evil glare. "Why did you stop?"

"Why is a kid trying to take me hostage?" Elyse countered.

The boy's lip curled in a sneer. "I am no kid."

Elyse looked him over from head to toe. "Then how do you explain that you look like a ten-year-old kid?"

The boy growled. "I am no kid."

Elyse just stared at him. "Then who are you?"

"Ben Piro," he replied as his body changed. He grew and filled out until he looked like a twenty-something man with dark hair and eyes that seemed to have fire in them. His fingers had claws at the end and the edges of his skin she could see appeared to be burning. The name gave her a start. *Where have I heard that before?*

Ben smiled, showing a set of very sharp teeth. "Josh and I were friends once upon a time. Until he betrayed me."

Elyse sucked in a sharp breath. *Ben … Josh's Ben, the one who was there when Mr. Pascal found him …* She bit her lip. Ben spoke of a betrayal, but she didn't know anything about that.

"Is that your plan?" she demanded, hoping if she prevented Ben from leaving the area long enough that Josh would wake up and discover she was gone. "To kidnap me so you can make Josh pay for the so-called betrayal?"

Ben's lips twitched as though he found her words funny. "Something along those lines. I'm not going to spoil the fun by telling you everything. Time to go now."

He shoved the gun in his belt and roughly grabbed her arm and tugged. Elyse opened her mouth to scream, and his free hand clamped itself over her mouth. The sensation of his hand on her mouth was painful. It felt like her skin was burning. Tears formed in her eyes. His hand hurt her.

"Are you going to behave?" he said tersely. Elyse nodded, blinking back tears, and the hand uncovered her mouth. "Let's go." Ben yanked her hard.

TWENTY
JOSH

Josh rolled over in bed and flung his arm out, expecting it to land on Elyse. His eyes flew open when it just hit the mattress. His whole body was tense until he heard the muffled sound of the shower running. *I wonder if she wants company*, he thought with a knowing smile, his cock already hardening. Josh made his way from the bedroom to the bathroom. The door was slightly ajar, and he could see steam drifting through the gap.

"Care if I join you?" he asked, projecting his voice so she should be able to hear it over the water. At the same time, he pushed the door open.

The shower was running, but to his shock Elyse was not in it. Josh rocked back on his heels, and the door swung toward him.

Boom!

Josh was thrown into the air as the apartment blew apart. The blast sent him through the window, and he landed hard on the street. When Josh came to, his first thought was that every inch of him hurt. He could feel the trickles of blood all over his body from going through the glass window. He also belatedly remembered that he was naked. Muttering curses, Josh slowly sat up.

Everything was spinning. He closed his eyes, hoping that would help. When he opened them, a tiger was straddling him.

Josh froze. He knew it had to be a shifter, but he wasn't sure who it was. *I shouldn't be surprised Terrance had someone nearby.* "Cory?" he asked, hoping fervently it was him and not one of the other tigers that he didn't really know.

The tiger gave a slight nod in confirmation, then cocked its head to the side as though waiting for something. Josh took a breath and started coughing. When he finally stopped, the tiger was still peering at him.

"If you don't want to shift, then I am not sure how well I can answer your questions," Josh muttered. The tiger let out a huff. "I took a nap. When I woke up, I thought Elyse was in the shower. I went to go speak to her."

The tiger gave a low growl. Josh sighed. He should have known that Cory would be able to smell Elyse's scent entwined with his. "Anyhow, she was not in the shower, and then the apartment exploded. I have no idea where she is or who would have taken her."

Josh took a deep breath. The benefit of having Cory in tiger form standing over him was it hid his nakedness from the other people who were coming by to see what had exploded. But Josh hurt and didn't really want to lie in the middle of the street any longer than necessary. "Can you please just shift so we can have a real conversation?"

Cory growled and then walked a few paces away and sat down. Once the tiger was sitting, he began to shift. A few seconds later, he was human.

"Was that so difficult?" Josh asked, slightly annoyed.

Cory gave him a scathing look. "I had my reasons to not want to shift. But we need to get you out of here. As soon as whoever set that bomb finds out that you're not dead, they're going to come back to finish the job, and I would rather not be here when that happens."

Josh braced himself on his hands, biting his lip as he felt shards of glass slicing deeper in them. He slowly stood up. His whole body shook. Once he was standing, the blood trickled down. He was sure he looked terrible.

"Do you have a healer?" he asked, unable to mask the pain in his voice any longer.

Cory gave him a sharp look. Josh swayed. As he lost his balance and almost fell over, the tiger shifter caught him.

"Why didn't you tell me you were hurt this badly?" Cory hissed.

Josh just gave him a weak smile and sagged as he lost consciousness.

Josh rubbed his eyes, trying to wake up all the way. He could hear his mom in the kitchen making breakfast, like she did every morning for him before he went to school and she went to work. His dad would eat and leave before Josh got up, so he wouldn't see him until after school.

His mom looked tired when he walked in. She gave him a smile, but it was not her usual cheery smile. Something is wrong, *he thought, but instead of saying anything, he sat down at the table, and she placed a large glass of orange juice and a plate heaped with pancakes in front of him.*

While he ate, he caught his mom staring at him a few times, but every time he opened his mouth to say something, she turned away as though she didn't want him to know she had been staring.

When he finished eating, he washed his plate and glass and put them back in the cupboard. She handed him his backpack and lunch, then gave him a quick hug.

"I love you, Josh." Her voice was oddly sad.

"I love you, Mom," he replied, hugging her tight.

The rest of the events of that day were blurry, until he got home from school. His dad was sitting at the table. Josh could tell as soon as he walked in that his dad was angry.

"Good afternoon, sir," Josh said.

His dad looked at him, eyes clouded with anger. "Sit down, Josh."

Josh sat hesitantly on the edge of the chair at the opposite side of the table. He was afraid to get too close in case his father decided to hit him.

"Your mom left," his dad said emotionlessly.

Josh shot a sharp look at his dad. "She went to work—"

His dad shook his head. "No, she left."

Josh's eyes narrowed. "How do you know?" His lip quivered slightly. This must be a trick, *he told himself.*

"Because she told me. The bitch came to my work and told me in front of everyone that she was done and not coming back," his dad growled.

Josh cringed. The change in his dad's tone and his use of the word bitch *spoke volumes of how angry he was.*

"I need to do my homework," Josh said softly, praying he could go to his room and let his dad cool down before facing him again.

His dad stared at him for a few moments before waving a hand in dismissal. "Fine, go do your homework, but you can't go out afterward."

Josh opened his eyes and found he was in a twin-size bed in a small gray room. Bandages of various sizes covered his body. Thankfully, though, the agonizing pain he had experienced immediately after the explosion had been reduced to a dull ache. He lifted the sheet and was pleased to see he was dressed in a white T-shirt and a pair of green athletic shorts. His hands were mostly wrapped in bandages, and there were smaller ones on his biceps and calves.

His dream was not a pleasant one, the day his mom had left. Thankfully, this time, he had only had to relive the first part, not what happened after dinner. He shuddered.

The door swung open. Josh struggled to sit up, not wanting to be in such a vulnerable position if it was another attack, and forcing himself to focus on something other than the dream.

Cory came through the door, eyebrow raised. "I don't think you're going to be fighting anytime soon," he said drily.

Josh scooted all the way to sitting and leaned against the wall. "I could fight if I had to," he replied, wincing.

"Uh-huh," Cory replied offhandedly.

"Do you know where Elyse is?" Josh asked. Elyse had disappeared, and then the apartment blew up. Getting her back was his number one priority.

Cory walked the rest of the way into the room and set a plate of food on the small table at the side of the bed. "Sort of."

"What is that supposed to mean?" Josh asked, voice rough.

"Ben Piro has her," Cory replied. Josh began cursing. "When Terrance found out Ben was involved, she felt it was in your best interest to not know. Clearly, that was a mistake."

Josh glared at him. "You knew Ben was here in Boise? How long have you known?"

Cory looked at Josh in the eyes. "A week."

Josh sputtered, "A week?" He threw off the covers and swung his legs out of the bed, then stood up. He swayed unsteadily, his legs protesting his weight. He took a shaky step forward.

"What are you doing?" Cory asked.

"I'm going to find Elyse, with or without you." Josh took another step forward and almost lost his balance. He grabbed the back of a chair to steady himself. His breath came in gasps. Each one created sharp pain in his chest, leading him to think he must have at least bruised some ribs along with whatever else had been injured.

"How do you expect to find Elyse and rescue her—if she needs rescuing—when you can't even walk?" Cory demanded.

"I will find a way. I heal quickly. I'm sure by the time I find her I will be able to fight," Josh said, trying to steady his voice. His attempt only partially worked.

"How about this? You rest, and I will bring you all the information I have. When my team finds Elyse, I'll let you know, and you can be there when we rescue her," Cory offered.

Josh bit his lip. Cory was right. He was in no shape to do anything. It just was hard to let go and allow someone he didn't know very well to spearhead the rescue. After being blindsided by the FBI assistant director's dark agenda, Josh was waiting for someone here to betray him, whether it was Catrina or Terrance or someone else.

"What about Terrance?" Josh asked. Usually, the two of them worked pretty closely together, and it seemed strange that Terrance had not come by to make sure he was okay after getting blown up, or at least to reassure him they were doing everything to find Elyse.

Cory shook his head. "She is on her way to Aerie. She should be back in a few hours, though, and will help with the search for Elyse. I told you I am on top of it. Now, be a good patient and get some rest so that you can heal and be ready to go in with us when we find her."

Josh sighed in resignation. "Fine, I will rest." He lay back down and pulled the sheet over his face, trying to convince himself to fall asleep and praying he would sleep in peace, without old memories haunting him.

TWENTY-ONE
TERRANCE

The train made its slow journey from the Plaza through the Boise foothills and up to Aerie. Terrance grimaced, showing her teeth, which were slightly longer than they should be—a sign for anyone looking that she was not in complete control of her tiger. Cory was right; she should have never accepted the job Trey had offered to acquire the Snowflake.

Nothing so far had gone as she had expected. After the attack Trey ordered on her at Rookwood, it had been clear her only option was to accept Governor Beechwood's offer. One hundred million dollars in exchange for the Snowflake. What Terrance hadn't considered was that the governor would want to handle the exchange in person at Aerie. Terrance had never trusted the governor, although his actions had always been aboveboard. She just got this feeling that everything wasn't as it seemed. Anytime she asked Agent Florence about it, the FBI agent ignored her query. Terrance had never figured out if that was because Agent Florence didn't believe her, or because she did but couldn't discuss it without drawing attention to herself.

Terrance let her eyelids shut and took a deep breath. *Everything will work out as it's meant to. I have to believe that,* she reminded herself. Earlier that morning, she had argued with Cory about who should go with her. He, of course, wanted to come, but she was concerned that having her mate there would make her seem weak and put the rest of their organization at risk if something were to go wrong. She also knew that Governor Beechwood would shoot anyone she sent if she wasn't there too. He would assume it was a trap.

Instead, I might be walking into a trap he set for me. She let her breath out and then opened her eyes. The train slowed as it started its climb into the foothills. Aerie was just on the other side. The small train station was operated by FBI agents and was right at the entrance to Aerie. No one got in or out without passing through those gates. Which also meant if anyone wanted to travel farther north than the station, they would have to go through the FBI, or travel the long way, trekking through the foothills on horseback or on foot, without the benefit of a road or train track to follow.

Terrance had carefully selected who would accompany her to Aerie. After a lengthy discussion with Cory, they had agreed that three to accompany her, putting the HAC representatives at a total of four, would be sufficient to show they meant business, but not so many to be perceived as a threat.

Pierre and Sienna were strong fighters in their human and shifted forms. Rounding out their group was Yolanda, who had proven over the years that she was reliable in high-stakes situations, so Terrance had not hesitated to ask her to come. Terrance wanted a mage because she knew that the governor was likely to have at least one mage, if not more, in his protection detail. Terrance knew of several who were employed by the government and worked primarily out of Aerie as well, and should conflict arise, she did not want to be caught unprepared.

All four of them wore an assortment of weapons. Terrance was openly wearing four guns and two knives. She had more underneath her clothing as well. They anticipated having to give up the weapons that were visible. Whether or not the governor would require a more thorough search was unknown.

"Are you ready?" she asked, meeting the eyes of each of them. They all nodded.

The train slowed to a halt and the doors slid open. Awaiting them on the small station platform were eight FBI agents in black suits with white shirts and dark sunglasses. The agents parted, and Agent Florence stepped forward.

"Good morning, Terrance," she said, offering her hand.

Terrance shook the offered hand. When Agent Florence withdrew, Terrance clenched her fist to hide the piece of paper that had been slipped into her hand. She was going to have to find a way to read it without one of the eight agents noticing. She gave Agent Florence a quick glance, but the woman kept her face blank, giving nothing away.

"We're ready when you are," Terrance said, and her group of four stepped all the way onto the platform. The train door snicked shut behind them.

Agent Florence nodded, and they began walking. Terrance and her crew were boxed in by the FBI agents. The train station at Aerie was a single level. They passed through automatic sliding glass doors and into a long hallway, at the end of which was an archway filled with lights. The FBI agents led the way, and everyone passed through the archway. An agent behind a desk stared intently at a computer screen, presumably at whatever the archway was scanning. The archway was new, and nothing on it gave Terrance any indication what exactly it was scanning for. She would have to remember to tell Cory about it so he could investigate what purpose it served.

Finally, the group cleared through the rest of the security measures and stepped onto the sidewalk. Terrance had not spent much time in Aerie and was always surprised by how it looked like stepping into a magazine ad from one hundred years ago. The paved streets were lined with well-manicured trees and bushes. The sidewalks were pristine, as though the concrete had been poured in the past six months rather than in a previous century. The area that made up the Aerie was mostly level. There were some slight elevation changes throughout the complex, but nothing major. The foothills surrounding Aerie, though, were a different matter. Perched at the top of the hills were row after row of wind turbines. They were strategically placed to capture the wind and turn it into energy, much like the solar farm west of downtown Atlanta. The wind farm here was used almost exclusively for Aerie. The excess power was stored in case any of the turbines failed and could not be repaired. Other regions in the Boise area also had wind turbines or a mix of turbines and solar panels.

Terrance could tell from the way the FBI agents were walking that they did not expect a threat now that they were within Aerie itself and out of the train station. Terrance was certain that the entire area was monitored by extensive audio and visual surveillance, which made it necessary for her group to use caution in what they spoke about or any actions they took that would cause someone at Aerie to notice. She brushed a finger over her thigh and the dagger she had strapped there, whether out of habit or a need for reassurance she wasn't sure. Yolanda was to her right, and the wolves were at her back.

Raising her hand to brush away a strand of hair, she snuck a peek at the piece of paper Agent Florence had pressed into her hand.

Be careful.

She tucked her hair back behind her ears and then shoved her hand in her pocket, depositing the scrap of paper there for disposal later. Obviously Agent Florence was warning her, but it was rather vague. She knew the FBI agent would expect them to already be on the alert for anything amiss, which left her wondering what had prompted Agent Florence to give her the note. The group walked for about ten minutes down the tree-lined street, passing several residences, before coming to a building with a large lawn spread before it. More agents were visible on the perimeter of the lawn, leading Terrance to believe that this must be the meeting place Governor Beechwood had chosen.

The building looked like it had been some sort of community clubhouse at some point, with large bay windows and what seemed to be an open meeting space inside. When they reached the door of the building, the eight agents who had made up their escort peeled off, leaving them with only Agent Florence to guide them inside.

Terrance could hear the distinct clicking of Agent Florence's heels on the ground. Terrance preferred her combat boots. They walked through the doors and stepped into the large room. The back wall had cabinets, a sink, and what might be a stove. The couches had been shoved to the side and a large conference table set in the center with executive-style chairs.

The governor was already seated at the head of the table. Governor Beechwood was an average, unremarkable man. He had short sandy-brown hair and a mustache that was shot with gray, brown eyes, and pale skin, as though he never went outside. He was wearing a dark-green suit with a pale-green button-up shirt underneath.

He gave her a smile that didn't reach his eyes. "I trust your train ride was uneventful?"

Terrance nodded. "Yes, it was fine."

Governor Beechwood made a gesture indicating they should sit. Terrance and Pierre took seats with Yolanda and Sienna standing against the wall, as were several FBI agents. If the choice to have two sitting and two standing ruffled the governor at all, he made no indication.

"Thank you for meeting me today. I am concerned that your possession of the Snowflake has caused a significant number of problems for me. As you know, its existence was discovered about six months ago. Since then, the president has been most keen on obtaining it to protect our country's ability to generate electricity.

"I am sure you are well aware what sort of disruption would be caused if someone within Hellfire and Chaos or another organization decided to use the Snowflake to take control of the electricity available in one or more cities," the governor explained.

"Yes, I am aware of the capabilities the Snowflake has," Terrance said.

The governor tapped his left index finger on the table. "One hundred million dollars is what we agreed upon. A hefty price in a world where it is difficult to spend such a large sum."

Terrance bit her lip to keep from responding. The deal the governor had proposed was ten times the one she had made with Trey. She wasn't sure if the governor was trying to get her to divulge what her plans were with the money or if he truly thought there wasn't anything that HAC could spend one hundred million dollars on. Not that the funds were going to HAC; this was still her private operation. The additional money had made it possible to justify the risk of backing out of the deal with Trey.

"You brought it with you, right?" the governor demanded.

"Of course," replied Terrance smoothly. "But I want to see the money first."

Governor Beechwood motioned with his hand and an agent walked over to Terrance with a black briefcase. He opened it and set it in front of her. "Two million cash, with the other ninety-eight million being wired into the account you provided."

Terrance quickly thumbed through the money, checking the bills and doing a rough count. She was also looking for any sort of booby trap that Beechwood might have decided to put in the briefcase. The case was clean, and the money was all there, as promised.

Terrance tugged on her left earlobe, and Yolanda stepped forward, taking a place beside Terrance and then placing her palm face-up on the table. There was a swirl of dark-purple threads that disappeared, and in their place was a tiny metal snowflake about the size of a thumbnail. Thin lines of black metal wove across the shiny chrome surface.

Terrance kept her eyes trained on Governor Beechwood, looking for any sign that he was going to betray her. Instead, he looked genuinely surprised. "That little thing is the Snowflake?"

"Yes," Terrance confirmed. "Would you like a demonstration to prove it?"

Governor Beechwood gave her a strange look that she couldn't interpret. Terrance gave a short nod of her head. Yolanda brought forth the tools needed to prove that the Snowflake in her hand was indeed *the* Snowflake. There was another swirl of dark purple magic, and an unremarkable computer appeared on the table in front of Yolanda. It was the same as most computers available, just a plain flat piece of glass. Yolanda lifted the Snowflake off her palm and set it on top of the computer. The screen lit up, and words began scrolling over it.

Yolanda raised her now-empty hands and made a few small gestures. Streams of dark-purple magic shot out of her hands. The FBI agents on the wall all reached for their guns; one even drew, aiming at Yolanda. Terrance wanted to roll her eyes. If her plan had been to attack the governor, she would have done so already.

The dark-purple magic formed a large rectangle, which then shimmered and solidified, creating a projection of the computer's screen. Yolanda lowered her hands, and the projection stayed suspended in the air.

An outline of the Snowflake was visible on the screen along with a control panel for the electrical grid tied to Aerie. Slider bars adjusted how much power each wind turbine could generate at any one time along with other, more finite controls required.

"Is that real?" asked the governor.

Terrance raised an eyebrow. "Yes. Let me demonstrate." She stood up and walked to the window at the back of the room, where she had a good view of two of the wind turbines. The governor reluctantly joined her at the window. Both turbines were slowly turning in the moderate breeze that had started since they came inside. "Yolanda, please shut them off."

196

A few moments ticked by, and the two wind turbines ground to a halt.

"You see, it works."

Just then, the governor's phone rang. Terrance could hear a worried voice on the other end but was not quite able to make out all of the words.

The governor rubbed his temple while he listened. "Stay on the line, and give me a moment." He turned his attention to Terrance. "Please turn it back on."

Terrance glanced over her shoulder at Yolanda, who then made some changes to the controls on the computer.

The governor held the phone back up to his ear and a small smile formed on his face as he listened to the person on the end of the phone. "Thank you. Goodbye," he said and stuffed the phone back in his pocket. "It seems as though you are telling the truth. That was just the director of operations at the turbine command center, calling to let me know that those two had randomly shut off, and they were not able to turn them on from their end. Then, when you turned them back on, the problem at the command center resolved."

Terrance let a small sigh escape from her lips. "Good. Then, you will wire the money?"

The governor nodded and walked back over to his seat at the table. "Yes."

When it was clear that the governor was satisfied with the demonstration, Yolanda got rid of the projection of the computer screen. It dissolved in a puff of purple magic. She then did a few more things with the computer before removing the Snowflake from the screen and sliding it into a case. She then put it in front of Terrance and stepped back to her place on the wall next to Sienna.

"The wire?" Terrance prompted.

The governor nodded and snapped his fingers. Instantly, the agents became of flurry of motion, then one stepped forward with another briefcase. The briefcase was set on the table in front of the governor, then opened. A few minutes later, the agent brought the briefcase over to Terrance. Inside was a computer, and it showed her account number and the ninety-eight million as having transferred.

Terrance slid her phone out of her pocket and quickly logged into her account, confirming that the transfer had indeed occurred. "All good on my end," she said before sliding the box with the Snowflake across the table.

The governor clapped his hand on top of the box before it slid off the table. Terrance turned her attention toward her people. It was time to go. They had nothing left to do at Aerie.

Terrance, Pierre, Yolanda, and Sienna were preparing to exit the clubhouse in Aerie. The governor was also preparing to depart. Terrance could see a convoy of vehicles lining up just outside. She wondered where they had been waiting since she hadn't seen them when they arrived. It did not surprise her that the governor was leaving, or at least giving a show of leaving. The exchange had happened, and they could move on with whatever other business each party had to attend to that day.

Terrance pushed open the door and stepped outside. A light wind mussed up her hair, sending small strands across her eyes. She swiped absently at them as she peered around. The agents were still monitoring the perimeter of the clubhouse, but the large escort from their arrival was nowhere to be seen. *Interesting.* She led the way onto the path from the clubhouse to the sidewalk.

The governor exited the building from the opposite side. It wasn't Terrance's concern. Pierre walked by her side with Yolanda and Sienna just behind them. Pierre opened his mouth to say something, but Terrance shook her head.

Behind them came the slam of a car door, followed by a strange, high-pitched whistle. Terrance winced, as did both wolves.

"What's wrong with you?" Yolanda asked as the three shifters stopped walking.

"You can't hear it?" Pierre growled

"No, I just hear the car doors shutting and—" Yolanda's response was cut off when a wisp of gray smoke flew through the air, and moments later, the car at the front of the convoy exploded.

"Rocket launcher!" shouted Yolanda.

Terrance squeezed her eyes shut. The whistle was getting louder and making it harder for her to focus.

"I'm going to shift. Pierre and Sienna, if you need to, then do it. Yolanda, you know what to do. Get us home."

Terrance watched Yolanda for a moment, dark-purple magic streaming from her fingers before Terrance closed her eyes and focused on her tiger form, praying that whatever the sound or attack was would be less of an issue once she was a tiger. She hit the ground with all four paws with a thud. Thankfully, the sound that had been excruciating to her human ears was much less irritating to her tiger ears. There was a brush of fur along her hip, and Pierre came to stand next to her. He was a large brown-and-gray timber wolf with dark-brown eyes. Like most shifters he was larger than a timber wolf found in the wild but smaller than Terrance's tiger.

Terrance started forward with Yolanda at her back and the two shifted wolves on her flanks. Two of the cars were in flames. FBI agents were scattered, some dead, and others seemed disoriented. She wasn't sure where the governor was but trusted Sienna would find him if he was somewhere he could be found.

Motion from behind the glass of the clubhouse had Terrance halting their progress toward the cars. *Maybe the governor withdrew into the building?* she wondered. She could feel eyes watching her from inside the clubhouse, but no one was making a move to come out and attack. Terrance slowly made her way around the perimeter, confirming that the governor and about ten FBI agents were inside.

A howl split the air, and Terrance sprinted toward it as a round of gunfire began. Pierre was fighting with a man in Kevlar armor. Terrance could see small tears in the armor as well as where Pierre's coat glistened with blood. Terrance let out a loud roar and leaped at the man, claws flashing as she sliced through his Kevlar like it was nothing. She landed hard on the pavement and spun, ready to make another pass. Pierre had been ready for her jump, and he was standing on the man's chest, his mouth around his throat. Waiting.

Waiting for my approval, Terrance reminded herself. She flicked her ears and turned away, looking for Sienna.

Terrance heard a sharp scream and then silence behind her as Pierre took the kill. *I might regret not having someone to interrogate later,* she thought, but they still had no idea what was going on, who was attacking, or if it was over.

She approached the smoking cars. The one in the back was the least damaged. Its hood showed some black scorch marks, but it looked as though it might be able to run if they needed it to. Tail swishing, Terrance moved to the second car. Nose to the ground, she almost missed the snick of the trigger. She dodged to the side as bullets peppered the spot she had just occupied. *Idiots.* While she was glad they were terrible shots, she was also surprised. Whoever they were, clearly hitting a target in one shot was not a high priority. In her human form, she made a much smaller target. As a four-hundred-pound tiger, she was harder to miss.

Growling, Terrance sprinted for a house across the street. She didn't have time to worry where the others had ended up or if they were following her. Sooner or later, the shooter would get lucky and hit their target. Her weaving path took her between two houses, where she was able to duck into the shadows of the bushes. Luckily, they were quite large and provided good cover. She belly-crawled around to the front of the house and peered at the scene before her.

Sienna had crawled underneath the third car in the convoy. Terrance winced in sympathy; it had to be a tight squeeze. It would protect the wolf from the shooter as long as they didn't have any more rockets. A light shimmered at the edge of her vision and she could make out the outline of Yolanda at the edge of the clubhouse against the only corner that wasn't glass. Yolanda's magic was obscuring her from the view of anyone who glanced her way. *Anyone without special goggles,* Terrance chided. Just as her closest HAC crew members had been given a magical implant that allowed them to see through most magical talents, others could have the ability as well. It was wickedly expensive, but not impossible.

Terrance absently washed her paw, keeping her eyes open for any sign of movement. After a while, the door to the clubhouse opened. *Now what?* She wondered what the governor was doing. He hadn't sent anyone to find the shooters, which meant they were still out there. There was no way they had just disappeared. It didn't make sense. After the trouble they had gone to get within Aerie's defenses, there had to be a greater plan. *Not my problem.*

"Terrance?" Pierre's voice was light in her mind. Usually, they refrained from speaking mind to mind when shifted because the government had a way of picking up on their conversations, as though they were transmitted on a radio wave.

"Did you find the shooters?" Terrance asked.

"Yes. But you're not going to like it," Pierre replied. Terrance let a small rumble escape from her mouth. More purr than growl. *"There is a large three-story house a few blocks away. They have two snipers. One has the rocket launcher and a huge stack of rockets."*

Terrance flexed her claws. Two snipers would be easy. They just had to get Yolanda close enough, and she could disable the guns.

"There are also blockades on both ends of the road. I can smell explosives, but I didn't want to get too close. I don't know where they are, only that they are there near the blockade."

This time a growl did escape her lips. A whine came from Sienna under the car. *Shit. If they have explosives by the blockades, where else have they set them?* Terrance briefly closed her eyes as she tried to figure out what was the best course of action. She snapped her head up, causing the bush to shake violently, when she heard the clubhouse door open and feet hitting the pavement. Her eyes became huge when she saw the FBI agents huddled around the governor, guns drawn.

"Boss, what do you want to do?" Pierre asked.

"We can't let the Snowflake get taken," Sienna said in a low growl.

"It's no longer our concern," Terrance replied tersely. She had already started extracting herself from the bush. *"I think we can sneak through the neighborhood without being detected."* She knew that Sienna would likely fight her on the decision. The wolf had not agreed with turning the device over to Governor Beechwood. *"Yolanda, provide cover for Pierre and Sienna to move toward the houses."*

Thankfully, Sienna kept silent. A cloud of dark-purple magic fell over Yolanda and the car where Sienna was hiding, obscuring both of them. Terrance watched as Sienna slid out from under the car and then quickly made her way to the house one door down. Yolanda stayed close to the wolf to maintain the magic.

"Stay in the shadows. Conserve your magic if you can, Yolanda," Terrance ordered. The three of them worked their way through the neighborhood, sticking to the shadows between the houses and under the trees.

Up ahead, Terrance could see the barricade of large orange-and-white cones blocking the road to the train station. Staying within the shadows meant that she couldn't see where the snipers were or if there were any others on the tops of additional houses. She knew Yolanda would spot any threats, but Terrance preferred to have a second set of eyes. She blinked. They hadn't expected to come under attack. If they had, then she might have had additional members as overwatch. For the moment, she would have to make do with the people she had brought and hope it would be enough to get them out.

They were hovering in the shadows of the last house before they had to cross the street or find a different route. Terrance sat still, as though she were a statue. Yolanda leaned against the wall, appearing as though she was just relaxing, not preparing to be attacked. Sienna was also sitting, but every so often her ears would twitch, presumably as she strained to hear any tell that an enemy was approaching. Across the way, a flicker of motion caught Terrance's attention. For a brief moment, she caught a glimpse of Pierre on the other side of the street near one of the houses. He seemed unharmed, which meant it was possible to get over to him. Except one wolf was far more likely to go undetected than three bodies moving together.

Terrance debated if it was better to run individually or as a group. Finally, decision made, she bumped Sienna with her shoulder and then ran her rough tongue over Yolanda's hand. *"All of us are going to sprint. I'll head straight across. Yolanda goes to the back corner of the house and Sienna to the front. I want both of you to run as fast as you can. If we're fast enough, then they might not even notice we've run past the barricade until it's too late for them to do anything about it."*

Terrance stood up and shook herself. There was a bush that had dark pink flowers on it. That would be her target. *"One, two ... three!"* As one, the tiger, wolf, and human took off. When Sienna and Yolanda were past the halfway point, Terrance sped up.

Pop! Pop! Pop! Bullets flew. Terrance was already running at top speed. She felt a burning sensation across her back as a bullet grazed her. Hissing and snarling, Terrance finally reached the shadows of the house. Unfortunately, since the shooters knew they were there, they didn't stop shooting. They were just concentrating along one wall. Terrance knew they had to keep moving or they would die.

A hiss rumbled through her as the burning along her back intensified. *"We need to keep moving. Stick to the plan."* The other two nodded in confirmation, and they made their way around to the back side of the house.

They heard a whirring sound coming down the street. Terrance spun, snarling. Her eyes went wide as she saw the car, the last one from the convoy, that the governor had gotten into, barreling down the street at over forty miles per hour, making a beeline for the barricade. She was about to order Yolanda to stop the car, when it exploded. The car flipped end over end past the barricade, triggering more explosions.

Boom! Boom!

The bombs, what Terrance now realized must be IEDs, had to have been chained together. The first explosion and continued movement of the car triggered more. The whole road was rubble. Pieces of pavement scattered everywhere, along with glass, siding from the houses that had been hit, and metal pieces from the car. There was a gasp behind Terrance. She turned and swore at the scene before her. Yolanda had a piece of metal in her forehead. Shards of metal and glass-like shrapnel peppered the rest of her body. Sienna had shifted and was sobbing, holding Yolanda's hand.

Unable to contain her emotions, Terrance shifted too. "What happened?"

Sienna took a raspy breath. "She shielded me and not herself when the car blew up."

Terrance bit her lip hard enough to draw blood. If Yolanda had only shielded one of them, she had to have been almost tapped out from using her magical talent. The mage always put others before herself. It was no surprise that she had shielded Sienna.

"We need to go," Terrance said firmly.

"But … what about Yolanda?" Sienna asked, a whine creeping into her voice.

"She's dead. If we try to carry her body out, there's a good chance we won't make it." Terrance paused. This discussion was wasting time they likely didn't have. She heard a sound approaching. Booted feet. *Shit!* "We're out of time. Let's go now," she ordered harshly. Now was not the time to let emotions get the better of them. Not if they wanted to leave without losing anyone else.

She felt fur under her hand. Pierre had come back to see what was slowing them down. "Stay a wolf. Stay alert, and let's go home," Terrance ordered. Pierre licked her hand and turned, leading the way.

Terrance had drawn her gun and cautiously followed Pierre. Behind them she could hear shouts as orders were given. Pierre led them around more houses and quickly scaled their fences. It was safer than going around the front and being completely exposed, but it slowed them down. Pierre could just leap over most of them, whereas Sienna and Terrance had to jump and then pull themselves over.

The bullet wound on Terrance's back continued to burn. She could feel her shirt clinging to it and knew it was likely going to stick when it was time to remove it. Going over numerous backyard fences was not helping, but she knew if she shifted again, it would be just as cumbersome. One advantage of keeping Pierre in wolf form was that he could smell any hidden explosives before they stumbled upon them, which was why they were not sprinting for the exit.

Behind them, Terrance could hear more orders being shouted and the fuzzy sound of a radio. The voices were coming from much closer than she had expected. They were going to have to fight if they didn't speed up their pace.

There was a scraping sound as shards of stucco sprayed outward from the house in front of them. Whoever was pursuing them had caught up.

"Shit," Sienna muttered. "Turn and fight or run, boss?"

Terrance sighed. Some days she hated being boss. "Run. It's the best shot we've got. If we can make it to the train, then we should be safe."

Sienna nodded, and they took off at a run. Instead of wasting time jumping backyard fences, Terrance led them around to the fronts of the houses. There was enough landscaping that it was better than running in the middle of the street, but not by much.

Pierre kept pace with them easily. For that, Terrance was glad. As soon as they cleared the light-pink house, bullets started flying again. But they weren't coming from behind them. They came from the sides as well. Terrance caught a flash of movement on one of the roofs and rolled. A bullet lodged itself in the grass right where she had been. Instead of running in a straight line, the three of them weaved. They ran through drills regularly for scenarios just like this one. Their paths were works of art; each stayed far enough away from the others so that they weren't making a larger target out of themselves, but the seemingly erratic movements made it very difficult to get a clean shot.

Terrance jumped over a low brick wall and almost fell to her knees when she heard a distinct click. She froze. A worm of terror worked its way through her. She was unfortunately confident that she had just stepped on an IED. If she stepped off it, best case scenario she lost her leg; worst case her life. She ground her teeth at the predicament.

Terrance and Cory had also drilled scenarios like this one into their crews. But unlike taking heavy gunfire, they had never, until today, had anyone step on an IED. Given the events that had already happened that morning, Terrance was not sure if Sienna and Pierre would follow their training or try to rescue her.

"Hello, Terrance," came a cold voice. Terrance snapped out of her thoughts and narrowed her eyes. It was her fellow HAC lieutenant, the vampire Catrina Fox.

Terrance frowned, unsure how to react to Catrina's sudden appearance. Catrina seldom had business in Boise—or the Pacific Northwest, for that matter.

Catrina was wearing a pendant with a large sapphire in it around her neck. Terrance wondered if that was why she seemed to not mind the sunlight. From what Catrina had told Terrance previously, sunlight was uncomfortable to all vampires; some couldn't even tolerate it at all.

"How kind of you to step on the IED," Catrina replied.

Terrance grimaced, thoughts churning. Catrina was acting strange. They were friends, or at least more than acquaintances, so her coldness was unexpected, as was her admitting to setting the IED. No matter what was going on, Terrance didn't harbor ill wishes for Catrina and didn't particularly want to find out how the vampire would handle it if she stepped off the IED and blew them both up.

Catrina must have noticed the shift in her stance. "Go ahead, step off," she challenged Terrance.

Terrance bit her lip and shook her head in refusal. "I don't want to die today, and if I know you at all, Catrina, I know that you don't want to die either."

"That's too bad." Catrina gave her a vicious grin, grabbed her arm, and gave a sharp tug. With nothing to brace against, Terrance let herself stumble forward, unable to fight the pull without moving off the IED. She squeezed her eyes shut, waiting for the blast. *Goodbye.*

Nothing happened. Terrance opened her eyes, confused. Catrina burst out laughing. She gasped, grabbing her sides. "You thought it was real," she sputtered.

"But …" Terrance said softly.

"It's fake," the Catrina said.

"How?" Terrance demanded.

"Just like you can make blank bullets, you can make a fake IED. It depresses just like a real IED, but there's nothing to explode, so when you step off it, nothing happens. Quite a handy device, don't you think?" Catrina said with a smirk.

"How did you know this one was fake? The one the car hit earlier was real," Terrance replied.

"I installed them myself, and I have a map of where they are," Catrina replied. "But enough chitchat. You're coming with me."

Terrance bristled. She wasn't going anywhere with Catrina if she had a say. Not after Catrina had just been cruel enough make Terrance believe she was on a real IED. A cold hand grabbed her, sharp nails digging in to her skin, and pinned her right arm behind her back, giving it a sharp twist. *I guess I don't have a say.* Catrina shoved her forward hard, almost forcing her to her knees.

"Terrance, we will get help!" Pierre's voice came through her mind. Unfortunately, unless she shifted, she could not reply. But they were at least following protocol. She also knew if Catrina wanted her dead, she would be dead. As soon as Terrance had stepped on the IED, fake or not, it made her an easy target for the snipers. But Catrina hadn't given that particular order. Which meant she either wanted something from Terrance or wasn't in control of the snipers. Terrance had turned the Snowflake over to the governor, and she assumed that the numerous explosions had vaporized it. Which meant Catrina had to want her for something else.

The grip on her arm did not let up as Terrance marched across Aerie. They did not go back toward the clubhouse or the train station. Instead, they went up a road that appeared to wind deeper into the compound. The houses they passed got larger and larger, their landscaping more and more elaborate. A few even had large bronze sculptures or fountains in the middle of huge circular driveways. Just like everything else in Aerie, these large residences seemed to be well taken care of. The fountains did not have water in them, the only obvious hint that the houses were likely unoccupied.

At the end of the upward-sloping street, which happened to be a cul-de-sac, was a sprawling mansion. Terrance thought it was likely Craftsman-style. When she was growing up, she had been fascinated by architecture and had made a point of learning about the different styles that could be found around Boise.

The entryway had large wooden columns topped with a truss and black metal hardware. The front door was a medium-colored wood that clearly showed its grain, adding to the character. A woman with blond hair pulled back in a severe bun and solid black body armor opened the door.

Inside, there was an oak floor with wide boards. It looked almost brand new, even though Terrance knew there was no way it could be. No construction had gone on at Aerie since COVID-50. Terrance swept her gaze over the entryway. It opened to a spacious, wide-open room. To the left was an open concept kitchen with a large black granite island. To the right was a great room, at the very end of which was a sizable stone-faced fireplace that appeared to take real wood logs. Flanking the fireplace were floor-to-ceiling windows, revealing the cobblestone patio and intricate landscaping that incorporated large boulders into a small, picturesque waterfall, with the foothills rising behind.

The great room did not have any furniture, which had Terrance wondering what exactly they used this house for. She was marched into the great room. In the time it took her to get from the entryway to the great room, a chair had been procured from somewhere. Catrina let go of her arm and roughly shoved Terrance into the chair. Terrance folded her hands in her lap and waited. She wanted to rub her arm to release some of the tight muscles but didn't want to show any sign of weakness. Part of her hoped Catrina would give her an explanation, but the vampire had disappeared.

After about ten minutes of waiting in silence, the air in front of the fireplace rippled slightly. A large man who had to be at least six foot six appeared. His dark-brown skin was almost black. He had bright red eyes and a thick black beard flecked with gray, and his bald head was covered in tattoos that were almost invisible, but she knew were there. Terrance shuddered. Gone was the black hooded robe he favored. In its place, he wore an immaculately tailored black suit.

Dariusz Sierżęga, vampire and leader of Hellfire and Chaos. It took an iron will to keep Terrance from reacting to his sudden presence. She was one of his lieutenants, although she rarely interacted with him directly. She wondered why he would not have just arranged a normal meeting with her when she belatedly remembered that the last time they had encountered one another had been in Atlanta at the masquerade ball when she had attacked him, and Elyse Hutchinson had gotten away.

Shit. The vampire in front of her was old—she had no idea how old—and he did not forgive or forget, ever. If he was angry with her for what happened in Atlanta, then she likely would never leave this house again. But it still didn't explain why he had gone to all this trouble. Why take her into custody here in Aerie of all places?

Dariusz gave her a cold smile, flashing all of his sharp teeth at her. "I'm sure you're wondering what this is about."

Terrance kept silent, her eyes trained on his shoulder.

"I heard a rumor that you had acquired the Snowflake. The Snowflake has been of interest to me for quite some time, so naturally I wanted to investigate this matter myself," Dariusz explained. "It was no big deal to convince Governor Beechwood to make you an even more enticing offer and set up the meeting here in Aerie." Dariusz took a step toward her. "Your demonstration of how it works was superb."

Terrance kept her face blank.

"What I found most interesting, though, is that the chip that Governor Beechwood had when his car was blown up ... that is not the real Snowflake."

Terrance was not prepared for Dariusz to say the Snowflake was fake. Her whole body tensed. She could feel her arms ripple as fur sprouted and then disappeared. "I don't know what you're talking about."

"Are you sure?" Dariusz replied, circling her chair. He started farther away but was slowly spiraling inward. Terrance had no illusions about what would happen if he stopped.

"Yes, I am sure. I gave Governor Beechwood the real Snowflake. We did not make a copy." Terrance hesitated, then decided that withholding information was useless at this point. "We tried to make a copy but couldn't get it to work. The files would transfer but then corrupt when we tried using them. Whoever made it put in some very complex tech to keep it from being duplicated successfully."

"Well." He pulled a box out of his pocket. Terrance recognized it immediately as the box she had put the Snowflake in before sliding it to Governor Beechwood. "This most definitely does not work."

Terrance wasn't sure what to say. Someone had swapped the Snowflake out after she had given it to Governor Beechwood. Or … Yolanda had swapped it. *That doesn't make any sense. What would Yolanda have to gain by keeping the Snowflake for herself?* Terrance bit her lip. *What wouldn't she have to gain … she could do exactly what I was trying to do, sell it to the highest bidder, or she could even use it.* She closed her eyes in frustration. *How did I miss this betrayal? Yolanda is dead. Can I even confirm that it* was *her and not someone on Governor Beechwood's team pulling the swap?*

"You see the predicament?" Dariusz said in a deep, sensuous voice. "Without knowing when it was swapped, it is impossible to know where to look."

Terrance scuffed her shoe across the floor. "I don't think I've ever heard you say something is impossible. You have infinite resources at your disposal."

Dariusz shrugged. "Not everything is as it seems."

"Then what do you want?" Terrance demanded. "You made quite the show of capturing me. There must have been a reason."

Dariusz stopped circling, and he tilted his head, regarding her. "Whoever stole the Snowflake must not be aware of my involvement."

"Or they are aware, and that's why they did it. To draw you out," Terrance retorted.

"I don't have enemies," Dariusz said firmly.

Terrance looked him over from head to toe in disbelief. "You are the oldest vampire in existence. I struggle to believe that you don't have enemies."

"I don't," Dariusz said and walked away.

I don't believe him. Terrance thought. *Or perhaps he truly believes he has no enemies, and that is why he is blind to whatever manipulation is going on here. Either way, I don't see how I fit into this.*

The chair dug into her back where the bullet had grazed her. Terrance was sure once again that if the intention was to kill her, it would have happened already. With that in mind, she stood up and stretched. No one was in the room with them; no indication that anyone else was even in the house, although she doubted that was the case. But Dariusz was also more than capable of handling himself. If he had wanted to kill her, he would have done it during their last fight at the masquerade ball. Maybe this meeting had been part of his plan all those weeks ago. She shook her head.

Dariusz made no move to indicate that she needed to return to the chair.

When it was obvious the vampire wasn't going to offer more information, Terrance cleared her throat. "What exactly is it that you want from me?"

Dariusz's red eyes bored into her. "I wanted the Snowflake."

Terrance clicked her tongue. "We have established that I am not in possession of it. It was swapped and now is in the wind."

"Yes, and since you were involved in its loss, it is now your responsibility to aid in recovering it," Dariusz replied, stepping toward her.

Terrance stood her ground; she wasn't going to let him intimidate her. "How do you expect me to aid you in recovering it? We have no idea who took it, and why would I want to?"

"I know you would like to see your mate again. I can ensure that you never see each other again. I have a man there now. All it would take is a phone call," Dariusz seethed.

Terrance bristled at the threat. "Fine, you have leverage. But how do you expect me to find the Snowflake?" she said.

"I have video footage," Dariusz said simply, as though she should have known that already.

"Video footage of what?" Terrance asked.

Dariusz tapped his index fingers together. "Aerie has cameras everywhere, and I tapped into their system. Governor Beechwood had tried to shut off the cameras for the meeting, but I ensured they were on and recording. I believe you will just need to carefully review them, and you should find something useful."

"Have you looked at them already?" Terrance asked.

Dariusz chuckled. "When would I have had time to do that? All of this has just happened. There is a computer with all the footage." He waved his hand at the wall and it disappeared, revealing a space with several monitors that were on and replaying the car being hit by the rocket launcher. "I will give you an hour, then I will be back to see what you have discovered."

Terrance sat at the computers, scanning through video footage. She had started with reviewing the footage when they entered the clubhouse. There was a moment when Yolanda had put the Snowflake back in its case that the case itself, at least on the footage, appeared to glow bright purple with Yolanda's talent for a few seconds, then the glow disappeared. It was the only thing off that Terrance could find between the demonstration and handing it over to Governor Beechwood. Though she did not recall seeing a flash of Yolanda's magic, perhaps the cameras had some sort of special filter to pick up on the subtle use of a talent that the naked eye could not see.

She continued to review the footage, looking for anything else that would give her a clue as to what Yolanda had done with the Snowflake, but there was no indication that the shadow mage had handed it off. Terrance watched Yolanda die from various camera angles, her anger bubbling to the surface.

I want to know why Yolanda did this, but that doesn't mean I wanted her to die.

Terrance was about to turn away from the computer screens when a movement caught her attention. She peered at the left corner of the footage. It was ten minutes after Yolanda had died. A figure was standing over her body. Then, the person picked Yolanda up and carried her into one of the houses.

Terrance's eyes widened. "Who was that?"

"Who was what?" Catrina asked from behind Terrance.

Terrance jumped and almost fell out of the chair, annoyed that Catrina had startled her and at her actions earlier with the IED. Terrance stood up and faced the vampire. She could feel herself losing control of her tiger as her teeth began to elongate and fur started to spread over her arms. She inhaled through her nose, trying to calm herself down enough to stop the shift.

"Why are you here, Catrina?" Terrance demanded.

"Dariusz gave me orders and I obeyed, just as you do," Catrina said.

"Did his orders involve being cruel? You could have just waved to me from one of the houses and I would have come," Terrance said, unable to keep the growl out of her voice.

Catrina rolled her eyes. "It must have occurred to you by now that there is more going on than meets the eye. Yolanda switched the real Snowflake for a fake one. We don't know who she is working for other than it's *not* Governor Beechwood. We must continue to proceed with caution. I couldn't just waltz in there and say hey, long time no see! Aerie is a government-operated location. Do you really think anyone would take it as anything less than a declaration of war if they knew Dariusz was here?"

Terrance closed her eyes and took a deep breath. When she opened them, she had returned to being fully human. Catrina had a very valid point, but she also left more questions. "Why is Dariusz setting up shop in Aerie?"

Catrina shrugged. "It was his idea. He thought being here under the nose of the government would be easier to help him stay off the radar of Nightshade Coven and the FBI than if he stayed at your headquarters."

Terrance nodded reluctantly. Everything the vampire was saying was true. She just didn't like being surprised, especially not by Dariusz. "I was watching this video, and I noticed that about ten minutes after Yolanda died, someone came and picked up her body and took it into that house." She pointed to the house on the screen. "Of course, the person was wearing dark clothing and kept their back to the cameras as though they knew exactly where they were. It would probably be worth investigating that house, although I doubt we will find anything useful," Terrance said.

"I will go check myself," Catrina said and then disappeared.

Terrance wrinkled her nose in distaste. She really disliked it when the vampires would just teleport in and out of a room without giving a warning. It was quite unnerving.

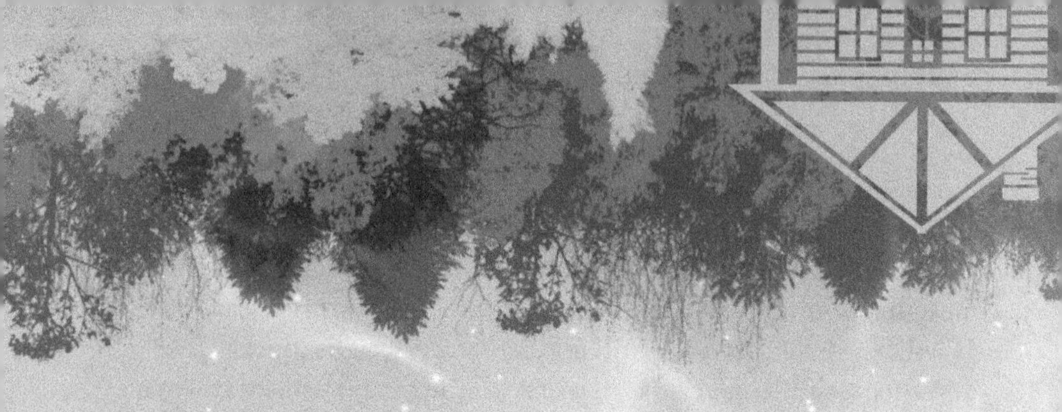

TWENTY-TWO
ELYSE

Elyse opened her eyes. She was lying on a moss-green couch. Ben must have done something that knocked her out because the last thing she remembered was struggling with him on the street just behind the apartment, and now they were most definitely somewhere else.

Elyse gazed at her surroundings. It appeared to be a cabin of sorts. Wide tongue-and-groove pine boards made up the walls and vaulted ceiling. The bits of the floor not covered in rugs were well worn and could be pine, though she wasn't sure since the boards were much narrower. On the center of the back wall was a wood stove and four doors, all shut, leading who knew where. Two windows were covered in forest-green drapes. An assortment of taxidermy—mix of deer and elk—decorated the walls. There was also the head of a brown bear and a full wolf body.

Elyse sat up all the way. She remembered how when they first arrived in Boise, she had wished that Catrina's idea of a safe haven for them was a cabin in the woods. *Well, I'm in a cabin like I wanted. Too bad it's not of my own free will.* The cabin was silent, but she knew that could mean she was the only one there or just that Ben was skilled at moving undetected, either using a magical

216

talent or just skills he had acquired. From discussions with Josh and her own previous experiences being captured, she had learned a few things that she sought to remind herself of. The first was that Ben was going to the trouble of keeping her alive, so he must want her for something. *I just need to figure out what.*

The door in the left corner opened, and Ben came through. He didn't bother to shut it, and behind him she could see what looked like a kitchen.

"You're awake. Good," he said, flashing his unnaturally sharp teeth in a grin that sent a shiver of fear down her spine. "I'm sure you have questions. I will permit you to ask me two."

Elyse was surprised he was allowing her to even ask questions instead of just demanding that she do something. She considered him and the cabin. "Why am I here?"

Ben raised a finger. "That's one. What's your second?"

"Can't you answer the first, then I can decide the second?" Elyse asked, annoyed. She pinched her hand, realizing she probably shouldn't do anything other than what he asked. Otherwise, it could go badly.

"No. My house, my rules. Tell me your two questions, and I will give you two answers. Then it's my turn," Ben said.

Elyse blew out a breath in resignation. "Fine. Question two is, where are we?"

"We are west of Boise, and you are here because I need you to get information for me about COVID-50 and … well, that was two answers," Ben finished—rather lamely, Elyse thought, wondering what he had been about to say. He was being decent to her right now, and Elyse was afraid to provoke him by asking more than two questions. She knew his "west of Boise" answer had been deliberately vague. She wasn't familiar enough with the geography of the area to know if it was common for cabins like this to just be in the western part of the city or if it meant that they were likely closer to the mountains.

Elyse was not surprised he wanted her to get information for him. It seemed like every time she had been captured, both by the Arañas Rojas and by Catrina Fox, that the objective had had something to do with her magical talent or family history. Subjects that Elyse was not an expert on and wasn't sure how what she currently knew would be useful to Ben.

"I want you to help me find the original vaccine that was used for COVID-50. I know that the box of Archibald's journals came with you from Atlanta. You should be able to use them to pinpoint a more specific timeframe, and then with your magical talent gather all the information I require to find it," Ben explained.

"Find the original vaccine? I don't think I understand," Elyse said.

"I am not sure what is confusing. Your talent will allow us to see events that happened in the past, including the last known location of the original vaccine. Then, we can go retrieve it," Ben replied.

"Why do you want the vaccine?" Elyse asked fearfully.

"To cure people of magical talents," Ben said, danger laced in his voice.

Elyse bit the inside of her lip. *Cure people? He says it as though magical talents are a disease. Maybe that is how he views his own, but what would happen if there were no magical talents in the United States anymore?* Elyse shuddered, wondering when she had begun to care about magical talents and why she thought something she hadn't even known existed just over a month ago was important. *I was naïve, and now that I know many of the things that still operate today do so because of magical talents ... the people like me who ranch or farm would manage without magic, but what about those who live in larger cities or are still dependent on electricity and other amenities that magic seems to be holding together? Or the processes that have been established using magic to help make up for the lack of supplies available?*

Ben sneered at her. "I don't care what you think. I did not capture you because I want your opinions. I simply want to use your magical talent."

Elyse sighed. Ben seemed confident she was able to control her magical talent.

"Hopefully I can," she muttered under her breath.

"What was that?" Ben asked, taking a step forward.

Elyse shook her head. "Nothing."

"I want you to start now," Ben ordered.

Elyse pinched her lips together and inhaled through her nose to keep herself from saying anything. He was dangerous, and pushing him would not do her any good. *I need to stay alive long enough for Josh to find me.*

"Here is the journal." Ben tossed her the journal she had been most recently reading—the one dated 2055/2056. "Is there anything else you need?"

"As much detail as you can give me," Elyse replied.

Ben shook his head. "I don't have more details. That's why I need you. If I had them, I would have just killed you."

Elyse ran her index finger over the edge of the journal. "I will do my best to get the information you are looking for."

"Good," Ben said, and took up a position leaning against the door frame and staring at her.

Elyse forced herself not to react. She needed to relax to get her talent to help her find the information he sought. The good thing was that finding information about the past was proving to be far more reliable than trying to see the future. Hopefully, that would work in her favor.

Elyse looked at Ben, then decided that she didn't need to worry about what he was doing and concentrated on what she must do to focus. She stood up and began a series of stretches. By the third set, she could finally feel her muscles starting to loosen up, but she did not stop. Instead, she went through her whole routine, which took about fifteen minutes. It was impossible to tell if Ben was annoyed at the delay or not because he didn't do anything other than watch.

When Elyse was done with the stretches, journal in hand, she walked around the room examining each chair and couch. A threadbare stuffed rocking chair looked promising. She sat down and was relieved to discover that her assumption had been correct; it was quite comfortable. Elyse closed her eyes and started taking deep breaths, counting to ten and letting them out. Slowly she sank into herself and found her talent. *Where is the COVID-50 vaccine from 2056?* Elyse could feel her arms and legs tingle as her magical talent started to spread through her body.

When she opened her eyes again, she was still in the cabin, but Ben was no longer in the doorway. As she gazed around, Elyse noticed that the three doors that had been closed were now open, the window curtains were pushed back, and sunlight was streaming inside. I guess this is a vision of the cabin. How strange.

Elyse stood up and started walking around. As she inspected the room, she noticed more differences. There were fewer animal heads on the wall; the bear was gone, as was the wolf. A yellow knit blanket was draped over the back of the couch. Out of the corner of her eye, she could see a flurry of movement.

Two people burst through the doorway from the kitchen. Elyse immediately recognized Dr. Basak, but the man was an unknown to her. He had a short stature, but she could see the hint of muscles rippling under his black-and-red plaid flannel shirt. He had gold-colored eyes, auburn hair, and a beard.

"You should destroy that while you have the chance!" the man shouted.

> *Dr. Basak took more steps back, hands up, fists slightly curled, as though she might throw a punch. "Don't you want a cure?"*
>
> *The man snarled. Elyse swore it sounded more animal than human. "Just because you think what happened is an abomination doesn't mean everyone feels the same way."*
>
> *"But everything can go back to normal," Dr. Basak protested.*
>
> *The man laughed harshly, "Nothing will go back to normal. You can't bring back the dead, Cecilia."*
>
> *When Dr. Basak didn't reply, the man kept talking. "How do you know it will work? Don't tell me you tested it on mice and are sure. Humans are not mice. I've read your notes that you thought were hidden, about how the virus and vaccine react differently with different types of blood. What if it doesn't cure someone who has been changed? What if it causes more problems?"*
>
> *"It won't!" protested Dr. Basak.*
>
> *"You are forbidden to use it on me or on my daughter," the man snarled. Just then a dog burst through the door. It took Elyse a moment to realize it wasn't a dog. It was a tiger cub. It ran in circles through their legs and then rolled around, chasing its own tail. Elyse could have sworn she heard it purring too.*

The room grew hazy, and Ben reappeared, though he was closer to her now, looking almost worried.

"What did you see? Does it normally take almost an hour?" Ben demanded.

Elyse blinked a few times, trying to settle her mind back into her body. "The amount of time it can take really varies. That is something I do not have control over." She paused, "As for what I saw ... I was in this cabin ..." Elyse launched into a summarized version of the vision.

"You have confirmed that the vaccine was also used as a cure for those who already had magical talents," Ben said, a pleased smile on his face. "The next thing I need you to determine is where it was kept."

"Dr. Basak lived here in Boise. Is your assumption that the vaccine was stored in Boise?" Elyse asked. She knew that the journal entries she had read had mentioned that further development of the vaccine would be relocated to Atlanta and the much larger lab there. Yet in the vision she just had, it was obvious Dr. Basak had continued some of her work locally.

"Yes, focus on Boise," Ben said, then moved back toward the kitchen doorway. "I will prepare a meal for you while you see what else you can find out."

Elyse was surprised but didn't want to annoy him, so she schooled her face into a neutral expression instead. "Food would be much appreciated," she said, then settled herself back onto the couch.

Elyse shut her eyes and focused on the task. *Vaccine cure in Boise.* She felt a slight tug as her talent began to engage.

Elyse opened her eyes and discovered she was in Dr. Basak's lab building. It would make sense that I would find the vaccine cure in a lab, *she reminded herself. She walked down the hallway and pushed open the door into the lab itself. It was empty. The lights had been turned off; only the soft glow from the refrigerators and other equipment provided just enough light to not run into things.*

She walked over to the row of refrigerators, assuming that a vaccine would need to be kept cold or at least climate controlled to have a prolonged shelf life. The inside was dark, making it difficult for her to deduce any details through the glass door other than there were row after row of vials. Elyse reached for the door handle, but her hand just passed through. Frustration bubbled up. How am I supposed to accomplish my task if I can't even see things properly?

She paced, trying to figure out how to solve her dilemma. I wonder if I can use my talent to influence the vision. *She took a deep breath, focusing on wanting to turn the lights on in the refrigerators. Nothing happened. Elyse sighed and walked away, hunting for something else that could be useful to her in the lab. She needed to bring Ben new information or he was going to get mad.*

After making an entire circuit of the lab and coming up empty-handed, Elyse stopped in front of the row of refrigerators again. To her surprise, the lights were now on in them. The shelves were filled with racks of vials. Each vial appeared to have a code on its lid that was tied to the code on the label at the front of each rack. Several labels started with C50. Elyse figured it was too much of a coincidence to be anything other than COVID-50 related. But none of the racks were labeled with anything to tell her what they were without knowing the codes. There must be a list of the codes somewhere in here. I can't imagine Dr. Basak had it all memorized or that Evermore Genetics would permit her to not have a written list of what the codes meant.

Elyse passed a desk with a nameplate sitting in the corner designating it as belonging to Dr. Basak. She figured that was as good a place as any to start looking for the list. She sat in the desk chair and riffled through the papers. For whatever reason, she could now physically move the papers, even though she couldn't open the refrigerator door earlier. She knew from Josh that talents did not always follow logic when it came to what one could and couldn't do.

She flipped through the papers on the desk, but they all seemed to be related to other things. Next, she checked the desk drawers, which had file folders alphabetically labeled by project. She came across one labeled COVID-50. Her talent appeared willing to allow her to interact with the objects in this vision and she slid the file out of the drawer and opened it on the desk.

The first sheet on top appeared to be an inventory list.

Fridge #1
C50-1A to Z
C50-5A to Z
C50-66B to M
Fridge #2
C50-AA100 to CC150
C50-IV40A to IV50Z

Elyse flipped through the pages till she found the first set of vials, C50-1A. Much to her excitement, at the top of the page was COVID-50 Vaccine 1A. A few lines down and the notes began: "First successful vaccine on mice. The vaccine suppressed COVID-50 and one percent of mice relapsed."

There were pages of notes on this first successful vaccine. Elyse had to skim her way through several of them until she found something useful. It seemed as though once Dr. Basak handed off the vaccine to Archibald for more in-depth research, she had still continued to experiment with it in mice and other small animals. Unfortunately, most of the experiments mentioned in the notes were referred to by codes. Which meant Elyse would have to find a list explaining what those meant.

She began riffling through the papers again when every-thing faded out.

Elyse growled under her throat as the cabin came back into focus. She had learned that the original vaccine was labeled C50-1A and was in the lab on whatever day her talent had taken her to. Whether or not it had stayed there, Elyse had no way of knowing.

Not without trying to narrow down the search in more visions with her talent.

"Did you learn anything new?" Ben demanded when he entered the room. She could smell something cooking in the kitchen that made her mouth water.

"I believe the original vaccine that you seek is also being called C50-1A," Elyse announced.

Ben smiled. "Good. Now, dinner is ready. Let's eat."

Ben departed immediately after they finished eating dinner, leaving Elyse to clean up the mess in the kitchen. He had mumbled something about investigating C50-1A and then left, slamming the door behind him. When his footsteps could not be heard, Elyse checked the door, but it was locked. Since he hadn't told her when he would be back, she was reluctant to let her guard down too much. After cleaning up the kitchen, she explored the cabin, making note of the bedroom he had given her with its bathroom and another door. She assumed it was to the bedroom he was staying in. She stared at the front door for a few minutes, wondering if he was going to come through it. When she was satisfied that Ben was not likely to randomly open the door and appear, she made a beeline for the door of his bedroom.

Elyse placed her hand on the doorknob and turned it. She was not expecting it to open. *I guess he forgot to lock it.* She cautiously pushed it open and turned on the light. There was a double bed, small chest of drawers, and a desk. On the desk was a large manila envelope with some papers sticking out of the top of it. Letting her curiosity get the better of her, Elyse walked over to the desk and pulled the papers out of the envelope.

Elyse was shocked to see it was on the letterhead of the president of the United States. Her mouth suddenly dry, she read the letter.

Mr. Piro,

While I find your argument about magical talents being dangerous insightful, I do not share your opinion that the government should endeavor to eradicate magical talents from the country.

Should a cure for COVID-50–generated magical talents exist, I would be interested in any information that you would be willing to share on the matter. Please do understand that I would need to verify that it is a legitimate discovery before a meeting can take place.

Thank you for reaching out, and do not hesitate to do so again.

Sincerely,
President Bradley Seagraves III

Elyse let go of the letter and it fluttered onto the desk. *Ben wrote to the president of the United States* and *got a reply from the president himself!* Her mind was spinning like crazy. She started to put the papers back into the envelope when the one at the bottom caught her eye.

Criteria to become president:

No magical talent
Never served time in a prison
Four years of military or bachelor's degree
Two years in a leadership position

The list had lots of smudges on it, as though it had been read many times over the years. It had no date, so she had no idea when it had been printed, but it looked like it was not recent. Worried that Ben would come back and catch her in his room, she finished replacing the papers in the envelope and retreated to the living room, making sure to shut the light off and close the door behind her.

Elyse sat on the couch and closed her eyes.

Ben, in his ten-year-old boy form, was sitting at a table looking out of a window at a huge wall. Elyse sat across from him. On the other side of the wall, Elyse could see the barest glimmer of water. Eyes wide, she realized that this was Ben somewhere in Manhattan.

Ben's face was red and blotched with anger. She could see steam starting to rise off of him. On the table was a letter. She recognized the letterhead for the president of the United States immediately and stood up, walking around the table so she could read the letter.

Mr. Piro,

President Seagraves has reviewed your request for a meeting to discuss removing the wall around Manhattan, but at this time he does not have room in his schedule to meet. He recommends that you reach out to your state representative.

Sincerely,
Secretary of State Valerie Merk

Elyse backed away from Ben as fire broke out along his body and claws elongated at the ends of his fingers. She knew this was just a vision, but she could feel the heat radiating from him.

Elyse gasped and opened her eyes. She was sitting on the couch in the dark. Ben had reached out to the president not once, but twice. *Maybe even more.* She knew some people would dream of meeting or becoming the president of the United States, but for her it had never sounded appealing. Apparently, it was an interest of Ben's, but Elyse wasn't sure how that factored into everything going on. *What does the president have to do with a cure for magical talents?*

Elyse paced the cabin. Ben had been gone almost twenty-four hours. She was on edge from waiting for so long. The cabin, much like the safe house apartment, had a fully stocked kitchen. Elyse's concern was more with Ben showing up unexpectedly and how she was going to escape.

Her gaze fell on Archibald's journal. She hadn't needed the journal to be able to lock on to the information Ben needed with her talent. But perhaps the journal had more information. Something that would be useful to her or Josh in the future.

The future … Elyse blew out a breath and picked up the journal. A few weeks ago, when Catrina had been teaching her the ropes of how to use her talent, the vampire had assumed it was only the ability to see the future. However, it turned out that Elyse could use her talent to see the past and the future. Unfortunately, the more people who knew, the larger the target it painted on her back.

She flipped through to about halfway through the journal and began reading.

October 6, 2056

The first COVID-50 vaccine is now being mass produced, and the first wave of people are being vaccinated. My neighbors and coworkers have all been vaccinated or have appointments to do so. But we are meeting resistance. Many people, especially those who are not working for the government, are refusing to use the vaccine.

No matter what I tell my mom, she flat-out refuses to be vaccinated. Since she now has full custody of the kids, she refuses to have them vaccinated too. We got into a big argument, and I said some things I shouldn't have. Hopefully one day she will forgive me.

October 31, 2056

Rumors have been circulating more frequently about possible occurrences of magic. I can't believe how stupid people are sometimes. Magic doesn't exist. Science does, and it is not difficult to learn how to manipulate light and sound to make it seem as though you are performing magic when it's just an intricate illusion.

One of my coworkers recently came back from Boise and swears that Dr. Basak has a pet tiger. Dr. Basak may be a little eccentric at times, but why would she have a pet tiger? In our few encounters, she didn't come across as someone who would do something that outlandish. I know there used to be these pop-up "zoos," illegally acquired wild animals that were treated like pets. But I thought after COVID-50 happened that most of them had been wiped out.

Elyse paused her reading. *Dr. Basak had a pet tiger?* That didn't sound right. Then, she remembered in her vision of Dr. Basak in this very cabin, there had been a young tiger. Elyse frowned. *Terrance is a tiger shifter; maybe the tiger isn't a pet, but it's just a young shifter.* Elyse debated if she should go back to reading the journal. Taking a deep breath, she stood up and set the journal face-down, open to the page she'd just been on.

Slowly, Elyse walked around the cabin. This was not the first time she had done this, but now she was looking for a hint that Dr. Basak had had a guest tiger shifter. Or something hidden she had missed before. Elyse followed the wall, running her hands over it, lifting objects one by one off the shelves as she came across them.

She hesitated at the first taxidermy elk. It was at about waist height. She knew it was dead, but the eyes creeped her out. They were the only objects she hadn't checked. Carefully, Elyse set her hands on either side of it and lifted. It slowly came off the hook it was attached to. She gently set it down on the floor and examined the space it had covered. Nothing was there, so she put it back and moved on to the next one.

Elyse rocked back on her heels, peering up at the bear's head. It was the last one she had to check, and she was nervous. It looked scary with its mouth open, teeth bared. It also was high on the wall. She was afraid it would fall on top of her if she didn't get something to stand on. She went to the kitchen and returned with a two-step ladder.

Swallowing hard and reminding herself the bear was dead and couldn't do anything to her, Elyse climbed the stool. The bear was even more intimidating face-to-face. She shuddered and set her hands on both sides of it, just as she had with the others, then lifted. It wouldn't budge.

She tried again but nothing happened. Sticking the tip of her tongue out of her mouth as she pondered what to do, she decided to run her hands around the edge and see if maybe it was stuck on something. The odd thing was that there was no edge. It just went into the wall. *That's not possible.* She ran her hands around it again, but there really was no edge. Then she tried lifting, which still didn't work. *Down?* she mused, not sure what other direction would make sense.

Hands on both sides, she pulled downward. There was a *whoosh*, and the bear head and the wall it was attached to swung away from her. Elyse threw her hands out, bracing on the wall to keep herself from toppling over the ladder. Once she was stable, she climbed back down and moved it out of the way, peering into the space beyond the secret door. She couldn't see much of anything.

Elyse recalled seeing a flashlight in one of the kitchen cabinets. She grabbed the flashlight, confirming that it worked, and then headed back to the door. *I should use the ladder to prop open the door.* Elyse shoved the ladder against the door and positioned it so hopefully if the door did start to swing shut, the ladder would prevent it from closing all the way.

Flashlight on, she walked past the secret door with the bear's head and into the hallway beyond. The hallway was short—maybe four or five feet—before it opened into a small room that felt almost like a closet. There was a desk and a tall filing cabinet, and shelves covered the wall space. The shelves were filled with a variety of things. The one directly above the desk had a feline skull about the size of a basketball.

"Not a house cat," Elyse said, startling herself. She hadn't intended to speak out loud. There was also a small model human skeleton as well as one of what Elyse surmised was a bobcat.

Her eyes dropped to the desk. There was a faded photo of Dr. Basak, the man that Elyse had seen in her vision, and a petite girl with long dark hair and golden eyes who was strangely familiar, though she couldn't place why The girl was between the two adults. A second photo showed the same man crouched next to a juvenile tiger; his arm thrown over the tiger's shoulders. *It is a tiger shifter.* Elyse smiled, feeling confident about her discovery.

She eagerly flipped over both frames and slid off the brads holding the back in place. She gently lifted the board with the stand off, revealing the back of the photos. Sure enough there was faded writing on both. Elyse held her flashlight close, trying to make sense of the script.

She thought the one with the three of them said "Cecelia, Jordan, and Terrance 2056," and then the one with the man and the tiger said "Jordan and Terrance 2065."

I know a Terrance who is a tiger shifter, but there's no way Terrance is almost seventy, is there? Her thoughts drifted back to the conversation a few days ago she had had with Terrance at HAC headquarters, when she had told Elyse that she had been married to Cory for thirty years and was older than she looked.

A wave of guilt hit her. Assuming it was the Terrance Basak she knew in the photo, then she was prying into a friend's family history. Elyse respected Terrance, and this felt like a violation of their friendship to be digging into the past without her say-so. Especially since she was here in this cabin, Terrance's family's cabin, at the behest of their enemy.

But what happens if I don't give Ben the information he needs? What if I am no longer useful? Would Terrance really be angry at me for only doing what is necessary to get out of a scary situation? Elyse wrung her hands. Her chest felt tight, and she didn't like the situation Ben had put her in. Her thoughts drifted to Josh. *What would Josh tell me if he were here?* She closed her eyes and took a few controlled breaths.

"If Josh were here, he would tell me to 'do what is necessary to get out of here and assume no help is coming,'" she said softly in a deeper voice, trying to mimic how Josh would sound. She giggled, knowing full well she sounded nothing like Josh.

A harsh chuckle came from behind her. Elyse spun, fists up.

"Josh would have been right that no help is coming," Ben said sharply. "You cannot escape. If you really want to test out the wards I have in place, you can try, but you'll regret it."

Elyse stayed silent. She had already tested the wards and found out, as Ben had said, that they hurt. She had blacked out for a few moments when she had managed to get the door to the porch unlocked. But she had been hoping that she could find a gap somewhere, like this secret room. Though as she looked around it, she realized there were no windows or other exits, just the door she had come in through, with the bear's head.

Ben started to head out of the room, then he half-turned and looked back at her. "The lab was a no-go. There is no C50-1A there." He turned away and walked out.

Elyse's mouth hung open, and she snapped it shut. *He had thought it would still be in the lab?* She shook her head. The chances that a viable sample of the C50-1A vaccine was in an Evermore Genetics lab in her opinion was almost zero. From what she knew—knowledge passed onto her by her Uncle Albert—unless samples were used in an ongoing project, they were only kept for one year before they were safely disposed of. Many had shelf lives significantly shorter than that.

Elyse ran a hand through her hair, debating what to do. Ben was back, and he hadn't said anything other than he had been unsuccessful. She assumed that meant she should just continue investigating the room and whatever else was necessary to acquire the information he needed.

She pulled out the desk chair and sat in it, wanting the same view Dr. Basak must have had when she was in the room. *Where would I store extra lab notes?* Lips pursed, Elyse studied the desk. It had a long, narrow drawer in the middle just above her legs and then two on either side of the chair. Scooting the chair back so she had enough space, she decided to start with the middle drawer.

She opened it, and a cloud of dust came billowing out. Sneezing, Elyse waved her hand through the air, trying to clear it. When the dust dispersed, she gazed into the drawer. Neatly arranged were an assortment of pens, pencils, a small notepad, paper clips, and even a stapler. She shut the drawer, and the motion released another cloud of dust.

"Achoo!"

Elyse wrinkled her nose, trying to prevent another sneeze. She reached for the top drawer on her left. It stuck, so she tugged harder, and it slowly came toward her. Inside was what looked like a portable safe. She reached in and pulled it out, setting it in the middle of the desk. The safe was black and about twelve inches square. The metal was icy-cold to touch, which seemed odd given the room was not cold. There was a keypad on the front. Elyse tugged on the lid, but as she had expected, it was locked. *Now I must find the code.*

Elyse returned her attention to the now-empty drawer, double-checking she hadn't missed anything before sliding it shut and moving to the drawer below it. This one had a few unopened but rather yellowed reams of paper. She turned her attention to the drawers on the right. The top one had a stack of drawings. She pulled them out and set them on top of the safe and perused them. The drawings were good; all of them contained animals, though the species varied. They were all appropriately proportioned. At the bottom of each was a very clear printed "Terrance." Her eyebrow arched. *Terrance can draw? She must have had some very good books to copy them from.*

When Elyse got to the end of stack, she picked it up and a photo of a group of grinning teenagers slid out. There were ten of them. Elyse gasped when she realized there were ten drawings. *Are these all shifters?* She stared at the photo, but it was hard to see any distinct features with just a flashlight. She put the photo on top of the safe and returned the drawings to the drawer, then checked the last desk drawer. It had a pile of composition notebooks. She diligently checked each one, confirming that they were all empty. But their presence led her to believe that it was possible there were notebooks that had information in them somewhere else. She just had to find them.

The filing cabinet looked promising. Elyse started at the top and worked her way down. The first drawer had hanging files neatly labeled by project. Unlike the ones in the lab, these had actual names. She flipped through them and found one labeled COVID-50. She pulled that one out and then shut the drawer. The remaining drawers had more hanging files and continued to be in alphabetical order. She did not find the composition notebooks.

Elyse yawned and stretched. She wasn't sure how long she'd been in here, but she at least wanted a glass of water. She set the file folder on top of the safe and the photo, then tucked the flashlight under her arm and picked up the safe. It was heavy. She had to adjust her grip and was surprised to feel a piece of paper taped to the bottom.

She made her way out of the room and walked into the kitchen. Ben was cooking something and turned in surprise when he saw her and the safe. "What's that?"

"A safe. It was in one of the drawers. There's something taped to the bottom," Elyse explained and set the safe down on the kitchen table. She set the folder and photo on the table and then tipped the safe onto its side. Sure enough, a piece of pink paper was taped to the bottom.

"Can you hand me a knife?" Elyse asked, expecting Ben to object since she could use it as a weapon.

He handed her a paring knife, and she used it to cut through the strips of tape holding the paper to the bottom. The paper floated to the table, and she set down the knife. Ben quickly snatched the knife out of her reach. Elyse shrugged and looked at the paper.

5842

"It might be the code for the safe," she said out loud since Ben hadn't come back over.

"Try it out," Ben suggested from his position at the stove.

Elyse settled the safe in an upright position and entered the four numbers into the keypad. She could hear the gears turning and then a click, and the lid popped open. Cold fog, or something that seemed like fog, poured out. She hastily shut the lid again. Her fingers tingled from the cold.

"What was that?" she asked Ben.

He had come over, spatula in hand. "I don't know. Was it cold?" Elyse nodded. "Yes."

"It could have been spelled to stay cold. Enhancing a cold pack or dry ice or something like that, allowing it to last longer than normal to preserve whatever is inside," Ben explained.

"Do you want me to open it and stick my hand in there? Or should we take precautions?" Elyse asked.

"I wouldn't stick your hand in there. Unless you don't mind losing it," Ben replied in a monotone.

Elyse gave him a dry look. "Then what would you suggest?"

"Tongs. There are some long ones over here." Ben walked away and reappeared with long tongs, like those Elyse had used on a grill. "This should give you enough room."

"What if what I pull out needs to stay cold?" Elyse asked.

"I will grab a bowl of ice," Ben replied and walked away again continuing to speak. "Then you can set the object on the ice, and hopefully if it does need to remain temperature controlled, that will buy us enough time to identify it at least."

"I like that plan," Elyse said.

As soon as Ben set the bowl of ice down next to the safe, Elyse re-entered the code and opened the lid again. She stuck the long tongs inside, being sure to not allow her hand to slide down the tongs and get touched by the fog coming out of the safe.

She felt the tongs scrape along something. It was tricky to grab an object when she couldn't see it, but she finally managed to grab it long enough to withdraw it completely from the safe. She gently placed what seemed to be a large vial in the bowl of ice. Then, she used the tongs to check if there was anything else. Sure enough, there were two more vials. She made sure to verify the rest of the safe was empty before shutting it and inspecting the contents of the bowl.

The vials were labeled in what she recognized as Dr. Basak's handwriting.

C50-1A, C50-66F, C50-IV42Z

Elyse blinked a few times, then rechecked the labels. "Those were on the list in my last vision. When I was in the lab."

Ben was grinning. "See, you did it. You helped me find a sample of the original vaccine. Now let's put these back in the safe." Instead of letting Elyse do it, Ben slid the safe over and opened it, then using his hands, not the tongs, he placed all three vials back into the safe and shut it.

"You got what you wanted. Let me go," Elyse said, trying to keep the pleading out of her voice.

Ben clicked his tongue. "It doesn't work like that. Yes, I have what I wanted from you. But I am not just going to let you walk out of here. No ... I will let you go when I am ready."

"Which will be when?" Elyse demanded, temper flaring.

"Whenever I say I am ready. Nothing you can do will change that. Now let's eat, and then I must go. I have work to do," Ben said.

They ate dinner in silence, and then Ben departed again.

TWENTY-THREE
TERRANCE

Terrance was still working directly with Dariusz in the house he had set up at Aerie. He refused to let her reach out to Cory to let him know she was fine. She knew how much her mate would worry. Hopefully, he could feel through their bond that she was not in danger and would not launch any sort of rescue attempt. She knew such an attempt would only piss off Dariusz, who for the moment was being rather amenable with her. He had drained three of the agents he had hired for protection because of their failure to obey even the simplest of orders. Though she had to admit she wasn't sure if he did it because he had needed to feed or because he was tired of listening to their lame excuses.

Either way, she didn't really blame him. She quickly threw anyone who showed signs of being that incompetent out of her HAC division.

Terrance scanned the two computer screens again. Dariusz was adamant that no one was alive from his past who would hold a grudge. She still felt as though that was a very plausible explanation for why someone would have taken the Snowflake from under the governor's nose.

Dariusz had ordered her to liaise with the government's office and make sure they were aware this was not a declaration of war from HAC on the Idaho or United States government, though it could be a good attempt at encouraging the two organizations to go after each other. She had to admit it would be a brilliant cover for anything else that was going on. Especially since it was well known that HAC did not think fondly of the current United States government. She could not recall a time when HAC had ever had a good opinion of the political leaders of the country.

The screen on the left had several photos of possible suspects. Even though Dariusz had protested vehemently, she chose to leave Willow Kelly's and Artur Hagi's photos up. She didn't care what Dariusz thought. Unless he did some sort of mind control shit on her, she was not going to remove them from the list. It felt like giving up too easily.

All told, they had six suspects, including her two. None of them, at least with the information she had, were very convincing. Willow likely had the most to gain since she was head of a large vampire coven and was not under the umbrella of HAC. Getting her hands on the Snowflake would be a pretty big statement and demonstrate to everyone that Nightshade Coven was a power to reckon with. Terrance felt her lip curling in distaste. As far as she knew, Nightshade Coven only had a foothold in Idaho and was not large enough of an organization to expand into nearby states. Unless there was a reason that Willow wanted leverage against the US government.

Heavy knocking on the front door disrupted her thoughts. Terrance started to walk toward the door when Dariusz appeared from who knew where and opened the door ahead of her. She was surprised when Pierre entered—surprised that Dariusz allowed him to come in and that her third-in-command had somehow figured out where she was.

She walked forward smiling. "Pierre, so good to see you." She brushed past Dariusz and gave Pierre a hug. She was not the hugging type. She was more likely to bite someone who tried, so she knew that Pierre would figure out that it was her way of showing him she was okay.

"It's good to see you … alive," he said in a rough almost-growl.

Dariusz hissed. "Terrance is my guest. I have no reason to kill her."

Pierre pulled out of her embrace and crossed his arms. "You don't usually need a reason to kill members of HAC. I have seen many die at your hand. Excuse me if I refuse to believe that you have suddenly decided you value Terrance enough to treat her with the respect she deserves for what she has accomplished as one of your lieutenants."

Terrance bit her tongue to keep from laughing. Dariusz looked appalled that Pierre had spoken to him but unsure of how to react. Terrance relished seeing him in this rare situation. But it also proved to her that he was not lying when he said he wanted her help. Otherwise, Pierre would have been dead for the way he had just spoken.

Unable to completely hide her amusement, Terrance stepped closer to Dariusz. "I am fine, Pierre. All in one piece. Dariusz even feeds me three meals a day."

Terrance could tell Pierre was still not convinced, but to her relief, he did not pursue the subject. "How did you find us?" she asked, knowing that Dariusz was wondering as well, unless he had just plucked the information from Pierre's head.

"I realized we had lost you before we hit the train station, but Sienna felt we should keep going and return later, once we had touched based with Cory on everything that happened. He was able to acquire satellite surveillance of Aerie, and it wasn't too difficult to figure out, once it came in, that something was going on in this house," Pierre explained.

Terrance nodded. His explanation made sense, and she assumed they hadn't come in guns blazing only because Cory had not sensed any distress from her. She was certain that Pierre had him on comms or something so that a squad on standby would move in if he gave the signal.

"Now that we've established that you are alive and well, can you tell me what exactly you're doing with Dariusz?" Pierre demanded.

"Trying to figure out who stole the Snowflake," Terrance replied.

Pierre gave her a toothy grin. "I can help with that."

Terrance raised her eyebrow. "You can?" She walked over to the sink and filled a glass of water, and took a sip.

"Yep. Ben Piro," Pierre replied with a smirk.

Terrance gasped and sprayed her mouthful of water everywhere, coughing and throwing out cuss words left and right. "What. The. Hell!"

Dariusz looked unnerved too, which bothered Terrance more. It took a lot to unsettle the ancient vampire and didn't bode well for those around him. "Last I checked he was at Darkwater Penitentiary," Dariusz commented.

"He's definitely not there anymore," Pierre said confidently.

"Who is he working with?" Terrance asked, mind churning with the new information. Ben Piro hadn't been on their list.

"We don't know yet. We have a list of potential people and groups but are still filtering through information. If Yolanda were still with us, it would go faster, but you're stuck with Sienna and Cory doing all the tech stuff," Pierre said.

"We were working on a list of suspects. Why don't I show you who we have on our list, and you can tell me if any of them are also on yours? It would be a good place to start," Terrance said.

Dariusz cleared his throat. "A moment before you get lost in research. Pierre, you need to tell your team to back off and return to your headquarters. I will permit you to come and go as you please if Terrance does not leave, but I do not appreciate the entire team lurking. They are bound to make a mistake, and if they do, well…" he said, studying his long claws, "I might have to reciprocate."

Pierre gulped. Terrance rolled her eyes. Dariusz was usually more subtle when making his threats, for she had no doubt it was a threat. "Go ahead and call the team off, Pierre. No need to stir up more trouble when we are close to figuring out this mess."

Pierre gave her a curt nod and walked a few paces away, hand touching his ear as he relayed the message to his team.

Dariusz stared at her. Taking a deep breath, she caught his eyes directly. "What's on your mind?"

"Why would Ben be involved in this?" Dariusz replied.

"How do you know Ben?" Terrance asked. She knew of Ben because she had looked up Josh, and it had come up in his FBI and personnel file, but she had never met him herself.

"I occasionally visit Darkwater Penitentiary. Given that's where the FBI stashes all their difficult-to-control talented, it is a good place to find recruits for HAC," Dariusz said.

Terrance's eyes narrowed. "The FBI put them there because they couldn't be recruited. Do I even want to know what you do to convince those people that they should join HAC?"

"Probably not," Dariusz admitted.

"How do you manage to keep control over them once they are free?" Terrance asked.

"When I make my offer, which I do compel them to take, the offer is made with the intention of keeping them interested in HAC. Some want money; others want a home to call their own. Things that are easy for me to give them," he explained.

"I am sure some of them have tried to betray you," Terrance said.

"Of course." Dariusz smiled. "It wouldn't be any fun if they all obeyed without question."

Terrance shuddered. Dariusz had recruited her when she was twenty. She had been angry with her Aunt Cecelia and had agreed to join HAC to get back at her, not knowing at the time that once in, it was very difficult, if not impossible, to get out. That was over fifty years ago. Over the years, she had witnessed what Dariusz did to people who crossed him many times.

"Ben ..." she prompted.

"Yes, Ben. When we met the first time, he sensed my presence before I had wanted to be known. His talent is significantly different than any that I have encountered before, and I am still unsure why it is so different. He can shift like you do, but when he does, his panther form shares a lot of properties with a volcano. I came across someone in Italy once who had a talent similar to a volcano, but from my experience shifters typically don't have another talent," Dariusz explained.

"A volcano? That seems far-fetched," Pierre said.

Dariusz shrugged. "You live in world where magical talents suddenly manifested in 2050. Previously no one believed magic was real. It took thirty years for the government to even openly acknowledge that COVID-50 changed that."

Terrance shot Pierre a look, which he blatantly ignored before continuing, "You say that as though you don't live in our world normally."

Dariusz put his full attention on Pierre. Terrance could see the wolf shifter visibly shrinking. "I am old. I have seen many things in my lifetime, including people believing and worshiping magic and then murdering people in cold blood because they were terrified of magic."

"You mean this has happened before?" Pierre replied.

"History tends to repeat itself," Dariusz replied and then focused on Terrance again. "While I am enjoying the chitchat, we need to get on with figuring things out. Ben has the Snowflake. We need to get it back as soon as possible."

Terrance agreed that letting Ben have something that powerful at his disposal was a scary thought. They didn't know enough about what motivated him to even begin to guess what he would do with it.

"Let's get started then," Dariusz said and motioned for them to head over to the computers.

TWENTY-FOUR

JOSH

Sienna had found a lead indicating that Artur Hagi would be at the Plaza around nine that night. When Cory had said he was putting together a group to trail Artur, Josh had volunteered. They still hadn't figured out where Ben was holding Elyse, and after two days of waiting, he desperately needed a distraction.

Josh and Sienna sat at opposite ends on a bench near the fountain in the Plaza. With the sun setting, the fountain lights were on, and music was playing. A few times, Josh thought that the water and music might have been choreographed, but then the water movements would get erratic.

Taylor, a great horned owl shifter, was perched in the large pine tree on the other side of the courtyard. Josh couldn't see him through the branches, but he knew that Taylor was there and was one of the shifters they had on overwatch. With the vampires' involvement, Cory had not wanted to send only shifters. There were twins George and Georgina, both with a talent for water. The twins were walking around the stores and shopping. Everyone had comm devices in their ears so that they could communicate as needed.

Josh took a sip of his drink, keeping his eyes peeled for Artur. He should be showing up any moment if the intel they had gotten was correct. The vampire was tall and skinny and favored black trench coats. He should be fairly easy to spot based on his build alone.

Josh caught a glimpse of a tall and skinny male on the other side of the fountain. He was about to comment into the comm when Taylor glided over the top of the fountain, narrowly missing getting his wings wet. He made one long pass and then returned to the tree.

Georgina's voice came over the comms. "Taylor confirms that Artur is on the far side of the fountain. Remember this is an observe and report assignment. We are *not* to engage."

Josh tapped his comm once, the signal that he understood but couldn't talk. He then slurped loudly on his drink and stood up, walking to a trash can to dispose of it. The trash took him in a straight line right for Artur and gave him the perfect excuse to get a better look at the vampire before retreating.

Josh slowly slurped his drink again, shook it, and slurped again. He made it look as though he was too focused on figuring out if his cup was really empty, while subtly watching Artur. The vampire took his time crossing from one side to the other. The path he took was straight, as though he did have a set destination but wasn't in a rush to get there.

Or he knows he's being watched, Josh mused. He slurped his drink one more time, then tossed it in the trash and walked back to the bench. Now Josh needed to make sure that Artur believed he was just a random bystander at the Plaza to enjoy the fountain and lights. Josh had also hoped that by drawing Artur's focus it would permit the rest of his team an opportunity to identify anyone that Artur might be meeting.

Josh sat down on the end of the bench and picked up his folded newspaper, opening it with a loud snap, then settling down and reading it. He ended up reading the same two lines over and over.

Cory had warned him not to interfere and if Georgina gave him an order, to obey it, even if he disagreed. Josh had said he would do his best. He refrained from making any set promises. Elyse was still missing. If the situation here at the Plaza changed, then Josh was going to do whatever was necessary to get Elyse back.

Josh lost track of how long he sat on the bench reading the same few lines when someone walked close enough that they brushed his newspaper.

"Hey!" called Josh, annoyed. He set down the paper, considering going after such a rude person, when he noticed a folded piece of paper with his name on it at his feet.

He stooped over and grabbed it. Flipping the paper open, he saw a few words were scribbled.

Jewelry store in 5

There was no signature. Not that Josh expected one given how the message was delivered. He glanced around but did not immediately see any of the HAC team. Deciding he could go to a meeting without anyone else holding his hand, Josh folded his newspaper and tucked it under his arm, then made his way to the jewelry store.

He'd never gone into one before, though lately he had begun contemplating whether or not he should look at engagement rings. Prior to Elyse, he'd never been in a relationship serious enough where he was thinking of proposing, and he wasn't the type to give a woman jewelry. He just didn't see the point in wasting money on gems. He'd rather spend time with them. *In bed,* the darker part of his mind pointed out. He wasn't denying it.

Josh reached the jewelry store. He tugged the door open and stepped inside. He was greeted by a refreshing blast of cold air. A smiling woman in a dark-purple pantsuit, wearing a diamond choker, huge sapphire earrings, and several bracelets in gemstones he didn't recognize, approached. He backed up a step. He wasn't in here to buy anything, and this saleswoman looked like she fully intended to make sure he left only after making a large purchase.

"How can I help you today? Let me guess, looking for an engagement ring?" the saleswoman said, setting a hand on Josh's elbow and attempting to guide him toward one of the cases. Josh dug his heels in and refused to budge. She tugged on his arm, before finally giving up and letting go.

"If you don't want to shop, why did you come in here?" the saleswoman asked.

"I'm meeting someone," Josh said. His eyes darted around the store, looking for whoever had given him the note. But other than a male sales associate sitting at a desk, there was no one else there.

"You could browse while you wait for the person to show up," the saleswoman suggested.

Josh peered into the case he had approached. It was full of earrings. "Can you show me the engagement rings?" he finally asked.

The saleswoman smiled broadly at him. "Yes, right this way. Now, are you wanting a diamond solitaire or something else?"

Josh scrunched up his face. He had no idea. He wasn't even sure he knew what a solitaire was. Instead of asking him more questions, the saleswoman stepped behind the case and pulled out several trays to show him. "These are all solitaires. As you can see, they have a single diamond on a simple band. Lots of shapes and sizes to choose from."

Josh leaned over, studying the different rings. He was intrigued by the diamonds that weren't round cut. He hadn't realized they could make them into such a wide range of shapes. *Do I even know anyone who is engaged or married?* Josh thought and then realized that if he did, he wasn't aware of it. Most of the people he knew were single or just casually dating. He realized Terrance and Cory were married, but he couldn't recall either of them wearing rings.

The next time I see Terrance I will have to remember to pay more attention.

There was a cough behind him. Josh turned, arm brushing one of the trays and sending it flying over the other side of the counter. "Shit!" he growled.

The saleswoman started screeching at him. Josh backed away, hands raised. He hadn't intentionally hit the tray. A soft chuckle came from his left and Josh pivoted to face it. "Pierre?" he said in surprise.

"Keep your voice down," Pierre ordered.

Josh sighed. "Why the secrecy?"

"It's complicated," the wolf shifter replied.

Josh shook his head. "That always seems to be the case. You're the one who gave me the note?"

Pierre nodded. "Yes. Ben Piro has Elyse and the Snowflake."

Josh's mouth dropped open. He forced himself to shut it so he didn't look stupid. "What does the Snowflake have to do with Elyse?"

Pierre shrugged. "We're still trying to figure that out. I just wanted you to know." Pierre took a step toward the door.

"What about Artur Hagi? Are we on the wrong trail?" Josh asked.

"It might be the right trail with Artur. I don't know yet. But I need to go. Bye!" Pierre rushed out the door and around the corner of the building.

The saleswoman gave Josh a scathing look. "It's time for you to go."

Josh kept his mouth shut, deciding it wasn't worth wasting his time trying to apologize. He quickly departed the jewelry store.

Once outside, Josh paused to get his thoughts more organized. He was stunned by the news that Ben Piro had acquired the Snowflake. From all of the time he had spent working on the black-market case, to his knowledge, the people involved with the creation and sale of it had been associates of Octavien Boutin. He now knew that Octavien's boss was Dariusz, which had added another layer of complications to everything.

Not only was Dariusz the head of HAC, he also had his claws in other matters as well. *But how does Ben fit into the equation?*

Josh rubbed his forehead, trying to recall his memories of Ben. One of the most prominent memories was the day he had discovered he had a magical talent when it unlocked and set his father's apartment on fire in Manhattan, New York. Taking a deep breath through his nostrils, he could almost smell the smoke.

He and Ben had argued about who would one day marry Celine, and the fight turned physical. They'd fought many times before, as best friends tend to do, but this fight was different. Josh had suspected for a while that although his friend appeared to be a ten-year-old boy, there was something about him not entirely human. When Josh awoke after the fight, the apartment was in flames, his skin had been burned and blistered from Ben's touch, and his side bore deep wounds from the metal claws that had sprouted from Ben's hands. Once he'd healed from his wounds, he learned about magical talents—including his own, which the fight with Ben had unlocked.

Josh shook his head. That memory of unlocking his talent was more about him than about Ben.

Thirteen-year-old Josh was walking down the street a few blocks from the apartment he lived in with his dad when he heard a rattling sound coming from the trash can in front of him. He stopped in his tracks, not sure whether he should approach or not. His dad had always drilled into him the need for caution. Many people in Manhattan would be eager to cause him harm.

"Help!" came a voice. Josh stepped closer to the trash can. "Help!" came the voice again. This time he was certain the voice belonged to someone inside of the trash can.

He quickly closed the gap and yanked the lid off. A scrawny kid peered up at him, a mixture of fear and relief in his eyes. Josh offered him a hand. "I'm Josh. Let's get you out of there."

The boy hesitated before taking Josh's hand. Josh gave a deft yank and popped the boy out of the can and into his arms. As soon as his arms were around the boy, he started to squirm and panic. "Let me go!"

Josh released his hold and the boy fell to the concrete. "Sorry, I didn't mean to scare you."

The boy glared at him, then stood up.

From what Josh could guess, he seemed about ten years old and looked like he needed a good meal or two. "When was the last time you ate?"

The boy shrugged, still acting as though he might bolt at a moment's notice. Josh slowly swung his backpack off of his shoulder and unzipped it, pulling out a sandwich. "Here, you can have this if you'd like."

The boy snatched the sandwich and demolished it in moments, then licked his fingers clean. "I'm Ben."

"Nice to meet you, Ben," Josh said, offering his hand. Ben shook it. Josh glanced at his watch.

"I need to get going. I'll see you around!" He gave a wave and kept walking toward his apartment. He was going to be late, and he was sure he'd get an earful from his dad about it, but he also knew that he had done two acts of kindness. Something he also got lectured on. He hoped that would be enough to satisfy his dad.

Josh leaned against the cool brick of the building, sifting through his memories of Ben. It had taken over six months before Ben had trusted him enough to open up some. After that, they had become fast friends, almost inseparable. When Josh had introduced Ben to Celine, they had hit it off right away too.

"What do you want to be when you grow up?" Celine, or Linney as they had nicknamed her, asked.

Josh debated how to answer the question. It had been on his mind lately. He knew when he turned eighteen in two years, he would have to decide if he was staying in Manhattan or venturing out.

"President of the United States!" Ben blurted out.

Josh looked at him in surprise. It was quite a big goal for a child to have, but he knew there was nothing wrong with dreaming big. "I'm sure if anyone can do that it's you, Ben."

Linney nodded, smiling in agreement. "Yep. What about you, Josh?"

He tapped his fingers on his thigh. "I want to help people and keep them safe from bad guys."

"An FBI agent?" Linney asked.

"Maybe, or something along those lines," he replied. "Linney, you asked the question, what is your dream?"

"Also to help people, but I want to be a surgeon," Linney replied.

"I'm sure your healing talent will help with that," Josh said, smiling.

Josh snapped out of his thoughts, eyes narrowed. *All those years ago, Ben said he wanted to be president of the United States. Does he have some crazy plan to use the Snowflake and Elyse to accomplish that?* He ran a hand over his face. To him it seemed like a strange way to go about ensuring his dream would happen. But then he realized that in his time as an FBI agent, he had come across cases where a man murdered a woman just because she gave him the wrong sandwich.

"Josh, what are you doing?" Georgina's voice sounded in his comm.

"Uh, just walking around," Josh replied.

"Then why were you in the jewelry store?" Georgina asked tartly.

"I walked in there … is there a problem? Do you need me somewhere else?" Josh asked. It irked him that she was watching his movements. *Cory and Terrance trust me. So why are my actions of interest to Georgina?*

"Artur is heading that way. I just wanted to make sure you're actually paying attention to our task," Georgina replied.

"Noted. I'll adjust my position." Josh walked across the street and headed for the little pop-up stand that was selling soda. He ordered a small drink. While he was paying, he saw Artur walking down the sidewalk where Josh had been minutes before.

By the time he paid and got the drink, Artur was far enough up the sidewalk that Josh felt like he could trail him. He assumed Georgina or George was not too far behind either.

Georgina's voice came over the comm. "Follow him, Josh. We are going to go the other way. I am worried he is getting suspicious."

Josh nodded to himself and crossed to the opposite sidewalk that Artur was on. He stayed far enough back and paused occasionally to window shop. He felt confident Artur didn't realize he was being followed. Artur headed up the street that went between the last two buildings and headed for the train station.

"He seems to be going for the train station. Can Taylor take over? Are we trying to follow him if he gets on a train?"

Josh did not turn up the street toward the train station; instead he continued back around the oval.

"We got what we need. Taylor will follow the train and take note of which station Artur gets off at, but the rest of us can return to headquarters," Georgina said.

Back in Cory's office, the computer screen showed images that one of the HAC members had been taking from one of the upper-story apartments during Artur's meeting. He was meeting with Trey, which had happened while Josh was in the jewelry store.

The photos showed the two of them talking and having some sort of hot beverage together, and then a handshake, which in

Josh's book implied a deal had been made. Cory studied the photos intently.

"Was anyone able to hear what kind of deal they were doing?" Josh asked when no one in the room seemed inclined to speak.

Georgina replied, "No, and that's what was puzzling. They were talking about the weather."

"The weather?" Josh said, perking up. "Do you recall the exact words?"

Georgina gave him a frown. "Yes, but I think they were just talking to make it look like they were there for a cup of coffee, not to broker a deal."

Cory growled, "Just tell him the words, Georgina. Quit messing around."

Josh bit his lip to keep from smiling.

Georgina glared at him before replying. "When they greeted each other, Artur said, 'Hello, what a beautiful sunny day.' Then, Trey replied, 'Not a cloud in the sky.' Then, Artur said, 'Tomorrow the forecast is showing thunderstorms.'"

Josh held up his hand, and Georgina stopped speaking. "I have heard phrases like this before. In fact, I wrote a lengthy report on them a few years ago since so many seemed rather common. Like criminals are too lazy to make original phrases up anymore. What you just recited means something like this. I have acquired the goods. I have the money. The meeting will be inside. I'll give you the exact location tomorrow."

Georgina didn't look convinced.

"I have found that usually references to good weather means that both parties have done whatever they agreed to do. Then, they discuss the meeting place. If bad weather comes up then the meeting is indoors, and if they talk about the seasons, like how lovely spring is, that the meeting will be outdoors. Did they say anything else?" Josh asked.

Georgina nodded. "Yes. Next Trey said, 'The train maintenance is scheduled for Wednesday,' and Artur replied, 'The maintenance crew has done a wonderful job with the landscaping here at the Plaza. Good luck.' Then, they shook and went their own ways."

Josh scratched his chin. The mention of the train was confusing. "Typically, when maintenance is discussed, they are referring to FBI or other parties being on alert. Maintenance on the train could just simply mean that the FBI is aware something is happening and be careful. Tomorrow is Wednesday, so that would fit. Or perhaps they need to use the train to get to the meeting location, and the trains are being watched more closely tomorrow."

Cory jumped in. "Well, based on what you just said about maintenance meaning being watched, I would say the last statement implied Artur knew you were tailing them, and he was informing Trey. Though neither one of them did anything about it. We must take into consideration that if Artur knew we were watching him tonight that he gave Trey a different message than the one he was originally supposed to."

"The only way we could confirm or deny that would be to talk to one of them directly. I don't know about you, but I am not sure I feel comfortable walking right up to Artur and declaring that I was eavesdropping, and could he please tell me more about the deal they have," Josh replied.

"Yes, I know that," said Cory. "However, we can't assume everything said was staged."

"What can you tell me about Trey?" Josh asked.

Cory blew out his breath and made a shooing motion with his hand. The room emptied of everyone but the two of them. Cory shut the door and then turned to face him. "Terrance made the original deal to find the Snowflake with Trey. She wanted to keep HAC out of it, and until her last meeting with Trey, everything seemed to be going well. When she retrieved the Snowflake, FBI Agent Florence then offered a deal from Governor Beechwood, who also wanted the Snowflake. Except the governor's offer was for one hundred million dollars, ten times what the deal was with Trey. Instead of immediately agreeing to the governor's offer she decided to try pushing Trey for double to see what his response was. He said either she'd be dead in twenty-four hours or have the money, and, well … you remember when she was attacked on your first day here. So she decided to proceed with accepting the governor's offer.

"The problem with the whole thing is that we still have no idea who Trey's boss is, so we don't really have a grasp of who is coming after Elyse. I suppose it's possible that Ben is the boss and was trying to keep his hands clean by acquiring the Snowflake through a simple purchase. Or it could be someone else entirely. Though I think with what Terrance has learned while she has been stuck in Aerie is that it definitely is not Dariusz." Cory took a deep breath, clenching and unclenching his fists. "The whole situation is annoying. We aren't exactly strapped for cash, so her reasoning for taking the initial contract didn't make much sense to me. But I have learned over the years when she decides she wants something, she will go for it with or without me. Does Elyse ever do that to you?"

Josh chuckled. "Occasionally."

"We of course also know now that Artur was one of the people who attacked her. He claimed at the attack he had nothing to do with Trey. This meeting tonight suggests otherwise," Cory explained.

Josh folded his arms across his chest. "Now you're wondering if the deal between Trey and Artur is still just that Trey ordered a hit on Terrance and hired Artur for the job. But Terrance is not here right now. Which means if they are meeting tomorrow to finish the deal that either Artur has killed her and we haven't received the news yet, he knows where she is and is planning on doing it before their meeting, or the deal is about something else altogether."

"Glad to know we're on the same page. What you just said is essentially where my thoughts have been going. Terrance is with Dariusz and as far as I know they are still at Aerie." Cory paused. "Except … we don't know if Trey or Artur is aware that Terrance sold the Snowflake to Governor Beechwood, and then it was stolen."

To Josh, it sounded like a colossal clusterfuck. He wondered what Terrance's real motive had been behind abandoning the deal with Trey and selling the Snowflake to the government. Had she discovered something else beyond just wanting a bigger payday and not felt like sharing it with everyone else?

Cory spoke, jarring Josh out of his thoughts. "Georgina said you left your post for a while and ended up in the jewelry store. Is everything okay?"

Josh sighed; it seemed nothing got past Cory. "Depends on your definition of okay. I got some new information."

"Oh," said Cory, seemingly intrigued.

"Yeah, Pierre asked me to meet him at the jewelry store," Josh said.

"My Pierre?" Cory asked.

Josh nodded. "Yes. At first when I got the note, I thought it was some sort of ruse of Artur's or something. But it was Pierre. Since I have not been around your people for very long, I am not sure what your dynamics are like, but it seemed as though Pierre didn't want anyone but me to get the information. I am going assume either you know it already or that he would consider it acceptable for me to share it with you as Terrance's mate. Anyhow … Pierre said that is has been confirmed that Ben has the Snowflake."

"That is a strange new development, but it would support the theory that Ben is Trey's boss," Cory replied.

"Yes. As you are probably aware, Ben and I were friends when we were young in Manhattan. I found him when I was thirteen, and we stayed friends until the day my talent was unlocked. I was sent away shortly after that to a school the government was running for magically talented youth," Josh explained.

"Okay. What does that have to do with what we're dealing with?" Cory asked.

"Well, we have been wondering what the motivation is for having the Snowflake. Or someone like Ben who does not have an organization to rally around him. I recalled a conversation I had with Ben when I was sixteen. We were talking about what our big dreams were of all things. He said that his was to be president of the United States," Josh said.

Cory gave him a look of disbelief. "You think that Ben is trying to become the president?"

Josh sighed. He knew it sounded ridiculous. "Possibly. Think about it. If he had the Snowflake to give him control over electricity in the entire country, he could force his way into office."

"And then what?" Cory demanded. "One of the first requirements that was put in place after the government admitted magical talents exist was that a president cannot have a magical talent."

"I have no idea. It's possible even Ben doesn't have a plan but is driven by anger at being forced into FBI control and then put into Darkwater Penitentiary. Anger and revenge can be very powerful motivators. Sometimes that's all it takes. Besides, you think it sounds ridiculous. Do you really think that the president would take him as a serious threat?" Josh replied.

"No. I don't think he would. Which means Ben could almost waltz right in and kill everyone. Especially since he looks like a ten-year-old boy most of the time. It's the perfect con," Cory replied.

"How do we stop him?" Josh asked.

Cory shook his head. "We are going to have to figure that out. Since he has no ties that we know of to anyone or anything, I believe it's safe to say he has nothing to lose and everything to gain. Which makes him even more dangerous. I need to update Terrance on these developments."

"What about Trey?" Josh asked. It seemed like they unraveled one part of the puzzle only to be left with another stray piece that didn't quite fit.

"I will make sure she has the warning about that too," Cory said.

Josh nodded and yawned. He was exhausted. "I'm going to head back to the apartment."

"Okay," said Cory. "I'll let you know as soon as any new information comes up."

Josh clapped Cory on the shoulder and showed himself out.

TWENTY-FIVE
TERRANCE

Terrance gazed at the computer screens, running over the information they had found. Pierre had left a few hours earlier, having confirmed what Dariusz had told her: that Ben Piro had the Snowflake and could be making a play to become president. Terrance found that tidbit hard to understand. Nothing she knew about Ben had led her to believe he would make a move against the president, not on his own. *Except if he organized stealing the Snowflake, then that means he was the mastermind behind blowing up Governor Beechwood's car.* It made her wish they knew where Elyse was. Being able to see the past would be incredibly helpful at that moment.

There was a knock on the front door. Terrance expected someone else to materialize and answer it, but by the fourth knock she realized that she must be alone in the house. She rose from her chair and pulled her gun out of the holster. The door was solid wood and did not have a peephole, so she had no idea who or what was on the other side. Cautiously, she opened the door. Her eyes widened when she saw Agent Florence on the other side.

"How did you find me?" Terrance asked before she could stop herself.

Agent Florence rolled her eyes. "I have access to the Aerie cameras too. Can I come in?"

Terrance couldn't think of any reason to not let Agent Florence in, so she stepped aside to give her room.

"What is this about?" she asked as she led the way to the counter where there were several stools.

"Governor Beechwood was in a car explosion after the exchange with the Snowflake. You were there. This is being classified as an assassination of a high-ranking government official. I find it difficult to believe that you would expect me to just let what happened go," Agent Florence said tersely.

Terrance's lips twitched. "I had nothing to do with his death."

"Do you really expect me to believe you?" Agent Florence demanded.

"Yes, because I was brought here to this very house after stepping on a fake IED. I did not orchestrate what happened immediately after the exchange with the Snowflake. I am sorry that Governor Beechwood died. I can't imagine how much upheaval that has caused for the FBI," Terrance said.

Agent Florence took a seat on one of the stools and folded her hands in her lap, facing Terrance. "A lot of upheaval. Lieutenant Governor Brian West has been sworn in, but he was not privy to the deal between you and Governor Beechwood and is demanding a full investigation with you as the top suspect, primarily because after the explosion, you disappeared. Unfortunately for us Governor West has been kept in the dark about the relationship between the FBI and HAC, and now that is coming back to bite us."

"Are you just here to tell me that Governor West wants to throw me in jail for assassinating Governor Beechwood?" Terrance asked. While she was not surprised about the news that she was the number one suspect in the governor's death, she was not entirely sure why Agent Florence had sought her out. Terrance certainly was not going to allow herself to be taken in for questioning, not when the research she was doing here was so critical.

"No, I was hoping you could throw me a bone that I can use to appease Governor West," Agent Florence replied.

Terrance smiled at the request. "Ben Piro."

Agent Florence pursed her lips. "I'm not familiar with that name."

Terrance shrugged. "I suggest you become familiar with it. He is responsible for orchestrating the attack at Aerie and stealing the Snowflake."

Agent Florence nodded and slid off her stool. "Very well. I will look into it. Hopefully I can put together enough information to convince Governor West to drop you as the top suspect."

"I am sure you will find enough as long as your presentation is convincing," Terrance replied.

"Thank you. I will reach out if I need anything else," Agent Florence said and then offered her hand. Terrance shook it and led Agent Florence back to the front door.

When Agent Florence's car departed, Terrance shut the door and headed back to her room for a shower.

Terrance stepped out of the shower, wrapping a towel around herself and then walking into the bedroom. She was still stuck at the house Dariusz had set up in Aerie. Catrina had stayed away though.

Terrance toweled herself off and slid on some pajamas. Normally, she slept in just a large T-shirt, but here in a house where her boss and other people she didn't know could appear at a whim, she did not want to walk around half-dressed.

There was a soft knock on the door. Terrance hung the towel up on a chair and opened the door. To her surprise, Dariusz was on the other side.

"Can I help you?" she asked formally. Catrina might have had a more friendly relationship with Dariusz, but Terrance did not. She had always kept a clear, well-defined line between herself and Dariusz.

"I heard that your members have been able to confirm that Trey and Artur Hagi are working together and that Ben seems to be working for himself," Dariusz said in a deep voice.

Terrance made sure to not lock eyes with him, which wasn't difficult given he was a foot taller than she was. "Yes."

"I am still not convinced that Artur is intentionally making a move against me. I believe that Nightshade Coven has more power in this situation than we have confirmed," Dariusz said.

Terrance kept silent. Dariusz was entitled to his opinion, and she did not think it was worth the risk of angering him to disagree. *Besides, if Artur is going after Dariusz, it is not my fight.*

"When we get confirmation of Elyse's location, I will allow you to return and assist in recovering her. I just feel as though you are of more use to me with the resources I have here at Aerie—especially when I can safely meet with you in-person—than if I let you go back to your headquarters. Nightshade Coven watches you just as closely as you watch them. They would most certainly catch wind of me being here if I were to show up at headquarters," Dariusz explained. Everything he said was true. Terrance nodded in agreement, not sure what else the vampire expected her to do.

Terrance started to yawn and covered her mouth to hide it.

Dariusz gave her a toothy smile. "I will let you retire. Good work." He turned on his heel and strode briskly down the hallway and around the corner.

Terrance yawned again and stepped back into her room and shut the door. She was about to slide under the covers when there was a soft tap on the door. She rolled her eyes. *Now what?*

Yanking the door open, she revealed Dariusz, eyes dancing with amusement. "A thought occurred to me."

Terrance tiredly ran a hand over her face. "Which is?"

"Contrary to what Archibald Cornelius believed, your aunt continued her research with the COVID-50 vaccine with samples she retained after Evermore Genetics transferred the research to the Atlanta lab," Dariusz explained.

Terrance shrugged. "She was always doing research. Why does this matter?"

Dariusz bared his teeth and hissed. "Remember who you're speaking to."

Terrance started to turn away. She was tired, and right now she didn't want to have a pissing contest with Dariusz; she just wanted to sleep, consequences be damned.

"Dr. Basak believed she found a cure," Dariusz said.

Terrance spun around in shock. "A cure?"

Dariusz nodded. "Yes. Now, since you are determined to go to sleep. I will allow you to do so and we can discuss this matter some other time." Without giving Terrance a chance to respond, he simply disappeared.

Terrance let out her breath, mind buzzing at the revelation that her aunt had believed she found a cure and the implications. She climbed onto the bed and under the covers, not sure if she'd be able to quiet her thoughts enough to even fall asleep now. She focused on Cory, who she missed, but she knew that they were getting close to figuring out where Elyse was being held and that soon it would all be over, one way or another.

TWENTY-SIX
ELYSE

When Elyse woke up the next morning, she decided she was going to try to escape. Staying in this cabin waiting for Ben was getting ridiculous. She had done everything he had asked. *There must be a way out. Something I missed.* She got dressed and ate a quick breakfast and searched the cabin again. Last time, when she had found the secret room, she had paid more attention to the walls. *What if I check the floors?*

As she scanned the floor along the edge of the wall, she stumbled as her foot caught the edge of the rug underneath the coffee table. She sat up, glad no one had seen her trip. The rug she was on drew her attention. Elyse pushed the coffee table out of the way and lifted the corner of the rug, folding it over on itself. To her surprise, there was a faint outline of a rectangle with a handle in the middle of it.

She wiggled her fingers under the metal ring till it was tipped at a high enough angle that she could get a good grip on it. Then, she tugged. Nothing happened. She tried again, and this time she felt it lift. Deciding the issue was just that she needed to put more weight into it, she slipped both hands around the ring and adjusted her legs. This time the door opened, and the momentum sent her toppling backward. The wood door slammed into the floor of the cabin with a thud.

The front door burst open, and Ben launched himself at her. Elyse scrambled backward, away from the heat that radiated from him.

"What are you doing!" he bellowed, fire coming out of his mouth.

Elyse's back hit the wall. She couldn't get any farther away. "Just exploring," she said.

Ben growled. "No, I think what you're doing is trying to escape. Which means you are just like everyone else, wanting to ruin my plans to destroy the president." He stood over her menacingly before turning and walking away. As he walked away, the flames disappeared, and his skin returned to a normal color. He kicked the trap door shut and ripped the handle off before sliding the rug back over the top.

Elyse watched him fearfully from her position on the floor. *Just my luck that he chose that moment to show up.* The room was uncomfortably hot, even though he had made the flames disappear. Elyse debated whether or not he would try to attack her if she stood up and turned on the fan.

When it was obvious that Ben was not paying attention to her anymore and retreated into his bedroom, Elyse stood up and turned on the ceiling fan. Then, she sat on the couch, running over what had just happened in her mind. She realized that Ben had let something slip in his anger: "my plans to destroy the president." Elyse's eyes widened as the implications of that statement came crashing down. *Is this what he is trying to do with the cure? Destroy the president? But according to that list I found yesterday, the president isn't permitted to have a magical talent, so how would a cure aid Ben in destroying the president?*

Elyse wished, not for the first time since being captured, that she could share her discovery with Josh. She was confident he would understand how everything fit together. With this new information, the only thing Elyse was now even more certain of was that

Ben was crazy, and the sooner she got away from him, the better off she would be.

As Elyse was cleaning up the kitchen after dinner, the file labeled COVID-50 sitting on the kitchen table caught her eye. She quickly finished drying the dishes and returned them to the cabinets. Then, she sat down, opened the file, and began reading.

C50-1A was successfully developed as a vaccine by Evermore Genetics in Atlanta, Georgia. EG did not support any theories indicating that C50-1A could be anything more than a vaccine. I was able to acquire tissue samples from individuals who had begun displaying signs of having talents that could not be scientifically explained. Experiments with the tissue samples indicated when C50-1A was administered to tissue samples from individuals with an unexplained talent, over the course of seventy-two hours, the tissues would return to normal human parameters. This promising information led me to ask for volunteers who possessed unexplained talents. Unfortunately, when C50-1A was administered to those individuals, no changes occurred. It appears that the changes experienced in small tissue samples were a fluke and not reproducible.

Mice and other non-human test subjects did not seem to develop any of the unexplained talents like humans did.

The other oddity of these unexplained talents is that they primarily occur in children whose mothers contracted COVID-50 during pregnancy and died in childbirth. Because I am not able to reproduce these unexplained talents in animal subjects, it is almost impossible to conduct any research on the phenomenon that appears to be happening. I doubt any pregnant woman would permit me to deliberately infect her with COVID-50 so that she could die and I could see whether or not the child always ended up with an unexplained talent.

It also remains to be seen if this first generation of children will go on to reproduce their unexplained talents or if it is just some weird fluke.

I find it rather disturbing that my niece can turn into a tiger. Her father is extremely protective of her and refuses to allow me to even get a blood sample. I suppose if I were in his shoes I would potentially behave the same way. But it is frustrating to have a family member who I see almost every day who has one of the unexplained talents, and yet I cannot use her in any of my research. Jordan has made it abundantly clear that if I ever try to coerce Terrance into allowing me to get a sample from her, he will prevent me from ever seeing her again. He doesn't make idle threats, so I will just have to figure out a different way.

Many of the families with affected children are terrified of the things their children are capable of and beg me to help them find a

cure. I have not had a shortage of samples.
Just not as large of a variety as I would
have liked. Rumors have been spreading, and I
have had quite a few families reach out from
the Midwest about curing their children.

I have noticed a trend that the unexplained
talents seem to vary by geographical region.
It's a similar pattern to how the COVID-50
virus originally spread and mutated, which
has led me to believe that each time it
mutated, it was moving across the country, and environmental factors tied to each
particular region had an influence on the
unexplained talents.

I have tried to reach out to Dr. Cornelius
about it again, but he has refused to
return my messages.

Elyse set the file down, her mind reeling. Dr. Basak had been actively trying to develop a cure for what she had called "unexplained talents." Elyse was not surprised that Ben had somehow discovered Dr. Basak's research mentioned somewhere and decided to pursue the cure for himself. Of course, the research was happening in the late 2050s. She wasn't sure how long Dr. Basak had continued to do her research, but she assumed it had not been picked up by anyone after Dr. Basak had retired. Otherwise, more people would have been aware of it.

Dr. Basak talked about Terrance and wanting to use her niece for her research. I wonder if Terrance was aware of this, that a cure could exist, or if her father had been able to keep her shielded from her aunt's endeavors, Elyse pondered. *I suppose the next time I see Terrance, I could ask her.* Yawning, she realized how tired she was. The stress from the pressure Ben was putting on her to find the answers he sought, repeatedly using her talent, and poor-quality sleep were catching up to her.

Elyse shut the folder and left it on the table before making her way to the bedroom. As she crossed the threshold, a pang of longing hit her. She missed Josh desperately. Tears stung her eyes as her emotions bubbled up. They had come to Boise because it was supposed to be safe, and now here she was, kidnapped *again.* The only solace she had was that unlike when the Arañas Rojas had kidnapped her at the hospital, Ben was not beating her for answers. In fact, as she thought about it, other than his kidnapping her and not letting her go, he was not treating her badly.

It could be way worse, she told herself.

Tears continued to trickle down her cheeks as she went through the motions of getting ready for bed. Ben had provided basic necessities and changes of clothing for her. At times, she could almost believe that she was on a romantic vacation with Josh in a cabin somewhere deep in the forest, except Josh never showed up.

She had finally felt like they were able to fully trust each other again. What had happened at the masquerade ball was behind them, and they were equally committed to their relationship now. *Will we ever get a chance to be a normal couple?* she wondered.

Elyse frowned as everything started to blur.

She wrinkled her nose as her vision cleared. Apparently, my talent decided to take my internal question as request for assistance.

> *She was standing in a meadow with oak trees, their leaves in brilliant fall foliage spreading out behind a wood trellis decorated in rust-colored roses. In front of the trellis, she saw herself, in a simple but elegant white A-line satin wedding gown. Her red hair cascaded down her back with tiny white flowers and crystals adorning it. She was able to pick out the faces of her close friends filling the seats. Jessica and Aunt*

Grace were there in the front row on the left. Terrance and Cory were in the front row on the right.

Elyse turned her attention to the man in front of her, Josh Everly. Blond hair neatly combed back, blue eyes meeting hers eagerly. He was handsome in a dark green suit with a rust rose boutonniere.

Sobs wracked Elyse's body as the vision faded. The vision had been similar to the first time she had seen her future wedding—but different in that she could see who she was marrying. She needed Josh more than she wanted to admit. She realized that now. She wasn't sure when it had happened, that she had fallen head over heels for him, but she was certain now that Josh was who she was meant to marry.

Slowly Elyse got ready for bed, trying to console herself that Josh would figure out where she was and get her out. Part of her knew that no matter what Ben said about being willing to exchange her the transaction would be dangerous.

She had discovered that Ben was a meticulous planner. She would not be surprised if he had prepared for a variety of outcomes regarding her cooperation and what information she was able to acquire with her talent.

Elyse climbed into bed and shut her eyes, willing her body to let her sleep.

There was a featherlight touch on her leg, then her breast, then back down her leg. Elyse moaned and rolled over. Josh's lips captured hers. As he deepened the kiss, his fingers teased her breasts until she could barely stand it. She could feel wetness between her legs and ran her hand down Josh's abdomen. His cock was hard. She ran her hands slowly up and down its length, smiling as Josh groaned in pleasure. Encouraged, she lifted herself on top of him. Josh gently raised her up by the hips and helped guide her on top of his cock. She almost came as he slid inside of her. It felt so good.

With some encouragement from Josh, she found her rhythm. She could feel the pressure building. She wasn't sure how much longer she'd be able to hold out. When she felt Josh's release explode inside her, she came moments later and sagged onto his chest. But Josh wasn't done with her yet. He flipped them over and slowly slid in and out. She was trying to figure out what he was doing when she felt his cock once again hardening inside her and her body eagerly responding in kind.

Shudders ran through Elyse as the orgasm washed through her. She blinked and reached for Josh, sure he was there beside her. But there was no one there. Her thighs were smeared with her fluids. Elyse was confused. She'd never had a dream that was as intense as that one had been. She bit her lip, trying not to dwell on it, and let herself drift back into much-needed sleep.

The next few hours she spent tossing and turning, never able to get back into the deep sleep. Finally, Elyse gave up, deciding to take a shower and then read more of the journals to waste time until Ben showed up again. She knew it was likely that he had what he had been looking for, the vaccine, and the next time he came back to the cabin, it would be to move her to wherever the meeting was. She was certain now that was his plan, to set up an in-person meeting with Josh to return her to him.

What was still nagging her, though, was what the purpose would be. Josh wasn't going to just agree to show up and take her home. In situations like these, there was always a trade involved. *Does Josh even have anything that Ben wants?* The water cascaded over her. It was as hot as she could make it, which was almost too hot if she was being honest with herself. *I'm sure there is something Josh has that Ben wants. I just don't know enough about their history to know what.* Instead of dwelling on Josh's end of the bargain, Elyse focused on lathering her hair and body with soap.

Elyse wasn't sure how long she spent in the shower, but the water was starting to cool off. Not wanting to go from a blazing hot to ice-cold shower, she took the hint and shut off the water. She dried off and then wrapped herself up in the towel. It was barely long enough to cover her. Just as she stepped back into the bedroom, a hand wrapped around her mouth, covering it with a cloth. Elyse tried to struggle but couldn't breathe and finally inhaled whatever was on the cloth, which knocked her out cold.

Elyse woke up and found herself tied to a chair somewhere near the middle of a massive warehouse. The building was primarily made of concrete and metal. Faded yellow support columns were in rows. She supposed the columns could have been used to split the space into various sections for different tasks. She was in awe of the sheer size of the building. To her surprise, the train tracks ran right through one side of the building, following the wall. There must be some sort of offshoot track that led to and from the building back to the main track, which would have been handy if this building had held inventory that needed to be shipped long distances.

She still had no idea how long she had been with Ben or how long she had been knocked out after her shower. He must have deemed it important for her to be dressed because she was clothed in a clean pair of jeans and a white T-shirt.

The rope around her hands was tight but not unbearable. Elyse thought she could probably free herself if she wanted, though without knowing what else was going on, she was not sure freeing herself was the best course of action. Ben had brought her here for a reason, and she needed to find out why.

Coming up with an idea, Elyse closed her eyes and took a deep breath, then reached for her talent.

Elyse opened her eyes and found herself on the train with Josh, Cory, and some others she didn't recognize.

Cory was speaking. "Josh, you are going to find Ben and Elyse. He specifically demanded you show up solo to retrieve her. We know it is a trap. He is planning to do something to you. You need to just play along with his demands, and once he has released Elyse, the rest of us will move in and take him out."

Josh nodded. "I'm assuming he plans to kill me. That was the threat he made the last time he confronted me before he was taken to Darkwater."

Elyse gasped at how calm Josh was as he spoke about Ben wanting to kill him, as though it were no big deal. Either he doesn't think Ben can do it, or he values my life that much more than his own. *She closed her eyes for a moment.* I must do everything I can to make sure we both get out alive and that my vision of our wedding someday can come to pass. *Mind made up, she focused on where exactly she was: in the front train car and rapidly approaching a huge, four-story-tall warehouse that the train tracks went right into.* Is this now? If so, then Josh is almost here! *Excitement filled her, rapidly followed by dread as she took in the size of the group Josh and Cory were with. Ten.* Why do they need so many people? *She walked around them, inspecting everyone. They were all wearing body armor and were loaded with weapons. Josh had handguns in holsters at his waist and thighs. Knives were strapped to his arms and lower legs.*

Claws dug painfully into her shoulder, and Elyse had to bite back a scream.

"What are you doing?" hissed Ben. His mouth was near her ear, and she could feel his hot breath on her neck.

"N … n … nothing," she sobbed.

Ben dug his claws in deeper, and Elyse screamed. It hurt too much.

"Liar. What are you doing?"

"Trying to find Josh," she said in the barest of whispers.

Ben yanked his claws out of her and paced. The air around him started to shimmer as heat rolled off him. Elyse felt sweat trickling down her forehead and back.

"You no longer have a magical talent."

"What do you mean?" Elyse gasped.

"I gave you the C50-1A vaccine … it was supposed to cure you and get rid of your magical talent," Ben said in a low growl.

"I would have known if you had given me anything. I haven't seen you since last night," Elyse said, tears dripping slowly down her face. *Except for when he knocked me out after the shower,* she realized. Her shoulder burned, and the heat radiating from Ben was almost too much to bear, especially since he had stopped pacing and was standing directly in front of her.

"Everything you discovered pointed to the vaccine being able to cure a magical talent. So why didn't it work?" Ben asked. His eyes had a far-off look.

"Maybe it just needs more time. Just like some medication takes a few days to work properly to help you not be sick," Elyse replied logically, hoping it would appease Ben's growing anger. To her relief, he began pacing again.

Did it not work because it takes time to work, or because there never was a cure … or because something is wrong with me? Elyse found she really hoped it was because it didn't work. Her thoughts drifted back to what she had read in the file after Ben had left. Dr. Basak's notes about how the vaccine cured tissue samples, but when it was tried with a real living human, nothing had happened. Relief coursed through her. If it hadn't worked on her, then it supported

Dr. Basak's findings. She was afraid to know what Ben or others would do if they could go around "curing" people of their magical talents without their knowledge or consent.

At the very end of the building, Elyse saw a flicker of movement in the opening for the train tracks. Which meant perhaps she really had just seen the present when she had seen Josh and the other HAC members riding a train.

A loud train horn echoed throughout the entire building. Elyse found herself whipping her head around. The sound had not come from the tracks in front of her, but from the tracks behind her. Chills ran down her spine, and for reasons she couldn't explain, she knew without question that Josh was not on the incoming train. *If it's not Josh or HAC, I don't want to find out who or what is on the train.* Ben's back was to her, and he seemed occupied by his thoughts. Elyse frantically picked at the rope around her hands. It fell to the floor within a few moments, and she quickly untied the rope around her feet and stood up.

She picked up the chair, debating if she should carry it with her as a weapon or use it against Ben, when he ran straight for her. Before she could react, his hand was wrapped around her throat, and she was lifted off the floor. She flung her arms and legs, trying to kick him, but his grip remained firm around her throat. His claws pricked her skin, and she could feel trickles of blood running down her throat.

A slow clap came from somewhere in the darkness. "How kind of you, Ben," came the distinctly male voice.

Ben ignored the newcomer. "Where the hell do you think you're going?"

Elyse drew a painful breath and coughed as Ben's grip on her throat tightened. Suddenly, he let go, and she fell hard onto the concrete. Her knees ached from the impact. Elyse took slow breaths, trying to recover from nearly being strangled. She closed her eyes, determined to work up the courage to stand up and face Ben and whoever had just shown up.

> *Instead, her talent had other ideas. Elyse found herself inside the train again. Everyone was armed to the teeth. She was having trouble spotting Josh with how tall the people were when Elyse realized this wasn't the same group of people. Neither Josh nor Cory was there. The individuals in this train all had pale skin and bloodred eyes. All except one, whose irises were bright blue, rimmed in red.* Vampires?

Elyse tumbled out of her magic when something slammed into her side, sending her rolling across the concrete like a discarded bottle. The warehouse was not well lit. The ceiling and walls had some holes allowing for natural light to filter in, but it made it difficult to see much unless it was directly in front of her.

Ben was sprawled near her, unmoving. Shadows swirled around him, and a tall, skinny man in a dark trench coat appeared.

"Who are you?" she asked softly.

The man's eyes met hers, and she gasped when she realized they were dark red. Then, he smiled, and she could see a full set of sharp teeth. "These days, I go by Artur Hagi," he replied lightly.

These days? Were there other days? Elyse wondered. The name was vaguely familiar, though it took her a few moments to realize he was the vampire who Josh had gone to Nightshade Coven to inquire about. "Artur, what do you want?"

"To destroy the world," he replied in a monotone voice.

"You're joking, right?" Elyse asked incredulously.

"Sure," Artur replied agreeably. The vampire straightened up from his crouch over Ben's prone body. Elyse thought he seemed much more menacing standing up than he did crouched.

Elyse put her palms flat on the concrete and pushed upward, giving herself the momentum she needed to get to her feet. She swayed slightly as her body adjusted to being completely upright. Her shoulder throbbed, and her knees ached. She was not going to let those things keep her from escaping or fighting her way out, whichever was necessary.

The train horn blared again, and Elyse jumped. She had completely forgotten about the train. Artur, it seemed, had not, for he was focused on the train that was lit up and speeding their way. Much faster than Elyse had expected.

The doors on the side slid open, and the people inside began leaping out, while the train kept going. Once the people hit the ground, they formed two groups, one on either side of Elyse. She twisted, trying to figure out who it was, and realized with a frown that it was the group of vampires.

"I didn't think you were going to come," Artur said, directing his words to someone on her left. Elyse pivoted and determined he must be talking to the blonde standing at the front of the group, the one who had had the blue eyes with red rims.

"You said you had the Snowflake. Why would I not come?" the blonde replied.

Artur chuckled. "Eager, Willow?"

There was a loud boom followed by a crack as the incoming train collided with another train on the tracks in front of it. Elyse could have sworn the track was empty a moment ago, but even as she watched, the second train flickered in and out of sight. It was hard to see in the dark, but it looked similar to the HAC train she and Josh had first ridden into Boise. With a terrible grinding noise, the train the vampires had jumped off surged sideways, flying off the tracks. Sparks went everywhere as the metal wheels scraped on the concrete. The train folded in two and continued to slide through the warehouse. To Elyse's horror, the first column it hit collapsed, then the next. Elyse found herself thrown backward with bits of metal and glass falling like rain around her. Because of her proximity to one of the columns, which was attached to the ceiling, she could feel tremors running down it as the remaining supports were pushed to their limits. Pieces of the ceiling where the fallen columns had been connected fell, littering the area with more pieces of concrete and rebar.

Where the two trains had collided, a fire had started, and the warehouse was filling with smoke. Artur had disappeared along with Ben, but the other vampires were still there, though scattered. A few might have been missing. There were some telltale piles of dust, leading Elyse to think that they had been impaled by the pieces that had come off the train.

Good, a few less vampires in the world.

The flames were growing. Elyse didn't know enough about trains to know if there were more parts that could explode, but she didn't want to be close by if they did. She scooted backward, keeping her eyes on the vampires in case they took notice of her. Fortunately, no one saw her slide deeper into the shadows.

TWENTY-SEVEN

JOSH
One hour earlier

Josh unwrapped the tape from his hands. Cory had agreed to another match at the gym in the HAC headquarters. Midway through their workout, an urgent message came in, informing Josh that if he didn't report to the abandoned warehouse on Franklin east of Garrity in an hour, Elyse would die. It had been signed *Ben Piro*. After three days of turning Boise upside down in their hunt for Ben, Josh had been relieved when the message arrived. It meant she was alive. He knew, just as Cory knew, that it was likely a trap. Ben had told him the last time they saw each other that he would get Josh back for betraying him—allowing the FBI to "recruit" Ben because of his magical talent—when he had refused the offer Josh had presented. Josh had never had the opportunity to explain because the FBI had whisked Ben away to some classified location that even with Josh's level of clearance, he hadn't been privy to. Now he knew that had been Darkwater Penitentiary.

Once Cory had explained about the Snowflake, Josh had begun to see that Boise was a pot threatening to boil over. The question was, when would it go and who would be caught in the crossfire? All fingers pointed toward Josh and Elyse. Though he still hadn't pieced together everything, the bigger picture was beginning to fall into place, especially since he had remembered that Ben's big dream was to become president of the United States. It seemed reasonable that Ben would not be able to accomplish his dream alone and would need help on the path to making his dream a reality, which created a plausible explanation for why he would have made a bargain with the local vampire coven to help him acquire the Snowflake.

"What can you tell me about the abandoned warehouse?" Josh asked as he walked toward the trash with the wad of tape in his hand.

"I had someone pull it up on the large screen in my office. Come on," Cory said, beckoning. Josh snagged his gym bag and water from the bench and followed Cory. They walked down the hallway to a door Josh swore hadn't been there during the tour the other day, because he would have noted where Cory's office was. Yet there in front of him was a door that had Cory's name on it. Sure enough, there was a table with some chairs arranged to face a large screen on the back wall. In the corner, there was also a desk.

Josh studied the image on the screen. It appeared to be a blueprint, though he was looking for something to tell him the scale. Railroad tracks ran through one side.

"I don't see dimensions. How big is it?" Josh finally inquired.

Cory tugged on his lip before replying. "It's huge. I don't know if you're familiar with some of the old popular sports? Well, it was reported that eleven football fields could easily fit inside this warehouse."

"How are we going to find her in a building that large?" Josh asked.

Cory tapped on the screen and some images came up showing the inside and outside of the building. "You can see from these images the building is largely just a huge open space with rows of columns. Which means there are very few rooms we would have to search. However, the sheer size will make it difficult to just gaze around the whole space and be certain of her location."

"Are you certain that there isn't anything inside? No furniture, shelving, old machinery, et cetera?" Josh asked.

Cory nodded. "Yes, as far as I know there are minimal things inside. To me, it seems like an odd choice simply because there is so much open space. It would be a challenge to set a trap that we wouldn't be aware of as soon as we set foot in the warehouse. That being said, I have sanctioned our use of full tactical gear, which will give us goggles that have the ability to see infrared and long distance. We will take a squad of ten with us. I think if we took more, it would be too cumbersome, but I want to have enough backup in case things go sideways."

"That sounds like a good plan. How much do you know about Ben?" Josh asked. He was thrilled to be working with someone like Cory who had a team on his side with experience in situations like this. Josh wouldn't have to do it alone or with people he didn't trust. Over the past week, Josh had found that he really liked and trusted Cory.

Cory tapped the computer screen again and several photos of Ben Piro appeared, as well as a profile. Josh was surprised to see the photos showed Ben not only in his form of a ten-year-old boy, but also when he was fully changed into a panther-like creature that looked like his skin was made of burning coals with long, sharp claws.

"Are these your photos?" Josh asked.

Cory shrugged. "Yes. I got into a tussle with him, and he fully shifted. I thought we were going to go into full-on battle mode, but then he just disappeared. I thought perhaps he had decided Boise wasn't worth his trouble. I'm sure you can imagine my surprise when he took Elyse and blew up the apartment."

Josh nodded absently as he ran through the information on the computer.

NAME: BEN PIRO
AGE: UNKNOWN
SPECIES: HUMAN
MAGICAL TALENT: SHAPESHIFTER WITH HEAT
MAGIC AND CLAWS
LAST KNOWN LOCATION: BOISE
HISTORY: WAS IN MANHATTAN FOR QUITE
A WHILE, THEN IN CALIFORNIA. FBI
RECRUITED IN CALIFORNIA, AND THEN HE
DISAPPEARED. RECORDS SURFACED A FEW
YEARS AGO SAYING HE HAD ESCAPED FROM
DARKWATER PENITENTIARY.

Josh paused. "Where is Darkwater Penitentiary?"

Cory shook his head. "I wish I knew. This is not the first time it has come up, but no one seems to know where it is. We've even asked Catrina, and she said she has not had success finding it either."

"It must be a supermax for talented or something like that because I am not sure that the FBI would have been able to keep Ben contained without a highly specialized facility. I've seen him melt stone before," Josh replied.

"Right now, it doesn't matter," Cory said dismissively. "The gear I've chosen has high heat and flame resistance. It's a little bit heavier than normal, but since we know Ben will be there, I wanted to give us as much protection as possible. Two of my guys will have flash bangs and smoke grenades."

"Who are you bringing as far as talented?" Josh asked.

Cory opened his mouth to reply when the door crashed open and Terrance rushed in. Josh watched as Cory vaulted over the table and swooped his mate into his arms, kissing her and simultaneously running his hands over her, checking for injuries.

"Where have you been?" Cory said in a low growl.

"Put me down," Terrance said halfheartedly.

Reluctantly, Cory obeyed, but Josh watched as their fingers intertwined. He knew the feeling, not wanting to let go once you had a loved one back.

"I know you're planning to go to the warehouse, but you can't," Terrance said resolutely.

"I'm going," Josh said harshly. There was nothing they could do to stop him. If Cory decided to not help that was fine, but Josh was not going to abandon Elyse.

"Dariusz Sierżęga is here," Terrance said in a rush.

Eyes widening, Josh took a few steps back, trying to process what she had just said. "Here?"

"Yes, he decided to leave his hideout in Aerie and come down into Boise," Terrance said, eyebrow arched as though daring him to challenge her further.

"What does Dariusz have to do with Ben?" Cory demanded.

"It has come to our knowledge that Ben has somehow managed to get his hands on the original COVID-50 vaccine. Dariusz is concerned that Ben found long-buried information that mentioned the first version of the vaccine was not just a vaccine for COVID-50, but also could cure people of their magical talents," Terrance explained.

Josh's mouth went slack at the thought of a cure. There was no way. "There has never been a cure."

Terrance shrugged. "Dariusz said there was at one point, but it did not have the desired result. He also mentioned my aunt's research, but my father made sure that I stayed as far away from that as possible, so I do not know anything about what she was working on or may have discovered."

"Did Ben get his hands on the supposed cure too?" Josh said, anger rising. He needed to get to Elyse before Ben killed her, on purpose or accidentally.

"I don't know. He has been moving around a lot recently, though he went back to Marsing, which is southwest of where we are now, several times, and our surveillance showed that at one point a cabin existed near where he had been in Marsing." She paused, then began cursing.

"What's wrong?" Josh asked.

"I should have made the connection before. I think that's my aunt's old cabin," Terrance replied.

"Is that a good or a bad thing?" Josh demanded.

Terrance shrugged. "It's good because we know precisely where it is, but there is no security or anything there that would help us. Now back to Ben. We know that if he has found the vaccine and evidence supporting that it is a viable cure, he will use it on Elyse and on anyone else he captures," Terrance explained.

"Which means it is even more critical that we get Elyse away from him," Josh said, taking a step toward the door.

Terrance cleared her throat. "I have still not established why Ben needs the cure and the Snowflake. Dariusz feels that they are linked. I am not sure why they would be, unless it has to do with the same people being involved with both."

Josh coughed, and both tiger shifters turned their attention on him. Their gazes when combined were quite intense. "I think I know what the connection between the two is. My working theory is that Ben wants to get close to the president and has decided that the best way of accomplishing his dream is to have the Snowflake and the cure at his disposal."

"Who stole the Snowflake from Governor Beechwood?" Cory asked.

"Who else has connections to Ben?" Josh asked at the same time.

Cory's lips twitched in amusement. While they waited for Terrance to answer their questions, Cory pulled up Ben's profile again and told the computer to initiate a search for Ben's known associates. While the computer conducted its search, a pacing Siberian tiger appeared on the screen.

Josh watched the pacing tiger until Terrance spoke again. He turned to face her so he could read her body language.

"Our best guess is that it is a crew hired by Nightshade Coven. Willow would not have attacked in broad daylight, especially when most of her coven is sensitive enough to sunlight that they risk death if they are caught in it," Terrance explained.

"One of the local crews, like UA?" Cory asked with excitement clear in his voice. Josh knew he was likely thinking that they kept tabs on all the local crews for hire and that it would not be too difficult to go investigate; worst case, they could head back out west to do a second interview with UA.

Terrance shook her head. "No. It's not local. After reviewing the videos of the attack, it became clear that they are highly trained and use tactics that are more common in eastern Europe. They also were speaking in Russian."

"I am not aware of any Russian mercenary groups that have been active in the United States since COVID-50. The FBI does have a list of mercenaries," Josh said.

"I think the FBI caused you to have too narrow of a focus," Terrance said in exasperation.

Josh frowned. "What do you mean?"

Cory jumped into the conversation then. "I think what Terrance is trying to say is that because the FBI's presence within the country is restricted to the areas that the government has a strong foothold in—cities such as Atlanta, Boise, and Los Angeles—that the information available to you is limited. HAC operates within the large cities too, as well as throughout the less habitable parts of the country. Which means the best places for a group of Russian mercenaries to hide would be away from the large cities, where they operate off of the government's radar. Honestly, that is where a good portion of HAC's operations occur too."

"There is a group of Russian mercenaries who use Yellowstone National Park as their base of operations, which means they are close enough to Boise to be a good choice, without the headache of the local politics," Terrance explained.

Josh blew out his breath in frustration. He wanted to just go get Elyse and not deal with these extra hurdles. Part of him knew if he ignored the information that Cory and Terrance were giving him that the odds of successfully rescuing Elyse would be slim to none. "I still don't see how the Snowflake has anything to do with Elyse."

Terrance curled her lip in annoyance. "Ben also has ties to the Russians. Which means that although Ben is claiming to want to give Elyse back to you, there could also be some sort of exchange happening with the Snowflake in the same location. There are way more players at the table than Ben." Terrance raised her hand and tapped a finger for each name she went through, "Ben, Russians, Dariusz, Nightshade Coven, Trey, and Artur. That's six, two of which are groups, not individuals."

Cory jumped in again. "If the Snowflake is at the center of this, then it would be wise to assume we could come up against *everyone* who has been involved in the past two weeks. So you see, now instead of one person, at best it would be ten; at worst we could be facing thirty people. *And* I'm not convinced they're all working together."

A thought occurred to Josh and apprehension filled him. "If he believes he has a cure for magical talents, what if this is Ben's plan? The Ben I knew as a teenager would not have orchestrated something like this, but I have come to the conclusion that I don't know this Ben. What if his plan is to lure everyone to the warehouse and then 'cure' us as a group? You said yourself it could be ten people, or it could be upward of thirty. What better way to make a statement than by curing a group all at once?"

Terrance looked at Josh in horror. He watched as she pulled herself tighter against Cory. "This is even more of a reason not to go! What if the cure works? Then you will no longer have a talent."

"I don't care about my talent if it means choosing between that and Elyse's life. I am worried about if the vaccine is not a cure. What if it does something else? Ben is *not* a scientist. I would not trust him to have thoroughly tested his cure before dosing that many people with it," Josh said, voice shaking. "If you don't want to come with me, that's fine. I will just go now." Josh turned and headed for the door.

He made it to the end of the hallway before Cory came after him.

"We will come. The Snowflake is our mess. Terrance wants us to wear face masks along with the full body suits, though. That was the compromise," Cory said.

"I am not opposed to the idea of full protection. We have no idea how Ben is planning to use the cure, so the more protection we have that gives him less accessibility to us, the better," Josh replied, relief filling his voice.

When Cory had said he was going to bring ten, Josh had thought that was a good number. He was not expecting Terrance's appearance to change the plan. Now there were twenty of them loading up on the train. He had to admit the changes to the plan were genius. Josh and Cory would take their ten and enter the warehouse using the train tracks that went through the building. Terrance with her ten, who were all shifters, would ride the train until about a quarter mile from the warehouse, where they would change and then run the rest of the way and enter through the northeastern corner. He knew they could still be outnumbered, but it was better than going by himself.

The train started moving. Josh found himself running through his prefight meditation routine, a set of mental exercises where he centered himself through breathing. It was not as easy as it used to be, before he met Elyse, to find the calm for an op. *I guess I've never had anyone I cared about this much.*

He opened his eyes when the train slowed to let Terrance's group disembark. Cory and Terrance were wrapped around each other in the corner. Josh squeezed his eyes shut as fear of losing Elyse forever slammed into him hard. *What if I never get to kiss her again? Never get to tell her I love her?*

A hand clamped down hard on his shoulder. "You okay?"

Josh found himself looking into the golden eyes of Pierre. "I will be better when we find Elyse."

"We will do our best," Pierre replied.

Josh swallowed. *I need to focus.* He squared his shoulders and stood straighter, then began running over the plan. The shifters unloaded quickly and then the door shut, and the train moved forward again. Now that Terrance's group was gone, the train had been put into stealth mode, created by a combination of magic and science. It allowed the train to move almost completely undetectably if it stayed under fifteen miles per hour.

The train slowed, and the warehouse got larger and larger until they could only see the concrete wall towering above them. Cory had not been kidding when he said how insane this warehouse was. As the nose of the train crossed into the building, he felt a glimmer of something, and then it was gone. It had almost felt like Elyse, but that wouldn't make any sense. *Elyse can't teleport.* He shrugged it off. The train was almost at a complete stop. The door slid open, and with Cory in the lead, one by one the team hopped out. When Josh was clear, the door slid back into place and the train stopped moving. He could only see it because he knew it was there. At the edges, there was a slight ripple, but otherwise the train was invisible.

Josh slid his goggles down over his face and was surprised to see that the train was not visible with the infrared setting either. He could see several heat signatures far off in the distance. To the side where the tracks were, another heat signature was rapidly approaching. Josh flicked out of the infrared setting and realized that it was another train, gaining speed and heading right for their invisible train.

"Run!" he shouted, no longer concerned about whether or not Ben knew he was there; if they didn't get away from their own train, they would get caught in the inevitable collision.

Josh took off at a sprint. He had flipped his goggles back into infrared mode. He headed diagonally away from the train, wanting to get closer to the center of the building but not run straight into whoever was waiting for them in the center.

Boom!

Suddenly, Josh found himself thrown through the air and into one of the columns. He slid to the ground with a thud, wincing. He stood, shaking out his arms and legs, reminding himself he had to keep moving. Keeping his eyes peeled for any members of their team who might need help, Josh continued his path closer to the middle of the warehouse. One of the downsides of using the goggles was that it hindered his peripheral vision.

A foot collided with his back and he tumbled forward. Josh took a few unsteady steps to regain his balance before whipping around with a right roundhouse kick. His attacker stumbled backward several steps. Josh grinned and shot forward, punching his assailant's stomach. It seemed his element of surprise was short-lived; each of his punches was blocked. He couldn't decide if the infrared view was helpful or not. He knew the warehouse was fairly dark, so he left the goggles on their current setting. He had trained in the past with a blindfold on. He did not need to be able to see to fight.

The woman—for Josh felt confident based on the fighting technique it was a woman—fighting him was also wearing some kind of tactical gear. She raised her hands to throw a punch in his face. Josh tipped his head to the side. Instead of her hand whistling by his face, a tendril of green magic snapped along his jaw, leaving burning pain in its wake. *Shit.*

Josh rocked back on his heels, then began a combo, left jab, right jab, followed by a left crescent kick. As his leg swung around for the kick, he heard the ringing of a gunshot, and the woman mage slumped to the ground. Josh had to pull up the kick so he wouldn't lose his balance now that the woman was no longer standing.

"Thanks," he called to the heat signature.

Whoever had fired the gun gave a slight wave of acknowledgement and kept moving.

TWENTY-EIGHT
ELYSE

Elyse ducked instinctively when she heard the gunshot. It had definitely gotten the attention of the vampires and Ben. Everyone was on edge. Willow started giving orders. Elyse could not hear all of them, but given the way several of the vampires departed, she hazarded an educated guess that it was for them to investigate the gunfire and eliminate the problem.

A thread of hope worked its way through Elyse. If there was gunfire, then it meant there were people who had survived the train collision.

In the shadows, she observed Ben and Willow having an intense discussion that involved Willow waving her arms around, perhaps to emphasize her anger. Elyse thought it was quite comical, especially since she couldn't hear anything being said. As she watched Ben, she became aware that occasionally he would flick his eyes up.

Why is he looking up? Elyse wondered. She looked at the air directly above Willow and Ben and could not see anything useful through the haze the smoke was creating. But she did discover that there were steel beams at about the two-story level, and one of them looked like it ran fairly close to the space Ben was in. *I wonder if I can get up there.* She recalled seeing some electrical wiring near some of the columns. It would make sense that there would be an access point to get up there.

The smoke was starting to make her eyes burn. Elyse closed them for a moment to see if she could get some relief while running the parts of the warehouse she had seen through her mind. She couldn't recall seeing any stairs near a column. Which meant she was going to have to go column by column and look for stairs or a ladder. *Maybe some of them have built-in rungs, like a power pole.*

For a moment, Elyse felt nauseous. *Just what I need—to start puking. That will surely draw unwanted attention to me.* Elyse opened her eyes and gasped in shock. She was standing on one of the beams, peering down at Ben and Willow. *What the hell!* Fear gripped her. She ran her hands over her arms and then pinched her elbow. She could feel it. She was certain that she had somehow transported herself from the ground onto the beam. *Josh never said anything about talents changing, not after they had been unlocked. Is this my talent changing, or a side effect of the vaccine Ben injected me with?*

Elyse closed her eyes, trying to get her mind to settle, to accept that she was standing on top of the beam she had been trying to figure out how to get to. *If I'm on the beam, then maybe I can see what Ben was looking at!* Elyse cautiously opened her eyes. The beam itself was about twelve inches wide, so she had room if she was careful. There was no railing to save her from falling, though.

Slowly Elyse surveyed her surroundings. She could see a network of beams like the one she was standing on, which seemed to run the whole building. She could also see the gaping hole where the columns had pulled free, revealing the moon in the dark night sky. The hole worried her; she could feel slight tremors along the beam and wasn't sure if they were because she was shaking with nerves or because the building was becoming unstable.

If she was feeling brave enough, she could likely use the beams as her pathway to find Josh and escape without Ben even knowing, as long as nobody looked up. Elyse glanced at the ceiling. At the very top of the ceiling, another two stories above her, she could see something. It looked like a series of canisters and wires. Without a way of casting light up there, she could not identify any specific details. She saw something that could be some sort of label, but it was unclear. Forcing herself to tear her eyes away from the canisters, Elyse inspected as much of the ceiling as she could and could not find any other area that had canisters like that. *It must be what Ben was looking at. Likely some kind of dispersal system for the vaccine.*

Elyse swallowed, trying to fight her instinct to run. She knew Josh was here somewhere, which meant he would keep looking for her no matter what. She had to find him and tell him about what she had seen on the ceiling and about the vampires. *If he hasn't come across them already.* She took a shaky breath and began walking across the beam in the general direction of the train explosion. Her pace was slow; she could not risk slipping. But it meant she was crossing above Ben and Willow for far longer than she would have liked.

Just as she reached the column that she would have to carefully skirt around, her foot slid out from under her and something small and shiny bounced, making little *ping* sounds along the beam until it fell off.

"You!" came a shout.

Shit! Elyse gasped; they had seen her. Afraid to run on the beam, she gripped the column, shimmying around it as quickly as she could. When she got to the next beam, she walked a hair faster than she had before. A blast of blue magic narrowly missed her feet, and she started running. She had no other choice. More blue magic flew past her. Whoever was throwing it had terrible aim. With her slow run, Elyse was barely able to stay ahead of it.

The air in front of her just before the next column swirled almost black. Elyse stopped in her tracks and had to throw her arms out to balance herself. A blast of blue magic sliced against the back of her calves. She hissed in pain and debated if she should go back or go through the black swirling magic.

The blonde vampire appeared in the middle of the dark magic, teeth bared, claws out, ready to strike. "You will not get away." The vampire launched herself at Elyse.

Elyse pivoted, and her feet went out from under her. Before she could catch herself, she slid off the beam. A quick grab with her left hand was all that kept her from falling into the vampires below her. Dangling by her fingertips, sure she was going to fall and become the next meal, Elyse found the only thing on her mind was that she regretted not telling Josh how much she loved him. Her fingers gave way, and Elyse squeezed her eyes shut.

She was expecting the impact of concrete or teeth. Instead, familiar arms wrapped around her. She opened her eyes and was staring into a gas mask. Elyse struggled.

"Elyse, it's Josh." The voice was slightly distorted.

"Truly?" she questioned but stopped squirming.

"I'm going to set you down and then take off my mask," he said, moving slowly, as though he was afraid to startle her into bolting.

Elyse stood, shaking slightly. Josh removed his mask and relief coursed through her, followed by many questions.

Josh pulled her close into a hug. "I'm here. You're fine." He glanced around before continuing to speak. "How did you get here? One moment I was keeping an eye out for another mercenary, and the next you're falling through the air and into my arms."

Elyse gave a nervous laugh. "I seem to have acquired a new talent."

Josh raised his eyebrow. "What do you mean?"

"I was thinking about you and wishing we'd had more time, and then I lost my grip on the beam, and I guess teleported myself here. The first time, I was trying to find a ladder or stairs to climb one of the columns and then I ended up on one of the upper beams," she said, gesturing overhead.

Josh narrowed his eyes and frowned. "I haven't heard of new talents developing once someone experienced the initial unlocking."

"Ben gave me the original COVID-50 vaccine. I guess he determined it is a cure for talents," Elyse explained.

Josh reached out and grabbed her arm. "Ben gave you the cure?"

Elyse nodded. "That's what he said. I believe he thinks it worked or is in the process of working."

"Other than teleporting yourself, has anything else changed?" Josh asked.

Elyse nodded. "As far as I can tell, that's the only thing. But … he has some sort of dispersal device, I think, strapped to the ceiling over where he was holding me. I think that he is planning on 'curing' everyone here."

Josh opened his mouth to speak when Elyse saw a flicker of movement behind him. She must have flinched or something because Josh spun around and fired two shots from his gun. There was a soft thud. "There are mercenaries here too. And Terrance is here with a group of shifters."

"The vampires are with Ben, back in the middle of the warehouse," Elyse replied. She tugged on Josh's arm. "We need to leave."

"I need to make sure Cory and Terrance know the danger they're in before I just vanish. I owe them that much. They would not have come otherwise," Josh replied.

Elyse sighed. The longer they were in the warehouse, the higher the risk that Ben would set off his device. While the vaccine had not cured her, she was deeply concerned about what would happen if it was sprayed on top of the various people in the building. She had not read through all of Dr. Basak's notes and research, which meant she likely had some large holes in her knowledge about the C50-1A vaccine that Ben had dosed her with. She knew Josh was right; they couldn't abandon their friends.

"I want you to follow me. I'm going to put the mask back on, since I can see better with the goggles," Josh said, then slid it back over his face, gun in hand. He led the way.

They made it about twenty feet before shadowy figures appeared out of the smoke. Elyse recognized some of them immediately. "They're vampires," she hissed to Josh under her breath. He nodded.

One of the vampires had blue magic swirling through his fingers. Another had two guns. The third— Elyse didn't get to finish the thought as a flash of sliver spun through the air. Josh raised his arm and blocked the knife with his gun, sending it clattering to the ground. Knife after knife was thrown, and Josh blocked each one. A vampire decided to join the fight and in between knife throws were blasts of blue magic.

Elyse stayed behind Josh, but when the magic hit his gun, she could see his whole body vibrating with the impact. She wasn't sure how long he could keep this up, not without a proper shield. She scanned the area around him, looking for something that could be used as a shield, but there was nothing. Out of the corner of her eye, she noticed movement. Hands up to defend herself, Elyse felt relief wash through her when she saw a large Siberian tiger flanked by two wolves.

The vampires started closing the distance between themselves and Josh, clearly not aware that Terrance was about to join the fray. With a loud roar, Terrance launched herself into the middle of the vampires. The wolves made a beeline for the knife-thrower and the vampire with the blue magic. The area erupted with snarls, howls, and screams. Elyse was not able to keep track of what was happening; in the dim light, combined with the number of individuals, it just looked like a writhing mass.

Josh occasionally fired a calculated shot into the group. Elyse was confident he hit his target and not one of their friends. Captivated by the fight, Elyse was shocked when the barrel of a gun was jabbed into the middle of her spine.

"Call off your team," came the harsh male voice with a heavy eastern European accent.

Josh spun gun raised. "You don't need Elyse."

"My orders say otherwise," replied the man with the gun in her back.

"Take me instead," Josh said, slightly lowering his gun.

Elyse gasped, and the European laughed. "Unfortunately, *you* are of no interest to me."

"Why do you want Elyse? What's so special about her?" Josh asked. Elyse realized she wanted to know the answer to that question too.

"I'm not paid to answer questions, I'm paid to execute orders, which includes getting custody of—" His words were cut short when he tipped forward and blood sprayed everywhere as his back was shredded by a large Siberian tiger.

Josh lowered his gun. "Thanks," he said to Terrance.

Elyse wasn't sure how long the tiger shifter would stay here before returning to the main fight. "Ben set up a dispersal system of the vaccine or cure, whatever you want to call it. We need to evacuate."

Terrance cocked her head as though studying Elyse before bounding away into the fight again.

"Did she understand what I said?" Elyse asked.

"Oh, I'm sure she understood. The question is whether she wants to leave or if she's going after the rest of the vampires first," Josh said. "We should go find Cory."

Elyse nodded. She could still hear the occasional snarl, but for the most part it seemed as though the shifters had demolished the vampires. But she wasn't sure if the European, whoever he was, had come solo or with a team. *Another group with a stake in this?* She still had a nagging feeling there was a piece that she was missing and that if she didn't figure out what it was, they were all doomed.

Once again, Josh led the way. Elyse's lungs were burning from the smoke, and her eyes were watering too. Josh was moving fast. She assumed he also wanted to get out of there as soon as possible. But with the low visibility and his dark clothing, Elyse was having trouble following him. Elyse could barely make out the yellow column just ahead. When Josh passed it, he disappeared completely.

The area around the column darkened. A pair of red-rimmed blue eyes appeared first, followed by the rest of the blonde vampire. Elyse took a few steps backward and stepped on something, and her foot slid out from under her. She had a flashback of the same thing happening on the beam when she had faced this vampire. Except this time, she wasn't falling; she was on the ground.

"Cute trick you played back there. Disappearing. Artur never mentioned you could teleport. Which makes me wonder what other secrets you've been hiding about your talent." The vampire swaggered closer. Elyse pulled herself to standing again.

"I'm Willow, by the way."

Elyse bit the inside of her lip. "Who is Artur, and why do either of you care about my magical talent?"

"Well, you see, vampires, unlike most of the other magically talented people, are able to create more vampires. Over the years, I have found that exceptional individuals, such as yourself, make the best vampires. Because … the magical talents in most cases stay with the individual through the transition. Why change ordinary humans when I can have a coven full of special vampires?" Willow explained.

Elyse gasped, face contorting. A malicious smile formed on Willow's face. "Oh … you didn't know that vampires can be created, did you?"

Elyse gulped, mouth feeling dry, but she could not bring herself to reply. Willow took the silence as confirmation. "I guess Josh never told you … well, perhaps he doesn't know. It *is* a rather personal thing, telling people how you became a vampire." Willow smiled, baring her teeth—her long, pointy, distinctly not human teeth. "The process is quite simple. I bite you, twenty-four hours later you almost die, and then I feed you my blood. You enter a coma, and three days later, you're a vampire."

Elyse shuddered. *There's no way it's that simple, otherwise there would be thousands of vampires running around the country. What she is leaving out doesn't matter though. I just need to get away from her. Or if I can keep her talking, Josh will come back.*

"Who is Artur?" Elyse asked, settling on a subject that might give her the information they're looking for, *if* Willow bit.

"You really don't know that either? Here I was thinking that the shifters seemed to be on top of the game, almost figuring everything out, and yet it seems like what they do know, they found out accidentally—not because they dug deep enough to learn all the details. What a shame," Willow said, clicking her tongue in disapproval. She was almost within arm's reach of Elyse. While the vampire talked, she kept moving closer.

"No, I don't know who Artur is," Elyse said firmly.

"Do you know who Dariusz Sierżęga is?" Willow demanded.

"Yes, he tried to kill me in Atlanta," Elyse replied.

Willow laughed. "If he tried to kill you, then he is stupid. Anyhow, Artur is Dariusz's sibling."

"Sibling?" Elyse asked.

"Yes. They have the same maker," Willow said. "About two hundred years ago, they had a big falling-out after Dariusz killed their maker."

"Vampires … vampires existed before COVID-50?" Elyse asked, unable to hide the quiver in her voice.

"Of course they did. But that is not what we're discussing. When Artur found out Dariusz wanted to get his hands on the Snowflake, he decided he wanted it too. Lucky for me, Artur wanted an ally to help, so here I am," Willow said, throwing her arms wide and posing.

"This is about the Snowflake?" Elyse asked, rubbing her hand over her face.

"Just think. If you could control the electricity in the entire country and had access to a cure for magical talents, then you would be in a position of utmost power. The government would have to bow to you or face massive consequences for the entire population of the country," Willow explained.

This whole thing is about a power play. I guess I shouldn't be sur-prised ... but Willow is talking like the Snowflake is here, in this building. Which means we can't leave till we find it. Elyse felt light-headed from the new information, even though she only loosely understood how she fit into the equation: her talent was desirable. Knowing that this was merely a power play was threatening to overwhelm her. Despair washed over her. She wasn't sure how to help, how to get her friends out of this mess that they were only in because of her.

Elyse's vision began to blur.

She blinked rapidly to clear it and found that Willow was no longer in front of her. Instead, she was floating above the shifters facing off against the mercenaries. The mercenaries had guns; the shifters, tooth and claw. Elyse found herself trying to turn away. She didn't want to watch her friends get slaughtered. But try as she might, she could not get this version of herself to change position at all.

Then, the mercenaries stumbled forward. The shifters, led by the two wolves, leaped as one into the mercenaries. A few shots rang out, but the two-pronged attack seemed to do the trick, and within a few minutes, the mercenaries were all dead.

Elyse blinked and realized she was no longer floating; Willow was close enough that they were almost bumping foreheads. The problem with the visions was she never knew how much time had passed. Whether it was moments or hours. The fact that Willow had not yet commented on her "disappearance" led Elyse to believe that it had only been moments.

Elyse felt a sense of calm and ease entering her. *If Cory and Terrance could come up with a plan, then so can I.* Her lips curved in a smile.

"Why are you smiling?" hissed Willow.

"You said earlier that Artur and Dariusz are brothers, but now they're on opposing sides and both gunning for possession of the Snowflake and the cure. Why are you not taking your own position?" Elyse asked.

Willow ran her fingers through her hair and took a step back, as though to get away from Elyse. "Why would I do that?"

"Do you owe either of them anything?" Elyse pressed.

"No," Willow replied, pursing her lips.

Elyse smirked. She was definitely unsettling Willow, as she had hoped. "Why not take it all for yourself?"

Willow gave her a suspicious look. "Why do you care?"

"I can help you. If you ensure my and Josh's safety, then I can get you the Snowflake and the cure," Elyse replied.

"How do you propose doing that?" Willow replied.

Elyse felt calm and focused, confident that with Willow's assistance she could play a critical role in getting herself, Josh, and the HAC members helping them out of the warehouse.

"You said that I can now teleport. Which means if it's anything like Catrina Fox's talent, I should be able to teleport to a location of my choosing. I can get the cure canisters and then I can get the Snowflake."

"That sounds good, but how do you expect to get the Snowflake? Ben has it on him," Willow said apprehensively.

Elyse tucked that away. The vampire was afraid of Ben. *Not that I blame her. He is terrifying when he gets angry.*

"You can distract him, and I will slip behind him and grab it," Elyse said confidently.

Willow nodded and reached her hand out. "Fine. Let's shake on it."

Elyse took Willow's hand and shook it. "I will get the canisters first," Elyse said. "I will alert you when I have them so you can distract them."

The vampire nodded and turned and walked away, leaving Elyse to figure out how to control her teleporting talent.

TWENTY-NINE
JOSH

Josh had been hiding behind one of the nearby columns. When he discovered Elyse was no longer following him, he backtracked and witnessed her entire encounter with Willow. When he saw that she was starting to panic, he almost opened fire on Willow. But then somehow, she regained control. He knew how difficult it was to do that, especially in a high-stress situation like they were in at the warehouse. He had years of experience to help him handle this. Elyse had none. He was certain back in Jackson County, nothing was ever this scary on the horse ranch.

What worried him was how Elyse planned to remove the canisters from the ceiling. She had told him she hadn't gotten a clear enough view, which concerned him. If the device they were attached to was similar to or based on a bomb, then Elyse risked setting it off in her attempts to free a canister. He knew she was smart enough to know this, which left him wondering what her *real* plan was. While he had been at the school for the talented in northern New York, he had taken several courses on bomb construction, including how to make and deactivate a variety of styles of devices. The knowledge had come in handy several times during his career at the FBI.

Willow finally disappeared in a swirl of her magic. When he was sure she was gone, Josh approached Elyse. He kept his movements slow so as not to startle her more than necessary. Once he knew she saw him, he slid the mask off his face and tied it to his belt. Sweat dripped down his forehead from wearing it for so long.

He was relieved when she smiled at him, and he closed the gap quickly and kissed her. She wrapped her hands in the straps of his armor, pulling him closer and deepening the kiss. Josh didn't need any more encouragement. Finally, he took a slight step back, separating their bodies and giving them both some breathing room.

"Hi," he said softly.

"Hi," replied Elyse, before blurting, "I love you."

Josh's eyes widened in surprise. He had not been expecting to hear those words coming out of Elyse's mouth for a long time yet. He knew how he felt about her but was never completely sure if she felt the same, or as deeply. "I love you too." He gave her a light kiss on the cheek. They were still in enemy territory, and Elyse had just shaken on a crazy plan with Willow.

"How are you hoping to execute your plan?" Josh asked.

Elyse shrugged. "I was hoping you could help me and that my new talent permits me to teleport others with me. Otherwise, I might need a way out of my agreement."

"I am fine having you experiment with me, but I must point out that we don't know what is happening in the middle of the warehouse anymore. There is no way of telling if Ben is even still there. I am assuming that Ben's plans are in shambles, but it's possible he has contingencies in place. We cannot afford to be complacent," Josh said.

Elyse nodded. "Yes, I know. I was thinking about trying to teleport us to the beam I was on before. I think when I went around the column there that I felt ladder rungs. Which means there's a good chance they go up as well as down."

"I was able to get a message to Cory. Everyone on our side should know about the canisters and be working on their own extraction," Josh said.

"Good, fewer people to worry about if this doesn't work," Elyse said. "Are you sure you want to do this? If the canisters release their contents, we have no way of knowing what will happen."

"Of course. I love you. You need me, Elyse, so I will be there by your side regardless of the outcome," Josh said firmly.

"Great. I was hoping you felt that way," Elyse replied.

"Before you try teleporting both of us onto a beam, how about we start with something simple. Can you see the column over there?" he asked, pointing to the one he had just been hiding behind.

Elyse nodded. "Okay."

Josh took Elyse's hands in his and waited. She closed her eyes and scrunched up her nose in concentration. Suddenly, Josh got really dizzy and his vision blurred. When he blinked, they were next to the column he had pointed out.

"It worked," he said with an encouraging smile.

"Do you feel okay?" Elyse asked. She looked a little green around the edges herself.

"Yep, I'm fine." He decided telling her that he was nauseous would not help boost her confidence for teleporting them on the beam. He needed her to focus on using her talent, not worrying about the side effects.

"Okay. Then let's go to the beam." She gave him a shaky smile.

Josh returned the smile and gave her hand an encouraging squeeze. Elyse closed her eyes and scrunched up her nose again. This time his vison went completely black before returning. He knew instantly they were higher up because he could make out hints of ducting and conduit in the ceiling above.

The beam they were on was about one foot wide. Plenty of space to maneuver. Josh had occasionally made himself practice kickboxing routines on the balance beam at the gym to ensure he was comfortable maneuvering on a narrow four-inch space. To him, the additional eight inches was more than what he needed—though a quick glance at Elyse's face made him realize that she was not relaxed at all with the narrowness of the beam. *Or maybe it's the heights, or both? It's not like we've had the discussion before about what our greatest fear is. At least not fears that would impact only her.* Elyse had not hesitated to share with him the fears she felt for her horse ranch, including one they had lived through—barn fire. Josh bit his lip. He couldn't afford to get distracted by his thoughts. Elyse had teleported them here so that he could get a better look at the canister.

"Where exactly was the ladder?" Josh asked Elyse.

"Follow me," Elyse said and carefully led the way to the column. Sure enough, there were metal rungs going up and down the column.

Josh studied them and then what was below them. There was a body, but it was too large to be Ben. It seemed, for the moment at least, that they had a chance to inspect the canisters without an audience.

"Do you want to go up there with me or be a lookout down here?" Josh asked.

"I'll stay. How about I whistle if someone is coming?" Elyse suggested.

The signal would be a little obvious, but it was better than shouting a word. "Sounds good. I will just take a look and then come back."

Elyse nodded. Not wanting to waste any more time, Josh quickly ascended the ladder. It took him all the way to the top of the building. The top of his hair was scraping the ceiling when he noticed there was a platform that ran diagonally between the column he was on and the next—and in the middle was the device. *This is how Ben got it up here. He didn't learn how to fly. He just had to climb like I did.* Josh had to pull himself onto the platform and crawl on hands and knees along it. The platform was about as wide as the amount of space he had to maneuver, roughly two feet. It was tight. Especially for someone of his size, but he would make do. He had been in worse situations before.

Josh crawled along the platform until he was directly underneath the device. A total of six separate cylinders were wired together. Each cylinder had a label on it with the biohazard symbol and C50-1A, as well as a date stamp: 8/1/2125, which meant they had been manufactured the day before. The wires went into a military-grade device that had a green light indicating it was on, but there was no visible timer. There was a receiver. Josh used his flashlight to inspect the individual wires and connections. He was surprised to find that only one of the six cylinders was truly wired to the device. The other five were decoys of some sort. What he was not sure about was whether or not they had trigger mechanisms underneath them, so that if he messed with one, it would explode anyhow.

Josh reached up and ran a finger along the edge of the canister. He could not feel anything that felt like a triggering mechanism. Which just left determining how to detach it from the ceiling. He debated what he should do. Initially, he had been planning to return to Elyse to tell her what he'd found. But now that he was here, he wanted to just go ahead and try to remove it. Sticking his flashlight in his mouth so he could see, he reached up again with both hands and gently tugged on the canister. To his surprise, it popped off the ceiling with just the small tug.

He sat up and inspected the canister. It was about five inches in diameter and ten inches long and surprisingly lightweight. Given that it was solid aluminum, he had no way of telling what was inside without trying to open it. He was not going to do that without proper protective equipment in a contained environment. Knowing Elyse was likely getting impatient, Josh turned around and crawled back to the column, then climbed down the ladder. It was more awkward this time with the canister in his hand, but he managed.

When he was on the beam where he'd left Elyse, she threw her arms around his neck, her relief clear.

"Careful," he warned her. "I brought one with me."

"But you said—" Elyse protested.

"Yes, I know what I said, but I decided to try removing one. It worked," Josh said dismissively.

"What would you have done if it hadn't worked?" Elyse demanded. "You didn't come back and tell me what you found so we could discuss it," she said, her voice rising. "Instead, you just went ahead without me."

Josh raised his hand as though surrendering. "I know, and I'm sorry. I just felt in the current situation it was the best course of action. Given there is a device overhead, this must be where Ben is herding everyone, which means we could have visitors any moment now. I'd rather get in and out as quickly as possible. Your plan with Willow involved letting her know or giving her the canister, and then she was going to provide a distraction. How exactly were you hoping to inform her that we have one? I know you can teleport now, but this is a huge warehouse. Bouncing around the whole place searching for her would exhaust you long before we found her," Josh asked. It was a problem with their plan that he hadn't considered until he said it.

He knew that Willow had magic. The swirling dark smoke was a giveaway, accompanied by her explanation of being able to make vampires, and wanting to choose people with magical talents also supported the theory. The swirling dark smoke was not any useful indication of the type of talent Willow had. In his experience, the color magic manifested as had more to do with the wielder than it did with enabling someone to identify the type of talent it belonged to. He had encountered someone with fire magic that appeared blue instead of the traditional reddish orange, and another who had water magic that was bright yellow.

"While you were investigating the device, I did consider this question of yours. I believe that if I focus on Willow, just like I focus on a question or certain words to help direct my talent to see the past or future, I could potentially teleport right to her," Elyse said.

Josh shook his head. "The problem with that is you have no way of knowing what you would be teleporting into. I want to come."

"No. She didn't know you were there eavesdropping on our conversation. I doubt she would take it well if you showed up with me. Besides, I think it would be prudent to leave the canister with you. Then I have leverage for her to keep her part of the bargain," Elyse said.

Josh smiled. Elyse was catching on to the strategies required for an operation like this. "That is a solid plan. I am still worried about you teleporting into the middle of something. We know there are vampires, mercenaries, and Ben running around here still. I'd hate for you to end up in the middle of a meeting."

"That is a risk I'm willing to take," Elyse replied. Before he could say anything else, she shut her eyes and disappeared. Josh sighed and ran a hand over his face. He was not going to wait for Elyse to come back. He wanted to find Terrance. He could hear voices below him, but he could not see who they belonged to. Josh moved quickly along the beam, working his way through the warehouse toward where he believed he would find Terrance. He had to admit that Elyse's idea for using the beams had been brilliant. He could move unhindered and undetected throughout the entire warehouse.

Finally, Josh found Terrance. Three gunshots had sent him running as fast as he dared across the beams in the direction of the train crash. He anticipated running into the mercenaries again but was relieved to see it was Terrance and her group of shifters down there instead. A wolf was sniffing the bodies on the ground, he presumed to ensure they were dead. Josh debated how to notify Terrance of his presence. He was worried if he made an obvious motion such as waving his arms or jumping from the beam to the ground that she might shoot him by mistake. He noticed that there was a ladder on the column closest to him, so he descended using it. By the time he reached the ground, the wolf was snarling a warning at him.

He raised his hands in the air, showing he was not holding a gun. "It's Josh Everly," he said, loud enough that Terrance and the wolf could hear him but hopefully not so loud as to draw unwanted attention.

"Josh!" called Terrance. The wolf stopped growling, and Josh lowered his hands and turned toward Terrance.

"I see you've met more of the mercenaries," he said casually.

Terrance shrugged. "They had just taken out some of the vampires and were not paying attention."

"That's great; the fewer people running around here wanting to kill us, the better. I have some news," Josh said and then launched into an explanation of the canisters, what they assumed Ben's grand plan was, and how Elyse hoped to stop him.

"Well, well, well, what do we have here," a high-pitched voice came from behind him. Josh dropped his hand to his gun but kept his eyes on Terrance's face. Her eyes were wide, and her jaw had dropped.

"You're dead!" Terrance said, a hitch in her voice. "I watched you die."

Josh bit his lip. The person behind him was dead. *A vampire?*

The voice giggled. It just sounded wrong to Josh. "You're wrong. You saw me fake my second death."

"Then how are you here, now?" Terrance asked.

Josh became concerned. Terrance was not making any move to attack whoever this person was. He still had not turned around to see the new enemy.

"I never knew that vampires could create more vampires. It's quite an impressive feat," the woman replied.

"They can't," came Terrance's whisper.

Josh knew better because he had just overheard Willow telling Elyse that vampires could create new vampires and that their preference was for talented humans since the talents could still work. *The person approaching is a talented vampire that Terrance knows.*

Slowly, Josh turned around. He made note of Terrance's other members, who had also stopped in their tracks and were gazing at the woman. Josh's eyes fell upon her, and though the voice was different than it had been when she was a human, he recognized the way she looked. It was Yolanda, the HAC shadow mage. Dark-purple magic swirled around her fingertips, though she had yet to make a move indicating she was going to harm them.

Josh very slowly removed his gun from its holster, keeping his movements slow to avoid detection. Yolanda seemed more interested in the way Terrance was reacting than in harming them for the time being. Josh raised his gun so it was level with his hip, pointing at her stomach. *Not the ideal shot.* His finger squeezed the trigger, when the whole building started to shake. He staggered to the side, and his grip slipped on his gun, pulling the trigger. The bullet ricocheted off the concrete and bounced back, hitting Yolanda in the leg.

Yolanda threw a ball of dark-purple magic at him, when the ground started to heave and buckle. Josh fell to the floor, unable to regain his balance. As the ground vibrated, Yolanda slid into the opening that was forming.

Josh turned his eyes away, unable to watch. The building pitched and rolled; columns broke loose from the ceiling. Pieces started falling, some larger than cars. Josh scrambled to get up, but every time he got to his knees, everything started moving again. Terrance and the wolves seemed to be faring somewhat better. They staggered away in various directions.

They heard a screeching sound that was becoming louder and louder. *The trains!* The back half of the train that had broken off in the collision was being tossed around as the ground heaved around it. It gained enough momentum to be thrown through the air, tumbling end over end, right for Josh.

The air next to him shimmered, and he felt Elyse's hands grab him. Before he could do anything, everything got blurry, and he found himself outside on a dirt road bathed in moonlight. The ground was vibrating but not to the extent it had been in the warehouse.

"Elyse?" he said, trying to get his eyes to focus. He thought she was still there but wasn't sure. Suddenly, he was bending, throwing up over and over. When his stomach muscles finally stopped contracting, he stood up shakily and looked around. In the distance, he could see what he thought might be the warehouse. Half of the building had completely collapsed. The rest of it was still shaking, and he could see even from here pieces continuing to fall.

Peppering the dirt road around him were members of the HAC teams that Cory and Terrance had been leading. Many of them were also puking. Josh took a deep breath, inhaling and trying to clear his nausea and the throbbing in his leg.

"Has anyone seen Elyse?" he called.

Terrance met his eyes. "She just went back to check for anyone else."

"What do you mean, went back?" Josh said.

"She is the only person who can teleport in our group. How did you think we got out here?" Terrance asked in an exhausted voice.

"I don't know. You were talking to Yolanda and then everything started shaking," Josh replied.

"That was an earthquake. There are still some aftershocks. That's why everything is still moving some," Cory replied.

"I didn't think Boise could get earthquakes," Josh said.

"We can. They just are rare. When we do get them, they're big fuckers," Cory replied with a growl.

"I need to get Elyse," Josh said. He took a few steps toward the warehouse and his leg almost gave out under his weight.

"You can't," said Terrance softly.

"You won't stop me," Josh said angrily.

Terrance gave him a sympathetic look. "Did you even look at yourself?"

Josh was confused. He felt fine, just a little nauseous, and his leg hurt a little. He was standing. When he looked down, he almost fell over in shock. There was a huge piece of rebar going straight through his leg. *How can I not feel that?*

"It's the adrenaline. As soon as it wears off, you are going to regret standing on it for so long," Cory said.

Josh gingerly sat down on the ground. The tiger shifter was right. His leg was starting to hurt. He examined the rebar and then had to look away. It was one thing to see someone else impaled, and another when it was himself.

The air shimmered slightly in front of him and Elyse appeared. Her eyes met his, and she gave him a tired smile.

"I couldn't find any other HAC survivors. This is everyone." They'd gone in with twenty-two and left with eight.

Elyse sat down next to him, and he wrapped his arm around her shoulder, pulling her close. "I love you," he said softly.

"I love you too," she replied.

THIRTY
TERRANCE

Terrance was snuggled tightly to Cory's chest in their bed. Or what was left of it. She couldn't help but smile at the memory of the sex that destroyed their bed. One moment she had been riding his cock hard, the next they were in the middle of the floor. It hadn't stopped them for more than a few moments.

Cory ran his fingers through her short hair. "Ter, are you okay?"

Terrance nodded. "Of course. Our bed and uh"—she glanced around—"room don't seem to be in the best shape though."

Cory shrugged. "It's just a room and furniture."

She turned so they were facing each other. "I can't believe we lost so many. Devin, Vic, Sienna …" Her voice faltered.

"I know. I am still having trouble wrapping my mind around what exactly happened last night. I just am grateful that you are safe," Cory said and wrapped his hands tightly around her waist, pressing their bodies firmly together.

"We need to make sure everyone is fine," Terrance protested. As much as she wanted to stay in his arms all day, she knew that as the leader of their clan, there were others, not just her mate, who needed to see for themselves that she was alive.

There was a light tap on the apartment door. Terrance scooted out of her mate's arms and stood up. "Give me a minute!" she called, hoping whoever was at the door wasn't going to just come in.

Cory turned on a lamp, casting light across the room. Terrance peered around, realizing how much damage they had really done. The bed and mattress were destroyed, the dresser was toppled over, pictures had fallen off the walls. She carefully stepped over pieces of the bed frame and made it to the dresser. Tugging on a corner, she got it upright and rummaged through the drawers, selecting bra, underwear, pants, and shirt.

Cory was watching her from his position on the bed. She cast one more look over the disaster, then she left the bedroom for their front door. She opened the door and the person on the other side stumbled forward. She held up a hand to catch them, and her golden eyes met Pierre's brown ones.

"What's wrong?" Terrance asked, pushing the door open wider and beckoning for Pierre to come in.

"Nothing … nothing new, I mean," Pierre said, stumbling over his words. "I just miss them."

Terrance blew out her breath. They had lost four of Pierre's pack yesterday at the warehouse, including Sienna, Pierre's sister. "I'm sorry. I know that it is a huge loss all at once. Especially Sienna."

Pierre threw himself on the sofa. Terrance was relieved to see that the living area of the apartment was mostly unscathed. "Have you been down to the healing suite?"

Pierre nodded. "Yes. Josh is out of surgery, and everyone else has been patched up. Though the healer is not entirely sure what to make of Elyse's new teleporting skills and that she was supposedly vaccinated with C50-1A. But I am not our clan leader, so perhaps there is additional information that is just not being shared with me."

Terrance tugged on her lip before responding. "Have you had a chance to go home yet to your wife, or did you just crash here at headquarters?"

Pierre shook his head. "I haven't gone home yet. I only told her I am alive and would give more details later."

"You should go home," Terrance suggested.

"Are you sure?" Pierre asked.

Terrance studied him. He appeared exhausted, though truthfully, she wasn't sure she looked much better. "Cory is here. I am sure we will be fine. Go home. I promise to call you if something changes and I need you to come back."

Pierre sat on the couch in silence for a few minutes. Finally, he stood up. "I will go home. Keep me posted."

Cory was in the kitchen cooking and Terrance was debating whether or not she should go down to the healer suite to see how Josh was doing when there was a knock on the door.

"Come in!" she yelled at the same time Cory did.

The door opened and Elyse stepped inside. Terrance took in Elyse's appearance, noting that it didn't seem as though the woman had taken any time to care for herself. *Not that I blame her. If it were Cory in the healer suite, I wouldn't have been willing to leave until I knew he was stable.*

"You look terrible. How's Josh?" Cory said. Terrance rolled her eyes; sometimes her mate could be so tactless.

Terrance watched as Elyse glanced down at herself before looking back at Cory and replying, "Josh is doing well. He's sleeping. I came because I wasn't sure where to go. I don't know where Josh has been staying since I was kidnapped."

Terrance set her hands on top of the table. "Josh has been staying in one of the apartments here. After you were kidnapped, a trap had been set to take out Josh, so the safe house no longer exists because it was blown up." She paused, letting that sink in.

"If you can tell me where it is, I can get out of your hair," Elyse said tiredly.

"How about you eat with us? Cory is almost done cooking, and then I can show you where it is?" Terrance offered.

Elyse nodded and then sat down at the table opposite Terrance. Terrance waited for Elyse to say anything else, but she did not seem interested in speaking, or at least not starting a conversation herself.

Terrance decided to give Elyse an update. "As you know, the earthquake sent everything at the warehouse into chaos. We are still trying to sort out exactly what happened. From what I can tell currently, Willow, Ben, and Artur are status unknown. I would love to believe they all died, but I think making that assumption without proof is too dangerous."

"What was the point of going there then?" Elyse said, breathing hitched as she appeared to fight back tears.

Terrance sighed. She hated that Elyse felt the whole thing was pointless. "We got you back."

"Am I really worth all those lives lost?" Elyse said, voice cracking. Tears flowed freely down her face.

Terrance reached over and gave Elyse's arm a squeeze. "Yes. You are worth it. But you are not the only thing we left with. We have one of the canisters of C50-1A."

Elyse hid her face in her hands. Terrance let her work through her feelings. She knew that the past few days had been extremely trying on Elyse, being held captive and whatever Ben had done to her, then being taken to the warehouse and discovering she had a new talent. It was a lot in such a short period of time.

A plate thumped onto the table, followed by another. Terrance glanced up at Cory, grateful he had brought food over. *Maybe it will help Elyse to eat.*

"Food is ready," Terrance announced and slid one of the plates closer to Elyse.

Both plates had a barbecued chicken thigh, ear of corn, and Caesar salad. Terrance selected a fork from the silverware holder at the middle of the table and dug into her food. A few moments later, Elyse followed suit. Cory soon joined them, and they ate in companionable silence.

"Elyse, if you would like, in the morning, I can escort you to see the horses," Cory said with a smile.

Elyse nodded. "Yes. I would like that very much. The healer said that as long as Josh continues to rest, he should be able to walk around headquarters tomorrow evening. I think she is being overly cautious. His wound looks fully healed to me. But if he is willing to follow the instructions, then I am not going to object."

When it was clear that no one was going for seconds, Terrance stood up and collected the plates. She made a move to start washing them, when Cory came up behind her and took the scrub brush out of her hand.

"You said you were going to escort her to Josh's apartment," Cory reminded her.

Terrance leaned back against him for a moment before standing up straight. "Yes. I will be right back." She ducked under his arm and over to where Elyse was still sitting at the table.

"I can take you to the apartment now. I'm sure you are desperate for a shower. We have lots of hot water," Terrance said with a smile.

Elyse nodded and gave a half-smile, then followed Terrance out of the apartment. Terrance led the way to the end of the hallway and, using her thumbprint, opened a door. She ushered Elyse inside ahead of her. "Here we are."

When Terrance was sure that Elyse was okay in the apartment, she headed back down the hallway to rejoin Cory. A tapping caught her attention, and it took her a moment to figure out where it was coming from—the foyer. She took a deep breath and threw her shoulders back, then strode down the hall toward the foyer. She had no idea who it was, but no matter how tired she was, she refused to show any weakness.

Terrance's eyes widened as she stepped into the foyer and saw who was on the other side of the glass doors: Tiny from UA. She could not recall the last time she had seen him away from his ranch. Which meant it must be important if he hadn't sent someone to speak for him. She quickly unlocked the door, but instead of inviting him inside, she stepped outside.

"Tiny, what can I do for you?" Terrance asked.

Tiny grimaced before responding, "I was not going to get in the middle of your affairs with Nightshade Coven, but after what went down at the warehouse, and the earthquake that hit the whole city, I feel like I don't have a choice."

Terrance exhaled, nostrils flaring, but stayed silent.

"Ben Piro has asked me to dig up information on President Seagraves and to let him know if he has any upcoming trips," Tiny explained.

"Shouldn't you be telling the FBI this information, not me?" Terrance asked, allowing her annoyance to creep into her voice.

Tiny shifted back and forth on his feet. "You're right, and I was planning on telling Agent Florence. However, I also know that Ben had kidnapped Elyse and was involved in the chaos at the warehouse, so I thought the information would be of interest to you as well. HAC isn't required to color inside the lines."

Terrance sighed. She knew he had a point. "Does the president have upcoming trips? Is he in immediate danger?"

She cared whether or not Ben succeeded in destroying the president, not because she cared about the president himself, but because she was afraid of what Ben would do if he seized control of the country armed with a cure and the Snowflake. The White House was well fortified. If Ben disposed of President Seagraves and then took up residence in the White House, it would be nearly impossible to eliminate him.

Which is likely the precise reason Ben has asked for information on the president's upcoming trips. If the president is outside of the White House, then he is far more vulnerable.

Tiny nodded. "Yes, he does. But from here in Boise, it is difficult to get any solid details. All I know is he will be on the move, and soon."

318

"Are you going to help?" Terrance asked.

Tiny stared at her for a few moments before responding. "This is me helping. Giving you this information free of charge."

Terrance rolled her eyes. "I will take that as a no. When it comes down to it, if we get a location on where the president is going and Ben is sure to follow, then you will not be aiding HAC in taking Ben down."

Tiny let out a low snarl. "You know I deal in information. I steer clear of the action. Are you going to be allowed to go after Ben?"

This time it was Terrance's turn to snarl, but she did not keep hers low. She let her displeasure be known. "I can go after whomever I want."

Tiny smirked. "Are you sure about that?"

Terrance curled her lip, baring her rapidly elongating canines. She felt the rush of cold air as the door opened behind her. She knew without looking that Cory was at her back. Tiny did not give up any ground, as she had expected. "If you do not have any more information to share, Tiny, then I bid you good day," Terrance said dismissively.

Tiny looked from her to Cory, and she could see his face change as he made his decision. "Good day." Tiny turned and walked away.

Terrance let out a sigh of relief as the bear shifter finally moved out of view. "Let's go back inside."

Terrance and Cory stepped into their apartment and the air shimmered. Both tiger shifters had guns trained on the space in front of them before whoever had chosen to teleport into their apartment— which should have not allowed anyone to teleport—materialized.

Catrina gave them cold smile and then turned her back on them, went over to the dining room table, and sat down.

"What are you doing here?" Terrance demanded.

Catrina shouldn't have been able to break through the warding on their apartment, which meant either her presence was urgent or she was just messing with Terrance.

Catrina patted the table. "Come sit."

"No, I don't want to sit, I want to know why you have shown up uninvited in my home," Terrance replied, her voice rough as she reined in the instinct to shift. She could feel Cory bristling beside her; her mate had never liked Catrina.

"Suit yourself," Catrina replied and turned her chair so she was facing them better.

"Why are you here now that the dust has settled and not when I could have used your help—for the actual fight?" Terrance asked.

Catrina rolled her eyes. "Dariusz sent me to Los Angeles to negotiate with one of the covens. If you have a problem with me not being at the warehouse, then you need to take it up with him."

Terrance sighed. At least she now knew that Catrina hadn't been ignoring her; she had just been busy attending her duties as an HAC lieutenant. "I think you have heard how things went at the warehouse. How did it go for you in Los Angeles?"

Catrina's eyes narrowed slightly before she replied, "The Blood Raiders said they would consider Dariusz's proposal, but they require more time."

Terrance gave a slight smirk. "Hopefully not too much." Catrina locked eyes with Terrance, something Terrance tried to avoid doing since she knew that some vampires, including Catrina, could use it as a way of mind control.

"You need to be careful, Terrance. Dariusz is not happy with how things have evolved here in Boise, particularly now that Ben Piro is in the wind," Catrina said.

"Ben was not my priority. Getting Elyse free was," Terrance snapped.

Catrina continued to hold her gaze. "Yes, I know that, and he knows that. The problem is I don't think he agrees with your decision to not prioritize Ben. If you were acting as an HAC lieutenant, then he should have been your priority. Dariusz is starting to question your loyalty, and I know that the two of you," she waved her hand to indicate Cory, "have witnessed firsthand what happens when he decides you are a threat."

Terrance felt her muscles tense as Cory growled from behind her. She blinked, hoping he would rein in his temper. Catrina was warning them to be careful, not threatening them in their own home. Terrance took a deep breath and blew it out slowly. "Thank you. Now, if you don't have any more information for us, we would like to clean up from dinner and go to sleep."

Catrina stood up. "That is all I have for now. Good night."

Before Terrance could say anything else, Catrina disappeared. Terrance's shoulders sagged in relief and she ran a hand over her face, trying to process everything she had just found out.

Cory's arms wrapped around her waist, and she leaned into his chest. "It will all work out one way or another," he said.

"I know it will," Terrance replied softly, then she turned around and stood on her tiptoes and kissed her mate deeply. She had known since she joined HAC that her job was dangerous whether she was doing an operation or not. It had taught her to live life in the moment because she never knew when it might be her last.

THIRTY-ONE
ELYSE

After taking a shower, Elyse wandered back down to the healer suite. Josh was sleeping, but she just needed the reassurance of seeing him before seeking out a bed.

She sat down in a plush chair that was about a foot away from the edge of the bed, close enough that she could touch Josh if she wanted to. Elyse leaned back in the chair and took a deep breath, letting her eyes flutter shut. *Only a moment,* she told herself.

Elyse opened her eyes and was surprised to find herself inside of what she assumed from Josh's description was the Nightshade Coven residence. A bedroom door was open from the hallway she stood in, and she peered inside. Yolanda was lying on the bed, unmoving. Elyse slipped through the door and edged closer. There was a wound on Yolanda's neck that looked like a bite that had been allowed to fester. The rest of the woman's skin was pale with a bluish tinge. Elyse realized with a start that Yolanda was likely in the middle of her transformation to become a vampire.

Elyse found herself trying to recall what Willow had said. Three days. With her limited knowledge of the transition a vampire went through, Elyse was uncertain what part of the three days Yolanda was in. Other than that, it was quite obvious she was still in a coma and not yet a vampire. Not sure what else to do, Elyse left the room and started walking down a hallway, deciding she could explore the rest of the building.

Unfortunately, the dream or vision started to fade the farther she went down the hallway.

Elyse's neck ached. She opened her eyes and found she was curled up in the chair, resting her head awkwardly on the armrest. A movement on the bed caught her eye, and she focused on it. Josh's eyes were open.

"Hi," he said softly.

"Hi," Elyse replied, reaching out to squeeze his hand.

"Why aren't you sleeping in a real bed?" Josh asked.

Elyse yawned. "I came to see you before doing that and sat down in the chair. I must have fallen asleep."

"Come here," Josh said, patting the side of the bed.

Elyse was about to protest that she would hurt him, but he gave her a pleading look that she couldn't resist. She carefully sat down on the side of the bed. Josh wrapped his arms around her and pulled her down beside him. Elyse snuggled into his side. "Better?"

"Definitely," Josh said.

"I love you," Elyse whispered into his ear. She waited for him to respond, but he didn't. She realized he had fallen back asleep. She knew she should probably leave but didn't have the heart to, not when Josh had asked for her to join him on the bed. Instead, she snuggled closer and shut her eyes, drifting off to sleep.

Forty-eight hours after the earthquake, Josh was cleared by the healer. The relief on Elyse's face as the healer gave them the news was palpable. She had only left his side to eat, shower, and go visit the horses with Cory. She was past being ready for a real bed, not a sliver of Josh's hospital one.

"You could have slept in the apartment," Josh said as though reading her thoughts.

Elyse stuck her tongue out at him. "You seemed quite content to have me sleeping in here."

"Well, you heard the healer. We can leave. So let's go before she comes up with another reason for me to stay longer," Josh said.

Elyse smiled and took his hand in hers. Side by side they walked through HAC headquarters until they reached the apartment.

"How much damage was there from the earthquake?" Josh asked, catching Elyse off guard.

"I think you know the safe house we started in was demolished from the bomb, but the houses on that block completely collapsed. HAC headquarters only had minor damage. Thanks to their stash of backup batteries and generators, the building did not lose power," Elyse explained as they stepped inside of the apartment.

"What about the nature of the earthquake? Was that investigated?" Josh asked.

Elyse giggled. "Why are you suddenly interested in all of this? You didn't ask me any questions about it while you were recovering."

Josh shrugged. "The healer said to keep things low-key. I figured questions that might be construed as work would get me in trouble."

"Well, for your information, Cory and Terrance verified that the earthquake was natural, not magical, and wreaked havoc across Boise," Elyse responded.

Elyse turned so she was facing Josh and stepped close to him, so they were almost touching. "Now, if you don't mind, there's something else I would like to do that doesn't involve talking."

Josh grinned and captured her lips with his, then grabbed her hand and tugged on it, leading her into the bedroom.

Unlike the safe house, this apartment had a single massive bed in the middle of the bedroom. The past forty-eight hours had been filled with uncertainty for Elyse: fear that the healer had been wrong and Josh would not be okay; longing for the physical contact that she craved that sleeping on his hospital bed could not quite satiate; and love—the realization that she was head over heels in love with Josh.

Elyse stood with the back of her legs lightly brushing the edge of the bed. When she had returned to the apartment to change clothes that morning, her choice had been very deliberate. Her fingers slowly worked their way down the buttons of her black silk shirt. As the shirt opened it revealed a bright red lace bra. Josh seemed unable to wait, because when she was about two-thirds of the way through the buttons, he took the bottom of the shirt in his hands and pulled. There was a loud rip and the buttons popped off.

"Oops," Josh murmured, pulling her close.

Elyse slid her hands between them, unbuckled his pants, and tugged both pants and boxers down. Josh stepped out of his pants and slid his shirt over his head. Then, he slid his fingers down the waistband of her skirt and smiled when he realized she was wearing a G-string.

Elyse stepped free of the skirt and gave Josh a scorching kiss, which he returned, pressing their bodies tightly together before he gently pushed her back onto the bed. Elyse scooted backward so her head was resting on the pillow. Josh straddled her, his cock brushing the inside of her thigh.

"I love you, Elyse Hutchinson," he said. She could hear the desire in his voice and see his emotions written clearly on his face.

"I love you too, Josh Everly," Elyse replied before setting her hands on his shoulders and pulling him down toward her. He shifted his hips ever so slightly and as their lips met, his cock slid inside of her.

As he started gliding in and out, Elyse felt a weird tingling sensation, like her talent was trying to work. She bit the inside of her cheek, hoping her magical talent would not choose now of all times to give her a vision. Josh trailed kisses down her neck toward her breast.

The tingling sensation increased and suddenly Elyse could no longer feel Josh's lips on her breast; instead her lips were on the breast, and she could feel the pleasure rising as she slid in and out. Elyse audibly gasped, and Josh immediately stopped and rolled off of her.

"What's wrong?" he said, worry in his voice.

Elyse squeezed her eyes shut and then opened them. The tingling sensation went away, and she wiggled her fingers; they moved when she told them. "I don't know. For a moment, it felt like I was going to get a vision, and then suddenly instead of me being me, I was you?" She knew how ridiculous it sounded.

Josh frowned. "I sort of had the same thing happen to me. I was sucking on your breast, and then I could feel your mouth on my breast, but also your weight on me."

"Like we switched bodies?" Elyse asked. She wondered if this was another side effect of Ben having given her the "cure."

"Maybe, but I haven't exactly heard of that happening before," Josh said and then with a featherlight touch began teasing her breasts.

Elyse couldn't stop the moan from escaping her lips as his touch set her body on fire. She reached over and ran her hand along his cock, which was already hard and slick with her fluids. Her touch was all the encouragement he needed. Bracing himself on his forearms, Josh returned to his position on top. She let go only when he was about to slide into her. As soon as he did, she did. It felt as though they had never stopped earlier.

The tingling on her arms began again, but this time Elyse ignored it, deciding if Josh wasn't worried and had experienced the same thing that it should not be a concern of hers either. As his strokes quickened, he slid his fingers inside her, teasing and heightening her pleasure even more. She knew she was close. Just as Josh sent her over the edge, their eyes locked, and she was looking at herself.

She gave one big thrust with her hips, her fingers matching each stroke, and then her seed exploded out of her cock. As her body spasmed, she found she was no longer able to brace and gently lowered herself.

Elyse blinked again as she felt Josh's weight settling on top of her. Except there was this new awareness of him. She could not only feel her own satisfaction at what they had just done, but she could feel his, and the love he felt for her enveloped her mind. Unsure what was going on, Elyse allowed herself to succumb to the wave of exhaustion that barreled into her.

When Elyse woke up, Josh was still on top of her. He was lightly snoring, and she was not entirely sure how she was going to get out from under him. She knew with the recent events that he needed as much sleep as possible. As she debated what she was going to do, she realized that she could feel a thread or something connecting the two of them. It hadn't been there yesterday when they had left the healer suite, so she was unsure what to make of it now.

Deciding that maybe Josh would know, she lifted her fingers and ran them gently along his back. That was when she recalled the conversation she had had with Terrance about the mating bond. *Terrance had said something about when it happened, it had almost been like they swapped bodies, and then after they were far more in tune with each other.* Under her light backrub, she could feel Josh starting to stir.

"Hello," she said softly. Before he could reply, she got a sense of love and warmth being projected along the thread that was now connecting them.

Josh smiled and rolled so he was no longer on top of her. "Hi."

Elyse considered the best way to tell him the news. "I am pretty sure we're mated," she said and waited for Josh's reaction.

"I know," he said, catching her off guard.

"How do you know?" Elyse replied suspiciously.

"Well … the whole temporary body swapping thing happens when the mating bond forms. When it occurred the second time,

I figured that was what was going on. And you know what, I am okay with it. I am madly in love with you, and if we are mated, then that only makes what I already know more true," Josh said before giving her a light kiss.

Elyse kissed him back, trying to work through this new development. "What does it mean to be mated exactly?"

Josh bit his lip in thought. "Well, it means a lot of different things. Usually, mates are more in tune to each other's emotions. Sometimes there is an additional magical talent involved, but usually it is just a deeper bond that two people share."

"Okay," Elyse replied, thinking maybe she would ask Terrance more about it or have to do some of her own research.

It had been a long two days, but everyone was finally feeling back to normal after the attack at the warehouse and the earthquake. Terrance had decided they needed an outing. Elyse trailed slightly behind Josh and Terrance. When Terrance had said that Dariusz wanted to meet one more time before he departed, she had been wary. Although the vampire had proven that he wasn't evil all the time, Elyse still didn't doubt that he wanted her for her talent, especially since it had continued to change after Ben used the vaccine on her. She wasn't sure if Dariusz knew that she and Josh were now mates and if that would make her more or less desirable to him.

Terrance hadn't told them where they were going, so Elyse had been in complete shock when they parked outside a large cemetery. "This is where we're meeting?"

"Yes. Dariusz sometimes has an odd sense of humor," Terrance replied.

Elyse tried to suppress a shudder. Cemeteries creeped her out. There were massive trees, branches spread out, casting shadows throughout the cemetery. Headstones in various sizes dotted the grass. There were even a few elaborate statues. The whole place was surrounded by a black wrought-iron fence. A large pair of gates stood open for them at the entrance.

They walked through. Dariusz had said he would meet them inside at a designated spot. As soon as Elyse stepped past the gate, the tips of her toes and the edges of her fingers tingled. At first, she thought maybe it was the mating bond doing something new. At the edge of her peripheral vision, she could see something white, but whenever she turned to look at it directly, it disappeared. The gap between her, Josh, and Terrance grew. Every few strides, Elyse would pause and turn her head this way and that. The tingling was spreading up her legs and arms.

"Are you okay?" asked Josh with a frown. "You're twitching."

Elyse shook her head. "No. My arms and legs are tingling, and I keep seeing things out of the corner of my eyes, yet when I turn to look at whatever it is straight on, it goes away."

"Tingling … like they're going to sleep? Or how it feels when you're trying to focus your talent to get a vision?" Josh asked.

"I guess it's more like when I get a vision," Elyse said.

"Okay," Josh said and took both of her hands in his. "I want you to close your eyes, and take a deep breath and let it out slowly to the count of ten. Then open your eyes. Ready? Go."

Elyse took a deep breath as instructed and let it out, counting backward from ten in her head. When she opened her eyes, instead of white fuzziness at the edge of her vision, there were half-defined shapes behind Josh. She took an involuntary step backward.

Josh gave her hands another squeeze. "Tell me what changed."

Elyse let out her breath slowly. "Instead of the white being at the edge of my vision, now there are shapes behind you."

Josh looked over his shoulder but quickly returned his gaze to meet hers. "I don't see anything. We need to catch up to Terrance so we can meet with Dariusz. I will protect you from whatever it is."

Elyse let Josh lead her. They wound their way through the cemetery and stopped next to Terrance. She was standing in front of one of the large statues. It had a winged horse balanced on the headstone. The white shapes seemed to be following them, though their details did not solidify anymore. It was unnerving that she was the only one that could see them.

"What took you so long?" Terrance said softly, not turning to look at them.

"Elyse seems to be manifesting another talent," Josh said, earning them both a sharp glance from Terrance.

"A talent tied to the cemetery?" Terrance asked, voice higher than normal. If Elyse knew her better, she'd say she detected a hint of fear in Terrance's voice.

"Yes. I'm seeing white shapes," Elyse replied.

Dariusz stepped out from behind the statue. Elyse wasn't sure if he had been hiding behind there or had just appeared and was giving off the illusion that he had been eavesdropping.

Dariusz smiled and licked his lips. "Ghosts. The white shapes are ghosts."

"How would you know?" Terrance asked.

"I can feel their presence. I just cannot see them," Dariusz replied.

Elyse had more questions. "How do you know I can see them?"

"Well," Dariusz replied drily. "We're in a cemetery, and you couldn't see them until you entered. Pretty safe bet that you're seeing ghosts."

"They're just white shapes. I can't tell if they are people or animals or anything," Elyse replied, her face heating up.

"You should know by now that each talent takes time to learn how to use it. I know you have gained some skill with seeing the past and future. But that did not happen the first time you discovered you had those talents. Seeing ghosts will be much the same," Dariusz explained.

"Will I be able to do anything other than see them?" Elyse asked.

"It would be rather helpful if you could command them," Dariusz replied.

"Helpful to who?" Josh interjected. "I don't think Elyse has a reason to speak to ghosts."

Dariusz opened his mouth to reply when a loud screech pierced the air. A huge, winged creature was diving straight toward them. Elyse stumbled backward. As it got closer, she could make out the details: pale skin, huge dark-red eyes, razor-sharp teeth. The head was human-like but with sharper angles than would be considered normal and short black hair. It also had huge black bat-like wings with silver veins running through them. Its hands and feet had long black claws.

Josh pulled Elyse farther back. Terrance was mid-shift when Dariusz leaped upward and, to her surprise, shifted. Huge black wings with silver veins sprouted from his back, his arms and legs elongated, and his face became more angled.

"What the hell are those?" Josh called to Terrance.

"Vampires," Terrance said roughly.

"That's not how they look," replied Elyse.

"The only one I know can shift like that is Dariusz," Terrance said. Then, she snapped her mouth shut and fell forward, completing the shift to Siberian tiger.

Elyse's mind whirled. *Why had no one ever said that vampires could shift? Or was it only old vampires could shift?* "Isn't Artur Hagi Dariusz's brother?"

Josh nodded. "Yes. That is what Willow said."

"Then would it make sense if that," she said, pointing to where the two vampires were fighting midair, "was Artur Hagi."

Josh looked at Terrance. "What do we do? They're fighting too close. If I start shooting, I'd risk hitting Dariusz. A few days ago, I probably wouldn't have minded if I killed him. Now I'm not so sure. I'm more afraid of the enemy we don't know—Artur Hagi."

Terrance closed her tiger eyes and shifted back. "Honestly, I think we should leave."

Snarls came from above them. Then, the entangled vampires were free-falling through the air. Black droplets of blood sprayed as they fell. Elyse shuddered as the blood droplets pelted her. Nausea hit her, and it was all she could do to keep her small lunch in her stomach.

Elyse found the longer the vampires fought and the more blood that landed on her, the clearer the ghosts were becoming, and they were angry. Many of them were shaking their fists at her or waving weapons around. They also seemed like they might be talking, but she could not hear anything.

"The ghosts are angry," she announced.

Josh gave her a sharp look. "That is really our cue to go. Angry ghosts and fighting vampires. C'mon!" He grabbed her hand and took off at a jog, heading as directly as possible back to the gate. Terrance matched her pace to theirs but kept glancing overhead.

They heard a loud crash and the ground beneath them vibrated. Gravel flew into the air around them. Elyse felt several pieces cut her arms and face.

The ghosts swirled around her, and she was just starting to make out sounds. They were screaming, "Fix it!"

Elyse gasped as a ghost grabbed her. The place where its hands touched her felt like ice and was flowing with her magical talent. She could feel it right at the surface of her skin.

"Fix what?" she demanded.

"The abominations," the ghost said, pointing to the two fallen vampires who were writhing on the ground.

"How do you expect me to fix it?" Elyse demanded.

"Who are you talking to?" Josh asked.

Elyse ignored him, focusing on the ghost.

"If you can see and talk to me, then you can also control me. I'm dead. Vampires are dead. Figure it out," the ghost said, glaring at her.

Elyse blinked a few times, trying to wrap her mind around what the ghost was suggesting. *It can't be that simple, can it? I can control the vampires and just tell them to cease to exist?* She rubbed the bridge of her nose. There had to be more to it. It couldn't be *that* easy.

"The ghost is talking to me. It says—" Elyse continued before the ghost interrupted her.

"I am not an *IT*. My name is Tom," the ghost hissed at her.

Elyse rolled her eyes. "Sorry. The ghost, his name is Tom. He says that I can control ghosts and other dead things. He wants me to get rid of the vampires."

Josh didn't look convinced. "Get rid of them by controlling them? It's not like you can order them to unmake themselves, can you?"

Terrance looked from one to the other. "You could try it," she suggested. "But I'd recommend doing that to Artur first, because you if you unmake Dariusz, then we will have to deal with Artur."

"Okay, so I'm really doing this?" Elyse said uncertainly.

"Yes. We will be here to back you up if it doesn't work," Terrance said and gave Elyse's arm an encouraging squeeze before shifting again.

Josh kissed her lightly on the lips, a promise for later. "I believe in you."

Elyse nodded. "Thank you."

Tom the ghost smacked her arm. "Are you done yet with your lollygagging? Now is your chance, while they are distracted!"

Elyse glared at the ghost but didn't reply. *First, I discovered I can now teleport, then that I have a mate, and now I can talk to ghosts. Do I even want to hazard a guess about what happens next?*

"Do either of you have any idea how to go about attempting this kind of talent?" Elyse asked, peering from Josh to Terrance and back.

"I have no clue," replied Josh. "Honestly, I didn't know anyone could talk to ghosts, let alone command them."

In her tiger form, Terrance shook her head.

"Okay then, I will figure something out," Elyse said. She let her eyes shut and took a deep breath, counting backward from ten. Tom seemed convinced she could command and unmake the two fighting vampires. *What's the worst that can happen?*

She took another deep breath and then focused on Artur Hagi. As a man, he was tall and skinny, preferred to wear a trench coat, and had dark-red eyes and razor-sharp teeth. As a shifted vampire, he had dark blueish-black skin, huge red eyes, clawed hands, and almost transparent wings with silver veins.

"Artur Hagi, I command you!" she shouted, deciding that using her mind might not be enough for her new talent to work properly.

The tips of Elyse's fingers tingled. She was tempted to open her eyes to see what was happening but was also afraid to know. "Artur Hagi, you do not exist!" as she said those words she poured all of her strength and willpower into the command, ordering her talent and Artur to obey. The tingling in her fingers intensified until it was almost painful and then vanished.

Elyse opened her eyes, not sure what she would find. Artur Hagi was gone, and Dariusz had changed back to human and was staring at her maliciously.

Josh quickly stepped in front of her. "She is mine," he said firmly.

Over his shoulder, Elyse could see Dariusz's furious expression. "This is not over." Before Elyse could think of how to reply, Dariusz vanished without a trace.

"Well … that did not go how I thought it would," Terrance said, giving Elyse an appraising look. "It seems as though you do have another new talent. You can command ghosts and vampires."

Josh stepped out of the way, so he was no longer blocking Elyse and slid her hand into his. "To unmake themselves," he said as though he still couldn't believe it.

"With Willow's presumed death, Nightshade Coven is in upheaval. If word gets out that Elyse can now unmake vampires … well. I would not recommend being anywhere that there is a significant vampire presence like there is here in Boise," Terrance said.

"You're sending us away?" Elyse said sadly.

"Not because I don't want you here. I want you to be safe. Nightshade Coven still has a lot of members. There are many places in this country that do not have large vampire populations. Atlanta is one of them. It could be worth considering returning. Since you can teleport, you don't need Catrina or anyone else to help you move from place to place," Terrance said.

"You think we should go back to Atlanta?" Josh said.

"It would be a good option. Everything you need is at your ranch," Terrance pointed out.

"But Dariusz knows where to find us if we go there," Josh replied.

"Yes, but he might be more willing to leave her in peace if she is obviously not trying to go after him," Terrance said. "I'm sure you can take a day to think about it and decide where you want to go for sure. But I would not wait much longer than that."

Elyse sighed. This was not the new development she had been hoping for. *I can kill vampires by unmaking them.* Josh squeezed her hand, trying to reassure her. "Okay. I will let you know what we decide," she said.

Elyse was standing with Josh in the sand paddock at the back of the stable in Boise where they had kept the horses. Terrance was leaning on the rail, watching them.

"Are you sure you want to go home?" Josh asked for the third time.

"Yes. We've already discussed the pros and cons. I think this is our best option for now," Elyse said.

"Okay. I support you. Are you ready?" Josh asked, loosely holding Fork's reins.

Elyse wrapped her fingers through Honey's reins and then gripped Josh's hand hard. "Yes."

"Me too," he said and gave her a quick kiss.

Elyse knew she was gripping his hand really tight, but she couldn't help it—she was nervous. *Home.* She focused on what the ranch looked like, the rolling hills, horses in the pastures, the new barn. She could tell it was working because she was starting to get nauseous, and her whole body was tingling from the magic.

When the tingling stopped, she opened her eyes, blinking rapidly. They were standing on a beach; the sun was reflecting off of the water and almost blinding her. Seagulls called overhead. She turned and saw several palm trees.

She met Josh's eyes; he was just as confused as she felt.

"Where are we?"

THIRTY-TWO
TERRANCE

As the shimmering faded from the sand paddock, Terrance let out a sigh of relief. It had worked; Josh and Elyse had teleported back to her ranch in Atlanta. She dusted her hands off on her pants and headed toward headquarters.

Since the development of Elyse's new talents, Terrance had been frantically doing as much research as she could, trying to figure out more about the ability to command ghosts. But she was coming up mostly empty-handed. There was a possible individual who had lived in Paris, but it was unclear if he was still alive. *I also don't have any way of getting to Paris to find out.* Part of her was tempted to ask Tiny if he could find anything. Another part of her was loath to give Tiny any information he might not already have. Since she didn't understand the nature of Elyse's new talent, she felt that it would keep her friend much safer if fewer people knew about it.

Just as she was rounding the corner to HAC headquarters, she spotted a familiar car on the corner. The window rolled down and sure enough, Agent Florence was sitting inside. The FBI agent waved Terrance over. "I was debating if I should go inside to find you, and here you are. Come sit in the car and let's chat."

Terrance opened the front passenger door and slid into the seat. When the door shut, all of the windows went completely black, preventing them from seeing out and anyone else from seeing inside.

"What is this about?" Terrance asked.

Agent Florence replied seriously, "Ben Piro."

"Did you find the information you needed to pin Governor Beechwood's assassination on him?" Terrance inquired.

"Yes. As I was digging into video footage around the city, I also found some showing him entering the warehouse before it got destroyed as well as slipping out another side after the earthquake. I was able to present it to Governor West, and he has dropped the case against you. I opened an official investigation into Ben Piro this morning. He accused of assassinating the governor and murdering the twenty dead found in the ruined warehouse. If we can catch him, we will be going for the death penalty," Agent Florence explained.

"I wish you luck catching him," Terrance said.

"We could do this operation together," Agent Florence offered.

Terrance bit her lip. Part of her wanted to say yes. She liked working with Agent Florence, and they had had good results in the past. Another part of her wanted to stay out of it. If she did not get a direct order from Dariusz, she had no reason to become further entangled in Ben and whatever insane plan he intended to carry out with the magical talent cure and the Snowflake.

"As much as I appreciate the offer, I am going to have to decline this time."

"Are you sure? Governor West has agreed to pay you a hefty sum if we are able to bring him in—dead or alive," Agent Florence said.

Terrance was a bit taken aback that Governor West would be willing to pay her for killing him. It was definitely not something Governor Beechwood would have done. "Yes, I am sure. I wish you luck." She put her hand on the door and it opened.

"Very well. I'll see you around," Agent Florence said and gave a slight wave.

Terrance nodded and shut the car door, then walked briskly the rest of the way to headquarters.

When she stepped inside the foyer, Cory waved at her. "Josh and Elyse?"

Terrance smiled. "They teleported home."

"Great. I made a pot of coffee," he replied and took her hand in his, leading her to their apartment.

Terrance felt her mouth watering in anticipation of a cup of hot coffee. They walked in the apartment, and the smell of fresh coffee hit her immediately, as well as—

"Coffee cake?" She sniffed the air and caught Cory grinning out of the corner of her eye.

"See, I can surprise you sometimes," he said and gave her a quick kiss before grabbing cups and plates. He set them on the table, a huge slice of coffee cake and a steaming cup of coffee for each of them.

Terrance licked her lips in anticipation. Fresh coffee cake was one of her favorite foods, especially when Cory made it from scratch. She took a big bite before noticing Cory took a much smaller one. She shrugged. She didn't care what he thought of her eating habits, not when it was just the two of them.

She swallowed her bite and then took a sip of coffee. "I know you too well to think this was for no reason. So, what is going on?"

Cory stuck his tongue out at her. "I can't be nice to you without there having to be a reason?" Instead of letting her reply, he kept speaking. "I wanted to continue our discussion from last week. The future, our future. You mentioned wanting to retire."

Terrance sighed and fiddled with a crumb on her plate. "Yes, I did."

"Has your opinion on that changed because of recent events?" Cory asked.

Terrance met his gaze. "Yes, no ... I'm not sure." She ran a hand through her hair. "So much has happened in the past couple of days that I no longer feel like I have the right answer."

"Maybe there won't ever be a right answer. It's just a decision we need to make, together," Cory pointed out.

"I know. Part of me thinks we should wait to bow out, to stop Ben before he runs rampant with the cure and destroys the president. But the other part of me is worried about what Dariusz is going to ask of us now that he knows Elyse can unmake him. If he gave us the order to kill her, I wouldn't be able to do it," Terrance said.

Cory laid his hand on top of hers and squeezed. "I know. I worry about that too. But would we be better off staying in the organization and making sure if that order about Elyse comes that it never gets fulfilled?"

"I'm not the only lieutenant he has. What if he gives the order to Catrina, Blaze, or Eduardo? I don't think I can count on even Catrina to not follow the order. Not if she finds out that Elyse can unmake her, which I'm sure she knows by now," Terrance said.

Cory took a sip of his coffee, eyes closed. He opened them before speaking. "Maybe we could stay for now, and you can start giving Pierre more control. He would be taking over for you if you left anyhow."

Terrance nodded. It was a good idea to let Pierre start to take more responsibility. "What are we going to do if the execution order comes for Elyse?"

"Then our retirement will begin," he said softly.

Terrance opened her eyes, which quickly adjusted to the darkness of the bedroom. Cory was snoring next to her. There was a tugging at her core. It was what had woken her up and was summoning her. She quietly slipped out of bed and out of the apartment. Once in the hallway, she shifted. Keeping to the shadows, she exited from headquarters.

Her path took her a few miles into the foothills. The tugging increased the closer she got to her destination. There was a small cave, and she felt certain that was where he was waiting. Terrance entered the cave. She saw the red eyes before she could make out any other features. Even with her superior vision in her tiger form, she knew she wouldn't see anything other than the eyes until he was ready. Slowly he stepped forward.

"It seems you are planning to leave me," Dariusz said in a cold voice.

Terrance could not help the shiver of fear that ran through her body. She didn't reply. There wasn't a reason to if he had overheard her discussion with Cory earlier.

"I thought you were satisfied. You even have the governor's hundred million dollars to keep you entertained," Dariusz continued. "Or perhaps you have realized that you now have a weapon at your disposal that will allow you to get out from my control."

Terrance curled her lip, baring her large canines, but still did not reply.

"This is the only warning you are going to get. If you prevent me from eliminating Elyse, then I will destroy everything you have built here. Everyone you care for will suffer." Dariusz bared his teeth. "You have been a loyal lieutenant for many years. I would hate to lose you over such a trivial matter as one insignificant human woman." Then, he vanished.

Terrance rocked back and sat down on her haunches, one thought foremost in her mind. *Dariusz's greatest mistake is underestimating the resilience of "insignificant humans." I will have to educate him.*

EPILOGUE

Catrina sat on top of the D, the only letter still fully upright on the legendary Hollywood sign in Southern California. She gazed out at the city, conflicting thoughts drifting through her mind. A long time ago this city had been her home, but over the years it had changed, just as she had changed. Now she wasn't sure if she wanted to belong here.

Dariusz had given her an assignment a few weeks ago to negotiate with the Blood Raiders, the largest vampire coven here. They had claimed to need more time, but now she was beginning to wonder if there was something else going on. She knew finding out would not be easy; many of the vampires in the Blood Raiders coven thought she had betrayed them. *How ironic that the coven I created no longer trusts me.*

Catrina stood up on the D, unfurling her wings. With a powerful push from her legs, she launched herself into the sky.

ABOUT THE AUTHOR

E.R. Jensen lives in Atlanta, GA with her husband and three sons. She began writing poetry in elementary school and at the end of 2020 decided to try writing her first novel. Aside from writing, she is also an avid horse enthusiast, and enjoys traveling.